PRA

MW01074762

"The Way up is Death *is just like your favorite dark ride- you hold your breath, your stomach drops and you wonder what is lurking around the next corner. When the ride ends, you want to get right back in line to ride it again. Again! Again!"*
Shannon Greiwe, Manager at Barnes & Noble Southcenter

Dan Hanks

THE WAY UP IS DEATH

ANGRY
ROBOT

ANGRY ROBOT
An imprint of Watkins Media Ltd

Unit 11, Shepperton House
89-93 Shepperton Road
London N1 3DF
UK

angryrobotbooks.com
twitter.com/angryrobotbooks
Get up and go!

An Angry Robot paperback original, 2025

Edited by Eleanor Teasdale and Jennifer Udden
Cover by Sarah O'Flaherty
Set in Meridien

ISBN 978 1 91520 294 9
Ebook ISBN 978 1 91520 295 6

Printed and bound in the United Kingdom by CPI Group (UK) Ltd, Croydon CR0 4YY.

9 8 7 6 5 4 3 2 1

MIX
Paper | Supporting responsible forestry
FSC® C171272
www.fsc.org

To those whose small acts of kindness, hope, and courage inspire the rest of us to keep climbing, when the tower of this strange world is so very tall.

And to Indy, my sweet shadow, and the very best and most adorable girl – thank you for saving us in so many ways, we will love you forever.

Prologue

The tower appeared in the skies above the UK on an otherwise unremarkable Saturday afternoon in the middle of May.

A tall, twisting fortress of the purest crimson, atop a floating island, it shimmered in the midst of swirling clouds tinged with blues and purples and pinks that were not of this world.

That it cast a shadow over the town of Hope, nestled in the lush hills of the Peak District, was a fact many would deliberate over later. But at the time they simply craned their necks and stared up at this illusion, this heavenly painting, thinking it a drone lightshow or a gigantic advertisement for a new cologne, or perhaps marketing for the latest streaming TV show that wouldn't last beyond a season.

Within twenty minutes of the tower's appearance, there were five car crashes along the wooded road through the hills to the town, fifty escaped sheep from an abandoned truck on the way to the slaughterhouse, and at least three dropped sandwiches at a family picnic. Within thirty minutes, the sight had become global news. Within an hour, the tower had become a meme. Within two hours, the constant sharing of the meme had brought down three social media platforms.

By midday the next day, two paranormal experts from the nearby town of Dark Peak had turned up, realised they were out of their depth, and left. Meanwhile, the prime minister of the UK had arrived to address the sight by megaphone, bluffing his way through a speech about shared values between us and whoever lived in the tower among the clouds. An hour later, with no response from the tower and a drop in his ratings among his rabid right-wing fanbase, he U-turned, and was on television declaring war.

Monday saw Hope cordoned off and the first armed vehicles arrive, while helicopters circled the behemoth in the skies above from a safe distance. Tuesday saw the first attempt by an airborne sniper to shoot the tower, only for the bullet to simply disappear before reaching it. Wednesday saw a fly-by by two Typhoon fighters, followed by a missile strike that again failed to do any conceivable damage.

Thursday saw a vote of no confidence in the prime minister, who resigned and was immediately replaced by his deputy, only for him to quit after being outed in a sex scandal that same lunchtime. At this point, the chancellor of the exchequer took over. She flew up to the Peak District, took one look at the tower, and also resigned.

For the entirety of Thursday night, the UK was leaderless. Some said it was the most stable the country had been in decades. Others put together a petition for Larry the Downing Street cat to take over. It reached forty million signatures by three in the morning.

By nine o'clock Friday morning, the foreign secretary had taken over and decided there was little to no threat, seeing as the tower hadn't actually done anything of note in all the time it had been hanging in the skies above middle England. He declared the country must "Keep Calm and Carry On", which, remarkably, everyone did.

And so, by Saturday afternoon, exactly one week later, the world had already forgotten about the floating tower, bored of its twisting, blood-red minarets and unwavering presence among the clouds.

Until a very definitive timer in bright golden light appeared on its façade. A timer that began a countdown, which experts quickly worked out would reach its zero hour in exactly two days.

And a single word appeared emblazoned over a foreboding, arched gateway everyone could see at its base. A word that spoke to the world of what the tower, and whoever sent it, required of them:

ASCEND.

CHAPTER ONE
Gone

Alden shifted nervously, a flicker of warmth rising in his chest as the woman reached across the pub table and placed her hand on his.

"It's not easy, is it?" she said, holding his gaze with the kind of casual confidence that seemed so easy for everyone else, but only ever found him after a couple of beers. Right now, his belief was still paddling around at the bottom of his first drink. "Life, I mean. It seems to be hard for everyone these days, don't you think? We're all a bit lost, struggling to find ourselves."

He nodded and took another sip, not daring to move the hand she held, lest she pull away. His chest was tight with that prickly, tingly, awful anxiety that haunted him relentlessly these days. But there was a gravity to the comfort of her touch, and he wanted to let it pull him in. After everything else lately, the relief of it was overwhelming.

Don't you dare cry, he warned himself. *Don't ruin the first glimmer of happiness you've had in months, you absolute tool.*

He took a deep breath, tried to centre himself.

"Do I have the look of the lost about me, then?" he said, jokingly. "Late twenties loser who needs his bandmates to set him up with women who are far too good for him. Or did Jess tell you my life story already?"

His date, Michelle, squeezed his fingers. "Jess told me that you're a teacher by day, rock star by night, but hinted you haven't had a great time for a while now and..." She paused. "Yeah, I could kind of sense it when you walked in. But isn't that the backstory of all lead singers in bands? I'd kind of be disappointed if you'd turned up cheery! The brooding look suits you, by the way."

Feeling his cheeks flush, he quickly hid his face behind another swig of beer. If only she knew it wasn't really brooding that kept him quiet these days and had his unkempt hair falling over his face most of the time.

"Gotta brood if you sing in a band," he agreed, then grinned. "Admittedly, it's less effective with the kids at school, who just think you're grumpy."

"You enjoy being a teacher?"

"Love it. Hard work, but it's the best."

"Inspiring, too, I bet?"

"Oh, for sure," he said, knowing it had been once. Right now? The feeling was like a colour he couldn't fathom in a monochrome world. He gave his spiel regardless. "It's a heck of a thing to know you're changing lives, even in a small way, watching kids learn and discover new ways of thinking that you're responsible for putting in front of them."

In truth, he hadn't been present in his classroom for weeks. There in person, sure, but his spirit set to autopilot. He didn't think he'd been missed, either, seeing as the children didn't pay that much attention even when he *was* engaged.

"And the band? You've played all around Manchester, haven't you?"

"We have. You name a sticky-carpeted dive in town, and I've sung there and had a pint or two spilled over me. Always fun."

"I've seen you at work online. You're good."

He smiled. "There's only so much of the beer-soaked experience you can get from YouTube, but thank you."

"And yet Jess tells me you guys haven't played for a while, because you've not been in the right headspace." She tilted her head. "Want to talk about it?"

Alden swirled his drink around a little before placing the glass down. He really didn't. Yet he didn't want the conversation to dry up, either. There was something happening he hadn't experienced in a while. A lightness he wanted to hold on to.

"I think that stuff is all second date conversation material?" he said tentatively, feeling buoyed by the idea he might see her again. Maybe it was the alcohol starting to work its magic, but there was a very small, very real sense of happiness forming inside him. Just a smidge of colour. Not enough for him to drop the façade, though. "I'm fine. I... uh..."

"I like the idea of a second date."

He looked up in surprise. "You do?"

"I do." Michelle held his gaze as she sipped her Guinness. "But you'd rather I talk about myself now, wouldn't you?"

"Ha... well, yes. Actually that would be pretty great."

Pulling her hand back, she swept her long blonde curls over her shoulders with a theatrical flourish and beamed at him. "OK, my friend, well, I can do *that* all night. It's probably the thing I'm best at, if I'm honest. But I have to warn you, you're in for quite the ride. Buckle up!"

His fingers flexed against the absence of her touch, but he quickly forgot as she proceeded to talk, her voice like the music he missed, her words like lyrics written for him. It was a symphony just loud and beautiful enough to distract him from the all-encompassing emptiness that had been burying him. The grief of what had been lost. The finality of the loneliness, and the terror that had tormented him with the likelihood he'd drift through life without purpose, departing this world without anyone or anything to miss him. Just one more insignificant soul who'd made no impact, no difference.

He'd just slip away and nobody would notice.

For a moment, he thought of the tree on the hill which he took his dog, Leia, on walks to sit beneath. Their place of solitude. Just them, away from the noise and chaos. And he realised that's when he'd last felt what he was feeling at that moment. That sense of companionship. Peace. Happiness.

He'd somehow caught a glimpse of it again here, with this person, in this pub, with the neon lights of the bar sparkling in the sticky rings across the table. Hope bloomed within him, along with the inevitable concern he might somehow ruin it, make it stop, cause her to up and leave. And then the emptiness would claim him again, wouldn't it?

Except, no. Stop that. He'd been watching a lot of therapy videos on Instagram and that wasn't the right way to be thinking, was it. Sometimes things just worked out! Wasn't that what those thirty-second therapists and endless memes said? What if this was one of those times? He'd had enough shit to last him a lifetime. He was due *something*. A new chapter. A turning of the page. To be at peace again.

In the end, though, it wasn't her who left.

As Michelle swept from one story into another, regaling him with the tale of how she'd first met Jess on a night out in Cambridge, a horrendous smashing of glass ripped through the bar.

Both swivelled their heads towards the noise, where a ponytailed barman had dropped a tray of drinks. But he was ignoring the liquid pooling at his boots and was instead gawping at the window.

Alden and Michelle turned to follow his gaze.

And as they peered out through the glass, beyond the city buildings, they saw something amazing.

Not the sight of the mysterious red tower suspended above the clouds over the distant hills. Everyone had grown bored of that already, thanks to the thousands of TikTok sensations who had made it the focus of their videos in the week since it had first appeared.

No. It was that the tower – until then completely lifeless – was suddenly glowing.

Strange, shimmering lights blazed up its sides, forming hundreds of rows that pulsated in time with the heartbeat thumping against Alden's ribcage. The rows looked very much like notches – markers of some kind. And, after a few moments, the very top one disappeared.

It's a countdown, Alden thought.

Which is when he felt a strange burning sensation rippling along the inside of his skin, from his feet, all the way up and out to his fingers.

He looked to Michelle for help and she saw his panic. But as she asked, "You all right?" and reached across to him again, he saw with horror that her hand, her body, the bar, and the entire world around him, was growing blurry and indistinct.

"Help?" he said, before he inexplicably faded into nothingness.

Nia sat with her back straight in her home office chair, as her slouched colleague Matt and the bearded film director Rupert stared blankly at her from their respective boxes on the laptop screen.

"I still don't get it," Rupert droned in his monotonous, bored voice, his mouth slightly out of sync with his words, as his reception struggled to cope with the video call. He pushed his glasses up his nose in staccato motion and Nia half hoped the connection would simply drop out so she could go back to drawing. The director had been talking about the design of a new fantastical city she was screen-sharing. The one she'd spent all last night reworking after being told the same thing yesterday. That he didn't *get it*... whatever that meant. How could she bloody well revise anything with such vague feedback?

"Perhaps if you tell me exactly what you don't get, I can better rework it for you?" she suggested patiently, like talking to a child. "Is it the world you don't understand, or the colours, or–"

Matt cut her off. His connection was irritatingly fine.

"Yeah, we've been hard at work on this one, boss, and we're dying to get it right for you! Doesn't matter if we pull more up-all-nighters, we'll get it done. Won't we, Nia?"

The pale, twirly-moustached man-child grinned at her as though they were some kind of partnership, a collaboration. But the truth of it was, he did nothing. He faffed about doing his own freelance work most days, while she revised and revised these designs as best she could, all by herself, because she couldn't trust him to hit deadline.

"Sure, Matt," she said, forcing a smile and not bothering to correct him. There was no point arguing the point; she was helpless, as she always was. No director she'd met ever listened, nor even cared what a lowly concept artist had to say. Which is why she preferred working from her tiny apartment in London, away from the chaos of the world, and had as little real-life interaction with people as possible. It was better that way. Just her, a digital pen and her imagination. That was a world she could control.

At least, it usually was. Creating art by committee was an entirely different story.

Holding in a sigh, she took a moment to gauge the likelihood of being interrupted again, then continued, "As I was saying, if you could just give me specifics about the design, maybe I could–"

Rupert cleared his throat, a disgusting phlegmy sound that dribbled through her speakers, just in advance of her seeing his jowls ripple on the screen. He then launched into a long monologue, ignoring her request for feedback and instead started telling her how to do her job. Nia just took it, too tired, overworked and over this process to fight her corner. She thought about faking an internet outage. It was tempting. But she knew they'd only have to pick it up later. It wouldn't make any difference to anything. She was locked into sitting there and doing as she was bid.

Her shoulders sagged as the emotional scaffolding she'd constructed to get through the day began to collapse. If she got anything through this round of concept art for the latest *Space Battles* movie, it'd be a miracle.

"...and here, what's this? A fountain? Why is there a fountain in this city? Is that something you've brought in from back home in India? No, sorry, I don't like it. I don't think we should have water features here."

"Once again, I'm British, sir," Nia sighed, wanting to strangle him force-style across the video connection. "And no, *you* said you wanted to see more of the gravity-defying water features in the city. *You* asked for them in the last iteration. Here, look, I've still got the notes you sent that prove—"

"I think we can all see what Nia was trying to do," Matt interrupted again. This time, she came very close to screaming at the screen. The dipshit leaned forward into his camera, elbows on the table, almost conspiratorially talking to the director. "She really went to town with including the upside-down fountains and those vertical pools, yeah. But too much, right? Far too much. That's not what you wanted, was it?"

She glared at him. *You little shit*, she thought.

The words wouldn't escape her mouth, though. Her lips almost formed them, but they'd almost formed them a hundred times before, and no matter how hard she wanted to say them, she couldn't. She didn't have the courage. She always felt stupid sticking up for herself, or chastising others for rudeness, or chasing those who didn't put the effort into her that she put into them. She was permanently helpless, at the mercy of the whim of others.

Her gaze drifted to the top of a framed photo at the back of the desk. Two heads, together. One hers, younger than she was now. The other a pair of brown eyes framed by similarly dark hair, only just visible over the clutter across Nia's workspace.

She didn't bother moving any of it to get a better look. She knew there was nothing but cheesy grins and regret lurking there.

"Continue, Matt," the director said with a nod.

"Right, well, what *I* envisaged was a little more subtle, less brash and on the nose, in keeping with your excellent notes. I think we can all agree that's the best way to go. Nia's stuff was probably pulling too obviously on her roots, but I've gone with something a little more normal. See what you think of this?"

Matt flushed Nia's work from the video screen and replaced it with his absolutely piss-poor efforts. It wasn't even finished in one corner of the image! It was as if he'd rushed sketching the revisions in the five minutes before the call – which she knew he probably had. There was also very little to distinguish it from the work he'd shown yesterday, other than maybe a few more scribbled pillars and a fountain that looked suspiciously like a breast.

Of course, *that's* what worked.

The director was leaning in. He nodded sagely and tapped his pen on the screen.

"Great work, my friend. Brilliant. Follow that line and make sure she does too, OK?"

"OK, boss, will do, thanks!" Matt said, as Rupert left the call. Matt then gave Nia a nod. "I think that went well, don't you? Now, can you get on to that for me? I'm swamped with all the art for the new spaceship. Thanks, Nia, you're a love!"

His face disappeared, too, and Nia's visage of resignation filled the screen.

"Ughhhhh," she groaned at herself, then shut the laptop lid.

This wasn't how her life was meant to have gone. She had started out with *dreams*, for fuck's sake. Had always wanted to seize the damn day. Perhaps even one day run her own business, make the decisions, be the one to say "no" when she bloody well wanted.

But regardless of the industry she'd stumbled hopefully into, it had always gone the same way. She was talented as anything, experienced as an artist in everything from movie production to video game design. Through her twenties and thirties she'd done the work, paid her dues, always felt that somewhere along the line it would just work out and she'd be allowed to finally control her own destiny.

Now the future was here, she was in her mid-forties, and still at the mercy of dickheads. What's worse, she knew there wasn't a damn thing that could change. She was too old. It was too late. She was screwed.

Feeling a sudden burning sensation around her chest, Nia very casually wondered if she was having a heart attack. There was no panic at all. No reaching for the phone in case she needed to call an ambulance. Given the amount of stress she endured, trying to just keep her head above water in the choppy seas of life, she knew it was long overdue. She almost welcomed the sweet release of eternal rest.

And yet, as she tentatively felt around and realised the pain was only skin deep, she realised she wasn't dying. With a frown, she tugged aside the nape of her blouse and looked down to see a strange mark appear on her chest.

It was in the shape of a leaf.

"Huh?" she said, touching a finger to it curiously.

Then her finger disappeared and so did she.

* * *

Dirk drew to a halt in the middle of the Yorkshire Dales, having just finished his brisk afternoon trail run. Barely out of breath, he checked his Garmin fēnix watch and grinned.

"Out-*fucking*-standing," he crowed, letting his voice carry over the hills. He'd outdone his personal best by a good ten minutes and the world needed to know it. He punched the air. "Fuck *yeah*, dawg! One hour fifteen? You are on fire!"

A couple of sheep in a nearby field looked up and Dirk could almost see the envy in their little beady eyes.

And why shouldn't they be envious of this exquisite statue of a man? He was Dirk Gentson, baller American, famous Instagram Reels comedian, and international bestselling celebrity children's author. He was the fittest, hottest fifty-five-year-old around – *way* more than any of the other scrawny, bumbling British authors he'd suffered on the UK leg of his book tour – and he had the world figured out and bent over, waiting to be pounded into submission.

Slipping his phone from his running backpack, he felt it prudent to mark the occasion, knowing he probably looked pretty great. He did, too, just a slight sheen of sweat dampening his well-trimmed, salt-and-pepper beard, and giving his chiselled cheekbones that glow women loved.

He took a photo of the stats on his watch, then gave his best smouldering look and took a dozen more selfies – ensuring his button-down T-shirt was pulled open enough to show off his chest tattoos in the afternoon light. Pausing to scroll through to the ones he figured would get his female following thirsty, he plastered them across his social media. The response was instant, and he couldn't help getting a bit of a semi as the notifications and likes began pouring in.

"Goddamn influencing *sensation*," he sung happily. He'd been milking his good looks all his life and was able to dazzle the entire world with the tap of a screen. Social media was magic. Designed to lift people like him above the masses. He felt it his God-given right to take advantage of that. Not only did it help sell his books, making him and his publisher even richer, but it was fun! He lived for that instant-gratification high, as well as the spicy DMs and conference encounters with hot single mums, flustered female interviewers – and, heck, even some of the event staff – that came with being famous and hot.

One hundred per cent wouldn't change a thing. Perfect life. No notes.

Dirk grinned as he scrolled today's incoming comments. He paused on one that said "Hottie" with several heart-eye emojis and checked the profile of the fan. He hadn't seen her before, but that wasn't unusual. He'd got to know most of the regulars who fawned over him, yet there were always new ones appearing daily. This one was a super-attractive redhead, striking a pose in her profile photo with a book on her lap and just enough hint of cleavage to make his shorts even tighter and get his pulse racing more than his watch suggested it had been.

He added her to his close friends list on Instagram – the one where he posted all his smouldering, sexier photos, for those women he fantasised about meeting for a future rendezvous. Then he swung his bag fully off his shoulder and on to the trail, lifted his T-shirt to show off his glistening abs, and pouted at the screen, ensuring the camera angle gave just a hint of his bulging shorts at the edge of the shot.

That one's for you, Red, he thought, as his finger hovered over the button to post to the carefully curated list he'd just added the woman to.

But his finger never found the phone. As he went to press down, he felt his head go light, a burning sensation in his arm, and he promptly vanished from the trail.

They weren't the only ones who disappeared from their lives that Saturday afternoon. Ten other people vanished inexplicably from across the UK, taken from what experts would conclude was approximately a three-hundred-mile radius of the tower, just after the moment when it came to life and the timer appeared.

There was the missing father and daughter, Earl and Rakie, who had been playing at a fairground in Llandudno in North Wales, one second standing at a claw machine, trying to win a *Jurassic World* plush dinosaur, the next second gone, just as the winning toy dropped into the hole.

There was the shaven-headed football fanatic, Mel, who was also a leading financier in London, dressed in the best suit money could buy, on his way to a football match.

A French air stewardess, Monique, was serving drinks aboard Flight 113 from Paris to New York, flying just over the edge of Cornwall, when suddenly she was no more. The drinks trolley rolled into first class and crashed into an open toilet door, spilling champagne everywhere.

Bryan, a famous-in-the-Eighties TV personality, was waiting to talk about his new show, pacing nervously in the green room of a London studio, when the producer popped his head around the door and discovered he'd gone.

A widow in her sixties, Kim, with grey hair and a penchant for after dinner mints, only got through half a box during her afternoon watch of *CSI: Miami*, before she vanished without finding out who killed the stripper.

A young Manchester lad, Dev, bright and funny, had been playing five-a-side football at the local Pitz when he completely missed an open goal and subsequently went missing himself.

A thirty-something model, Mason, and a twenty-something PR executive, Casey, vanished on their way to very different photo shoots in Leeds and Liverpool.

And a bright-eyed, bushy-tailed priest was preparing for that evening's Mass when he felt the warmth of the Lord marking him. He held his breath as he accepted it – he was being called home.

CHAPTER TWO
The Thirteen

Thirteen people was how they started.

Alden counted them not long after they all materialised at the base of the tower. It had taken him a few minutes to gather himself, one second sitting at a table feeling something akin to happiness, the next falling backwards onto a patch of grass. *Materialised.* That was the word that popped into his head as he dug his fingers into the mud and stared out over the Peak District from like a mile above it. *Materialised,* like in some kind of science fiction show.

He squeezed his eyes shut tight, then opened them again, but it made no difference to the view, nor the fierce brightness of the sky, nor the chill wind whipping strands of his dark hair across his face.

Nor the fact that rising above them all, about fifty feet away, was *the tower.*

Beneath the low howls of the wind, a symphony of shocked groans crescendoed around him.

"What the hell…?"

"Where are we?"

"Dad, *Dad,* what's going on?"

And then a very clear, very loud American, "The *fuck* was that?"

Alden stared around the island at the base of the tower, seeing figures in various states of distress and confusion. Thirteen people, including him. Mostly adult. Some elderly. A variety of races. One teenage girl and a man he assumed must be her father. A woman in a flight attendant's uniform. There was even a priest.

All of them either were collapsed on the grass, or climbing to their feet and staring around at one another or the tower.

Alden let his gaze be drawn back along with them. His head tilted back as he took it all in. Seeing the tower disappear as it grew higher, its summit swathed in billows of purple and pink clouds. Yeah, *shit*, this was actually happening. He really was here! This was the tower he'd seen on TV all week, the same tower he'd literally just been looking at through the pub window in Manchester – a city shimmering in the distance.

"What the hell just happened?"

It was a woman's voice, and Alden realised after a moment that the question was directed at him. He glanced to the side, where a cockney-sounding British-Indian woman in a blouse and jeans was sitting on the grass, staring between him and the tower as if neither might be real.

"I… have no idea," he said honestly.

They both looked back to the tower and this time Alden noticed the medieval fortress doorway at its base. The kind of huge, arched nightmare that might as well have been ripped straight from the cover of some horror novel about vampires.

The two door panels were black as the night, crisscrossed with bands of blood-red metal, each carved with an impossible variety of patterns that, as Alden watched, seemed to change with every blink of his eyes. One moment swirling, with impressions of screaming faces ensconced in the depths of hell. The next, there were motifs of cities and stars and other depictions he didn't understand.

And above the arch, a single word was afire. Six simple letters glowing with the power of the sun, branding themselves onto his consciousness.

ASCEND.

Alden had seen this place on the television. Online. In GIFs. In comedy video reels. Even in graffiti around his city. The tower in the clouds had very quickly become a well-worn meme. But as with everything in life, in reality it was far, *far* different.

He felt small. A speck in the shadow of a boot. A mote of dust at the mercy of the universe. Waiting to be extinguished.

Yet in his insignificance – for that was the truth of it; in the face of such huge horror, he was nothing – he also sensed an awakening. A siren song whispering in his ear, mouthing its intention to his face, telling him what was needed. What fate was asking him to do. *No, not asking*, he thought, *but commanding*. Urging him. Driving him to get to his feet and take action, make his mark, do what needed to be done… before it was too late.

"*Ascend*," he said loudly.

The letters seemed to grow brighter for a moment, echoing the breath that carried the word away on the wind. Within them was movement, too. Was something in there? He could see the brightness pulsing, sending tendrils of light thrashing and twitching into the surrounding façade like veins. They stretched up, connecting to the rows of lights branded on the side of the tower – notches that Alden could see had already started to disappear. Counting down.

The entire tower shimmered as he watched. The sight sent a shiver of electricity up his spine, churned nausea in his gut, and made his skin crawl. The thing seemed alive. Eager. Hungry.

For them?

Shit, he thought again.

Alden very badly wanted to go home. Back to the pub. Back to his date. The happiness he'd been feeling had been drowned beneath the torrent of fear coursing through his body, choking him and pulling him under. His head spun as he tried to keep himself afloat in his own mind. He struggled awkwardly to his feet, noticing the woman near him had already done the same. The wind buffeted him as he tried to hold firm, keep his legs from giving way under him.

Ahead, the tower continued to taunt and encourage and beckon. It grew in his mind. No longer just a building, but an immovable monolith of impossible truth, becoming more real than anything he'd ever known. It wasn't just a physical presence, either. He could *feel* the thing in his head, under his skin, writhing within his bones.

It *was* alive. And that didn't make sense, but it didn't need to.

It was alive and this was happening. All of it.

He shuffled away from the tower, away from the people, and turned towards the edge of the island. He didn't know what he expected to see, but there was no real "end" to the grass. No cut in the soil. It just sort of faded away into a light, translucent mist.

He could see over the edge, though. To the ground, far, far below. The sight made his balls tighten and his stomach drop straight through him, becoming a metaphysical puddle between his legs.

There was no way to get back down there.

He felt light-headed and for a moment he teetered on the brink, before a hand grabbed his shoulder.

"Careful, it's a long way down."

The woman's wavy black hair, greying at the sides, snaked around her face like Medusa as she stared at him. The dark, wary pools of her eyes carried the weight of middle age to them, as did the lines creasing her tawny skin. Yet there was an attractive, calm energy to her presence that immediately put him at ease.

He leaned into her fingers as they eased him away from the edge. The trace of a smile faded as she saw how pale he must have looked.

"Christ, you OK? You going to be sick?"

Alden shrugged unconvincingly. "I'm good."

"Nice try," she said, giving him a squeeze before letting him go. "But I don't think any of us are really very good right now. This is all nuts, quite frankly."

"You're not wrong."

She offered her hand. "Nia."

He shook it, grateful for some normality to cling to in the madness. "Alden."

For a moment after that they stood silently, looking around at the group of people brought here with them. Different faces pulled taut with the same fear, as they looked between the imposing tower and the fall to their deaths beyond the island. A couple of them were talking, one crying. The priest seemed to be consoling the flight attendant.

The fifty-something American, in his tight white T-shirt and running shorts, was looking around as though he'd lost something. As he caught Nia's eye, Alden felt a flash of something familiar about the man, before he nodded – as though used to people staring at him – and strode over.

"My fucking bag's gone," he said. "My bag and my phone. You pair got a phone on you?"

Alden checked his pockets, but the comforting rectangular weight of his was missing. Had it fallen out getting up here? Had the tower taken it?

Nia shook her head, too. "Sorry, no."

"Well, then." The American grimaced. "Fuck this *all* to hell, I can't even call my agent!" He reached out and offered his hand to Nia – then Alden, as an afterthought – and shook vigorously. "The name's Dirk, by the way. Dirk Gentson. Sure as shit I don't need to tell you that, but I'm telling you anyway."

Alden found the man's grip far too forceful, as if he was trying to prove a point. Not that he needed to, given the kind of physique and leading-man swagger he possessed, all of which had probably been honed over the years in whatever reflective surface he'd come across.

Dirk's thick, tattooed arms crossed over his chest, and he struck a pose of turning and assessing their surroundings with the kind of confidence befitting so many men ill-deserving of it. His shoulder rubbed up against Nia's and she immediately stiffened and stepped away. Not that he seemed to notice.

"This is entirely fucked *up*, my dudes. Feels like we've been drugged and thrown into some kind of reality TV show." He didn't wait for a response before barrelling on. "I swear to Christ, my agent's been trying to get me into one of them for years and I knew he'd fucking do it somehow. But *this*? This is batshit."

Alden cringed as he realised how he knew this man.

"Dirk Gentson," he said. "You're the children's author?"

Dirk gave a shit-eating grin, like a lighthouse trying to

beckon ships onto the rocks, and he slapped Alden on the back. "You got it in one, buddy. Instagram influencer and now inter*national* bestseller of the 'Whimsy Whizz' series! I'm sorry, though, who are you? Where do I know you from?" He looked around again. "Am I the only celebrity on this show?"

"I really don't think this is a show," Nia said.

"Nia, baby, if you're wondering where the cameras are, they're not going to have them out for us to see, are they? Come on, girl, *think*! They hide them places. In the grass. In that shit-stack of a tower. There might be drones flying around us, too, with zoom lenses, getting our reactions to whatever this is." He stopped, frowned, and looked at Nia and Alden more intently. "You two *are* famous, aren't you?"

"I'm in a band," Alden said, almost defensively. "Monkey on a Wall. I can't imagine you've heard of us, though."

"No, definitely haven't. And how about you, sweetheart? You've got to be an influencer, right?"

Nia's expression remained impassive. "I influence very little in life, I've discovered."

Alden smiled, but Dirk seemed nonplussed. He ran a hand over his hair and looked around him again, clearly for more interesting people to talk to. "Well, fuck. I don't know what to make of any of this, then. If it was a show, we'd all need to be celebrities of some description, making it a level playing field. What's the point otherwise?" Dirk then spotted a tall, spindly, white-haired man with a moustache close by. He brightened. "Oh, wait a minute. There's one!" He rushed off without sparing either of them a backward glance.

"So he's an author?" Nia asked Alden quietly.

"Unfortunately, yes. Was a comedian who did those voiceover skits on Instagram, then got a multi-million-pound book deal because he was famous and, well, good-looking, I guess. Although there's questions over whether that jawline is real. Anyway, he's a real treat. A publisher's dream. Who now writes vapid guff for kids."

"Ouch! You don't like his books, then?"

"I don't like the adults who are too caught up in the hype to see through his bullshit." Alden's cheeks grew warm. "Sorry, it's just that my kids have to read his books. It's in the curriculum. Even at eleven and twelve they understand his work is inane faff, but I still hate that they're subjected to it at all."

"So you're a teacher as well as in a band?"

"Primary school teacher by day. Unknown and underpaid singer-songwriter by night."

"Nice to meet another downbeat creative spirit." She smiled. "I'm a designer. Games. Movies. Whatever pays."

Alden nodded thoughtfully, looking around the group again. His eyes, though, were drawn back to the tower. He couldn't help it. The thing had an inexorable pull to it, like the passage of time, like the future. Reeling him in.

The word continued blazing above the doorway.

ASCEND.

"Why are we here?" he asked.

"That's the billion-dollar question, isn't it?" Nia replied. She gestured with unease to the sign. "I'd hazard a pretty educated guess that we're being given directions, though. Ascend. Climb. That's as clear as narrative design gets."

"Reckon there's a golden-egg-laying goose at the top?"

"I don't know, Alden. I get the feeling we're more likely to run into the giant."

The wind picked up, whistling through the grass, sweeping around the thirteen people, carrying whispers of shock and confusion and fear. Two of the people – a tall, impossibly good-looking model and a shorter, blonde woman in a sharp suit – were busy peering over the edge of the island as Alden had been doing.

Yet he couldn't help but feel escaping that way – even if they could safely – wasn't even an option. There was something in the air surrounding them. Almost a hum. An energy. Enveloping them. He had the worst feeling that even if they tried to jump, they might not make it past that strange mist.

Nia was right. The tower had told them what to do. And he couldn't help but feel it was going to make them do it.

He stared at the building again, trying to figure it out. Even up close, it eluded definition. It wasn't the kind of imposing fortress that warranted the moniker of "citadel", but neither was it a straight up-and-down tower, seeing as the main trunk of it branched out into smaller minarets, with bridges and walkways connecting them.

Or… Wait, did they? He blinked and suddenly they disappeared, then reappeared in different places. The more he watched, the more it seemed to shift and bend and twist, just like the light that moved within it. It was almost natural, as though the tower was blowing against some unseeable cosmic wind.

Voices rising close by drew his attention.

"Dad, *please*, can't we just go talk to him?"

"No, Rakie. I don't care how famous he is."

"But, *Dad*."

"I told you, this isn't the time."

Alden's gaze shifted to the man and girl arguing to his right.

The man was rugged, Black, with greying stubble and kind eyes, and wearing an open-necked shirt beneath a waistcoat. He stood tall, carrying himself with poise, as though doing his best to remain unfazed by the situation.

The young teenage girl, maybe thirteen, was in a grey sports hoodie and jeans, and was pouting.

"But it's Dirk Gentson! He's *huge* on Instagram and he wrote those books I read in primary school! Maybe I can ask him for tips, or maybe he'll even want to read my work. Come *on*, Dad! Please?"

"Shit, girl, leave it alone."

The man kept his voice level, though the frustration in his gravelly Welsh accent was still perceptible beneath the breeze as he spoke to his daughter. He glanced over to Alden and Nia.

"You two friends of that author?"

Nia shook her head. "I try not to have friends. Especially not people like that."

The father seemed in on her joke. Despite his daughter's awe, he didn't seem to hold much love for Dirk either. "So, at the risk of repeating what we've all been asking... any idea what the hell is going on?" he asked.

"Our acquaintance Dirk thinks it's some kind of reality TV show," Alden said.

"You think that?"

Alden gestured to the tower. "I can't imagine there's a TV budget big enough for *this*."

The man considered that for a moment. He then introduced himself as Earl, and beckoned his daughter, Rakie, over to meet them. Alden and Nia introduced themselves, too. Alden felt a little better for the company as the four of them stood together in the face of the impossible. Confusion still reigned in his head, along with a heady sense of fear, but he wasn't alone anymore. He wasn't facing the monstrosity of a tower by himself. That was something.

"Is that a tree?" Rakie asked suddenly. She pointed to the centre of the tower, in between the lights marking the countdown. Their faces peered upwards, trying to make it out. And the more Alden looked, the more the lines grew distinct and visible, as if sensing they'd been seen.

"Well, I'll be…" Earl muttered. "It certainly looks like one. Carved into the front of the building and everything."

"But how?" Nia said. "I've seen pictures of this tower all over the news for the last week, but didn't ever notice that on it. Did it just appear?"

"Maybe it's showing us," Alden said quietly. "Now we're up here. Maybe the tower is showing us something important."

Rakie didn't think much of that suggestion. "What's important about a tree?"

"I've no idea. But there it is. A tree, of sorts." He tilted his head and squinted. "I think."

"It's definitely an attempt at designing a tree," Nia said, sounding puzzled. "But it's almost like it's been carved by someone not familiar with trees… if that makes sense. The details are all wrong. This is meant to be a tree, but it's all spiralling trunk like a unicorn's horn, and far too many twisting branches flowing and fluttering around it."

"And there are thirteen leaves that I can see," Earl said, his curious tone growing flat, serious. His eyes flickered from Nia to Alden. "Thirteen leaves. Thirteen of us." He drew up the sleeve of his shirt. "And then there's this. Just before we were brought here, something appeared on my forearm. It was a tattoo of a leaf. Rakie's got one, too."

Rakie scrunched up the sleeve of her hoody to reveal her arm. "I got a sycamore!"

Alden felt his blood run cold. He slowly offered his own wrist, studying the marking properly. "Oak... I think." He looked to Nia, who was already pulling across the nape of her blouse. She had an ash leaf. Delicate. Deft. Drawn as though blowing across her collarbone.

She looked at them all. "So what does *this* mean?"

"We got matching tattoos!" Rakie said brightly, as though it explained everything. Earl put a hand on her shoulder, but there was concern in his eyes as he looked at the two adults.

Alden did his best to give the man a reassuring smile. He'd always found the children in his classes to be pretty resilient to changes in life. There was often shock, but they'd settle into the new normal much faster than the adults, who'd still be reeling and panicking and overthinking. He had particularly strong memories of one class he'd loved, who when he'd told them he was leaving to move to another school, presented him with a small four-leaf clover they'd found that lunchtime. It was to wish him luck.

They'd barely handed it over before they were already chatting with one another about which teacher might replace him.

Rakie's focus on a mundane detail of this insanity was probably a good thing. At least it was keeping her calm for the moment.

The same couldn't be said for the rest of the group of people growing more agitated by the second. Alden wondered if someone was going to step up, take charge. He hoped one of the people was maybe a former soldier, or secret agent, or firefighter, or any other role where protecting and saving people from terrifying experiences was the norm. Wasn't that how these scenarios usually played out in the movies?

When a voice finally spoke up above the chatter, he looked expectantly across the grass island. His heart sank.

It was the priest.

"My friends, there is no need for panic and fear!" the pale, mousy-haired man called, a crooked smile of confidence shining upon them all. "Clearly, positive things are occurring. You should be grateful, not scared. Hopeful, not hopeless." He began walking backwards, towards the doorway, both hands raised aloft. "This is divine intervention made real. We have been plucked from our lives and chosen to be here. People, good people, we have been selected as representatives!"

"Representing what exactly?" the stylish Black woman in the flight attendant's outfit asked, in what sounded like a French accent.

"Humanity!" the priest responded.

Then, as he took another step closer to the tower, the entire island began to shake. Alden felt his flesh pinch, as though a thousand invisible hooks had snared him and were reeling him in.

Towards the doorway.

Where the doors were beginning to open.

CHAPTER THREE
A Doorway Beckons

Nia swallowed back the bile in her throat, trying not to panic over the momentary ache that had racked her body. She knew she wasn't the only one to have felt whatever the hell that was. Alden had shuddered beside her simultaneously, his already pale face almost completely drained of colour. Even the white priest had stopped his monologuing, looking even more like a ghost as the doors had opened and the tower called to them.

Was it a call, though? Or a hungered yearning?

She could almost feel the tower salivating, its mouth gaping wide, drawing them in with each breath. It wanted them. Like an overeager producer on a film set, or a studio head, or any number of men she'd had the displeasure of working with over the years.

I might not get to say no this time, she thought, staring up at the building, feeling her chest tighten with anxiety.

She tugged at her ear and took six short breaths, inhaling deeply on the seventh and holding it for a moment. Trying to trigger her parasympathetic nervous system to cancel the fight-or-flight response her body was locked in.

It helped, a little. Or maybe the wave of intense *need* that had just spilled out from the tower had dissipated. Either way, the rush of adrenaline was subsiding, even if the tingles in her arms were still there.

She looked to Alden, his eyes wide beneath his dark hair.

"You OK?" he asked.

"That was *extreme*," she said, trying to find the logic to any of this. "It felt strange – maybe something in the air that just escaped from those doors. Something poisonous."

He looked as though he might be sick. "Toxic, maybe."

Neither of them was convinced, though. Nia already knew she was clutching at straws, trying to find an alternative explanation. Something that made more sense than: *the tower wants us inside*.

The priest composed himself again, straightening his collar, the smile plastered back to his face. He made a show of laughing a little, as though trying to convince everyone this was all fine.

"Well, then, *behold*, my friends, the way to God is upon us!" he called, letting his voice echo around the island. He indicated the darkness beyond the doorway. "And He has opened the way Himself!"

He turned and walked towards the entrance, arms held aloft as if in greeting to whatever they might find in there. Despite the pull still tugging at her to follow him, Nia felt only apprehension. This wasn't right, nor safe. They were all vulnerable, on the cusp of being forced into a situation none of them wanted to be in. There was nothing heavenly about any of this.

"Mark 13, 26! It was foretold there will be a coming in the clouds with great power and glory. Thessalonians 4, 17! We who are still alive and are left will be caught up together with them in the clouds to meet the Lord in the air." The priest's words were smooth, firm and loud, as befitting a role in life trying to convince people to believe in what they considered the unbelievable. He beamed at them. "My friends, the entrance to Heaven we have been seeking our entire lives is here. I can barely believe it, yet it is clear, absolutely crystal clear, that this is the right moment, the right time. Finally, our benevolent God has spoken. The Rapture is upon us. And we will ascend!"

Nia wasn't religious, and even if she had been, the slick sense of terror coating her insides would have rejected the priest's notion that any of this was to do with a kind and caring deity. The tower had brought them here, that much couldn't be argued. The leaves carved in its stone and the leaves marking them weren't coincidence.

Yet she could barely look at the darkness beckoning her into that doorway. Nothing good lay in there.

"The Lord is good. He has shown us, the worthy, a way forward. A way *up*!"

Nia looked around the gathering, wondering if anybody was going to speak up. Dirk seemed unhappy about not being in the spotlight, but so far he was keeping his mouth shut. There was a bald white man in a tight-fitting suit she didn't like the look of, but even he was keeping silent, perhaps waiting to see where this was going.

We're all waiting for the priest to go inside first, she thought.

Alden, Earl and Rakie all tensed beside her as the priest continued towards the tower, his preached words reverberating around them as though the speech was trapped on this sky island with them. It lent power to his conviction that this might be some kind of religious miracle, an act of God, and that they were the chosen ones.

Nia wanted to cover her ears, run – anything to get away from all this. But there was nowhere to go. She was trapped in the horror of the moment, as she so often was in life.

Except this time she wasn't in control of the fantastical locale, she had been placed *within* it.

"It is true, it is true, and it is beautiful this truth I see before me." The priest's hands were alive with movement, weaving his words through the air as he voiced them. "A truth that *we* see before *us*! Not as individuals, but as a collective! A *community* of different folk of shapes, sizes and colours. This is it, my friends. We have been brought here to meet our maker. To revel in the hereafter. For the hereafter has been granted to us all!"

Earl had his hands on his daughter's shoulders, almost as protecting her. "You're saying that these are the end times and we've been chosen to survive? You really think this is the rapture?"

"Yes, *yes*! But we are not here merely to survive, my friend. We will transcend! Evolve beyond this life. Join the heavenly hosts."

Nia couldn't help herself. This was all too ridiculous.

"There are only thirteen of us here on this rock, Father," she said pointedly. "Of all the people in the world, you think only the thirteen of us were good enough to get into heaven? You can't possibly believe that?"

There was a moment of silence. The voice in her head noted she'd managed to say what she wanted without being interrupted. Perhaps these were the end times after all.

"I can believe it," the priest responded in a confident, sweeping voice, and Nia could see it in his eyes. Where everyone else here was fearful, concerned by what the tower represented, this man relished the idea that somehow he'd bested his brethren. He had been chosen above all others who had devoted their lives to his faith – even the Pope! – to lead and encourage the winners of life into the hereafter.

God had selected *him* for this task. Given him charge of humanity's fate.

The idea that even in the end times she wasn't in control of her own destiny, and was being shepherded by such an egotistical man of God, made her want to punch something.

"Who is to say what is believable and what is not, my child," he said to her again, a patronising tone creeping to the surface. "Only a few minutes ago I was preparing to speak to my parishioners. And now I am here, among the clouds, ready to brave my final journey to a destination I have longed for my entire life. God's ways are mysterious! Who am I to question them?" He cleared his throat and raised his voice. "My friends, my family, don't you see? We have been chosen to ascend to Heaven through this tower of God. This representative of the first tree, the one in the Garden of Eden, the first Paradise. That must be what awaits us up there, if only we find it in our hearts to believe the word of God as He has instructed!" He laughed and pointed to the instruction glowing brightly across the top of the open doorway. "*Ascend!* It could not be clearer. He made sure there would be no doubt we would believe Him and do as He asked. Come, friends, you should hurry and make your decisions to accept this great gift as it has been granted. Who is to say how long we are allowed to tarry here."

He began to stride forward again, leading the way with confidence, as if walking into the sea and expecting it to part for him. His arms were wide, like Jesus on the cross. Opening himself to his heavenly fate, utterly unafraid.

Only then did Nia see the darkness through the doorway take form. It was as if it had been waiting for the first, the bravest, the most reckless, to step forward.

There were gasps among them, shocked whispers, as they could see shapes growing more distinct, almost like the details were being loaded into existence. Then there were dashes of colour. Although none of it was bright or welcoming. Along with the others, Nia couldn't help but take a step or two towards the doorway, her curiosity overcoming her wariness, trying to see what awaited them. Rakie was beside her; Earl and Alden, too.

Within seconds she could see wet, mossy stone. An entire corridor of it, disappearing into the distance, while barely discernible torches on the walls suddenly exploded into flame, lighting everything in an eerie glow.

"It's… a medieval castle," Nia said, confused. Not just because that wasn't what she'd expected to see inside this spectacular, otherworldly tower, but because it seemed so… stereotypically mundane. A caricature. The kind of thing a designer might cobble together over a weekend for a low-budget game.

The surprise of it was enough of a distraction to let her continue moving forward. More details appeared moment by moment.

The weighted points of a portcullis hanging from the ceiling.

Small, rusted bars set in a wooden cell door.

A wooden treasure chest pushed up against the wall.

Nia found herself pulling a face as she saw it all pop into being, still walking forward, until she and the rest of the group were spread out in a semicircle before the opening.

They all had similar looks of puzzlement – especially Earl and his daughter.

"Dad?" Rakie said.

"Yeah, I see it too, kiddo."

"The treasure…"

"Yeah, I know."

Nia looked back to the chest and saw there were gold coins spilling out of it, each one glittering and enticing. It was clichéd and silly, and too obviously *not right*.

The priest, delighted to see his flock following him, stepped closer to the treasure.

"I think you need to wait," Earl said, with a sudden conviction that came out of nowhere. Nia felt it in his tone, his stance. There were murmurs of discontent among the others, who must have been feeling the same. A little elderly Asian woman was nodding. Even the bullish man in the suit didn't look particularly happy at what he saw in there.

Nia wanted to speak, to back Earl up. She straightened, gathering her courage.

"I think–" was all she managed.

"And *I* think we should let our God-fearing fellow lead the way and at least have a little look inside," Dirk said, stepping up beside her. "This is all very strange, but he is a priest and this is a tower that leads up to…" He gestured in the direction of the bizarre clouds swirling around the tower above them. "Well, it leads up, at least. Who knows where? Heaven? Sure. Maybe. It's possible. So how about we let the guy check it out while we wait for a helicopter or whatever to come along and rescue us?"

"What are you doing?" Nia whispered.

"Do *you* want to be first in, sweetheart?" Dirk hissed out of the side of his mouth. "Let him go and we'll see what happens."

The priest laughed, not hearing either of them nor bothering to care. He strode forward with renewed vigour, crossing the threshold of the doorway onto the dungeon stones. The light of the word hung above him blazed stronger.

ASCEND.

"Rescue?" he called back. "Goodness! The signs are as clear as can be. This is our time, my friends. Do not doubt. Have faith! Let us rejoice and ascend to the heavenly planes that await us."

Standing beside the treasure chest, he reached down to grab a handful of coins. Rakie made an uncomfortable noise and pushed herself back into her father's embrace. Even Nia felt herself tensing, waiting for something to happen, somehow knowing it was coming.

Then there was a noise.

It was a grinding. Stone upon metal. Or metal upon stone. Either way, it pierced the air, just as the priest held out his hand to the others, letting them watch the coins spill through his fingers with glee.

"The treasure of the L–" he began.

In the blink of an eye, the torchlight in the corridor flickered and grew behind him, until the man became just a silhouette.

Then he became several silhouettes.

As the scythes swung back into the wall, the priest's body fell apart in a pool of blood and unholy matter, sloshing across the cobbles of the dungeon's floor, spilling out of the doorway into the grass, painting it all a deep, deathly red.

Nia's mouth hung open, willing a scream out, but there was nothing but a void of shock inside her. Others managed to emit noises. Crying, wailing. Earl covered Rakie's eyes and spun her around so she couldn't keep watching, although it was far too late for that. Alden bent over and began to dry heave.

Dirk let loose a ton of expletives in his Southern American

drawl, then headed for the edge of the island, where he lifted his arms to the sky like the priest had and began screaming for help.

Nia did not hesitate to join him.

CHAPTER FOUR
Ascend

Alden stared at the remains of the priest as the panic surged around him.

It was like standing on a cliff edge on the coast, hearing the ocean waves crash over each other, beating ceaselessly against the rockface. So much noise and energy – people crying, screaming at one another. Nia and Dirk crying for help behind him. Earl consoling his daughter. None of it changing the facts of what they had seen.

Or what he was coming to understand lay ahead.

He stood alone in the chaos, feeling like he might be sick again but knowing there was nothing left inside him. He dragged his gaze away from the bloody mulch and studied the tower. It continued to move and change as it had been doing, like a living dream, while those weird swirls of cloud – like a crazily colourful aurora borealis – continued to waft and circle behind and around it. The countdown lights flickered impatiently, as though the thing seemed to be waiting for the group to reach the inevitable conclusion.

"This is like a bad trip, huh?" a young man said, sidling up to Alden. His hair was a mass of dark brown curls and he had a slightly unkempt, youthful moustache, which he smoothed down nervously. "I do *not* know what any of us are doing here, but if it turns out we somehow all took some bad drugs and are living out a collective delusion, it would be mad. In fact, I kinda hope we are, because it's gotta be better than whatever the fuck that was!" He offered his hand to Alden. "I'm Dev. Real name Bhasker, but my friends always thought I looked like that actor guy, Dev whatshisname, and I kinda liked being compared to him, so, yeah."

"Dev," Alden repeated. "Nice to meet you. I'm… uh… Alden."

"Woah, almost forget your own name there? You must be dealing with this worse than me!"

Alden felt the corner of his lips lift at the humour, despite the utter mess of the situation. He gestured to what was left of the priest. "There's a lot going on. I don't think my brain is keeping up."

"No shit, man. Any thoughts on, uh, everything?"

"A few."

"Anything that gets us out of here without going in *there*?"

Alden's hair dropped over his eyes as he shook his head. He brushed it back behind his ears with a frown, wishing he had an inkling of an idea that didn't involve the tower. But it was all-encompassing. A pervasive force in his mind.

By the noise coming from the others, he figured they all understood. The tower had made it clear what it wanted from them upon their arrival. Then it had shown them the risks of doing so, the cost of getting it wrong.

"Look, what if we just don't go in there?" Dev continued. "We could sit out here, wait to be rescued, like that guy said before. There are TV cameras all over this place, right? So someone's got to have seen us appear here. Maybe the government will send helicopters and shit."

Alden didn't say anything for a moment. The idea was a nice one. Normal. Safe. Yet the tower continued pulling.

There was a gravity to it, and you couldn't ignore gravity, no matter how much you wanted.

"I just don't think we have a choice," he said, hating the words even as he let them slip out. "We were brought here. We've been given an instruction. The doorway opened and the tower is counting down. I think the truth is... we need to go inside and climb the thing. Something important is at the top. It must be, if we need to risk our lives to reach it."

Behind him, Dirk and Nia had stopped shouting for help. The author must have heard him, because he laughed hysterically.

"You want to go in so badly, *you* do it," Dirk called over. "I'm not going near that deathtrap. We're just lucky the priest led the way, showed us what was waiting for us!"

Nia frowned at him. "Yeah, and you encouraged him to do it."

"Better him than us, sweetheart. Now we know not to go in and suffer the same fate. You're welcome!"

"Why would the tower bring us here, tell us to climb it, and then kill us all before we've even had a chance to try? That doesn't make sense. He must have done something wrong. Triggered a trap."

Dirk's face turned a bright shade of red. "*None* of this makes any fucking sense! Maybe it's all a big prank. Maybe wherever this tower is from, the word 'Ascend' means 'don't step through the fucking doorway we just opened or we'll dice you like a human carrot'. Who knows what the thinking is behind this, or even if there *is* any thinking? I still say we wait out here, and hope the army or SAS or whoever the fuck you guys have looking after the country comes and gets us. They'll send helicopters or drones or something soon. I'm sure of it."

"And what if we're the only ones left?" Alden said.

He hadn't meant to be so loud, yet his words carried outwards in a ripple across the group, leaving silence behind. Everyone turned to stare at him.

"You're saying you believe that fucking dipshit of a priest?" Dirk blurted out. He ran a hand over his closely cropped hair, looking as though he wished it was long enough to tear out. "Dude, *no*. The world didn't end and we're not the only ones left. This isn't the motherfucking rapture, bitch. At least the priest had a reason to try to bullshit us into following him in there. You're just a shitty musician – what's your excuse?"

Alden shrunk under the accusation and the gazes of the others on him. He wanted to defend himself, but there was little left in the tank. He was running on empty, and he just didn't have the words to argue against the man's insults. What was the point?

Perhaps realising there was no fight in him, Nia spoke up.

"So, if everyone is still out there, where are they all?" she asked. "Because we've been here a while now and there have been cameras trained on this tower the whole of the last week. They should have seen the lights up there come to life. They would surely have seen us. Shouldn't we have seen an acknowledgement of that by now?"

Another man stepped forward into the fray. The elderly gentleman Dirk had been excited about before. Tall and stick-thin, with lank white hair swept backwards like an ageing show dog. He must have been about seventy, and was a little stooped of shoulder, but he seemed to straighten and grow taller as the spotlight found him.

Alden could see why Dirk had gone to meet him. It was another celebrity. Not one he knew well, but he'd seen enough memes to recognise him as a TV presenter named Bryan, from some 1980s or 1990s Saturday morning show.

"The Yank is right, you know," Bryan said. "There's no RAF base for several miles in any direction from here. Nearest is near Liverpool. Played there once, in fact, in the Eighties. Good crowd. Was nice to enjoy banter that would get you cancelled today! Anyway, they'll be here to save us soon, mark my words."

"How can you be–?" Nia started to ask, and Alden saw her recoil in frustration as she was cut off again.

"We just need a little patience, my love. A bit of resolve. This country was built on such things – 'Keep Calm and Carry On' and all that! In my day, that motto was in the DNA of those of us who saw the horrors of war. It was how we survived. Blitz spirit, you know. Not that you millennials would know."

Nia's face hardened. "I'm Gen X, and with the greatest respect, you don't seem old enough to have been in the bloody Blitz."

"Oi, leave it out! This man's a bloody legend. If he says he was in the Blitz, then he was in the Blitz, all right?"

The new voice belonged to the businessman thug in his smart blue suit and salmon shirt. Maybe late thirties, ruddy-cheeked, and with faint wisps of eyebrows the only hair anywhere on his face or head. He was like a giant, angry thumb.

He stepped up and slung a meaty arm over Bryan's shoulder. A chunky gold watch jangled at his wrist.

"*This* guy is a national treasure and was on one of the best British shows of all time. You show him some fucking respect."

"Thank you," Bryan said, looking a little uncomfortable.

"'S all right, mate. I got you. Name's Mel."

"Bryan Cherub."

"Oh, I know who you are, Mr Cherub. Fuck it, *everyone* knows who you are! *Crazy Town* on BBC1, Saturday morning in the late Eighties. Never missed an episode, me." He suddenly guffawed, a verbal shotgun that made Bryan jump. "That sketch with the bees' nest and the branch and the fake tits! Ha! Classic."

His thick fingers tightened on the comedian's shoulders and the taller man's smile broke for a second. A glimmer of fear surfaced beneath the reflection of a well-practised television grin.

"Yes, well, thank you. Always good to meet a fan."

"So we're agreed, then!" Dirk announced, trying to wrestle himself back into the spotlight. "We're gonna stay here on the grass and wait to be saved, yeah? Only a matter of time, as the man said. Whatever this tower is, it's nothing to do with us. Let's leave it be."

There were more than a few nods around the group.

As the others discussed finding themselves a spot to sit and wait, Alden turned back to the tower, letting his eyes drift over its shapeless, ever-moving form, down towards the doorway. The dungeon could still be seen inside, even more distinct than it had been before.

The terror of it still filled him completely and he badly wanted to join the rest of the group. But the inescapable pull still had him. He knew waiting was pointless.

"There's no rescue coming, is there?" Nia said, joining him. "Forget the military – the TV crews and their drones would have been here by now for an exclusive."

Alden nodded. "Either they're not there anymore or they can't see us for some reason. Maybe the tower is hiding our presence."

"What for, though? What do you think this all means?"

"I… have no clue." He sighed. "But I think you've felt what I have, haven't you? And as I tell my kids, sometimes you have to trust your feelings when you don't have anything else to go on. It's like with music – there are patterns and chord progressions and inevitabilities in every song. You get a feel for it. It's instinct. It might be fate. Who knows." He looked down to the leaf on his wrist again. "This is all for a reason. And in order to know this song, I think we have to start playing. We have to go in."

"Bloody hell, Alden, I was hoping you'd reassure me."

"Sorry, I'm not very good at this. Never had to convince a whole bunch of people I had a feeling we had to climb a tower that just eviscerated a man of God."

"Yeah, you definitely need practice," she said, clearly trying not to look at the priest's remains. "But you're not the only one with that feeling, Alden. I think you're right about this. We have to go in."

They stood there in silence for a few moments, Alden realising that most had gathered with Dirk at the edge of the island. Most chatting. Some waving for help.

Only Earl, Rakie and Dev stood close by.

The cliques were forming already. It was like a microcosm of humanity up here.

Or secondary school.

He stared through the doorway, trying to understand what exactly waited for them in there. "You know, that dungeon looks strange. A little off… if that makes sense?"

"Clichéd?"

"Yeah, that's it exactly. It's clichéd. Like it's been ripped straight from the cover of an old fantasy novel or game poster. I keep expecting a pixelated dragon to stumble out."

She nodded along. "And that treasure feels planted. Like some kind of bait to draw us in. It just all feels odd. Weirdly designed. Who'd put the pile of gold coins immediately inside the doorway like that?"

"Loot crate," Rakie said, stepping up beside them. "That's what gamers call them. Although this one was only designed to look like a loot crate in *Forbidden Fortress*. Really, it was a trick crate to test the noobs, wasn't it, Dad? You got tricked by it first time you played, didn't you?"

"Rakie, I'm not sure this is..." Earl realised his daughter was staring at the priest again, and he turned her around to face him. "Yes, that trick loot crate got me in the game. And maybe this looks a bit similar, but it's not the same, you understand?"

She rolled her eyes theatrically and pulled away. "Look, I know, but *there* are the handcuff things on the wall where your character gets locked up at the start. What do you call them? Shackles?" Earl nodded and she pointed to the loot crate the priest had touched. "And *that's* the trick crate designed to kill you the first time you play. I saw how to get past them in a walkthrough. All the loot crates with that smudge on the lid are traps."

Alden saw Nia's face light up in recognition. "You're saying this is a level from a video game?"

"Uh-huh. A classic one, famous for being a real kick to the tits to play. You die in the game, you die for good. You don't get spare lives. You have to start over."

"I see."

Earl gave Nia an incredulous look. "You're not seriously buying all this, are you? Listen, I recognise it looks a bit like that game, but it can't possibly be the same thing. Up here? In this tower?" He looked around, presumably for some kind of hidden camera. "This has got to be some kind of billionaire's prank. Some reality race to the top."

"No billionaire can make an island fly," Nia said.

"Right. Then… what? My daughter is right about this?"

Nia shrugged. Alden looked up again to the countdown lights. Another one was snuffed out as he watched.

"If she recognises it, that's a good thing," he offered, trying to find a way for this to make sense. To find some detail they could all cling to. "We'll have to figure out the 'why' later. But if that dungeon is like the one in your video game, what matters most right now is that you've both played it, right? Because we need to go in there without dying."

"I beat it," Rakie said.

"You did?"

"Yeah. It's hard. I had to do a walkthrough, but I did it."

Nia bit her lip thoughtfully. "Was it set in a tower like this?"

"Nope."

"Huh. OK. But you know your way through this bit?"

"Yeah."

Earl placed a protective hand on her shoulder. "Rakie knows it backwards. Inside and out. But she can't go in there. It's too dangerous."

I don't think we have a choice, Alden thought. But how could he say that out loud? And what if he was wrong? What if he convinced the man to take the girl along with them and they ended up getting hurt?

"Maybe we should tell the others what we've discovered," Nia said, seeing they were at an impasse. She looked between the two men. "We could let them know what we're thinking and discuss it as a group, at least."

"You think they'll listen?" Alden asked doubtfully.

She smiled and shook her head, gesturing for him to take the lead. "Not to me. But you're in a band. The stage is all yours."

But as he wondered if she was mocking him, a noise pierced the air.

A scream.

"Get back!" the short woman with the blonde pixie-cut hair cried. She had been standing near the edge of the island, but jumped into the embrace of the impossibly handsome man, who was surely a model, and pushed them both towards the tower. "The ground's vanishing – go, *go*!"

Even from there, Alden could see the grass falling away. But it wasn't crumbling. The island holding them up was just… disappearing.

"Everyone, run!" Earl yelled. He pointed at the tower. "In there, quickly!"

"What makes you think *that's* any safer?" Dirk whined, running past them.

"You got a better idea?"

The thug, Mel, his suit straining against his bulk, hurried forward as fast as any of them, pushing the elderly Asian woman out of the way. He glared at Alden and Nia as he ran past. "What did you fucking do?"

Alden glanced at Nia. *Did we do anything?* There wasn't time to ask, though. She grabbed his arm and pulled him along with the wave of people, sprinting as fast as they could towards the doorway. Someone slid on the priest's intestines; someone else crunched what sounded like bone underfoot. Bodies ran into one another and collapsed on the other side of where the priest had met his end, falling to the flagstones in the middle of the fantasy dungeon corridor, giving the treasure chest a wide berth.

Alden fell against the wall with Nia. Huddled together, they watched the last of the grass verge of the island disappear, before their view of the world vanished as the heavy doors swung shut with a thunderous crash.

CHAPTER FIVE
Torture

Alden felt the cold and damp press against his skin. As the ghost of a breeze blew up the corridor, he shivered. He moved closer to the torches on the wall, trying to warm himself, noting the identical make-up of each implement, right down to the grain of the wooden handles.

The others followed him. In the flickering light, their faces were glistening with sweat, hair plastered to foreheads, eyes wide and anxious at what they'd just witnessed. The echoes of their murmurs, to each other and to themselves, flitted around them like spirits. Shoes crunched against the flagstones and slid over bloody footprints. There was a steady drip of water nearby.

Alden had never been one for claustrophobia, but there was something in the chamber that filled him with dread. It was like being buried alive.

Perhaps they had been.

He moved further into the skybound tomb, steering clear of another fantasy dungeon loot crate that looked exactly like the one that had killed the priest. The spilled coins were awfully tempting, sparkling as they were in the light.

"It was an easy mistake to make," Earl said, drawing up alongside him. He reached out to touch the shackles on the wall they'd seen earlier. "The game was designed to kill your confidence from the start."

"Except here you actually die," Alden said.

"Exactly."

"So which loot crates do we avoid? The ones with the smudges, isn't that what you said, Rakie?"

The girl shrugged. "Yeah, the chests with that little dirty mark on top are the trick ones. They usually have coins, but not always. Everything else is fine."

"OK, thanks."

He took a breath, then another, trying to think through this impossible situation. In the back of his mind, he was almost glad for the distraction from his recent woes. It was good to have something to focus on.

As a heated conversation grew around him, Dirk grabbed a torch from the wall and waved it about his head, trying to get everyone's attention. A snake tattoo wove around one of his muscled, hairless forearms.

"Hey, y'all, shut the fuck up! No, we didn't want to come into the tower, and for some motherfucking great reasons. But now we're here, I think we just need to sit tight and wait to be rescued, OK? We're alive right where we are, and as long as nobody triggers any other booby traps, we should be fine. People are out there looking for me. My agent is *tenacious*, you understand? Any minute now, someone is going to drill through those doors and come get us. I promise."

There were enough nods and mumbles to suggest most people were going to be swayed the author's way. Mel and the 1980s TV host, Bryan, were already scoping out the cleanest sections of wall to sit down against, and as they did so, others followed. Dev looked to Alden, then almost apologetically sat down alongside them.

Alden knew it wasn't going to work. The tower had pushed them inside. It *wanted* them to climb it. Why else would they have been forced in here? Why else would the tower have made the island vanish? Sitting around was just going to cost them time, and who knew what other tricks it might use to push them to do its bidding? Better they get going now.

"Listen, I–I don't think we can just hang out," Alden suggested tentatively. "The tower wants us to ascend. It told us that above the door, and it just showed us what it could do if we don't listen."

"Wanker," Mel snorted. "I'm staying here."

Dirk's lips twitched as though he wanted to grin. He placed a hand on Alden's shoulder and composed himself. "Sorry, my man, but he's not wrong. Also, I think you've gone a tiny bit crazy. Because you're speaking like this place is conscious. It's not. It's just a big, weird building."

"A big, weird building on a floating island in a portal in the sky that magicked us onto it," Alden said, feeling as though he really shouldn't have to be convincing anybody of this. "You're a children's author, Dirk. You're famed for your imagination. How can you discount everything that's happening here? Yeah, it's all nuts, but we need to be careful where we draw the line about what to accept and what to ignore. I agree we need to stick together, but not here. We have to move forwards. We have to climb each floor to the top and try to find answers along the way. There must be a reason we're being made to do this."

"But you saw what happened to that lovely priest," the elderly woman said. "This place is bad. We can't trust it."

"Yeah," Bryan said. "The old lady's right, you know."

"My name is Kim."

Bryan ignored her. "Whatever, love. Listen, this place is a deathtrap and our friend Dirk is bang on the money. We should stay here, near the entrance, where we're safe."

Rakie raised her hand. "I know the way through, if that helps. I've played this game before." She looked up to Earl. "Right, Dad?"

"Ah, Rakie, honey, maybe you shouldn't–"

"Game?" Dirk said, pulling a face. "What d'you mean, *game*?"

Alden could see from the reaction of the group that this might be the straw that broke their brains. Rakie backed into her father's arms as they all stared at her.

"It's from a video game," Earl said, reluctantly but firmly. He raised his chin defiantly as all eyes turned to him. "Yeah, I know how it sounds. But it is what it is. This place has been designed to look like a game Rakie plays. No idea why or how, but the main thing is – this girl knows how to beat the level." He hesitated and looked down at his daughter. "And... yeah, I'm pretty sure we're not allowed to linger in one place, are we?"

"Oh shit," Rakie said, eyes wide. "I forgot. The Driller! We need to go, Dad. *Now.*"

She began dragging Earl up the corridor with such desperation, Alden felt his skin crawl at the thought of staying behind.

Nobody else moved.

"This is a game?" the male model said.

"What's a driller?" Kim asked.

Alden wanted to say something, to rally them into moving, but could he even do that with these people? He was used to encouraging children to get shit done – and some of the time it even worked – but this was an entirely different class he was facing.

The kind that would probably seek answers in someone like Dirk, as much as it curdled his soul to admit it.

"Listen, Dirk, we all need to go together," Alden urged, trying to dampen his panic as Rakie and Earl moved away. "If the girl recognises this place and knows how to survive here, it's more than the rest of us do. Please, say something. We need to follow them."

Dirk held his hands up. "Hey, man, it's a free country, talk to them yourself. I ain't stopping you."

"Oh, for fuck's sake," Nia said impatiently, stepping up beside Alden and shooting Dirk a withering look. "Put that influencer charm to good use and convince the others to come with us, or you're probably going to find out that 'driller' isn't some new dating site for you to scroll through for hookups."

"You don't know that," he said, a sly smile creeping over his lips.

"I don't, no. But see that smart girl over there, the one running away from here as fast as she can? She seems to know it. And given that nobody else in here can say for certain what's going on, I'm going to place all bets on her. Come on, Alden. Let's go with them and try to find whatever takes us up to the next floor."

She turned on her heels and started up the stone-clad corridor, side-stepping the drips and the strands of moss, hastening after the father and daughter. Alden held Dirk's gaze for a moment longer, before going after her.

Behind him, Dirk swore under his breath. Then there was silence. Then the man addressed the others in a low tone.

Whatever he said, worked. Alden heard the scrapes of shoes and grunts of exertion as the rest of the group got to their feet and followed them.

The power of celebrity, he thought.

They moved slowly through the damp, torchlit corridor. Alden noted the others occasionally reached out to inspect their surroundings, gauging its touch, feel and authenticity, perhaps still not believing this was all real. He couldn't blame them. It seemed like wandering through a dream at times.

The space was only big enough for pairs of them to walk side by side – three abreast at a push – so it was inevitable that the group split into little groups, with those walking together introducing themselves in hushed voices.

Alden caught snippets of their conversations as he walked. He found out the handsome male model with a swish of sandy hair was Mason, who'd been asleep on a train only to wake up and find himself here. The blonde woman in the suit was Casey, a PR executive, who'd been driving down the M62 to Leeds, singing at the top of her lungs to Taylor Swift, when she'd been taken. They briefly wondered what might have become of her car after she disappeared from driving it.

The elderly woman, Kim, was originally from Indonesia and had moved to the UK with her now-deceased husband some forty years ago. She was chatting with Dev, who was from Manchester, and whose bright demeanour and little jokes Alden could tell were likely covering for a severe bout of panic

The suited and booted Mel was regaling Bryan with information about the football match he'd been on his way to watch. Meanwhile, Bryan was trying to politely end the conversation and chat instead to Dirk, who was otherwise engaged flirting with the French flight attendant, Monique. She had appeared here from a plane between Paris and New York, which just happened to be passing over the UK at the moment the tower had plucked them from their lives.

Alden listened to it all, feeling a little more at ease now they were moving again and all together. He lifted his gaze to Earl and Rakie ahead, moving with a familiarity about the dungeons that suggested what they'd said about recognising this place was true.

He still couldn't quite get to grips with what that might mean.

Nia walked beside him. They moved silently at first, and he wondered if maybe they were happy enough in each other's company to do so, or whether she was simply not in the mood to talk. But as the conversations continued around them, their silence grew more awkward and obvious, until he had to break it.

"So where were you before this?"

"Me?" she asked. "Oh, I was at work."

"On a Saturday?"

"Yeah, you tend to work all hours when you do what I do. Which is follow the lead of men who have no idea where they're going." Alden blinked, unable to know how to respond, and she sighed. "Sorry, just feeling a little bit at the whim of life right now."

He gestured ahead. "At least we're being led by a girl."

Her laugh was brief, but sincere. "What were you doing when the tower beamed you up?"

"I was on a date."

"Going well?"

"Yeah, I was actually enjoying myself for the first time in a while. Nice to know it was still possible."

"I'm sorry it had to end, then. You've had a tough time lately, I assume?"

Alden's chest tightened as he nodded, the black hole of grief inside making its presence known again. What he wouldn't give to get out of here, back to his date and that whisper of colour he'd felt.

"That would be one way of putting it," he said. "My, uh, dog Leia died a few months ago."

Spoken aloud in this dank dungeon, trapped in a tower in the sky, the words sounded silly, trivial, ridiculous. The loss of a pet compared to all this?

But it's not just that, he reminded himself. *It wasn't just her you lost.*

He was rewarded with a flash of images of his family in the garden, Leia bounding around, jumping on his mum and dad. All light and fun, and full of warmth. Before he was confronted with pale faces on an iPad screen. Breathing tubes. Beeping. Masks. And then there was just Leia and him, alone in a cold house, and then—

Hold it together, mate, he thought, shaking himself out of the spiral.

"Oh, I'm so sorry," Nia said, genuine concern etched in the lines at the corner of her eyes as she touched his arm. It almost broke him.

"Thank you," he said, forcing a smile. "But it's fine. It's just… maybe not the best time to be ripped from existence and told to climb a tower of death, you know? Although I can't imagine there is *any* good time for this shit."

She nodded and gave the dungeons a look of contempt. "You got that right."

* * *

The corridor remained long and narrow and straight, the barred cells on either side all empty, save for a few shadowy skeletons covered in tattered and indistinct rags that spoke of no discernible origin. All very generic, especially when you considered they kept passing the same collection of loot crates – trick ones and otherwise – plus some amphorae Alden suspected might also contain some game-related treasure.

"If some of these are booby traps," he asked Earl, who remained ahead of him, "what about the others? Is it worth having a look inside those ones?"

"I wouldn't touch anything at all," the man replied over his shoulder. "This all feels familiar, but I don't know if I want to stake my life, or yours, on thinking anything here is safe."

"It's so repetitive," Nia said, noting yet another collection of the same stuff. "Did someone get bored designing this thing?"

"It was like this in the game," Rakie said.

"She's not wrong," Earl added. "I think it was going for that classic feel. So this is all in keeping with what we remember of *Forbidden Fortress*, except for one thing… Why the hell is it in this tower, and why are we being forced to experience it in real life?"

Dev's voice drifted from behind them. "Not just that, though! Has anybody noticed how this corridor is wayyyy longer than the tower looked from the outside? We should have been through the back of the building by now. Yet we keep going through these same boring tunnels. Seriously, why?"

As if responding to being called out, the single corridor soon started branching out into side corridors. Alden peered down these offshoots as they passed them and saw even more routes leading off. What had started as a simple dungeon corridor had become a sprawling labyrinthine maze, all of it stretching far, far beyond the footprint of the tower and the island it had been resting on.

He'd never been one for physics or science, yet he had noted the way the tower flitted in and out of reality outside, its shape malleable, its physicality inconsistent, and assumed the same must be true inside, too. None of it was logical or tied to any reality they understood. They needed to be prepared for anything.

Earl and Rakie eventually stopped at a crossroads that seemed remarkably similar to several others they'd passed. Ahead was the same. To the right, there was a carved symbol of a wolf's head at the end of the corridor. To the left, there was nothing out of the ordinary that Alden could see, other than a strange, slick moss coating the ceiling.

"If this is a game," Nia said, tilting her head left, "then I'd wager we go that way."

Rakie looked back in surprise. "Yeah, we need to stay beneath the moss. How did you know?"

"Just a designer's hunch."

"You sure we weren't supposed to head towards that symbol?" Earl asked his daughter, looking into the right tunnel.

"That's there to tempt you. Don't you remember finding it and then dying immediately? It's a trap, luring the basic players."

"You calling me basic?"

Rakie laughed. "You know it. Come on, Nia's right, we go this way."

Earl didn't argue. He let his daughter take them to the left.

Along this corridor the walls changed; the stone became darker, damper. With what, Alden didn't know. It looked in the flickering torchlight like it might be blood. But if the walls were bleeding, he didn't really want to know it. Overhead, the moss had been lost beneath a thick tangle of vines and roots breaking through the ceiling. He wondered if there were insects in there and pulled his shirt collar tighter around his neck.

He kept following the father and daughter, checking over his shoulder to make sure the others were following. Several pairs of eyes blinked back at him in the eerie light. A caravan of the lost and confused. Only Dirk held his gaze and blew him a kiss. Alden ignored him.

"Here we go," Rakie said, pulling up ahead.

The corridor ended in a doorway beyond which Alden could see very little. It felt like it was opening into a cavernous room, but no matter how hard he stared into it, the space remained indistinct and cloaked in a haze. He couldn't tell if it was in the room itself, or his eyes literally couldn't focus on whatever was in there.

He didn't like how it made him feel.

"What's this place, then?" Dirk said, leaning between Alden and Nia, doing his best to nudge Alden out of the way. His breath was uncomfortably warm, with the slight scent of peppermint. "I can't see any goddamn thing in there, kid. Is this part of that game of yours?"

"No… this is new," Rakie said.

The note of confusion in her voice gave Alden pause. She'd been confident at the start, leading them at pace through this weird place. Now she was hesitant. Unwilling to step forward into the room. It made him not want to step inside either.

"Maybe we should double back and–" Nia started.

It was Mel in the back who forced them forward. Shoved his big meaty hands into backs and growled angrily at everyone. "Oi, what's the holdup? If we get out of this fucking cellar in time, I might make the second half. Get a move on!"

Dev was pushed into Dirk, who stumbled against Alden, who teetered and fell forward against Earl.

The man crossed the threshold, pulling his daughter with him. As soon as he did, the momentum forced everyone else in, too.

Then everything changed.

The plain, sterile air suddenly grew thick with bitter, acrid stink. Noise enveloped them, a vast cacophony of screaming slicing through the chamber like chainsaws through a corpse. Multiple voices of suffering and agony.

Alden's knees wobbled and he clasped his hands to his ears. He could see other people shimmering into existence around them, each one connected to some kind of machine, bloodshot eyes bulging from their faces, lips pulled taut with agony, letting loose horrific sounds.

A figure to his right was strapped to a rack. The spoked wheels were turning themselves. Her entire body shuddered, and she moaned as one of her arms popped from its socket. Rakie saw it and screamed, burying her face into her father's chest.

Beside them, Dirk was staring up at a man being lowered by chains from an unseeable ceiling onto a chair with a long, rusted spike placed dead centre. While on the other side of Alden, Nia was covering her mouth with horror at a woman chained to the wall, her head covered with a hessian sack that was bulging and chittering with the sounds of rodents inside it. With every movement, it grew more stained with blood.

Then a vision appeared directly before Alden.

It was a man in a chair. Dark hair all mussed up and head held upright in a vice. A wire was slung across his throat, tied to some kind of clockwork cog. As Alden watched, the cog turned of its own accord and the man gurgled as a thin red line began to appear across his neck, drawing further and further in, even as the man's head convulsed and his eyes sought Alden's for help.

That's when Alden realised.

It was *him* in the chair.

He was watching himself be garrotted.

The other Alden reached out desperately. Fingers grabbed at the sleeve of his jacket, tugging at it. Physical contact that was far too real for what had been empty space a few seconds ago.

"It's us!" Alden gasped, backing away, trying to force air down his own throat, into his lungs, keeping himself alive, while the other him was slowly murdered in front of his eyes. He started hyperventilating and doubled over. A panic attack. He blinked as his vision blurred, hearing the cries around him, realising everyone else was facing the same horror.

They were all watching themselves die in the worst possible ways.

How could *this* be part of the game?

Alden tried to get a bearing on Earl again, saw the man

barely holding it together as his daughter screeched into his chest. It was clear neither of them had been expecting this.

Something touched his wrist and he jerked back. It was him again. The vision had somehow moved, followed him the few steps he'd taken. The other hand reached for him again and, this time, tightened around his forearm. The knuckles whitened. He was yanked closer to himself, towards the blood spilling from the wound, the soft sound of flesh and muscle being cut.

His other eyes were red and wild. His jaw locked. His lips moving.

"*Help… me…*" he mouthed.

Alden wanted to curl up into a ball and squeeze his eyes shut, but something forced him to keep going. To try to help. He grabbed the turning cog, felt the wood ice-cold beneath his fingers, pouring the depths of winter up into him. He gritted his teeth against the pain and pulled as hard as he could, feeling his skin begin to blister, before a burst of cold, hard nothingness blew up through the metal, emptied into his bones, and threw him backwards.

He could have sworn in that moment he had been killed. For this was surely death. Being overcome with the loneliest, emptiest feeling, as though he had somehow reached out and touched the eternal void at the end of the universe… and it had touched him back.

But then his tumble through the air came to an abrupt end, as he slammed into the stone wall and slid down to the floor. Still alive. Even though death was making its presence felt all around him.

Nobody came to his aid. Nobody could. They were all fighting the same battles. Those trying to save themselves were flung across the room. Nia was tossed into Earl and his daughter. Mel hit the ceiling and fell to the floor in a heap. Dirk was begging the others to save his doppelgänger from being slowly impaled on the spike.

Then, in the midst of the chaos, Alden saw calm.

Kim, slight of figure, with her neatly brushed grey hair, was standing across the room before her other self. There was no urgency to her movement, even as she talked, head bowed before her alternative self in a copper bath, drowning. Alden could see prune fingers gripped the rusting rim, trying to pull herself out, fighting whatever force was holding her under.

Water splashed over the side. Over Kim.

But the tiny woman remained the essence of calm within this nightmare. A port in this storm for Alden to look towards. Gently reaching out to herself, Kim placed a palm upon her dying self's hand.

Not to help her out.

Just to let her know she was there.

The fingers flexed and strained under her, but Kim held still and this energy seemed to flow into her dying self. The scrabbling at the rusted metal ceased. The fingers relaxed.

Then the entire bathtub disappeared.

Kim's shoulders lifted and sagged, as though she was taking a deep breath, then she turned. Through the chaos, she saw Alden.

Nodded to him.

His other self grabbed for his arm again, but this time Alden let him. He felt the hand clamp down on his forearm, and even as he avoided looking at himself, he let his own fingers wrap around the other. He wanted to vomit as he felt his double shudder, continuing to hear the slow, precise tearing of wire through skin, unable to stop breathing in the metallic, rusting stench of the blood soaking into the other's clothes.

The fingers gripped him even tighter, bruising his skin, fingernails digging in.

Still Alden held fast to his other. Adrenaline coursing through him, pulse racing, brain screaming. Horrified at his own helplessness. Hoping this was going to work, that he'd understood what Kim had done. That he needed to stand fast, not fight the visions.

Then it happened.

There was a warmth. A soothing beneath his fingers.

He looked over to see the wire simply vanish. Then the immovable cog. And finally, with a sigh of peace that bubbled more blood from the still-gaping wound, the other him faded into the ether.

Alden's hands dropped away, twitching. He stepped back in shock.

"We need to accept it," he said, his voice barely a whisper. He cleared his throat and tried to rise above the screams and shouts of the others. "Hey, listen, everybody *listen*! Don't fight this. Don't try to help yourselves. You can't save them. You just have to stay strong and accept this."

"Not just accept, but embrace," Kim added, lifting her voice as much as she could to be heard. "Offer yourself comfort. Understand that this is death, and it comes to us all."

Dirk laughed hysterically, hands covering his eyes as the other him reached the spike and began a blood-curdling cry of agony. "What are you two fucking talking about? I'm not going to accept *shit*! This is insane. Someone fucking *do* something!"

One by one, the others understood, though. They must have seen Alden and Kim weren't being haunted by visions anymore. Acceptance rippled outwards across the room. Earl grabbed Rakie and spun her around to face their own personal traumas hanging from the ceiling. He whispered something in her ear and both of them reached out to their kicking legs above. After a few seconds, the flailing stopped, and their other selves dissipated. Nia touched her hand to the arm of the woman with the bloodied bag on her head and the movement in the bag grew still before the figure disappeared entirely.

Eventually, Dirk had no choice but to blindly reach out his hand to place it on the struggling man's shoulder. He kept looking away, face pinched in revulsion, until finally, mercifully, the screaming stopped. The other Dirk grew calm and fell away from reality.

"Fuck all the way off," Dirk whimpered, dropping to his knees.

Nia pulled him back up, as Alden stared around the room at the others, seeing his own terror and confusion mirrored in their faces. Especially as a new noise echoed around the room. A grinding of stone on stone.

What now? he thought with despair, forcing himself to stand ready for whatever hell came next.

On the other side of the chamber, a door opened to let them out.

"I want to go home," he muttered, staggering along with the others towards the flickering dungeon light.

CHAPTER SIX
Questions of Death

Fuck this place.

Nia fell against the stone wall in the new corridor and slid to the ground. Her breath was still coming in gasps. Her heart pounding so loud she could barely hear herself think, let alone the others talk. All she could discern were sounds that seemed like they might be words, distant and indistinct. The whimpers, though, were louder.

As was the weeping.

What did we just see?

The rest of the group had caught up and were collapsing, too. The flight attendant kicked off her heels and sat down beside her, crinkling her otherwise immaculate navy trouser suit, with a L'Espoir Air logo emblazoned on a badge. Her deep brown eyes, matching the colour of her perfect skin, regarded Nia with weariness.

"*Tu vas bien*?" she asked, breathless. Then in English, "Are you OK?"

Nia brushed her hair from her face, wiped her eyes. "I honestly don't know. You?"

"Yes. The same."

"Fuck," Nia said again, and put her head between her knees, unable to get the sound of the chittering rats, or the image of the blood slowly soaking into the bag on the woman's head, out of her mind. She was close to vomiting.

The flight attendant's hand found her back and rubbed.

"My name is Monique."

"Nia."

"Well, Nia, we have each other in this… whatever this place is." Monique took in a low, long breath. Then another, as though trying to calm herself. "I might have said it was a godforsaken realm, but I do not believe this tower exists in a place our gods could find to forsake it. Nothing is real here. That chamber… Those people…?"

"They were us."

Monique nodded. "Yes. And they came out of nowhere and returned to nowhere. Why?"

A shadow fell over them, and Nia looked up to see Alden joining them. His scruffy hair was mostly tucked behind his ears, revealing a haunted look on his face. She imagined it probably reflected her own. She didn't think she'd ever forget what had just happened, could still see the images every time she blinked.

"Earl and Rakie said it wasn't part of the game," he said, before someone burst through the group and grabbed him.

It was Mel, the gammon in the business suit. His face was beetroot red, a violent mix of terrified and raging. "What kind of game are you playing here, you little wanker?" he spat, spinning Alden around to face him. "How did you know what to do in there? If this is some kind of fucked-up prank, if you're one of those influencers doing all this shit for views, I'm going to cave your fucking head in."

"What?" Alden said, clearly confused. He looked to Dirk. "He's the inf–"

His face snapped to the side as Mel's fleshy fist connected with his jaw. Alden fell back, but the thug wasn't done with him yet. He held him tightly in place and wound up to strike again.

"What was that?"

Nia scrambled to her feet to stop him somehow. But it was Dirk who stepped in.

The children's author slid in between the two men, the buttons of his white T-shirt pulling open at his chest, while his running shorts rode up, revealing a muscled runner's thigh. It was an odd sight, seeing this preening man square up to a gorilla in a business suit. But Nia was grateful for the intervention.

"Hey, dude, let's just chill for a moment, yeah?" Dirk cooed to Mel. "I'm on your side here. This is all *supremely* fucked up, but just have a think about what you're saying. You think this little idiot managed to build a tower in the sky and magic us all here? You think he conjured those…? Nah, I don't even know what those were. Visions? Acid trips? Whatever. *I'm* one of those rich-as-fuck influencers on social media, and I can tell you now, there ain't no amount of money got the buying power to pull this shit off. Wannabe rock star Michael Bubbles here doesn't have the reach or the dollars to build a tower of Lego, let alone whatever the fuck this place is. He's a nobody."

Wincing, Alden leaned over to spit blood onto the stone floor. "None taken."

"Hey, buddy, I'm saving your life here," Dirk snapped, before focusing on Mel again, giving him a slap on the shoulder of solidarity. "We good, dawg?"

Mel rubbed his knuckles, then let go. "For now," he said, as Alden collapsed to the floor.

As Dirk led the arsehole away, Nia quickly rushed to Alden. He groaned while she inspected his face, lifting his chin up gently so she could get a look at him in the torchlight.

"Shit, that must have hurt."

"Uh-huh."

"You going to be OK, slugger?"

Alden laughed, then winced. "Pretty sure I'm the slug*ee* here. Sorry, no gold star for you."

"That's the concussion speaking." She gave him the middle finger. "Can you see straight? How many am I holding up?"

"Very funny."

She used her sleeve to wipe a little blood from the corner of his lip and then helped him back up again. A small part of her hated that she had to ask the same question as Mel after what had just happened, but the thick-necked arsehole had been on to something. This was important. They all needed to know.

"So…" she began awkwardly.

"Go on, ask."

"How *did* you know how to get us out of that chamber of horrors?"

"It wasn't me." He faced the group, looking to someone at the back of the corridor. The little old woman, Kim. "I watched what she was doing, the only thing I saw working. We were all trying to save ourselves, weren't we? I couldn't. No matter how hard I tried, something kept knocking me back."

Nia nodded, remembering it for herself. The intense cold, as though she was caught outside naked in the middle of winter. Just a sheer, brutal shock.

"Yeah… *that*," Alden said, seeing it in her eyes. He looked around him, meeting the faces of the other interlopers in this monstrous tower. "Every time I tried to save the other me, I felt it see me. And I saw the rest of you experience the same. It was like we touched something we shouldn't have and were violently rejected. As though whatever we were doing was wrong." He gestured to Kim again. The woman gave him a kindly smile. "And then I saw her. Everyone else was trying to save themselves, but I saw Kim just stand there, offering comfort. And it worked." He raised his voice, addressing her directly. "How did you know that's what *it* wanted, Kim?"

Bryan unfolded himself like a praying mantis from the shadows. "Dare I ask what *it* is, exactly?"

"The tower," Alden said. "I think it's sentient. Can't you feel it?"

There was quiet for a moment and Nia felt the tension intensify between the players in the group. Yes, that's what they all were in her mind. Players in this game. Some of them making their moves. Others sitting back, likely waiting their turn.

"Kim?" Alden persisted.

For her part, Kim clasped her frail fingers together in front of her, every bit the polite, quiet old lady who might live down the street from you, who would always wave hello and sometimes offered the neighbourhood children an ice lolly in the summer.

"At my age, you realise death is inevitable," she said softly, her words like crinkling paper. "I could do nothing for the woman in the bath, even if she was me. I had no strength to pull her out, you see? No effort of mine could have saved her. And then I understood. Because when you get to my age, you come to know death. It becomes a friend. You must not fear it. You must only accept it. Death is an inevitable part of this journey and without it there is no journey. If something lives, it must surely die. There is a great peace in knowing that."

"I'm sorry, I do not understand," Monique said, looking around to make sure she wasn't alone.

Alden answered.

"We weren't in that room to try to save ourselves. I think we were there to learn to accept our mortality. To accept death."

The word *death* echoed through the claustrophobic corridor and disappeared into the darkness beyond the torchlight. Nobody in the group moved or spoke.

Nia didn't know what to make of all this. But she did know she'd felt that sense of calm and acceptance when she had been back in that room, and she had reached out against all her instincts – not to free her other self, but to comfort her. To let her know she wasn't alone.

Where the cold had been previously, warmth had then followed. Like discovering a lit pub fire on a winter's evening.

That's what the tower had wanted from them. The acceptance of death.

But why?

The question raised its head again, and she wanted to scream it at these people and these stones and the flames of the torches and the fabric of the tower itself. *Why why why?* It was the only question that mattered. Other than maybe *how the hell do we get out of here?* But, even then – even if she was suddenly, magically, transported home again to her frustrating, helpless existence – she knew she would go the rest of her days asking that very same question. *Why?*

Nia was an artist. There was a need within her to create, to craft, to conjure art from ideas. To try to capture the feelings and emotions of people, moments, locations, and pour them into a tangible form. It was a way of taking the world around her and controlling it in some way. It was perhaps the only way she knew of exerting power over her life, without other people fucking it up.

It bugged her beyond reason that she needed to know the answer to *why*, and that any answers would rely on this group of strangers. The only upside was that she could see they were all asking themselves the same question.

There would be no answers, though. For in the distance there was a *thump-thump-thump* and a screech of metal tearing through stone, and Earl's daughter cried out in familiarity and terror as she turned to her father.

"Oh no," she whispered. "It's here."

CHAPTER SEVEN
The Driller

The twelve ran from the horrendous noise.

Towards what, Alden didn't think any of them had an idea.

But he currently didn't care. The discordant echoes behind them were enough to convince him they had to get away, and *fast*.

Rakie led the way, dragging her dad along. They'd made their escape as soon as they'd heard the noise and the others had been panicked enough to follow. Dirk had pushed past everyone until he was trailing the father and daughter, while Alden and Nia hurried behind him.

"Do we really need to move at such a rush?" Bryan moaned from the back. "We don't even know what we're running from! That noise could be us being rescued."

Dev shot back, "Does that shit *sound* like a rescue, mate?"

"It's not a rescue," Rakie called. "It's a monster in the game. The Driller."

A moment of silence followed, in which Dirk muttered what they were probably all thinking. "For *fuck's* sake, you were being serious about that?"

Earl looked back at them as another shrill noise echoed in their wake. "In case you're wondering, yes, it's exactly what the name suggests. And that sound you can hear is exactly how it sounds in the game. This isn't a rescue, it's an attack. Please, let's just keep going."

Bryan, though, was clearly not one to give up or listen to those with experience. Alden sighed inwardly, knowing the type. His old headmaster had been similar. A man who knew what he knew and be damned with anybody else's lived experience. A façade of confidence, with little of note behind the walls.

"I'm just saying–" he began indignantly.

"Well, don't!" Nia said, the frustration evident in her voice. "Save your breath for walking and don't drop behind."

Alden raised an eyebrow as he glanced over, catching her eye as she brushed her wavy dark hair from her face, looking a little flushed. She shrugged, a little sheepishly, confirming she didn't really speak to people like that usually. He didn't care, though. If her nerves were shot, she wasn't the only one. He gave her a grin of solidarity. Of all the people around him, she was the one he felt the most comfortable with. She had a good energy, and he knew if Leia was around, she'd agree. His dog had always been great at reading people. Nia would have been found to be one of the good ones and curled up on; he could just picture it.

They continued moving at a jog, Dev helping the elderly Kim along as fast as he could, while Bryan bluntly told Mason as he swiped him away, "I'm old, not dead," when the model tried to help.

Through the corridors they went, back in the game environment they'd been in before, with the same walls and shackles and mass of greenery on the ceiling. Numerous side tunnels led off the main corridor, and Alden could see doorways leading to rooms where blocks and ladders and rope bridges and clockwork dials sat swathed in a maudlin gloom, as if waiting to be activated.

"Do we not need to go in any of those?" Casey called across the group.

"Side quests," Rakie said. "We can't get distracted. That's how he gets you."

"And how do we get him?" Alden asked.

"You can't."

"Oh... but it's a boss in a game, right? It's there to be beaten, otherwise what's the point?"

"*That's* the point. It's why *Forbidden Fortress* is so cool. It's full of unbeatable bad guys and the Driller is the worst of them. You just have to avoid it in order to get through the level..."

Rakie's words trailed into a frustrated sigh as they passed another crossroads and she dropped her pace, letting go of her father's hand. She looked around the corridor with frustration. "Except we should have reached the end by now. There's a staircase at the end of the dungeon and you take it up to the next level." She looked to her dad, tired, confused, her eyes welling up. "Did I do it wrong?"

"No, Rakie, this isn't on you. It's not exactly the same game we've played. What happened back in that torture chamber proves something else is at work here. It's been made to feel like that game, but it isn't. It's like... got the same vibe."

The tail end of the group caught up and Bryan moaned again. "Why've we stopped? For pity's sake, keep going, all of you!"

"Look who's a believer now," Nia muttered, rolling her eyes.

Another scrape echoed through the gloom behind them.

A thud. Another screech of metal on stone. The noises were inconsistent, as though the villain was rambling after them, but the echoes made them constant, irrepressible, as if the nightmare would never, ever stop following.

"Seriously, what *is* that thing?" Dirk hissed loudly. "I write books, kid. I know how supremely weird a storyteller's imagination can get, and right now mine is in overdrive. How bad is this *Driller*?"

"Oh, well, I'm a writer, too, actu–" Rakie began.

He cut her off with a sigh of derision. "Look, I would just *love* to chat about books and stories, and maybe I can do a school visit for you later, but right now can we focus on the thing that's going to try to kill everyone, yeah? What is it, kid? What are we about to face?"

"I, uh, it's a big thing made of metal and it drills people, I guess."

Dirk ran his fingers over his face with barely concealed frustration. "Jesus," he said, then ushered the girl and her father to keep moving. The noise was growing steadily louder and a low roar filled the tunnel. "OK, let's just fucking shift gears, you two. Where now?"

Rakie looked like she was about to break. Alden had seen so many children deal with pressure over the last few years, especially during the pandemic, but this was something else entirely. Not only having been cut off by someone she clearly admired, she was also responsible for saving the lives of eleven other people. For leading them through this impossible maze. He could only imagine how she was feeling.

"I'm so sorry," the girl responded quietly. "I think I'm lost. Maybe we took a wrong turn back there or something."

Mel grumbled from the back. "Should never have let a fucking kid take charge."

Earl ignored him and grabbed her hand, pulling her onwards.

"Is there anything else you remember about the game that might help? You said you did a walkthrough."

"There are usually signs in games like this, Rakie," Nia said to the girl, trying to encourage her. "I've designed them myself. Where you sprinkle little clues to show you where to go. Was there anything like that?"

"No, I don't think so."

"There wasn't a hidden trail or anything?"

"Oh, shit, the moss!" the girl exclaimed, then craned her neck up to the ceiling. She pointed to the tangled mass of undergrowth carpeting the roof of the corridor. "Look for the moss we saw earlier! That's what you have to follow to get out of here. It's special."

They all looked up to see undergrowth that was thick and twisted, full of roots and stalks and leaves.

"How the fuck can you even tell *what's* up there?" Dirk shouted, trying to make himself heard over the approaching noise. "And what's special about the moss?"

Rakie broke free of Earl's grasp and ran to the wall, wrenching the nearest torch free. As the flame danced above the club handle, she jumped and shoved it upwards as high as she could. Then again. The fire flickered against the leaves, before something ignited with a vigorous *WHOOSH*. A river of flame quickly snaked out across the ceiling, engulfing everything in its path, until it hit a crossroads and diverted into the corridor on the right.

"It's flammable!" the girl said, dropping the torch, grabbing both Nia and her dad, and following the lit trail, ducking as she went.

As the others followed, Alden noticed Kim dropping

behind. He took the old lady's arm and helped her along as fast as she could go, having to duck as the fire grew. The moss stank as it burned, a thick and bitter smell, while the blanket of heat that covered the ceiling quickly became unbearable.

It was like trying to run beneath a grill.

"Come on, Kim, just a little further," Alden urged, covering his mouth and nose with his arm, hoping he was right.

He stumbled forward after the others, feeling the vibrations of the tunnel shaking around him. The sound behind them was so close, he half expected to be able to glance over his shoulder and see its source.

Then Rakie shouted, "There it is!"

The fire had finally led them to the end of the corridor. But where Alden had expected stone stairs leading them out of the dungeon, there was only a tree.

It grew from the flagstones, roots spreading out from its base like a skirt. The trunk twisted upwards, branches curling off it at intervals, and it disappeared into a hole in the fire above.

"A fucking *tree*?" Mel shouted, panicked and angry. Alden and Kim reached the others, just as he pushed his way to the front. "It's a dead end! Where are the stairs?"

With his forearm shielding his face against the heat, Earl moved closer and looked up. "There's a hole in the ceiling! It's just big enough for us to climb through one at a time. Quickly, use the branches, pull yourself up!"

"But how do we know it's safe?" Bryan said, shoving his way through to stand beside Mel. The two were taking strength from each other's dickish tendencies.

"It's safe. The fire led us here, right, Rakie?"

The girl nodded, squinting against the intense light.

"Well, I'm not going up there and, quite frankly, I think this is crazy. This whole thing is–"

Bryan was cut off by another horrific noise as the corridor shook again and Alden fell backwards, finally catching sight of what had been chasing them.

A figure of bone and flesh and metal stood there, as tall as the corridor, its triangular skull half-immersed in the flames engulfing the roof. Two oversized arms fell from its shoulders to the floor, except each fleshy mass of muscles ended in hands with drills for fingers. They flexed and scraped along the flagstones, churning up clouds of dust and grit as they bit into the rock.

The group fell upon the tree in a swell of screams. Dirk and Bryan pushed Earl aside to reach it first, scrambling up the branches and hauling themselves through the hole in the roof, as the others followed.

The floor shook again as the Driller stomped towards them.

Alden saw Kim had fallen against the far wall. As they locked eyes he could see the fear in the crinkled lines of her face. And the exhaustion. He couldn't see her being able to go much further.

The Driller must have seen it, too, and diverted towards her, its feet cracking the flagstones with such force Alden stumbled into the wall himself.

If I can just reach her, he thought desperately, not knowing where the end of that sentence lay. But he knew he couldn't just leave her here.

He scrambled upright.

There's no time, his brain argued again.

His river of thoughts trickled to a slow drip as he stepped towards her.

You are going to DIE!

The heat above continued to burn sweat from his flushed skin. His eyes stung and his throat was raw and his hair was plastered to his forehead. He could hear the crunch of people scrabbling up the bark of the tree behind him and his heart shook with the vibrations of the creature's anvil-shaped feet as they shattered the stones beneath them.

He noticed the glimmer of hope in Kim's gaze as she saw him trying to reach her. That was probably the worst of it, he realised. His action had instilled hope. She actually believed he might be able to help.

"Alden, no!" Nia's voice rang out.

He didn't stop. Even as he saw the Driller's limbs lift from the floor and reach out, growing, extending towards the woman, the robot's long drill fingers spinning with murderous intent, his focus stayed on her. Every fibre of his being pushed him in that direction, using the wall for support, clawing himself forward.

He didn't have a plan. This was all instinct. Because the logic of it made no sense. He couldn't fight this towering killing machine. The best he could hope was to distract the thing, but even then, how could he do that? He was alone. Unarmed.

Then he saw the loot crate between him and his inevitable death.

They'd passed a hundred of them since entering the tower. Most had the smudge on the lid of the chest or coins spilling out of them. But Earl's warning had stuck with him. He'd stopped paying attention to them all, even the ones that were supposedly *not* trick crates.

This one had no smudge, no coins.

What have I got to lose?

Nia called another warning from behind him. Mel was swearing at Casey to climb up the tree faster. But Alden's focus was on reaching the chest. He grabbed the lid, feeling the splinters of wood rough against his fingers, and threw it up with no expectation as to what he was going to find in there. Only hope.

What he found was a *big fucking gun*.

It shouldn't have been in the dungeon. It was out of place, out of time – a futuristic, pump-action bazooka of a weapon, with glowing green goop contained within the barrel.

Alden didn't care. He grabbed the thing, struggling under the weight as he heaved it up and tucked it under his arm, feeling the power of it humming beneath his touch. Then, as he swung it around to face the beast, like one of those cheesy 1980s action heroes his dad used to talk about, his finger slipped over the trigger and–

A sinewy, cyborg arm slammed into his chest, lifting him off his feet and rocketing him into the opposite wall. The gun flew from his grip and he heard it clattering across the flagstones as he hit yet more stone and slid to the floor.

It would have been a blessing had everything gone dark. The agony of the impact was enough to make him want to lie down and give up. But then he heard Kim crying. His eyes opened, blinking away the tears, and he saw her staring at him. Her pitiful saviour.

The abject humiliation burned hotter than the heat of his injuries. Until it was lost in the horror of watching one of the drill fingers flex and push against her arm, tearing into her coat.

Alden looked away, knowing what was coming next.

Which is when he saw the gun, lying near the tree. And the man standing over it, picking it up with the kind of violent glint in his eyes that spoke of a lifetime of fantasising about big weapons and using them to maim and kill and sate the insecurity in his soul.

Mel stepped forward like some kind of science-fiction gangster, all tight-fitting suit and futuristic gun.

"Oi!" he said. A man of few words.

Alden watched him train the gun on the Driller, knowing, ridiculously, that the man wasn't being driven by a need to save Kim. He just wanted to get his weapon off. He stepped forward again, then again, any fear he'd had gone.

Suddenly:

BLAM.

Mel fired. A shock wave of green energy exploded from the gun, shaking the corridor and blowing a channel through the raging fire above as it shot towards the creature. Alden's ears rang as he recoiled, then twisted to see the creature take the hit.

Except it didn't.

Mel had missed.

The fury in the man's eyes grew more intense. There was no embarrassment, though. His shoulders were back, his chin was strong and set. He stepped forward again, confident, cocky, clearly fuelled by the power he cradled in his hands, ready to fire again.

"Consider that a warning shot, you big bastard."

The Driller withdrew from Kim and faced him, head tilted.

Alden looked to Kim and gestured towards the tree. *Go*, he mouthed.

She slid along the wall, while Mel stepped past her, grinning like a maniac.

"Now," he growled. "Eat shit!"

He squeezed the trigger again as he spoke, only this time, nothing happened. Alden saw the green glow immediately fade from the glass barrel and the gun fell apart in Mel's hands. His face drooped in confusion for a moment, then grew back angrier. He moved towards the Driller anyway, a real "fuck it" look on his face. His eyes were filled with a primal fury, a deep and ancient rage. It was pouring out of every pore of his body. The guy wanted his blood.

The Driller did too, though. One of its metal feet slammed down, shaking the corridor again. The fire above them flickered intensely with the waft of movement. It came forward to meet the man.

Mel didn't flinch. Didn't try to run.

To his shame, Alden did.

He slipped, trying to get back to his feet. His shoulder ached and his legs were almost numb with shock, and he fell hard against the wall again, trying to rationalise what he was doing.

I can't help him, he told himself. *I can barely stand.*

As Nia grabbed Kim and was helping her up the tree, Alden saw Mel throw out a fist as one of the creature's long arms shot out towards him. The drills glanced off the man's right knuckles, slicing through his skin, sending a shower of blood across Mel's bald pink head.

The man barely noticed. Instead, he went in with his left, aiming for his opponent's triangular skull of a head.

It connected.

The creature didn't move.

Alden knew then, as multiple other arms suddenly grew from the Driller's back and swept through the air to grab the man, that the contest was already over.

To his credit, Mel didn't shout at Alden or call him a coward as he ran away. Even though Alden felt a deep shame dragging at his guts as he forced his legs to move, to get away from what was about to go down, nothing was voiced. Mel was either still fixated on the killing machine, or he had simply accepted Alden was making the smart choice.

Alden reached the tree as Nia's trainers disappeared above him, following Kim into the hole in the roof, just as the drilling sounds filling the corridor were suddenly muffled by suit and flesh.

Mel started screaming.

There were leaves on the tree, Alden noticed as he climbed, trying to focus on anything but the agony filling the corridor. Iridescent leaves hanging from the branches like festive ornaments. More leaves, just like their tattoos. What did they mean?

Behind him, the screaming was taken to a horrifying new pitch.

Alden had always been scared of death. Even as a child the idea had frightened him silly, kept him up at night worrying about it, wondering when and how it might happen.

Everything that had happened in the last few years had worked to confirm he was right to fear death, because it was everywhere. The pandemic had brought that home to Alden. Showing him, even when it didn't happen to you, it had the power to affect you, break you, claim your life for its own as if you *had* died. Making you feel insignificant, irrelevant, unseen. Taunting you with the fear that you'll always be alone. That, in the end, you'll die alone too.

Leia had been able to hold him together for a while,

distracting him with the loving companionship only possible with a dog. But with her gone, he had drifted – grief and fear and loneliness taking him for a plaything.

Climbing this impossible tree in this tower of death, with Mel's tortured screams filling his ears, Alden realised now how badly he still wanted to live.

It was a glorious and terrible moment. Suddenly he had purpose again, but the terror was made exponentially worse because of it. He didn't want to die alone. He wanted to find himself again, feel that spark of happiness and company he'd felt in the bar with Michelle. He wanted to make sure his new friend Nia was safe. And Dev. And Kim. He wanted them all to get out of this fucking tower and survive and live again.

Resting his hand on the topmost branch, Alden braced himself, knowing what he had to do. Because he couldn't let this bastard of a man suffer the very thing that terrified him.

He had to bear witness to Mel's fate. He couldn't let him die alone.

So he turned around... and immediately wished he hadn't.

The Driller had wrapped the man up in its limbs and buried every single one of its spinning fingers into his body. Bloodied tatters of his suit and skin were flying in all directions as he was lifted off his feet. His bald head was blistering as it was dragged through the flames on the roof, before he was pulled slowly – deliberately – towards the Driller's face.

It regarded him with curiosity for a moment, before its jaw split open and a spiralling, sinewy tongue appeared.

Mel's eyes bulged as he realised where this was heading.

He screamed again, a wordless noise of terror, before the tongue burst out of the creature and entered his mouth. His scream morphed into something altogether worse, and only then did his gaze swing Alden's way.

A plea. Far, far too late.

Alden scrambled up the tree as fast as he fucking could, heaving himself into the hole.

CHAPTER EIGHT
Poseidon

The nothingness within the hole lasted only a moment.

Then Nia found herself crawling across a platform, its cold, wet metal slick beneath her fingers. She collapsed on it, gasping for breath, her brain racing to catch up. Nothing made sense. There had been no physical transition between pulling herself up from the tree to wherever she was now. She had simply ceased to exist, the bond between her atoms blinking out, before reforming again in this new place.

It was gloomy and damp. She heard the lapping of water amid the groans around her from the others, though her eyes hadn't yet adjusted to be able to see much. She knew instantly, though, that it wasn't like the dungeon they'd just left, with its torches and stone and fire-covered roof. The sounds were tinny, and as she lifted her head to scope out her surroundings, she saw long, thin stretches of neon lamps attached to the stark white metal walls. It was modern, realistic. More so than the fantasy dungeon they'd just escaped.

We've jumped genres, the designer's voice in her mind told her. *Switched movies. There's a glitch in the Matrix.*

She saw the shadowy figures of the group around her. Brief glimpses of faces in the half-light. Their collective gasps and heavy breathing after the tree climb created a cushion of noise around her that she found only partly comforting. She hadn't ever been one for spending time with strangers where she could help it, and these people *were* still strangers. Thrown together into the worst possible experience.

She supposed she should be grateful she wasn't alone, at least.

Someone's boots clanked on the metal floor as they shifted, sending echoes of the impact rippling around them in a very different corridor from the one they'd just escaped. Then someone burst the surface of a pool of water beside her, and through the coughing and spluttering she realised it was Alden.

She lunged for his flailing arm and grabbed it, hauling him onto the metal platform with Dev's help. The teacher's black hair was plastered to his pale face, like trees hiding a ghost.

"You're OK, Alden," she breathed, surprised at the relief she felt that he'd made it. "You're safe now."

Was that true? Probably not.

She held him close to her, trying to let her warmth overcome the cold in him. She'd seen what he had tried to do in the dungeon, going up against that slasher villain like that. He must have been absolutely nuts. But it marked him as someone she could trust, and *that* was a rare thing in life. Nia hadn't known many men who fitted the bill and she resolved to protect him in this foul place.

"Where's Mel?" Bryan snapped. The accusation hung clearly in the air, as the man's beady eyes fixed on Alden and his moustache quivered with indignation. "The boy and Mel were the only ones left to come through. What's he done with him?"

Nia let go her grip on Alden as he twisted and retched loudly twice, gushing swallowed water back into the pool. His face then fell against the metal.

"Dead," Alden said, still gasping for air.

"What's that, boy? Speak up and answer me! Did you leave him behind?"

Nia bristled, the adrenaline still surging through her from their dungeon escape. "His name is Alden and he said your friend is dead. OK? Now shut up and leave him alone, you irrelevant dinosaur." She was surprised by the bite in her voice, but she was fed up with biting her tongue, bottling up the frustration of existing in a world run by these dickheads, channelling her outbursts inward, just so she wasn't seen as emotional or a bitch. Here? Fuck that. She had nothing to lose. "If you hadn't been so busy pushing everyone out of the way to save your pasty, ancient behind, you would have seen Alden try to fight that monster to save Kim. And then Mel got involved, too. Kim and Alden managed to get away. Clearly Mel wasn't able to. Right, Alden?"

Alden sat up on his elbows. When he looked up at her, giving the briefest of nods, she saw the revulsion in his eyes and was unable to help the shiver that scurried up her spine.

She badly wanted to go home. Away from this nightmare. Shut herself away from other people and towers and terrifying killer robots and go back to existing from behind a screen. This was all a reality she didn't want to have to deal with.

"You're OK," she repeated to herself, as much as to Alden. She patted his hand and gave it a squeeze. "We'll get through this."

Dev was looking at her in earnest. "So what do we do now, Nia?" he asked.

He was a young lad – perhaps nineteen, maybe twenty. Short black hair and a few spots across his barely whiskered olive skin. He was just about holding things together, but from the fidgeting of his fingers, rubbing them over one another, she sensed he was maybe a scare away from losing his mind.

That he was looking to her to take control made her wonder if he already had.

Her gaze drifted from his face to the platform they were both sitting on. It had simply been splashed with water before, but it seemed the water was rising, lapping over the edges of the pool Alden had just appeared from.

"First thing we need to do is get up and move to higher ground," she said. When nobody argued, she got to her feet and led by example. One by one, the other survivors followed suit, collectively accepting the need to make a move.

That's how she thought of them. *Survivors*. Although of what, Nia still didn't really understand.

She hauled Alden up, who continued coughing up water. Dev threw his arm around Kim to comfort her. Earl was reassuring Rakie. The tall – and, so far, painfully quiet – Mason was holding the shorter blonde woman, Casey. Nia wondered who might be reassuring whom there, as neither was saying a word.

Unsurprisingly, Dirk was looking after himself, adjusting his T-shirt and rubbing down his broad forearms as though he might be cold. Nia caught a nod between him and Monique, who looked similarly chilly.

Bryan was busying himself brushing his long, wrinkled fingers down his damp tweed jacket to straighten it.

"So come on then, self-proclaimed leaders of the group," he muttered. "Which way do we need to go?"

Nia had already made up her mind which direction to head in. But she needed to check in with Earl and Rakie first. The girl was staring at something she held in her hands, turning it over. The barest glint of light bounced off it, before she saw Nia looking and tucked it into her hoody pocket quickly.

"Rakie? This place isn't in your game, is it?"

"No, sorry." Rakie shook her head. "Never seen any of this before."

"Earl?"

"Sorry, no. This isn't any game I've played."

Bryan grunted under his breath as if expecting as much, then raised his eyebrows at Nia. "Great. So I guess it's up to you to make the call, seeing as you seem to be trying to take charge here. And I, for one, am not going to stand in the way of the woke brigade!"

Nia set her jaw, resisting the urge to visibly clench her fists at her side. There was always one arsehole, everywhere she went. Every job. Every social gathering. Why did the tower have to beam one up here, too?

The thing was, she had a strong sense she knew exactly where to go. The environmental clues were striking and her creative instincts were on alert. She'd bet good money she could lead them through, no matter what anyone thought or said.

Thankfully, she didn't have to say a damn thing in the end.

"Eat a bag of dicks, you old fart," Rakie said to the man, before walking over, taking Nia's arm, and gesturing for her to lead them onwards.

Nia allowed herself a small smile as she chose a direction and heard the others fall in line behind her.

* * *

Design had always come naturally to Nia. Whether it be creating elaborate Lego playsets for games with her young brother and sister, or building collapsible blanket forts to dive into, steal the teddy bear treasure, and fight your way out as your siblings chucked cushions at you, she was always creating and crafting for fun. Inevitably, she ended up falling in love with art, where, with a few swishes of a pen or pencil, you could bring *anything* to life.

From there, she got jobs with advertising agencies and branding companies, and eventually Hollywood came calling. But it was her stint as a game designer that had been speaking to her since they'd set foot in the tower.

Her time in that high-intensity industry had only lasted a couple of years, but she'd learned enough in those long, stressful days about the psychology of designing a journey. How to work in subtle signs and clues to get people unfamiliar with an environment to pay attention to what you wanted them to look at. To instinctively move where they needed to go. These barest touches of guidance were so slight, nobody else would recognise them as such unless they thought long and hard about it or discovered them by accident.

The moss in the dungeons had been a sneaky trick – a trail hidden almost in plain sight, above their heads the entire time. That was definitely a design of the latter sensibility, requiring an inadvertent spark, or perhaps a cheat code, to discover it.

Here, though, treading carefully along the unusual metal floor, jumping across where parts of it had gone missing, and avoiding the dripping water overhead, Nia realised there was something more deliberate about the design.

We're being funnelled, she thought.

It was the light.

The place where they'd appeared had been cast in shadows, lit only by the stuttering neon lamps fixed strangely low along a wall in only one direction. Nobody had mentioned it, but the other direction had been much less well lit. Gloomy. A mood board of all your worst fears.

As awful as the flickering neon was, it provided a visible path for them to follow. Had she been designing some kind of game in which she wanted a group of exhausted, terrified people to go in a particular direction, she would have done the same thing.

There was something comforting about not being familiar with the strange aesthetic of their surroundings and yet still understanding the purpose of its design. She still had no idea what this place was supposed to be, but there was a measure of satisfaction in knowing at least they were heading the way they needed to be heading.

If only she could trust they weren't being led to their deaths.

The strange corridor with the metal floor and low-level lamps on the walls soon came to an end, and they stepped around a corner to find another, much longer corridor stretching out ahead of them. Here, the lights didn't flicker and there were lots of doors in the walls, all set at regular intervals and weirdly positioned a couple of feet off the floor, so you'd have to step up and over just to get inside.

And then she realised.

"We're upside down!" she said, looking up at the ceiling to see a long stretch of red, orange and black material coating every inch of it. An old-fashioned carpet, sitting right above their heads.

Suddenly everything else made sense. As they passed the first open door, Nia saw through the curtain of water falling half across it and noted a cabin bed and standing sink both bolted to the ceiling, along with a broken mirror stretching to the floor. Everything was inverted.

Bryan's arrogant, confrontational tone had deserted him for the moment.

"This is a film," he said, his voice cracking a little under the weight of growing confusion. "This is all from a film. I'm sure it is. I saw it years ago, when I was working at a holiday camp and they were showing it in a room next to the theatre where I'd perform. I'd do my bit for the kids at lunchtime and then I'd have a couple of hours to kill before the evening show. So, I'd pop next door. And this one time, the film was about a ship that capsizes in the ocean..."

"I know that movie!" Dev said excitedly. "My dad brought me up on all the films he liked when he was growing up. So many bloody musicals, but also a shedload of seventies disaster movies. Seriously, what was their problem back then?" He rolled his eyes. "Anyway, I remember this one, too. *The Poseidon Adventure*, right?"

It clearly pained Bryan to agree with someone who was still young enough to have all his faculties, but he nodded anyway. "It was a cruise liner that sank. A big one. A floating palace all decked up with finery and decorations, because I think it was Christmas, wasn't it?"

"Yeah, and when it gets hit by a tsunami, a group of survivors have to find their way out. Except the ship is upside down, so they travel upwards to the bottom of the ship where there's an air pocket, and they can bang on the hull for the rescuers to hear them."

"We stick to our plan, then," Nia said. "Keep going and look for a way up?"

Dev nodded, Alden too, and even Bryan managed a slight shrug, which she supposed was his way of agreeing without admitting that was what he was doing. Nobody else in the group had anything to say. Even Dirk stayed quiet, too busy peering into another cabin, looking distinctly uncomfortable with everything.

Nia led them on, and now she knew where they were, she was able to better understand what she was looking for. They were clearly on a cabin deck, which meant there would be stairwells nearby. She looked to Alden, who was still pale, and nudged her shoulder against his, offering an encouraging smile. He returned it, albeit distantly, and she sighed inwardly, hoping he'd shake off whatever he'd seen. She didn't like admitting such things, but she couldn't be alone. She needed him back.

"I don't like this place," Casey said a little further behind them.

"Nobody does, sweetheart," Dirk said. "Whining won't help it go any faster."

"Hey," Mason said.

"What, Studly McStudmuffin? You finally got something to say?"

Mason didn't respond, and for a moment there was a tense silence. Then Monique said, "I agree with Casey. Also, I think the lights are going out behind us. It's dark back there."

They all looked over their shoulders. The woman was right. The lamps had all died or blown out further than ten yards behind them.

All by design. Pushing us onwards.

Kim was still being helped along by Dev. "Please, we should not fight," she urged everybody. "We must stay together. Find the way up. Yes, Nia?"

Nia began to pick up the pace. "Yes, I think that's all we can do. Let's find the nearest stairwell and climb it. At least that's in keeping with what the designers of the tower wanted us to do."

Bryan harrumphed.

"I thought you were on board with this idea?" she asked. "What now?"

"Yes, well, in the film they went up. And perhaps we have no choice here. But you keep talking about what the tower wants. Who's to say what it or the people who built the tower really wanted? Who's to say their plan wasn't just to bring us here to torment and kill us?" He sniffed loudly. "Or, more likely, this is some kind of collective delusion. A government experiment, perhaps."

"Now *that's* delusional," Earl muttered.

"You may think that, sir," Bryan shot back, straightening to his full height. "But who is to say what's right and what's wrong, what's real and what's not? A tower appears from out of nowhere, *floating* above the Earth. And not in Hollywood or New York or London, mind, but in the middle of the blasted English countryside! And it's not really a tower, but rather a dungeon, and then an underwater ship, and God knows what else next. Sorry, no. This is all insane and I am struggling to believe that any of it can possibly be real."

Alden made a point of wandering to one of the cabin doors and pushing it open. It swung with a creak that reverberated down the endless corridor, then smacked the wall with a clang. He then put his hand under a stream of water, letting it splash off his palm.

"We can all see this. We can all hear it. And I can *feel* it." He knocked on the wall to emphasise his point. "You're saying this is all in our heads? Some kind of government conspiracy?"

"Well… why not?"

"Because it's nuts," Alden said, wrinkling his nose and pushing his hair away from his face. "Have you seen the governments of the world lately? Very few of them are capable of even doing what they were elected to do. No way could they pull this off."

Bryan stayed quiet after that.

Nia picked up the pace as best she could, aware that the tower was pushing them onwards, but not wanting to rush into any danger. She hadn't wanted the responsibility of leading these people through anything. Hell, she would have baulked at spending any amount of time with most of them, even in a safe environment. But they had a child with them, and she wasn't about to let the confident personality with zero smarts make the decisions. Not here. That shit had to be suffered in the real world, sure. Governments and billion-dollar organisations were all run by the Bryans of the world. Here, though, she knew she had to make a stand if they had a chance of escape. She saw the environmental cues and her mind was open to the rules of the design. That gave them a chance.

The corridor of cabins soon ended at a pair of double doors, over which they climbed into what had been a bar. The group traipsed over and around fallen tables and chairs, kicking away bottles and splashing through the pooling water. Nobody said a word. The only sounds were their breathing and the occasional crunch of broken glass.

As Nia continued looking for clues to their predicament, her eyes were drawn to the paintings on the wall, most of which were the wrong way up, while others had tilted and were barely clinging to their fixtures.

At first glance, they seemed the kind of generic paintings you might get in any public space, where more concern is given to the budget than the décor. Landscapes with horses and carts. Sailing boats cresting waves. Portraits of people going about their lives.

But as she approached one in particular – that of a couple of people in old-fashioned coats and top hats holding hands on the deck of a ship – she saw that the details of the figures were all wrong. Their faces were blurred and inhuman. Their arms were too long, and their fingers were too many and interwoven like tangles of spaghetti. And the rest of the people on the deck around them, all seemingly studying the couple in the centre, were similarly wrong. Smudged faces, multiple mouths and noses, necks that didn't quite join with their heads. They were a collection of haunted streaks and missing faces.

It was like looking at an AI-generated image. A semblance of art, until you looked closer to see the hideousness inhumanity of the detail.

"I do not like those," Rakie said, clutching her father tightly and pulling him away from them. "Whoever painted them didn't do it right. They don't feel good."

"Like everything else in this place," Nia said, feeling an energy lurking beneath the canvas, beneath this entire level, just waiting.

But for what?

CHAPTER NINE
Rats

Nia led the group across the destroyed bar. There were multiple exits, but again the flickering lights seemed to draw them in a particular direction, through another set of double doors, one of which was hanging off its hinges.

One by one they helped each other over the door frame until they gathered in a new corridor. The same tasteless carpet adorned the ceiling, but there were no rooms leading off. There were two directions, left and right. Both were lit, but to the right she felt the lights were stronger. Nia turned that way.

"Hey, why not left?" Dirk said.

His voice carried the length and breadth of the space, bounced off the walls, and made everyone pause. Nia stopped with her back to everyone, that familiar sinking feeling in her gut. Bryan had shut up, so it was Dirk's turn to question her judgement.

"Just saying, my dude," he continued, "you were *very* quick to turn right just then. Do you know something we don't? What if we decided to go left instead?"

Nia turned to note a very definable split in the group. Alden, Earl and Rakie had started along after her. Dev and Kim were in the centre. Bryan, Casey, Mason and Monique were standing on the other side. It might have just been the way of things, but Nia couldn't help but sense the scene represented how much faith everyone had in her.

Just for once, she thought, *I wish people would trust that I know what I'm doing.*

Of course, these people didn't know her and she didn't know them. They had every right not to trust her. But hadn't she spent so many years following others, only to find out later they were just making shit up as they went? It was unfair she wasn't being given the same kind of trust. She was bloody well due.

Dirk stood at the far end of the group, arms on his hips like some kind of explorer. "Well, honey, whadda you say?"

He's just trying to make himself feel bigger, Nia told herself, chewing the inside of her cheek, trying not to spit out expletives. *This little act of mutiny is simply him trying to feel more powerful in a powerless situation.*

She could understand that. But she also knew she was making excuses for him and that didn't sit well. Taking a moment to settle herself, she ran her hands through her hair, slipping on the hairband she always carried on her wrist to tie it back into a ponytail.

"Look, I appreciate none of us really knows where we're going," she said as calmly as she could, gesturing to the corridor to the left. It held more shadow, more puddles of water gleaming in the half-light. "But we have two choices here, and the way to the right is better lit and looks drier."

"What makes you so sure that's the right way, though?"

"Because I'm following the light, Dirk. Using light to guide people to where you want them to go is one of countless game design techniques. Subtle cues to push a player through a level without overtly telling them where to go. It's not much to go on here, sure, but it's enough. We were brought here with a purpose, and I think whatever built this place understood we needed at least a fighting chance of finding our way through it."

Rakie was staring at her with a sense of wonder. "That's so cool!"

"And it makes sense," Earl replied, his eyes drifting across Dirk's side of the group.

Dirk himself shrugged with a well-practised air of dismissiveness. At once charming and irrefutably stubborn. A natural-born prick.

"I thought we established that nothing..." He pulled a face. "...*nothing* makes sense here! We're in a fucking upside-down ship from the 1970s after escaping a video game dungeon. So why use that kind of logic? Why use *any* kind of logic? What do you even think this place is?"

"I honestly don't know," Nia said.

"Well then, sweetheart."

She bristled. "We've been brought here to complete a goal. We need to climb each level and thus the tower. The moss in the dungeon lit the way to the exit. And here, in this ship, the lights always seem to be brighter in a particular direction. We're being led – I'd stake my life on it."

"Yeah, and all of ours, too," Bryan muttered.

Alden's voice was still a little shaky, his eyes watery and red. But he held firm beside Nia. "Why bring us here only to kill us? There are tests and consequences here, sure. But the tower had to provide us with a fighting chance of making it to the top. Otherwise, what's the point? Nia's right, the tower must be showing us the way."

"And how'd you know anything about anything, Baby BTS?" Dirk said, letting go a barked laugh. Monique and Casey smiled at the nickname, and Nia shot them all a glare.

"No, sorry, Nia here is just going by gut feeling, like we all are. Which puts us at kind of an impasse, wouldn't you say?" He looked at her. "Your gut feeling versus mine."

"OK, enough," she snapped. "No more arguments."

It was oppressive and miserably damp, and Nia was uncomfortably cold and hungry. Dirk had got one thing right: this was an impasse, and she couldn't see how they were going to overcome it. Any arguments were just going to further entrench everyone in the views they already had. Or, if they didn't know what to believe, they certainly had already made their mind up about *who* to believe, regardless of who wielded the logic.

Nia could almost see the "likes" in the eyes of those stood with the handsome author. They had subscribed to his charm and would not be convinced by a nobody like her. She'd seen it in the world more than enough these last few years. It was the era of influencers. Video Pied Pipers with perfectly filtered smiles and ring-light glows, peddling their celebrity to win hearts and minds and money – and Dirk was the personification of that whole movement.

"We're left with the only thing humans ever have in life," she continued. "A choice. I can see you've made yours and I wish you luck heading into the dark."

Dirk grinned, victorious, and raised his hands to the others. "Beautiful. Come on, then, *my kin*. Let's take matters into our own hands." He glanced at Nia. "Race you to the top!"

She watched as he turned and began walking left. His ego was such, he didn't even check to make sure anybody was going with him. The arrogant tit just knew they would. And they did. One by one. Some with apologetic glances in her direction, and one smug grin from Bryan.

Monique, at least, hesitated for a moment. But then she, too, turned to go with the others.

Thanks for the solidarity, Nia thought.

She turned to her little band: Alden, Earl, Rakie, Dev and Kim. Alden gave her a grin of encouragement – possibly even relief that Dirk had finally pissed off.

"Shall we go, then?" he asked.

And as they did, trudging up the corridor, following the light, Nia wondering if she should have done more to save the others. If perhaps the tower sensed the split and would react in some way against one or both groups.

"Do you think–" she started to ask, of Alden, of all of them. But she didn't get to finish, for there was an almighty cacophony of cries far behind them, followed by the tiles beneath them trembling with running.

They turned to witness the shadows of Dirk's group racing towards them, Dirk himself pushing through the others and leaving them behind.

"Change of plan!" he yelled. "Run, you slow fucks, *run*!"

A horrendous sound followed in their wake. A wave of scratching claws and chittering, which instantly conjured images for Nia of her other self with the bloodied bag on her head and a creature she knew must be in it, trying to chew its way through her face to escape.

Taking a step backwards, she caught a glimpse of a thrashing shadow moving behind the other group, blanketing the ceiling, defying gravity.

Rats. Thousands of them.

It shouldn't have been possible, but as the groups collided and merged into a collective panic, the carpet above their heads was suddenly overrun with a warm of long, sleek, dripping rats, all running upside down.

As the humans ducked and stumbled forwards, screams ringing in their ears from Earl's daughter and Monique and even Dirk, too, the rats mirrored their escape.

Long tails flicked down and whipped above the group as the moving mass of grey fur bundled its way overhead, bodies leaping and writhing over and around one another. A stink of rot followed them and engulfed the people beneath. Nia gagged and threw a sleeve over her mouth as she ran, bumping into Alden and almost falling. He caught her and held on to her arm, pulling her forward.

"Keep going!" he yelled.

The rats began scurrying down the walls either side of them.

There were just so many of them. Wave upon wave of the animals, crashing upon one another, growing in swells. The corridor was so thick with their slick, lithe bodies that the space was growing smaller. Until Dirk – having pushed past everyone else – had to slow down and crouch, covering his head with his arms. The others bundled next to him, ducking, pulling tight against the force of nature that had surrounded them, growing closer on all sides.

Alden's other hand still held Nia's. He'd been shaken out of his shock, eyes wide and his attention present, fixed on surviving their current horror. She was grateful for the normalcy of his touch in that moment, but something continued to nag at her about all this.

She could tell Alden felt it, too. "The rats aren't attacking us," he said.

A pause, and they both looked back.

They're running from something.

There came a rumble of thunder in the distance. One that became a thick, fierce roar, shaking the floor beneath their feet.

A wall of water crashed around the corner of the corridor behind them, smashing into lamps, blowing out the electrics, and swallowing the corridor whole.

CHAPTER TEN
The River

Nia stayed hunched up, knowing they could never outrun the rushing water. Even the rats, past them and pushing ahead at speed, were going to be overwhelmed by the deluge.

She wondered then what it might be like to drown in this upside-down ship, in a tower hanging above the skies of England, with the only witnesses an army of gravity-defying, soon-to-be-drowned rats. Would she be missed back home? She didn't think so. Her parents, maybe, if they looked up from their own retirement long enough to give a shit. Her younger brother and sister were busy with their own lives. She had no real friends anymore, nor work colleagues who'd even care if she never appeared on a video call again.

As the tumultuous growl of approaching death grew, she wondered if back home was even a thing still. What if they *were* the only ones left? Just a bunch of strangers who'd been plucked from the apocalypse to undertake this huge mindfuck of an obstacle course in the hope of proving something.

The rampaging waters were almost upon them. She watched the frothing crests curling and ripping the walls apart as they passed, seemingly excited to wrap around her throat. There was an eagerness to them that felt deliberate, intentional. Something wanted them to die. Maybe death wasn't the point of the tower, but it seemed like it was hungry for it, regardless.

"We're going to die," she whispered.

"No," was all Alden said back. An instinctive rejection of the idea, though there was no fire in it. Even he didn't know how they were going to get out of this.

She wondered if Alden would miss her if she was the one to go next. It was a strange thought, given they didn't know each other and they were probably both about to die anyway. But if she died and he survived, would he think about her? He had a good energy to him. They'd formed an understanding. A sense of friendship. And that was something she hadn't wanted in a good long time. If only they'd had more time to get to know each other. He seemed a little lost and lonely, and clearly he'd arrived with grief weighing him down. She could have helped him. Talked to him. Made him feel less alone. Now she wouldn't get the chance. It all felt unfair.

She continued watching the corridor be torn apart and eaten up in the torrent. They were next. They'd frozen in its path, with nowhere to go.

Her thoughts churned with the water, time moving slower in these last moments, as she'd always heard it would.

What would happen if they all died at once? Would a new batch of people get beamed up to compete, or would the tower disappear? Would the world end through their failure to ascend it? Or was the priest right, and this was the path to heaven, in which case... what awaited them after this? Hell?

She didn't think it could be worse than this.

The sheer volume of noise was incredible. It was like Poseidon himself was barrelling through the ship to devour them. Yet... there was a different noise cutting through it all. A strange sound for the situation.

A dog barking.

Alden tensed and leapt up. Nia's side was suddenly cold from where he'd been crouched. The dog barked again and she frowned, confused. Rats she could understand, but why was a dog on the ship?

A word echoed distantly in her mind, like a bubble trapped beneath the violent water rushing their way. She couldn't make it out at first. Nor when it sounded again, a little louder this time.

Then the bubble burst.

Nia.

Her name.

She was about to be swept away. The corridor behind them was almost gone, consumed by the hungry river. She could see no light beyond the water. Nothing but emptiness. The water was just the messenger. It was the void at its back that was the danger.

The void was coming to claim them all.

Nia!

The calling was more distinct. It was quickly followed up by her world shifting suddenly, as her arm was yanked back.

"*NIA!*" Alden yelled.

She spun to face him, her hair whipping around her cheeks, as he yanked her over to the wall, where a pair of legs were crawling over the edge of a doorway she was sure hadn't been there before. The door had been flung open, an emergency bar on the inside and *Fire Door* scrawled upside down below it. A stairwell lay beyond, where most of the group were scrambling up the sloped roof of the stairs.

"Climb over," Alden urged, pushing her ahead of him to where Dirk and Earl were waiting. She was still in a daze as she held her hands up, and was grabbed roughly and lifted clean off her feet.

The roar of water peaked as she landed on her knees on the other side and was dragged away from the immediate danger. Earl let go, turning back to the open doorway. Dirk continued to hold her tightly, his fingers comforting against her arm.

"You're OK," he said, pulling her upright. The words were strange in their sincerity. The echo of them was lost as the thunderous explosion of water tore past the open doorway.

Earl fell against the tall lip of it, leaning over the edge to grab Alden as the torrent smacked into him and tried to carry him away. Nia could only see the top of his hair bobbing beyond the door as the water grew in volume. Then it started pouring over the edge. Dirk pulled Nia along with him, up the slope of the stairwell ceiling.

"No," she said, echoing Alden, wanting to fight Dirk off, wanting to go back and help, even though she didn't know how. But she had no strength to argue. She let him guide her up the white plasterboard, digging dents with the heels of her trainers as she fought to avoid sliding back down.

At the top, she looked back. Alden was only barely hanging on to Earl and Dev. The water wanted him. The *tower* wanted him. Nia could feel its need as it tried to snatch him away.

The water was pouring through, over his head, over his rescuers, filling the stairwell.

"Shut the door!" Bryan yelled from the safety of the midpoint of the stairs, where they doubled back on themselves to rise to the next floor. In the back of Nia's mind she realised they'd gone up, climbed, but were still in the level. They must not have found the proper way up yet.

Fuck.

Bryan pushed her aside to call again. "Let him go and shut it before we all drown, damn you!"

"No," she said again, too weak to be heard by anyone. She didn't want Alden to die. She didn't want to go on this journey without him.

But...

There was a small, guilty part of her that knew what followed the water. She'd seen it in there as it devoured the corridor behind. It was darkness. An empty nothing. *The* empty nothing. And it scared the shit out of her, enough for a sliver of guilt to snake through her mind, wondering if it might be best to listen to Bryan and shut the door before *it* could get through.

As if a crappy stairwell door could shut out the eternal void.

She glanced back again, terrified that's what she'd see. Alden and the other two men gone, having been consumed. Ceasing to exist, as the water and its deadly driver rose to take her too.

But Dev had both hands on Alden, his eyes squeezed shut against the spray, as he and Earl hauled his body over the edge. All three fell back into the fast-rising pool, before the pair got up and staggered through the water to drag the half-drowned Alden up the stairwell with them.

Bryan was still moaning about closing the door as he pushed past Nia and continued upwards. Dirk made to follow, but Nia held there and for some reason he stayed, too, helping the three stragglers up to safety. Alden was as white as a ghost, eyes pinched tightly together, nose running and water still spilling from his lips. Nia grabbed his arm and hoisted him up into a hug, and they fell back against the wall with a thud. Dirk reached out for Earl and Dev to help them the rest of the way.

"You OK?" Alden muttered against Nia's ear. She couldn't help herself, and burst out laughing.

"You got me out of there and you're the one who just got dunked. Are *you* OK?"

She felt him shiver against her. A whole-body shake that spoke of more than just the cold water soaking his clothes.

"Scared," he whispered. Ashamed. Embarrassed. "I don't want to die."

Nia looked over his shoulder to see Dirk listening in. She gave him a thumbs up.

"I've got you," she said to Alden.

He went quiet for a moment. "I heard my dog."

"Your dog?"

"That's when I saw the door. The barking was coming from in here."

She didn't know what to say to that. Had she heard it, too? It seemed like it might have been in her mind. There had been so much noise, she wasn't thinking straight.

"I'm not going crazy, am I, Nia?"

She felt the weight of him lift from her as Dirk leaned over the pair, pulling Alden up by the waist of his jeans. "No time to get cosy with the lady – water's still coming." He shoved Alden aside and held out a hand for Nia. She took it and let him help her up.

"Should've shut the damn door," Bryan called from above.

The stragglers moved quickly, scrambling up to the next floor to join the others, while death continued rising to meet them. Nia felt they didn't think the water was ever going to stop chasing them. Not until it had taken someone, or they reached whatever exit would allow them to escape this bloody ship.

Mason and Casey were the first to reach the doors on the next level, but they were locked shut. They started trying to break through.

Nia looked down and could have sworn she saw shadows moving in the water.

"Keep going up," she said.

Bryan, who appeared defeated by the short climb already, looked aghast. "We've just gone up! Shouldn't we have been taken to the next level of the tower by now? We're doing what it wants, just like you said. Why are we still in this place?"

"Maybe we need to find another tree to climb," Dev suggested.

Nia knew it was supposed to be a joke, but nobody laughed. Rakie was actually nodding, as though she had been thinking the same. The girl's fingers twitched against the pocket of her jacket, pressing against whatever was inside to check it was still there.

"A tree got us up here before," Rakie said. "And there was a tree on the tower outside, remember? Trees bring life."

"Maybe they bring escape, too?" Kim added, leaning against the wall.

Nia looked back down the stairwell. They didn't have time to think on this too much. "We'll have to keep moving and see what we find. Keep following the signs. And this is one – if this door is locked, we're not meant to go through it. The tower wants us to keep going. We'll know the way out when we see it, I'm guessing."

So they kept going up. Scrambling and slipping their way up the ceiling of the stairwell from one floor to another. The next door they came across was completely dark behind it. The floor after that had no door. And the one after that was barred and locked.

"We should be at the top of the fucking tower by now," Dirk complained.

Still they could see and hear the water rising up the stairwell behind them.

They were four floors up when they finally came across an open door. Light shone through and it seemed mercifully devoid of moving shadows, rats, killer cyborgs, or anything else that might present a threat. The stairwell above them was shrouded in darkness, too, the lamps all seemingly broken.

"We go through here," Nia said.

Nobody argued with her this time. Too tired for it. Or perhaps remembering the last time they'd chosen to ignore her.

Good thing, too. Because as they climbed through the door, she saw what they had been hoping to find.

CHAPTER ELEVEN
A Very Merry Christmas

The ship's theatre was dome shaped, with hundreds of plush red seats circling the outside and the stage in the centre. With the ship upside down, everything was above them, the chairs on the ceiling rising to the wooden platform that hung in the middle of the venue.

But it was what lay below the stage that had Nia's attention.

A towering Christmas tree, at least as high as the theatre was tall, had it not been lying across broken light rigs.

"Told you," Dev said, sounding a little shocked he'd been right. "A fucking tree, mate."

Bryan's moustache twisted with the derision of his words. "We can't climb that, you moron. That tree is broken. Kaput. On its side and full of broken ornaments. How the hell is that going to take us to whatever level we need to go to next, eh? Think before you speak."

"Tree looks in one piece to me," Alden said. "Maybe we just need to raise it up again. Can anybody see anything in that stage overhead? A trapdoor, or something we might need to climb to?"

Dev pointed excitedly. "Look, there's something up there in the wood! A hatch, I think. You can see the outline and there's some kind of handle. That's got to be where we need to go, right?"

"To get out of the ship and move to the next level," Earl said. "Yep, that's got to be it."

"But how?" Casey said. She was bedraggled and terrified, her blue eyes desperately seeking reassurance. Still she clung to Mason.

He looked down at her and shrugged. "I don't know," he said helplessly.

Nia couldn't tell if he was being honest or if the quiet persona was to keep himself under the radar. Either way, he'd been no real help so far. What was the tower thinking in bringing a male model? Come to think of it, what could it want from a reclusive artist like her? Or from any of them?

There was nothing special about any of them. How come *they* had been chosen – was it just happenstance, being in the wrong place at the wrong time? Or were they lab rats in a maze, deliberately thrown together at random to see how they got on?

Dirk stepped forward, throwing his arm around Casey and puffing out his chest. Nia couldn't help but see him as a fancy bird, trying to arouse a mate. He was attractive, of that there was no doubt, but she could tell he was a man wrapped up in his own little mind games and insecurities. At that moment, he had spotted an opportunity to show himself as better than the younger, taller, more handsome Mason.

"Shouldn't be difficult, sweetheart," he said, gesturing to the ceiling. "We just need to lift that tree up between us and hold it steady. If we can find a rope of some kind, someone can tie it between the hatch handle and the top of the tree, and *bingo*, that's your escape." He looked around, trying not to let his glance linger too long on the ageing figures of Bryan and Kim. "If it's long enough, perhaps we can tie it around those who can't climb up and pull them to the top?"

"You cannot be serious!" Bryan said. Even upside down, the theatre was clearly still capable of producing some terrifyingly powerful acoustics, and the indignant outburst boomed around them. "I will not be made to climb another bloody tree or be hoisted like some kind of elderly pensioner. Do you even remember me from TV, any of you? There's no way you'd be suggesting this if you did. You simply can't do this! Where's the respect, I ask you – *where*?" He drew himself up even taller, like a lamppost with a sour face. "No, sorry. I'm not putting up with this any longer. I'm going to go and find a proper way out of this place. There will be one somewhere and I shall find it."

Nia caught Alden looking at her. *No time*, he mouthed, tapping his wrist.

He was right – they couldn't stand there arguing any longer. The water they'd left behind wouldn't be too long in following them in.

"Bryan, you have to stick with us," she said. "We were led here and I can't see another way to go. This feels like the way out."

He held up his finger to shush her. "No. You've led us nowhere. I'm going to look after myself, thank you very much. You, my friends, are generations incapable of doing anything useful. There is no way you would have made it through the war."

"*You* didn't make it through the war," Nia snapped.

But Bryan was already staggering off with that old-fashioned gait he had, all long limbs and looking down at everyone and everything he saw.

She wondered for a moment if she should go after him, trying harder to convince him he was making a mistake. Then Dirk touched her arm. "Let him go, honey."

Nia let the sickly term of endearment go. "You think he'll come back?"

"I think… he's made his mind up," Dirk said. There was a strange look in his eyes as he glanced at Bryan. Then his grip on her skin firmed a little, encouraging her to turn away. "Come on, leave him. Time is of the fucking essence, right?"

She glanced one last time back at the old man as he walked towards a set of locked doors. They inexplicably had a chain wrapped through the handles on the inside, but Bryan shook them anyway to try to prise them open. He banged his fists against the doors for a moment, the impacts echoing through the theatre. Then he moved to another door with a frosted window.

Nia stopped as Dirk tried to pull her with him.

There was some kind of movement behind the window in the door Bryan was about to open.

Shadows shifting. Swirling.

"Bryan, don't!" she shouted, as he grabbed the handle.

He looked over his shoulder. "Oh, do fuck off!" he said, yanking the door open.

The wave that hit him was like a bullet. A wall of water that took its chance the second the door gave way, as though it had been waiting for this moment its entire existence.

The door blew off its hinges and cartwheeled past the group. So did Bryan's body, which was flung backwards across the entire theatre, coming to a stop only when it smacked into the wall on the other side.

The back of Bryan's head exploded, his right arm snapped in two, and he crumpled like a rag doll into the spray.

Nia cried out, in fear more than anything, as the water gushed into the theatre, released from its prison, looking for victims. She felt the cold death swirling around her feet, seeping into her trainers again, tainting her with its chill. It swept up through her bones, teasing her, testing her, seeing if she'd freeze and give herself up to it or be spurred to action.

"Get to the tree," she shouted. It seemed a strange thing to say, but they had no choice but to go all in with the idea that the Christmas tree was their escape. The water was spilling in around them so fast, they didn't have much time to do anything else.

Then someone screamed, "Shark!"

Nia heard something knock into a row of chairs behind her. It was a heavy thud and she couldn't help but glance back as she splashed over the lighting rig, reaching for the tree, only to see a whole *row* of conjoined theatre chairs being dragged across the water.

Big fucking shark.

Scrambling up the tree, pushing through baubles and tinsel and some leaflike decorations, Nia did her best to ignore the pine needles stabbing her hands and wrists, poking through her shirt and sodden jeans. She hadn't expected it to be a real Christmas tree. As she pulled herself to safety, she wondered how the cruise line staff had got the thing on board in the first place. Then she remembered none of this could possibly be real and those people didn't exist. This was all a design construct, so why not have a real tree in this drowning place if you could have one? And throw in a real shark, too.

"Nia, give me your hand," Dirk said. He'd already made it to the top of the felled tree before everyone else. She reached out and took it, letting him drag her roughly the rest of the way.

Her trainers found purchase alongside him, but she let go of his hand quickly enough to reach for Kim behind her.

That's when her eyes glanced past the old woman, to the shape cutting through the flood.

"Holy shit," she breathed.

The shark was enormous. Far larger than seemed normal, even for this place. How could it possibly have squeezed through the door Bryan had opened? Screw that – how could it have got inside the ship in the first place? There was no way it would have been able to swim down the corridors they'd been through.

Its fin sliced through the water with purpose as the creature split another row of fallen chairs in half, making a beeline for the far wall. Nia noticed Bryan's limp body still there, floating face up, blood pooling around his injured head.

The shark's nose lifted from the water. Its mouth opened, revealing teeth as white as stars on a dark night.

Then they bit down on Bryan's legs.

Turned out, he was still alive.

The TV personality's arms shot out. His head tipped backwards and he let out a horrendous wail of horror, even as his midriff folded with the impact of being bitten in half.

If it had been clean, it might have been over quickly. But there was nothing clean about this attack. After the initial chomp, it became slow, deliberate, the shark gently thrashing him about as if actively savouring the taste of him.

Nia knew enough to understand this wasn't accurate. Like the AI paintings in the restaurant, this was only a semblance of the truth. A picture crafted by a mind that didn't understand what it was painting, only saw the colours on the surface with no conception of the inner meaning. No appreciation for the inner workings.

Bryan's screams filled the theatre when, by rights, he should have passed out from shock long before. The acoustics didn't care for such trivialities. They took the agony and built a symphony of his last moments, the last performance this theatre would ever see, spilling out the man's torment for the audience of ten as they clung to the Christmas tree.

Even as their improbable life raft was carried aloft by the rising waters, they were unable to look away.

The shark continued its meal. Shearing the man apart. Until the screams peaked and were mercifully silenced.

Bryan's head lolled. And his torso detached and slowly drifted away from the shark.

"Fuck this shit," Dev moaned, scrambling up the side of the tree some more. "I'm done. Over and out. I'm not a fucking chew toy."

Nia felt the entire tree wobble as Dev panicked. Earl reached down from where he, Rakie and Kim were clinging, and lifted him up to where they were. "Hold still, boy," he warned. "Or else you're going to spin us all back into the water."

Dev's shoulders sagged and he began crying. Kim slipped her arm around him and let him sob into her shoulder. Near them, Casey and Mason huddled together – him slack-jawed, his hair slicked to his forehead. Her curls were dishevelled and trails of mascara ran down her cheeks, onto her neck.

The water continued rising, taking the tree with it. Soon the theatre was half drowned and the shark disappeared. Bobbing chairs on the surface were the only signs of movement, shadows breaking the reflections of the fading light. It was eerily quiet, too, only the sounds of lapping water and their pinched, hyperventilating gasps. Alden's shoulder rubbed against Nia's, the warmth of him reminding her she wasn't alone. But he said nothing. The group held to their branches in the Christmas tree, not daring to move or speak.

Then:

"It's coming," Monique whispered through chattering teeth, hunched in the branches, her once immaculate navy-blue uniform soaked and clinging to her shoulders. She pointed to the other side of the tree.

"You saw it?" Dirk asked.

"Yes. I think so. But now it's gone. It's–"

"There it is!" Rakie shouted.

The fin had reappeared, slicing above the water suddenly only feet from them. It moved quickly along the length of the giant tree, almost the size of it, then pulled around the other side.

"It's circling us," Dirk said, watching the tip of the fin move past the thick foliage, brushing the end of a floating piece of tinsel. "It fucking knows we're here."

Alden looked up, towards the stage above them.

"We just need a few more minutes. We're nearly at the hatch!"

Nia saw he was right. They were floating so close to the ceiling and the hatch was directly above them, a small handle on its left-hand side.

"Can you reach it, Alden?" she asked.

"Maybe."

"Maybes won't get us out of this," Dirk muttered.

Alden glared at him and tried to stand upright, but his arms barely stretched above his head before one of his feet slipped off the branch and he fell backwards. Only an outstretched hand from Dirk on his other side saved him. Gasping, Alden was hauled by him and Nia back into the pine needles, where he grabbed on tightly.

"You were too short to try that," Dirk said.

"You want to give it a go?"

"Fuck no."

"Fine," Nia said. "Then we're just going to have to wait a moment until we're in reach. And then be quick about getting through before the entire place is underwater and–"

All went dark.

The lights had finally blown and Nia's world was reduced to noise alone. The screams around her. The scrape of the pine needles as the others shifted and tightened their grips on the tree.

A shark's fin slicing through the surface.

"Alden?" Nia said.

"I'm here."

"Can you remember exactly where the hatch was?"

"I think so. We were being lifted directly towards it."

Almost like it was on purpose.

Were they meant to have climbed on the tree? Was Bryan meant to have sacrificed himself to flood this place and float the others to the exit? How could the designers of the tower have known either of those things would come to pass?

There was no time to dwell on it. "Listen, we're going to run out of time if we leave it much longer. Dirk, if you're not going to do it, at least help me hold Alden as he does."

She felt Alden slowly, deliberately stretch his body in a way that felt like him trying to reach up. Nia quickly slipped her hand around his back to steady him. She felt Dirk's there, too.

There was a knock above her.

"I can feel the stage," Alden said.

"Be fucking quick, dude," Dirk shot back.

He's trying, she wanted to shout. But she didn't. She couldn't risk breaking the fragile truce that seemed to be in play. She could hear Alden's hand patting across the wood desperately and silently urged him on. *Come on, Alden. Let's get out of here.*

"Got it!"

There was a creak. A grunt of effort. And a rush of air blew down through Nia's damp hair, sending a shiver down the back of her shirt.

The breeze arrived with a glow from above. Just enough for her to see the edges of metal rungs inside the opening of the hatch.

"Everyone, move to me," Alden shouted. "Go slowly, so you don't rock the tree. There's a ladder up there. Reach up, grab the rungs, pull yourself up." He leaned in to Nia. "You go first?"

She badly wanted to get out of here, but she refused to be like the others in the dungeon, jostling one another to get away from danger. "No, let me stay and help," she said.

He didn't argue. And neither said a thing when a shadowy figure she assumed was Dirk tutted loudly, brushed past and pulled himself up through the hatch. She'd expected nothing less.

For a moment the bulk of Dirk's muscled frame blocked the glow and Nia held her breath. Then the glow reappeared as he simply vanished.

"This is it!" she shouted. "Keep moving!"

One by one, the others inched through the branches, spilling the soft brushing sounds out into the sliver of air that was trapped there. Nia helped up Casey, who then took a moment to reach back and pull up Kim, as Mason and Nia pushed her up from below. Alden, meanwhile, was holding the hatch open, pushing it back as the tree lifted even closer, until he was able to wedge it behind a branch. As Dev followed Mason and Monique, and Earl and Rakie squeezed up after them, Nia and Alden were pressed up between the tree and against the stage. She felt the water rising up her legs.

"Quickly," Alden said. "Get up here–"

The tree suddenly shuddered and spun as the shark smacked into it.

Nia lost her balance and fell into the water, slipping away, trying to stop herself moving away from the glow above. The glow was the way out. If she lost that, she was dead.

The shark crashed into the tree again.

It knew they were trying to escape.

Nia's head broke the surface as her foot found the trunk, and she pushed herself upwards, back towards the light.

"Nia!"

Alden was half into the hatch, hanging off the ladder. His hand swiped across her back, grabbing her collar. Her shirt bit into her neck as he wrenched her up after him, holding on long enough for her to reach up and find purchase on the rungs.

The branches whipped into their legs as the tree was hit again.

Then there was a loud snap; Nia felt it as much as she heard it. The tree had broken. Their shield was gone.

Alden helped her up, ahead of him. Then came up close behind, pushing her to go faster with his shoulders.

"Go, Nia."

There was the scrape of a fin against the hatch.

"Faster!"

A smash as she imagined the shark's head following them through the opening.

"Please."

Alden's words collapsed into themselves as the glow above became an overwhelming flash of white, and Nia temporarily ceased to exist.

CHAPTER TWELVE
A Haunting in Suburbia

There was a split second when Dirk had no conception of anything.

It was over in the blink of an eye, and as soon as he existed again, he realised it had been a moment of calm, not having to worry about any number of thoughts fighting for attention in his brain.

On the other hand, it had also been horrific knowing you didn't exist, and even – just momentarily – were not significant in any way.

He felt like Schrödinger's Cat, existing simultaneously inside and outside of the box. A feeling much the same as the first time they'd climbed between levels of this fucking tower, except that this time he'd been mentally preparing for the transition and it had *still* been a bag of dicks.

He fell off the ladder... upwards? Sideways? *Through?* Whatever. All he really knew was that he was spilling onto the black and white tiles of a badly decorated hallway. His cheek coming to rest on the cold sheen of the ceramic, his bare arms and legs splayed unceremoniously outwards.

"*Fuuuuuuck,*" he announced.

It was dimly lit, wherever they were. With the kind of diffused light whose sole purpose was to make darkness even worse by creating shadows within it.

He shivered and rolled onto his back.

A cheap, gaudy chandelier hung in the gloom above him, dangling from an Artexed ceiling. It didn't look like it had been used in a while. Cobwebs were strung between once fine crystals. Glass lamps were frosted and cracked. It was all... lifeless. That was the word. A lifeless decoration, a skeleton of a formerly living thing. He wondered when it had last felt electricity powering through it, lighting up this dreadfully mediocre place.

He sat up and cracked his knuckles. "Where the fuck are we now?"

The crumpled heaps around him were all groaning upon arrival. He didn't bother counting. Whoever had survived had survived. Nobody answered him immediately, but that he wasn't alone was at least something. Fodder for the cannons ahead.

They were in a house, of a sort. The way an old 1970s home movie featuring your family could be considered a theatrical feature film. It was small, claustrophobic and tasteless. Unable to keep the disgust from creeping over his face, he realised this was actually the kind of house you'd *see* in a 1970s home movie. It had flowery brown and green wallpapered walls, a hypnotically dull tiled hallway. And, before them, rising into the dark, a staircase resplendent in a worn yellow shag carpet.

Doorways stood silently on either side of them, the doors cream-coloured and slightly ajar, revealing more darkness beyond. Same for the end of the corridor, past the stairs, and also the understairs cupboard. All not quite closed. Not quite safe.

A shiver ran up his spine.

Nope. Don't like this at all.

A childhood fear began writhing beneath his skin. He much preferred his doors shut, closed, pulled so fucking tight there was no way a creeping evil on the other side could be seen approaching. No space for ethereal fingers to slip through and reach for him. No gap for red, unblinking eyes to hold his gaze and freeze him in place, awaiting the inevitable desecration of his soul.

Doors ajar held the possibility of letting something in.

Something bad.

As the hairs across his skin stood on end, he remembered seeing a house like this before. In an old show, perhaps? Maybe one of those "True Hauntings" on cable his parents wouldn't let him watch as a kid. He'd only get a glimpse of some old man with glasses introducing this week's case in some dull-ass house like this, before being shooed off to bed.

Yeah, this felt like one of those places. The kind of low-key suburban homes where your grandma lived, next door to someone else's grandma. On the outside, every garden was pristine. People chatted over fences. You learned to ride your bike in the streets outside and everybody knew everyone else. A place that looked like this was dull and safe. Nostalgically so.

But Dirk knew the unremarkable had a way of hiding evil in plain sight. He'd never held much stock in the clichéd abandoned mansions as the scenes of the most frightening horror stories. These suburban houses were where the real, terrible shit went down. Inside these houses, things were seen. Heard. Felt. Children possessed. People harmed. Some even dying of fright.

He had some *baaaaad* memories of reading books at his school library with such stories in it. Horrifying tales of real hauntings and supernatural deaths. He remembered seeing a pair of legs in a black-and-white photo in one of those books, from what was spontaneous human combustion. They had belonged to some little old lady, who'd been sitting at home in her front room, knitting or some shit, and then *BANG*, she was gone, all the way down to her rolled-up stockings.

Dirk felt the cold of the air pick at his skin as he thought back to the photo. Yeah, this was *that* kind of place. Where demons were waiting behind terrible wallpaper, and there was always the possibility you could just explode in flames and die.

As, one by one, the others slowly sat up, their dumb faces checking out their new surroundings, he noted with silent panic the hanging lamp at the top of the stairs flicker into life, casting the hallway in a pallid, sickly light.

He froze. His breath grew shallow.

I remember that story. It's how the ghost would let the owners know he was coming for them.

The lamp started swinging.

Fuck.

Dirk nearly shit himself as Kim suddenly shrieked.

"Oh my God!" The stupid old woman was looking up at the wall just above his head, at a picture he was sure hadn't been there a second ago. There were several paintings adorning the hall, in fact. All filled with rather ordinary portraits of people smiling.

Wait, no. Shit, what was *this* now?

They were changing as he watched them. The swirls of paint beginning to run down the canvas. Melting the images. Twisting the mouths of the figures into grimaces.

Kim began wailing, still pointing at the picture above him. Jabbing her finger as if to shoo it away. "It's him. My husband. Jiang!" Her eyes were streaming tears. "B–but I don't understand. How can he be up there in this place? Why is my beautiful Jiang here?"

Dirk watched as that painting, too, deteriorated. The eyes of Kim's husband went first. Then the nose. Until whatever had been there before was no longer human. Just a blank-faced figure with a mouth twisted in fear. Lips curled, as if on the verge of begging for help.

"That can't be good," the teacher and wannabe musician, Alden, said.

Dev stood up and put his arms around Kim, as he had been doing a lot, clearly suffering some kind of grandma fetish. "Hey, it's OK," he lied. "It's not really him, don't worry."

Whether it was him or not, Dirk didn't really care. He was more interested in getting to his feet and examining the other paintings.

He'd seen those in the ship, noting the strange design, a style of art he was seeing a lot more of these days. The covers of his books were AI-generated, mainly because his publisher was cheap, but he'd also developed a bit of a liking for the weird, messed-up shit they came up with. It was art through a different, non-human lens.

This was like that. The paintings had been crafted by another hand. One that did not see things as humans might, but was doing its best to pass itself off as one.

Kim continued wailing as her beloved Jiang's entire figure melted off the canvas.

"Is this your house, Kim?" Nia asked gently. "Is that where we are right now?"

It took a moment for the question to register, but the old lady slowly took her eyes off the painting and looked at their surroundings. If she recognised the other paintings on the wall, she didn't show it, although they were so messed up, that didn't mean much.

"It feels... familiar. But, no, this isn't my home."

"But that was your husband?"

"Yes! Jiang was his name. He's been dead many years now, though. He grew sick and I couldn't hold on to him. Why is he here? Why?"

She began to cry again and Alden, doing his best to continue being a perfect prissy fuck, wandered over and whispered something to her. She nodded and wiped her eyes.

Dirk's lips thinned as he saw Nia watching. This was the kind of thing women always said they loved in a man – seeing them all kind and sensitive. The reality was different, in his experience. At least with the women he tended to see. But there was something about Nia that he liked, and he didn't want her to be fucking around chasing the weedy teacher.

Yeah, she was blunt and stubborn and the type of woman he really couldn't care less for in the real world. He much preferred those who were a little broken, vulnerable, or just lonely. Women he might befriend online, jumping into their DMs and letting them get all giddy over his celebrity status. Didn't matter he was a kids' author playing – and ploughing – the field like that. Fame was a powerful shield. He had all kinds of other famous authors blurbing his books and joking around with him online. That kind of status bought him enough trust to do pretty much what he pleased behind the scenes back home.

But this wasn't back home, and Nia wasn't the kind of woman who would fall for that shtick. Wherever they were – and he had a bad feeling this location had been ripped straight from those ghostly books at his school library – the group was trapped. Ten of them left. And Nia was by far the most attractive. If he was going to be stuck for fuck-knows how long, he was going to stake his claim before she opted for anyone else.

Time to give her the Alpha Male rizzzzzz, baby!

Dirk leaned over and put his hand on her shoulder. Nia looked surprised, but didn't flinch. That was half the battle, he'd discovered over the years. Get a touch in, gauge their reaction. Then you knew how much work was needed before they would submit.

"You OK?" he asked with as much sincerity as he could muster.

"Fine," Nia replied, clearly confused. Good. He operated best in the cracks of that confusion. "Why?"

"Oh. You know. Just this whole thing, right?" He gave her the barest hint of a smile. Just enough not to scare her off. But enough to stir her curiosity. "What made you ask if this was her house, anyway? Do you know something we don't?"

The others were paying attention to the pair of them, including Alden. The frown across the kid's goofy face was a treat.

Good, let him watch me work.

Nia's shoulders lifted in a shrug. "Fine. Well, I was just thinking that the two levels we've been through were both recognisable to someone in the group. The dungeon was like the game Rakie plays. The ship was the one from the movie Bryan and Dev told us about."

Dirk felt the chill return. He didn't know if it was in the air or inside him.

The lamp at the top of the stairs started swinging more wildly.

"What are you saying?" he asked, trying not to look at it.

"Kim just saw her husband in that picture. She thinks she recognises the house. What if these memories are being drawn from us somehow? Used by the tower to create these experiences?"

"But how would that even be possible? And *why* the fuck would the tower even do that?"

"I've no idea," Nia said. "But it's probably not outside the realm of possibility, is it? Given everything that's happened, it's at least a logical explanation. And if it's true, it may well be we're creating the tower as we climb it."

Dirk smiled, trying to feign understanding, acknowledgement, confidence. But his brain was flipping back through the pages of his life, straight to those haunted house books from his childhood. Had the tower been *inside his fucking mind*?

Get out!

He covered his rising terror with a barked laugh that probably came out a little more forced than he'd intended. "Oh, come now, sweetheart! The tower was already built when we saw it outside. And, no offence, Kim, but that weird picture was barely recognisable as human. I don't think it was *anybody's* husband. Nah, sorry, I don't buy it."

But you *recognise this place, don't you?*

Dirk felt the cold sweat across the back of his neck as the others deliberated over his words.

You recognise it from the books and stories. The ghost stories that clearly fucked you up as a child.

He got quickly to his feet, brushed himself down.

This is that house, you stupid fuck. You can't just ignore it.

You know what this is. And that lamp there? It's still swinging. It means death is coming!

As if hearing his thoughts, the lamp at the top of the stairs stopped dead. The light was constant, allowing the mundane dread of the 1970s suburban house to seep into his brain.

In some ways, the stillness was even worse.

"We should get moving," he said, eyeing the twisted portrait next to him.

Its smile seemed to grow wider.

CHAPTER THIRTEEN
There's Somebody at the Door

To his surprise and annoyance, Dirk somehow ended up leading the group through the narrow hallway of the house.

As they passed the slightly open doors, he pulled them closed just to be on the safe side. Each time, he waited for the reassurance of the latch clicking into place. It never came.

Just another thing to mess with your head, he told himself. *Don't focus on that shit, dawg. Keep going, you got this.*

There was zero debate about where they needed to go. The last two levels had demanded upwards movement and they all seemed wearily accepting of the need to continue that tactic. Dirk gestured up the stairs. Several of the ragtag bunch of losers he'd been trapped with nodded their heads back.

Alden was among them. "We need to follow the light," he said, probably as a reminder of what had happened the last time they hadn't.

Dirk bristled at the thought of proving Justin Dimberlake right. Yet, as he eyed the door at the end of the hallway on this floor, beyond the stairs – the only other option, really – he saw through the crack into the kitchen. And, in the gloom, he could see a cupboard door slowly start to open.

He immediately took the stairs, feeling the hardness of each step beneath the threadbare carpet. The wood groaned beneath his running shoes. Not pleasantly, like in his own home – which he'd paid more money for than this bunch would probably make in their entire lives, combined. No, each sound was a warning. A threat. The slow creak of a bone just before it shattered.

It was difficult to resist glancing back to make sure he wasn't alone. This was a narrow staircase, so he took each step by himself, the others having to follow one by one. He moved reluctantly, not willing to get upstairs any faster than he had to. The unknown waiting for him on the landing, beneath that deathly still lamp, made it feel like he was trying to wade through a nightmare.

"Hey, Mr Gentson," a voice behind him, far too bright for this place. It was the girl, Rakie. He glanced back to see she'd pushed herself up the queue to get to him. "How do you come up with the ideas for your books?"

Jesus Christ.

Dirk tried to focus on his breath, keeping it steady. He resisted noticing the closeness of that fucking hell-lamp above him.

"You know I'm a writer, too, and I'd love–"

"Dude," he said, cutting her off. "Can you not? We're kinda in the middle of something here. Just… when we get through this, contact my agent and we'll get a coffee or something, yeah?"

"Oh, *really*?"

Not a fucking chance, he thought.

Eyes held low, he fixed on the last few steps. Slowly. Steadily. Forwards and upwards. Approaching death? He hoped not.

Suddenly it was done. He was upstairs.

He looked around.

This should have been a nondescript, everyday house. A two-up, two-down, with the bare minimum floor space between rooms. That's what it looked like below. And, sure, in a way, that's what it was up here.

The décor, at least, held fast to its humdrum horror.

But now they were up here, he saw once again that nothing was as it should be. There was another door slightly ajar to his left – which he quickly shut – but then he turned to the stretch of landing bending around the railings at the top of the stairs and realised it branched off into at least *ten* different narrow hallways.

"Come the fuck on, that's not fair," he muttered under his breath. Which way were they supposed to go?

"Follow the light," Nia said quietly as she reached the top of the stairs and saw his confusion.

Dirk waited on the landing until everyone was up the stairs. He noted Mason bringing up the rear and saw him hurry the last few steps, as though the darkness below was chasing him up. He was almost pushing Casey in front of him to make her go faster.

Meanwhile, Dev was all sweaty nose and cheeks as he continued helping Kim. The boy's not-quite-a-beard was pulled taut in an almost permanent grimace.

"You look like shit," Dirk whispered.

It made him feel a little better, stronger for it. Always did when you projected your own crap onto others. He didn't even care that Dev ignored him, clearly far too busy trying to control his bowels to respond.

Dirk then looked to the hallways. Following the light was easier said than done, given that most of the routes leading away were glowing in some way, as though someone had forgotten to turn off a nightlight somewhere along them. There was a leading contender, though – the third hallway along, one that held a lighter, brighter glow.

He looked across to Nia, unwilling to speak over the group, to loudly break the pact of quiet that the house seemed to be asking of them. He asked the question with his eyes.

That hallway?

She nodded.

They moved on and turned down it.

It was narrow, like the one downstairs. Cramped, even. The carpet was a different colour – a sticky crimson – but similarly worn in patches, just as on the stairs. There was wallpaper, too, adorned with more old-fashioned flowers, though these colours were faded and ghostlike.

As they moved, Dirk realised this hallway led to yet more branching off it, between which there were yet more slightly open doors, behind which he was sure evil waited. He pulled shut every single one he came across – again, not hearing any definitive click of the latch – suddenly knowing this was why he'd let himself lead: so he could make sure nobody else pushed the doors open and let out whatever was in those rooms.

They walked slowly, carefully, Dirk growing more uncomfortable, if that were even possible. This house was oppressive and claustrophobic, and what few windows he saw illogically placed in the middle of hallways showed nothing but indistinct shapes in a mist "outside".

He supposed the tower must be trying to replicate the idea of a house in a suburban street shrouded in fog. There was a certain menace to it, but he was far more concerned about the doors – *so many fucking doors* – and the fact this was yet another never-ending series of hallways for them to wander.

Were they walking in circles again? He'd been following the goddamn lights, as Nia had said. Why hadn't they got anywhere yet?

"What kind of haunted house is this?" Casey said, the sound of her slightly irritated voice dampened by the lack of space around them. "It's big enough for a mansion, but it's just the same crappy hallways. Surely we should have been beamed into a fancy abandoned stately home – you know, with big foyers, sweeping staircases, balconies and entire wings of rooms for ghosts to hide in? There should be freaky statues and grandfather clocks ticking. Long curtains. Candles. Mammoth fireplaces with secret passageways inside. Where's all that stuff?"

"What makes you think it's supposed to be a haunted house?" Mason asked, his beautiful but blank features ever so slightly pinched in confusion. Dirk envied the way the light caught his cheekbones, but otherwise there was little about the man that carried anything of note. He actually kept forgetting he was there.

"Are you kidding?" Casey said. "Doesn't this feel haunted to you, Mason?"

The model went quiet. Dirk saw his perfect skin flush with embarrassment, and with good reason. Because, honestly, how could any of them *not* feel the air of terror? Its taint was almost palpable. You could feel its fingers on your skin, tugging at your hair, its tongue slow and deliberate as it savoured your fear, its teeth sinking into your flesh.

Something evil lurked here. Dirk was sure of it.

"Maybe the tower got this one wrong," Monique said.

Dirk shook his head, closing another door. "Actually, they did it perfectly. If you'd read that stupid book on hauntings I'd read as a kid, you'd know. This is all on point."

"Usborne's *Ghosts*," Nia said, half to herself. "That's the book that did it for me growing up. I didn't even read the thing, but the cover alone gave me nightmares." She glanced over. "Was that the one?"

"Nah, don't think so. It was something else. But it doesn't matter really. No real-life haunting shit like that should *ever* be found in the elementary school library."

"I saw mine at school, too. Nuts, right?"

She gets me, Dirk decided, and there was a split second where he felt a genuine connection between them. He found himself smiling at her. It was perhaps the sincerest moment he'd ever had with a woman.

Until Alden broke the spell.

"What if this is all a test?" the little prick said.

As Nia's attention was drawn away from him, Dirk had a vision in his head of pushing the kid through one of the open doors into the clutches of whatever was lurking there. Leaving him alone in the dark and taken, possessed, torn apart… whatever it was this level did to people.

The good humour leached from his smile. "You're the one who told us we had to climb the tower, dude. Are you only just fucking realising what this is all about? I thought you were a teacher!"

There were a couple of laughs among the group.

"That's not what I meant," Alden said, his face twitching at the reaction. "These levels… there's something about them. Maybe we *are* creating them as we climb. Maybe the tower is drawing experiences from us to build our journey. But if that's the case, why is it doing that? Why is it forcing us to live through them?"

"You think the reason is to test us?" Nia asked.

"Could be. Maybe it's not just about getting to the top of

the tower, but what we're experiencing and dealing with is part of it, too. Part of the test set by whoever, or whatever, sent the tower."

"I swear to God, if you say it's aliens..." Dirk muttered.

Alden didn't respond, but he didn't deny it either. The others noticed. Glances were shared among the group, as silent questions were posed. Dirk wanted to laugh at them all, but something stopped him.

What else but aliens would put a tower in the sky filled with nonsensical experiences and make a bunch of random people struggle through it or die trying?

He started walking again, as much to lead them all onwards as to try to outrun the thought. Unfortunately, there was another thought following close behind. A musing about the three people so far who had been killed by the tower.

Death had found them on each level.

What if...? he began to think.

Before he realised, in his musing, he'd passed by one of the doors. Leaving it open.

He spun to see Mason, the beautiful moron, steering towards it.

"Mason, *no!*"

The sound of Dirk's voice was lost beneath the creak of the door opening. A ghastly whine that turned all heads towards the sound, as Mason pushed it to get a look through.

What lay beyond, Dirk couldn't see and would never find out. All he knew was that a whisper of cold blew outwards as something suddenly yanked the door all the way inwards, slamming it against the inside of the room. A guttural noise burst forth from the darkness.

"MINE!"

It wasn't a voice so much as a tearing sound. A rip in the fabric of reality.

Mason fell back, flailing as though something was trying to grab him. To his horror, Dirk saw the man's clothes being tugged at, pulled into the room by invisible hands. As the model screamed and was dragged across the hallway by the unseen force, Casey made a desperate lunge for him, but only Earl got any real purchase, grabbing Mason's arm just as he was about to disappear.

The man shoved his boot on the door frame, holding them both out of danger. But not for long.

"Help," Earl gasped.

Dirk's entire body was frozen to the spot. He'd known it. He'd fucking *known* there was something behind those doors and it was out, loose, and it was going to have one of them. And he couldn't even run away, because he was too petrified to move.

All he could do was stare. Realising that whatever held Mason was too strong. The wooden frame was splitting around Earl's boot, and the man almost slipped as Mason was yanked forward again. Casey stumbled and let go. Had Alden not thrown his hands around Mason's waist in that moment, Dirk knew all three of them would have been lost.

"*MINNNNNNE!*" came the voice again. Louder this time. The walls seemed to shake with its power.

Rakie was wailing, hands over her ears. Monique wrapped her in a hug and bundled her up the hallway with Kim. But this left Dev cowering in absolute terror on the other side of the hallway from the fight to save Mason.

"Shiiiit!" Dev yelled, staring through the doorway and trying to push himself as far into the wall as possible to get away from it. "What *is* that?"

Dirk didn't want to look. He knew he'd never recover if he saw whatever it was. But as he turned away, he saw something else happening.

Bubbles were appearing in the wallpaper around them, growing larger by the second. Dark welts forming within each one. They spread out from the open doorway like a virus.

"Jesus, what's that?" Nia said.

One of them grew large enough to burst. A thick molasses of dark red liquid dripped down the wall.

Blood. It's blood.

The rest of the blistered wallpaper began to erupt in waves, splattering the survivors. A glob of it smacked Dirk in the forehead and he let out an involuntary moan, wiping his forearm across his face, trying to get it off him.

He backed away from the doorway, just as the lamp above their heads shattered, showering glass around them and dropping them into near darkness.

The only light lay up the corridor. If those lamps began to blow out, too, they'd all be fucking stuck in the dark with the thing in the room and the blood pouring from the walls.

"Dirk," Alden wheezed desperately, still clutching Mason. "Help."

Dirk saw every sinew in the boy's neck stretching to its limit. Earl's, too. Even as Nia and Casey joined them, pulling at Mason's belt, he saw they were only just holding on to him, his wails now terrified sobs. Invisible hands continued to grab at his clothes. The T-shirt ripped once, then twice, as the spirit's aggression grew.

Leave them, the voice in Dirk's head said.

He looked back towards the light. Monique, Kim and Rakie were waiting, staring back in horror, yelling at them to hurry.

Someone has to die here, the voice continued, giving form to the vague thought he'd had before. *People have died on each level. This is how it needs to be.*

Did he really know that, though?

Let Mason die, and get out.

Alden's face was strained, blossoming red beneath his flop of dark hair. He must know he was going to lose this tug of war, but he hadn't let go yet. Stupid kid. All of them, stupid. Their compassion was going to get them killed. Didn't they know anything about the world? They couldn't win. They were idiots for even trying.

What's more, he knew the voice in his head was right. It was as primal an instinct as any he'd ever had, and he half wondered if the tower was talking to him.

Someone had to die. It might as well be Mason. Better him than someone important.

Like me.

He was tempted to at least pull Nia after him. They could escape together. It would probably leave the evil entity to take Alden, Mason, Earl and Casey, but screw it. They should have known they couldn't win this fight. Let the tower have them.

His fingers flexed, ready to make his move, just as a splatter of blood flew through his lips and smacked against the inside of his cheek.

It tasted of ruin. Of decay. A pungent, thick ooze that quickly dripped onto his tongue and down his throat. He clutched his neck and gagged, stumbling against the back wall, sending a jolt of pain through his shoulder, yet barely caring as more blood blisters burst against his T-shirt, seeping through the material against his skin.

It was in his *mouth*. In *him*. Dirk fought the need to breathe, knowing if he did, he'd swallow it. His stomach began heaving, the bile rising. He was bent double, ready to spew it all over the carpet but too scared to see the evil pass his lips.

For a moment he was incapacitated, ready to fall to his knees and hope for the end.

Whatever was in the room sensed his vulnerability. He fucking *felt* it. The thing knew he was giving up. It stopped fighting for Mason and reached out its invisible tendrils for Dirk.

The others cried out as they stumbled back, thinking they'd somehow won. They knocked into Dirk, pushing him further away from the door.

It saved his life.

As he felt his own T-shirt being tugged towards the door, their combined mass got in the way. The connection with the thing inside the room was severed.

He was able to turn and run, just as the lamp ahead exploded, shrouding the corridor in darkness.

Dirk's eyes were watering, his body convulsing, coughing and spitting the rancid discharge out of him. Dribbling down his lips and the front of his clothes. His shoulders scraped against the walls, trying to keep himself upright. He heard the others behind him, felt the evil escape from the room and follow them through the shadows, ready to smother them and never let go.

"We're not going to make it," Dirk said, his voice whiny and pathetic, though he didn't give a shit. They turned a corner and raced towards the next lamp, just as that one exploded. Fuck. They were being too slow.

Another staircase rose ahead, much the same as the one on the ground floor. The light at the top of it was lit and swinging wildly. They raced up anyway, taking the steps two at a time.

Dirk looked back to see the blistering walls and waves of spraying blood catching up with them. Along with something else. A force riding the wave of darkness. Eager to feed.

"How far is it?" Monique cried as they reached another landing. She was still cradling Rakie, but they drew to a halt as a dozen more hallways stretched out from this place.

Dirk realised with dread they were all unlit.

The only source of light came from around the edges of a doorway in front of them.

He didn't want to go in. He didn't want to open that door and see what might be lurking inside.

But he knew that was exactly what they were going to have to do.

CHAPTER FOURTEEN
A Way Out

Dirk's feet wouldn't move. Even as the others brushed past and Alden pushed through the door into the light beyond, he stayed where he was. Caught between what might lie ahead and what was coming after them.

Move, you stupid fuck, or you'll *be the one who dies here!*

His brain knew the truth of it, and still he could only stare as the door opened and the others streamed through. What was he waiting for? Logic told him the light was leading the way, just as Nia had said. But the light was in one of these rooms. A haunted fucking room, the likes of which they'd just seen try to devour Mason. Maybe the light was a trap. Like that fish in the ocean that dangled a glowing antenna in front of its mouth to lure its food inside. Maybe they were going to hurl themselves towards it, only to be chewed up by the tower.

The whole tower is *a trap, jackass. Just follow the others and fucking hurry!*

It was the silence that finally broke him. The absolute quiet behind him.

Everyone else was in the room. He was alone.

Dirk blinked, the cold sweat trickling down his brow, and seeping into the corners of his eyes. He could feel the darkness, swallowing up the floor below them and creeping up the stairs, inevitably, inexorably, towards him. An emptiness he knew wouldn't simply kill him. It would wipe him from existence, cancelling him forever.

He drew a breath and fell forward. His right leg instinctively shot forward to cushion the impact. It was like learning to walk again. Fear had wiped him clean and here he was, trying to move in a way he'd taken for granted for the last fifty-five years, all in an effort to walk into a room.

If only his followers could see him now.

"Dirk, what are you doing?" a voice urged from the doorway. He couldn't see who it was – the glow from the room had turned them all into silhouettes inside. Perhaps they had been consumed after all, only their shadows left to torment him. Then Nia's face turned and caught the light from the hallway, and he saw she was real and alive. She reached out. "Get in here now, it's behind you!"

They would never speak of what *it* was. Would never get the chance. But he knew they both felt what was at risk if they failed to climb the tower. What awaited them if they simply stopped moving. A something in the nothing.

Time slowed as he crossed the corridor, an infant in a man's body, relearning everything fear had just wiped clean from him. It was like that time he'd had to build a new Instagram account from scratch after someone had hacked his old one. *How do I do this? How did I do this the first time? It's not going fast enough!*

He wasn't going fast enough. His steps were awkward. The cold grew at his back.

His face turned to the side, instinctively wanting to glance over his shoulder to see what it was that was going to kill him. A strange, morbidly human need to know his death. Yet something else caught his eye. A glimmer down the hallway, ghostly white but not a ghost. It had been real for a moment, solid and true.

A short, slender being held suspended in the centre of a mass of whiplike limbs stretching out to edges of the hallway. It had been moving, swinging through the dark. But then, just for a moment, it had paused, swaying, as if it had seen him.

The vision rippled and vanished.

That was all Dirk got to see before Nia leaned further out, grabbed him by the arm, and yanked him so forcefully into the room with the others that he tumbled onto a dirty carpet and rolled into a baby's cot.

He heard the door slam shut and the beautiful sound of a key turning, sliding a lock into place. Then someone slid to the floor with a sigh, their back against it, letting out a tense sigh.

"What the fuck were you *doing* out there, Dirk?" Nia asked. "Why did you just stop dead like that?"

He peered through the low light of the room, pushing himself away from the cot in what appeared to be a dingy nursery. The adrenaline that had been building up inside him threatened to pour out in the form of tears and screams. He tensed his core, unwilling to lose his shit in front of everyone.

"I–I don't fucking know, OK?" he snapped, getting to his feet and brushing himself off. "Why is any of this happening? My legs just stopped working for a moment. Maybe the tower had a hold of me somehow, stopped me from thinking straight. Who the fuck knows?"

The others were all looking at him. Alden leaned by the door, Nia slunk on her backside next to him. Dev was on a three-legged stool, while Rakie and Monique were sitting on a threadbare couch, Earl perched on the curled armrest next to his daughter. Casey had even stopped inspecting Mason's finely toned torso under his T-shirt to make sure the evil hadn't done any damage, and both were staring at him, too.

Everyone's expressions varied from pity to scorn. Dirk didn't know which he hated the most.

Only the old lady, Kim, was distracted. She stood apart from the group at the back of the room in front of a bookshelf, where a dusty brick of a baby monitor sat alone. As she went to touch it, there was a sudden burst of static, and from within the horrific scratching, another sound emerged.

A baby crying.

Dirk had been resting his hand lightly on the cot guard rail, so when he felt it shudder at the same time as the crying began, he almost shed his skin clean off. Then he looked down to see a small bundle of blankets on the mattress. They were hospital wraps, dirty and stained.

His blood turned cold as something moved beneath and a small face appeared. A baby. Surprisingly healthy looking, except for one glaring issue.

As it opened its mouth to scream, not a sound emerged.

It was coming out of the baby monitor instead.

"Fuck this, fuck this, fuck this," Dirk gasped, scrambling backwards. He bumped into Alden, who was staring in shock at Kim and the baby monitor.

"This happened in a book once and it didn't end well. We need to get out of here!"

"And go where? We're stuck in this room!"

The slow creak of a door cut suddenly through the din, and again Dirk's insides nearly tried to escape him.

It wasn't the main door, though. It was Kim at the back of the room. She'd found a door that yet again he was sure hadn't been there a few seconds ago, and the crazy bitch had opened it without consulting any of them. He wanted to scream. *Haven't you been paying attention to literally anything going on here?* But then the crying from the monitor grew fiercer. The baby's torment becoming the epicentre of a storm of noise.

And the baby in the crib started to lift from the stained mattress.

Fuuuuuuuck offfffffff!

Dirk sprinted towards Kim, along with the others. Knocking had started at the door behind them, from the hallway they'd come from, but there was too much happening for Dirk to give a shit about the eternal void. They all bundled past the cot and forced themselves through Kim's door at the far end of the room.

Openly weeping, Dev was the last one through and he pulled the door shut. The baby's cry instantly disappeared, which would have been a relief if they hadn't found themselves squeezed into a small bathroom in the middle of a poltergeist event.

Cabinet doors beneath the bathroom mirror opened and shut, again and again. The shower curtain hanging over the porcelain bath billowed as though something was trying to push through it. Ghostly white tiles behind it were shattering, one by one.

Then the taps spun themselves on with fury, and as steam engulfed the mirror, a slowly drawn invisible finger wrote two words:

GET OUT

"We're trying!" Dirk yelled back.

The message disappeared as the glass itself began to run, rivulets of silver dripping into the basin, which was matted with hair and fuck knows what else. Blood began bubbling up through the coarse fibres. Dirk felt vomit rising the same way in his throat. He pushed to the centre of the group, forcing himself to some kind of safety.

"Where do we go?" Casey cried.

The answer revealed itself as the wall ahead began to shake and crumble. Suddenly there was a rent in the tiles, a long split that pulled wider, revealing light beyond.

In any normal situation, Dirk would have resisted the idea of diving through a hole in the wall into the unknown, but this was the kind of situation that called for it.

He pushed Kim and Alden ahead of him, forcing them towards what he hoped was their escape.

"Go there! Quicker! Move it, you bag of dicks!"

Alden didn't hesitate. He was either brave or stupid, but he turned sideways when he reached the wall and crawled through without thinking, taking care not to snag himself on the broken tiles lining the split like jagged teeth.

The kid reached back to help Kim through after him, then Dirk pushed forward to make sure he was next. Monique screamed behind him. He tried to move faster, but slipped and fell against the ripped wall. Bricks and old pipes stuck out at awkward angles, digging into his chest. The corner of a snapped timber joint scraped his face. He moaned as he scrambled through this illogically deep wall. Until, finally, he fell through into another room and landed on a rug.

Dust puffed up and out, clouding him in its dry, choking embrace. He rolled away and found himself on a wooden floor. A cold breeze crept through the timbers, fingers of it teasing him, brushing against his face, letting him know death was circling.

It would have been easy to lie there and accept it. He was fit as fuck, physically speaking, but this place was taking an emotional toll, too. He was exhausted from the terror of the dungeon and the sinking ship, and a haunted house straight out of his childhood fears.

But then the breeze grew through the floorboards, and he pictured it opening up and swallowing him face first, and that was enough to push him to his feet.

This room wasn't like the rest, he realised. Gone was the shabby suburban chic, as if they'd crawled through the wall into an entirely new house. This was more like it. A far more stereotypical haunted mansion, with the kind of stately reading room you found within those sprawling estates. Full of ancient furniture and paintings and rugs. There was even a gigantic fireplace with a low, smouldering fire that seemed on the edge of going out.

"Did we transition?" Monique asked, looking around the group. "I didn't feel it. And we didn't go up? So this is the same level, right?"

"And still fucking creepy," Dev said, jiggling from side to side nervously, making one of the floorboards creak. He wiped his eyes, glancing back to the hole in the wall they'd crawled through, probably to make sure nothing was coming through after them. "We need to get out of here, OK? *I* need to get out. I'm fucking done, man. Over it. Please just find the way out, OK? Please?"

Monique put her arm around him and he sobbed into her shoulder.

It was Nia who gestured to a shape in the shadows on

the other side of the room. It was indistinct for a moment, before Dirk's eyes adjusted and he saw it materialise into a spiral staircase.

"Ask and ye shall receive," Nia said.

Slipping from her father's grasp, Rakie wandered over and lightly touched the metal handrail that circled upwards. She followed its curve, frowning as she looked up.

"But it doesn't go anywhere," she said, confused. "The steps just go to the ceiling." She drew her hand back and then studied the iron filigree design of intertwined branches and leaves. Nature again, Dirk realised, just like the tree in the dungeon and the Christmas tree in the ship. Except that it was lifeless. Rakie looked to her father. "This is all wrong, Dad. This is the way up, but it's not ready. It doesn't feel right."

Dirk stayed where he was as the rest of the group wandered over to join the father and daughter. Mason and Casey refusing to let each other go. Monique stuck close to Dev. Alden and Nia together, too. The cliques were forming. An inevitable consequence of this dire situation, but Dirk wasn't used to being on the outside of any group.

Though he noticed he wasn't the only one.

To one side, Kim had drifted away to stand before a tall painting that hung from ceiling to floor. It seemed fitting for such a room. Imposing and solemn.

"It's him again," she said wistfully.

Her voice was so low, only Dirk heard her.

The image she was transfixed by was again a figure, although this one was mercifully still human for the moment. A short man with a sweep of grey hair across his scalp and a little curly moustache atop thin lips. He wore a grey suit with a red tie, and there was a newspaper tucked under his arm.

As Dirk watched, the newspaper suddenly dropped and rolled out of the painting.

He was too aghast to cry out, as he might have. Too busy reeling from everything else to react in a normal, human way to this act of supernatural fuckery. He simply stood there, mouth agape and a cold shiver electrifying every inch of his skin, as the man in the painting began to move.

Arms twitching, then lifting up. Hands flexing. Pink fingers pushing at the canvas, stretching the material.

Before the man's elongated arms stretched fully into the room towards Kim.

Strange thing was, the woman didn't even flinch.

She was *waiting* for him to take her.

Dirk's shout of warning – *Get the fuck away from there!* – stuck in his throat. He looked over to the others surrounding the staircase, staring up it in case it might suddenly open for them. He looked at the lifeless leaves in the iron design. Then he looked back to Kim and her painted husband coming to life.

A shadow flitted across his mind. A sickly knowledge of what might be at play in this death tower, and how he might bend it to his advantage.

They'd agreed the tower was challenging them, testing them, and death was a consequence. It had succeeded in killing three of them across two levels, and on both levels they'd found their escape without anything blocking their exit. But this time? Nobody had died yet and the way up was blocked. As the girl said, something wasn't right.

The voice in his head returned.

Someone has to die here, it repeated.

It was a concept he hadn't liked the first time it had unfolded in his mind, beckoning him closer, whispering in his ear. He should have scrunched it up and set it on fire, then buried the ashes in the vault where he kept all his darkest thoughts.

But he still couldn't get past the truth of it.

What if the tower needed blood? What if that was the only way for them to get out?

Get a grip. You can't tell the others this, they'll think you're crazy.

Dirk chewed his lip, scratching the thick stubble across his jaw. He took a step towards the stairs. Towards the others.

It would take him past Kim.

What if you tell them and they believe you? They might try to kill YOU.

He took another step, his eyes on the other eight people in the room, all of whom were still inspecting the staircase, staring up at the ceiling, trying to find a button or a lever or something that would let them escape.

Nobody was thinking.

More importantly, nobody was paying attention.

He moved within a couple of feet of Kim. She had her back to him, engrossed in the coming-alive painting of her dead husband. There was no terror in her posture. She wasn't trying to lean away. She just stood there as this oil painting pushed through the fabric and reached for her, as if this was the most normal thing in the world. Maybe even something she'd long dreamed of him doing.

Dirk's hands clenched as he hesitated. *She's a sweet old lady who just misses her husband*, he told himself.

A sting of envy punctured the thought. He recognised the warmth and familiarity of this moment, but only from a distance. He was on the periphery of love, as he always was. He'd never experienced a romantic relationship, never found a sense of home in another person. Sex? Sure. Lots of it. Sometimes with women who'd pursued his celebrity, sometimes women he'd pursued using his celebrity. But it never went beyond that first, brief, messy encounter. He'd never let it. And only now, in this fucked-up place, did he understand what he'd been missing.

He was within touching distance, watching Kim's grey hair swishing at the back of her neck as she tilted her head upwards, towards the outstretched painted hands of her dead husband. As paint flaked off the canvas, dropping like colourful rain, he wondered what it must be like. To experience that bond with another person. To feel something with someone, for longer than it took to get off. To yearn for someone so fucking *much* that the supernatural vision of them coming to life to kill you was something to embrace.

Dirk envied her life, envied her love, envied her moment.

He would tell himself time and again, until his own death, that it would have happened anyway. That she was waiting for the painting to grab her, not realising this was the tower doing its work. It wasn't her husband. It was something pretending to be him, to coax her into letting herself be taken.

He found a little solace in that lie. It was enough to look the others in the eye later.

The truth was, with nobody looking, he reached out with his left hand as he walked past and nudged Kim in the back with enough force to send her stumbling forwards to meet the outstretched hands.

She made a noise of surprise. Just a soft little gasp he would never forget, but it was quickly muffled as she fell into the painting's embrace.

The arms wrapped around her with a smooth, swift motion. One around her neck. The other around her waist.

Dirk wasted no time in walking on, pausing only to kick the rolled-up newspaper into the fire.

Behind him he heard the faintest snaps, like brittle twigs underfoot in autumn, as Kim's body was squeezed and folded and pulled into the painting.

By the time any of the other heads turned, Dirk was already among them.

"Where's Kim?" Dev asked, peering back into the rest of the room. Dirk didn't see what he saw, and he certainly wasn't going to look back and give himself away.

Fortunately, he didn't need to.

Because he was right. *He was right.*

As Kim's body had been squeezed into human paint in whatever dimension she'd been taken to, the staircase came to life. The leaves, until then seemingly withered, unfurled and grew in colour. Except one, which fell to the floor. But the rest burst into emerald green from the ground up, as if there was some technicolour filter being rolled upwards in front of his eyes. Up and up they wove, around the railings of the spiral staircase, until they reached the hole in the ceiling, and then suddenly there was a change in the atmosphere of the room. A shift in tone. In spirit.

Dirk knew it had worked. Kim's death had opened the way out.

Huh, he thought.

Yet he had no time to dwell on what advantages this knowledge was going to give him. Even as Alden and Nia high-fived, and Rakie picked up the dead leaf and slid it into her jacket, a tremendous sound boomed across the walls all around them. The tower knew they were about to escape again, and it wanted more blood. It wasn't sated by the old lady. Her frail body hadn't lasted long.

It needed another sacrifice.

Dirk pushed through the group and leapt onto the iron steps. He half ran, half pulled himself up by the handrail as he circled the staircase up to the hole in the ceiling and pushed himself into oblivion, not waiting to see if anybody else followed.

Not today, Satan, he thought, as he jumped to the next level.

CHAPTER FIFTEEN
Paradise

Alden had never seen a man run so fast as Dirk did to get out of the haunted house.

He didn't blame him. He couldn't, because he was similarly petrified as the ghosts began trying to beat their way through the walls. But he still held firm at the bottom of the spiral staircase and urged the others up ahead of him. Because it was the right thing to do. Even if he wanted to buckle and crumble under the sheer fright of it all.

As he ran up last, he could feel something enter the room and snap at his heels. Not a firm physical being. A presence. *An evil.*

It was enough to push him up faster. Shoving at Nia's back to make sure she was able to leap through the black hole to oblivion, before following her through.

Something touched his leg as he leapt. He didn't care to ever know what it was.

The next thing he knew he was on sand.

The change was jarring, like leaping from the depths of winter into the heat of summer. There were warm, soft grains beneath his fingers as he fell upon a beach and had to squeeze his eyes shut against the blindingly beautiful sunshine dazzling the air, as though it was on fire. Nearby there were birds chirping. Water lapping gently. The soft whisper of a breeze.

Alden let his head loll for a moment, licking his lips, tasting the salty ocean air, embracing the temporary respite.

Then he rolled onto his backside and sat up, opening his eyes as much as he could.

Wow.

They were on a glorious tropical coastline. It stretched out in either direction, perhaps for half a mile or so, then disappeared, giving the impression they were on an island. That's how it felt, too. There was a sense of isolation to the paradise that was almost tangible.

He got up and noticed the others looking dazed – but not unhappy – at the extreme shift in surroundings. One minute in the worst of all haunted houses, the next in bright sunshine, with turquoise waters lapping nearby.

"A beach house," Casey said, pulling at Mason's arms as she pointed towards the shore behind them. Alden turned to see a stunning glass-fronted building nestled in the palm trees. It had two storeys, with a porch area at the front and what looked like a bar and seats underneath. As Alden peered at it, he could almost hear music begin to drift towards them and the distinct smell of a barbecue.

"Paradise," Dev moaned, with a glazed look of ecstasy on his face as he looked between the house and the sea and the beach. "Thank fuck. Now this is *my* kind of level."

Casey continued pulling at Mason, trying to drag him back there. There was a smile on her lips that Alden hadn't seen since they'd arrived. A genuinely lovely expression of hope. It suited her.

"Come on," she said. "We should go see if they have water. And maybe some food, while we're at it."

But Mason held fast – the only one of the group to do

so. There was a weird look of recognition on his face that Alden understood instantly. The man knew what they were looking at, because of course he did. That's how things worked here, wasn't it? Each jump up the tower spoke to at least one of them on a very personal level.

"I'm home," Mason said.

"*This* is your home?" Dev exclaimed, almost falling over in the sand. "Holy shit, Mason."

Earl rolled his sleeves up, getting as much of his skin under the warmth of the sun as possible. He slipped a forearm across the perspiration on his forehead. "This is a hell of a place for anyone to live, son. You sure you didn't knock your head in that house we just escaped?"

Mason didn't answer. He was transfixed by the house on the beach and allowed himself to be led by Casey across the sand, towards the place he claimed was his home.

They began to follow in pairs.

"We're one short," Nia said quietly to Alden. "Kim didn't appear with us."

"Shit – she didn't?"

Alden's insides constricted; he quickly scanned the shoreline in case somehow she'd appeared after the rest of them. But there was nothing. How'd he let that happen? Hadn't he ushered the kindly old lady up the stairs with the others ahead of him? *Shit.* Now he thought of it, he couldn't remember seeing her on the stairs at all. She was usually pretty slow, and one of them would have had to help her.

"She was in the room with us, wasn't she? We all made it into the reading room, I'm sure we were all there."

Nia nodded. "Yeah, me too. But the staircase woke up so suddenly and then that banging started, we left in a rush. Is there a chance we left her behind?"

"I don't think so?" Alden said, hoping it was true. Then he shook the burgeoning guilt away. "No, I was the last one out. I know I looked around and there was nobody else. I waited until everyone was on the stairs."

Dirk brushed past them, head up, giving them a broad smile. Alden expected the man to make some kind of joke, but he seemed too happy, too confident in where they were, to care for such things. He hurried onwards, leaving the pair alone again, before Dev brought up the rear. The sunshine beaming out of his face a minute ago had temporarily disappeared behind a cloud.

"Were you two just talking about Kim?"

Alden and Nia glanced at each other.

"Yeah, sorry mate," Alden said. "She's not here. We... don't think she made it."

Dev's face crumbled, his shoulders sagged. He did exactly what Alden had done – scanning the coastline, spinning in circles, to try to prove them wrong. But he saw nothing that disputed what Alden had said.

He spat in the sand. "Fuck this tower."

Alden reached over and squeezed his shoulder, but there was really nothing else to say. He'd been so sure they'd all made it out of that level. And Kim? She'd saved them all in that torture chamber. Had it not been for her calm and understanding, they would been killed on the first level of the tower, failed its challenge, and who knows what that might have meant? Maybe it would have disappeared to test another thirteen people in another place and time. Maybe it would have exploded and blown the world to pieces.

Kim had made sure they were still in this. It wasn't fair she hadn't made it to paradise, along with the rest of them.

Except this probably isn't paradise, he thought.

He trudged a little slower towards the idyllic beach house.

Alden's wariness subsided a little once they reached Mason's home and wandered inside. It was just as nice inside as out, all clean lines and catalogue-style decoration. The kitchen was open plan with the living room, and this is where they all stayed. Even Mason, who seemed reluctant to go further into the house.

Being together with everyone, with the comforting chatter wrapping around him, should have helped Alden's mood. But it didn't. Kim's loss had hit him harder than he thought possible. The guilt that he might have missed something, failed in his chance to save that lovely woman, stirred up other feelings he'd been keeping at bay throughout the ship, throughout the house.

Grief continued to haunt him, even in these sunnier climes.

He stood at the rear of the kitchen as the others hunted for snacks and poured water from the apparently authentic tap. The window before him opened up to the interior of the island, the waving palms and the darkness of the forest.

It would be easy to lose yourself in those shadows. To allow them to hold and shape whatever emotions you were feeling. The dark between the trees was always like that.

He could almost see Leia bounding among them on one of their walks.

"How you doing, Alden?"

Nia had come to stand by him, sipping water from a pristine crystal glass. Mason's home was not without its finery, it seemed, even in the tower's version.

"Yeah, I'm fine," he lied, then laughed. "F. I. N. E. Freaked out. Insecure. Neurotic. Emotional. That's what my therapist always says when I tell her I'm fine. She never believes me."

Nia smiled a little. "I think, after what we've been through, we're probably all F. I. N. E. But, seriously, are you, though? Are you fine?"

Alden went back to staring out at the forest shadows, finding safety there. "I heard my dog barking in the ship," he said. "I know it sounds crazy, but I heard her. Not just any dog. *Her.*"

"I believe you."

"We were about to get hit with that river, and then she barks and I look up to see the door. It hadn't been there before, I'm sure of it. Yet there it was, and we managed to get out. Because of her." His gaze flickered to hers in the reflection. "You heard her too, didn't you?"

Nia's shoulders inched up. Not quite a shrug, not quite a dismissal. "Maybe. There was a lot happening, a lot of noise. It's possible I heard a dog. Leia, right?"

Her remembering the name was enough to set him off. He nodded, as the tears welled in his eyes and he tried to blink them away. Why would the tower be making him hear Leia? What kind of cruel trick was that after all he'd been through?

Nia's hand slipped around his waist and she rested against him. The human touch almost broke him. "I had a dog growing up," she said. "A schnauzer. He was a bundle of joy and energy and he never ever stopped. So, when he eventually did, I felt like life itself stopped for a while. Everything was muted, pointless, colourless. I was... Yeah, I was devastated. It was the worst feeling I think I'd ever experienced. But you come through it, Alden. There's always another sunset, I promise."

He leaned into her embrace, trying not to let the sobs rack his body, not wanting anybody else in the room to notice or say anything. When he spoke, his voice was a whisper, the faintest breath.

"I don't have anyone back home, Nia. Leia was my family since the pandemic. Since I lost my parents. She was the last link to who I was, who *we* were together. When she died, I was... I was cut adrift. Yeah, that's it. *Adrift*. I had teaching and the band, but I couldn't handle it anymore. I couldn't hold on to it all. I didn't *want* to hold on to it. Does that make sense?" He felt Nia's head nodding against him. "I'd only barely managed to cling on to my shit during the lockdowns, without my folks, without music, trying to do my job via fucking *video*. Leia was who got me through it. And now it's just me. I'm no good as just me, Nia. I don't want to be alone."

There. That was the truth of it. A weight lifted as he pulled the truth from himself and laid it bare for someone – anyone – to see. And it felt... better. A little.

"I'm so sorry, Alden."

Blinking through the tears, he straightened, cleared his throat. "It's fine. I'm fine. Thank you."

"You're not alone, though." She glanced at him and then gestured over her shoulder, jokingly. "You have us now."

And he laughed, despite the pain inside. Because it was true. The tower had brought him to this place to break him. It had given him purpose instead. A found family he had become irrevocably tied to. People he wanted to help. Along with a reminder that he wanted to survive for himself, to get back to the world and explore that glimmer of happiness he'd felt just before being brought here.

He wanted to live for that next sunset.

* * *

"*This* is where you lived?" Casey asked Mason again.

Alden had dried his eyes and stood in the kitchen, having a drink of water that Nia had got for him. They stood together, no longer talking, content to listen to the others.

Mason stood in the open-plan kitchen, leaning a little stiffly against the countertop, his long fingers tapping lightly on the sleek charcoal surface. "Yeah, this is where I grew up. The house, the island... It's all exactly as it was." He nodded at the clock on the wall, which only had one hand. It was pointing straight down. "Even that thing is accurate. It fell off the wall in a storm and the minute hand came off, never to be seen again, so we just kept it as it was. Mum's excuse was that at least we'd know what hour it was. This is... ridiculous. I can't believe it. Do you think this place is real?"

Nobody answered. Alden was almost sure they were still in the tower, but even as he thought it, he wondered if he could trust himself. Could he be sure of anything anymore? What if the tower had sent them back in time, or zapped them across the world to wherever this island was? Who knew what the hell it was capable of doing?

He noticed Dev had regained a little of his spirit as he returned from the toilet, took a seat at the breakfast bench, and poured himself a shot of whisky from the bottle on the counter. "Did anybody find any food?"

"I think there was some takeaway in the fridge," Mason offered.

Dev laughed. "Where the fuck did you get takeaway food around *here*? You have it shipped in by helicopter or something?"

"Sometimes," Mason said with half a smile. "Most of the time we took the boat around the coast to the town, though. It's about a mile away. Driving would have been faster, but the roads are pretty awful and it was far more scenic on the water. Often coasted a little and ate half of the order on the way back."

"Jesus, I want your life."

Mason's good humour faded. He inspected the water in his glass, swirling it around. "I was here alone a lot of the time. My parents were both successful, busy with their pursuits. And then when I brought my boyfriend home, they suddenly became even busier. I never saw them again. Texts at Christmas. Sometimes on my birthday, when they remembered. They said nothing when I moved out, and not even when Tom and I got married." He blew out his cheeks and took a sip of his drink. "But, yeah, I got to grow up here and got everything I physically needed to live, so I guess I can't really complain."

Alden could see the pain in Mason's eyes as he looked around at this luxury home, seeing what the others couldn't. As he watched, the house suddenly grew a little darker, and he couldn't help but turn to the window to see if the sun had vanished behind a cloud.

No. The skies were still clear.

Something in *here* had changed.

He glanced around. Nobody else seemed to care, but the stunning beachside house was a little less warm and inviting, a little colder. He felt the loneliness and shivered. Mason noticed, nodding, as if acknowledging he felt it, too.

If Casey was disappointed to learn Mason was married to another man, she didn't let slip too much. There was the slightest sag in her shoulders, but as she sensed his mood dip she gave his strong, tanned arm a squeeze before resting her cheek against his skin. She said nothing, offering only reassurance. Mason stroked her hair.

Meanwhile, Earl and Rakie were helping themselves to some biscuits they'd found, Monique had taken a seat near the window, lying her head back on the numerous cushions scattered across it, and Dirk was slumped in an armchair near her, staring into the distance.

Alden was grateful Nia held fast next to him in the kitchen, drinking thoughtfully as she stared at a stack of books on the counter next to a fake plant.

Dev kept swinging on his stool, forcing the good cheer of the whisky down his throat.

"Mate, this place is immense. It's *so* nice. You should come visit the place *I* grew up! Arse end of Manchester, one of the few places that hasn't been torn down and had fancy apartments shoved up its arse, though I reckon it needs it. Hell, man, if I'd grown up here, I'd never bloody leave! The beach on your doorstep, you can swim any time you want. Sunbathe, too. And no bastards around to rob you. It's perfect."

Mason grinned around chewing the biscuit Rakie had offered him, seemingly unconcerned it might not be entirely real.

"Well, when all this is over, Dev, I'll take you to the real beach house, OK? The place is probably still empty, aside from the odd housekeeper keeping it in check. We'll fly there and have a week or two in the sun. Deal?"

Dev slipped off the stool as he raised his glass and burst out laughing. "Why wait until then? We're here already! I say we kick back and chill. Who's to say this place isn't the real deal, anyway? Maybe we passed the tower's test and this is the reward. We won, baby. We beat the tower. And we get a free stay in paradise for our troubles!"

Alden wished he could join in the fantasy, but he knew Dev was clutching at straws. Finding solace in the lie.

His gaze drifted to where Nia was sliding one of the books out of the pile next to the whisky bottle. It had a colourful green spine and bold letters, making it stand out from the rest with their dull covers.

He read the title as she turned it over to read the back cover copy.

The Meaning of Life, it said. It was written above the silhouette of a tree stretching its branches out in all directions, letting leaves fall from its branches.

Alden's skin prickled with recognition.

A tree.

Leaves.

As Nia turned the book over to better study the front cover, she realised it, too. She looked up and their eyes met. "A recurring theme," she said quietly, tapping the tree with her forefinger. As the book shifted in her hands, it caught the sunlight and the leaves gleamed a variety of different colours. Alden stared, entranced, as her finger moved from the tree to the title.

"Bit of a coincidence you pulled that book out of the pile," he said, knowing that perhaps there was no coincidence at all.

She nodded as though she was thinking the same. "There was something about it that drew my eye, much like the light in the ship and in the house. I bet the others here aren't even real books." Holding hers in one hand, she lifted the others from the top and placed them on the kitchen counter one by one. Alden stared, confused, as he saw the rest of the stack was filled with nonsense. Plain covers and garbled shapes that at a glance might be words, but were definitely none he recognised, in any language. Nia opened the cover of one of them. It was entirely blank inside. She closed it again and held up the one in her hands. "We were meant to see this. Although… the meaning of life? I can't see how that helps us much."

She turned it over again, as if trying to loosen its secrets, and again the leaves on the front sparkled in the light.

Alden chewed his lip, suddenly having a thought. "How many leaves are on the front?"

"Huh?"

"The leaves falling from the tree. How many are there?"

She counted them. "Nine."

Of course there were. Patterns were starting to be revealed, even though nothing made sense yet. As Nia tilted her head, wondering what he was getting at, Alden made a point of looking around the room from person to person. Then he held her gaze as he let the unspoken truth of the connection find its way to her.

"Nine leaves," he said.

"Nine people," she replied, eyes widening. She brushed her hair away from her face and tucked it behind her ears as she studied the cover, then opened it up to check out the contents. As she scanned what lay within the pages, a frown grew.

"Anything?" he asked.

"Enough for me to think we need to set up here for the night," she said, waving the tome at him. "We should get some rest, and eat and drink what we can. Because I have a feeling this is going to give us a lot to talk about."

CHAPTER SIXTEEN
The Answer is 42

It was a strange little camp they had created by mid-afternoon.

While Nia grabbed a space on the couch and sat engrossed in the book, Alden encouraged the others to do the same – to chill, eat, hang out. Whatever they wanted to do, as long as they stayed close to the house. So far this level hadn't suggested anything dangerous was hunting them, but he wasn't about to take the chance. The guilt over Kim hung heavy, and although he wasn't the oldest or strongest or even the loudest in the group, he felt an obligation to these people. He would do what he could to make sure they made it out of here.

He pulled in two wicker chairs from the porch patio, making sure there were seats for everyone in the living room. Then he sat down in one on the opposite side of the coffee table upon which Mason and Earl were playing The Game of Life – although Mason insisted he'd never owned it – with Rakie, Casey and, surprisingly, Dirk.

Monique was still asleep. Nia was reading the book.

Only Dev had kept himself separate. Drinking another couple of shots in the kitchen, then making his way outside to soak up the sun.

"Artificially generated or a figment of my imagination,

it doesn't make any difference," he had argued, when Alden tried to get him to stay in the house. "This is a bloody paradise! There is sun! I'm going to make the most of it before we have to carry on this game of trying not to die as we climb an alien tower."

"Just stay where we can see you, OK?"

"Fine, *Dad.*"

Alden could see him, bare feet planted firmly in the sand, with his shirt off, his eyes closed and his face lifted to the heavens. To anybody else, it looked like he'd found his own little sanctuary and was going to make the most of it. It was the stereotypical British holiday in the sun, before returning to the daily grind in the cold and wet for another year.

But there were cracks in the cheery façade. Alden had seen it in Dev's bloodshot eyes as he'd pushed past him to get outside.

"I should go and bring him back in," he said, as much to himself as anyone else in the room.

"I think you are worried too much," Monique murmured from the couch, opening a lazy eye as he shifted the extra seats into the circle. "Let him have his sun."

Dirk rolled his dice, then moved his little family car a couple of spaces on the board game. "She's right, kid, there's nothing here to hurt us. It's an island paradise, right? A paradise pulled from Mason's brain, and I don't think there's anything of note in there we need to be worried about." He looked up at Mason with a grin. "No offence, dude."

Mason rolled his eyes and glanced at Alden. "Maybe he's right, Alden. We seem to be OK for the moment. Maybe you should try to rest a moment, too. Go outside with Dev and get some vitamin D. The water and food have been real enough, and the sun must be, too. It might help."

Alden didn't know, though. He was on edge, dreading whatever was surely coming next, and no amount of sunbathing would help that. He looked to Nia to see if she agreed with Mason's diagnosis, but she was still chewing through the book. One by one the pages turned with a sweep of her fingers, and her brow creased with focus as she slipped further and further into the text.

Only when Earl threw his hands up in the air to celebrate winning the board game – getting married, having seven kids, three dogs, and somehow still having money – did Nia let out a long, loud breath and place the open book on the curve of her knee.

"Well, shit," she said.

"Good shit or bad?" Alden asked.

"Not sure. Maybe both. It's fascinating, though. And I think it was put here for a reason. The tower wanted me to see it, wanted us to find it."

"Why?"

"To sate our curiosity as to why we were brought here."

The game players stopped chatting and looked over. Monique pulled herself upright on the couch. To Alden's relief, even Dev had returned and wandered in from outside, plonking himself into the seat next to Alden.

"So what's the deal?" Earl asked.

"Yeah, any clues in there about how to get the fuck outta here?" Dirk added.

"No," Nia said. "But it does offer up some interesting implications. That the tower isn't all it seems. That these levels aren't entirely randomly pulled from us. There seems to be more of a design to the whole thing than I'd considered." She picked up the book and flicked to a double-page spread, holding it up for the group to see. On the left-hand page was a series of bullet points, all led by dotted lines to a diagram on the right-hand side. It was a tall rectangle, split up into nine sections. She tapped it twice. "I think this is our tower."

"What are those lines?" Rakie asked. "Are they the levels that we're climbing?"

"I think that is exactly what they are, Rakie. Nine levels, split into three distinct sections. You see, the book–" Dirk opened his mouth to say something, but Nia held up a firm finger and glared at him. "*No*. Let me finish and then you'll find out. You see, the book presents a theory based on research by philosophers and scientists, and probably a few other very clever people. And the theory is that the meaning of life is split into three distinct parts. They name them as coherence, purpose and significance." She tapped the first of the stages on the illustration. "This one is coherence. It's all about life making sense. Or not, I guess." Her finger moved up the page. "And this one is purpose, where it's all about people having and working towards goals and aims in life."

Alden shifted his chair closer to get a better look. "And that last one, at the top of the tower – that's significance?"

"Yeah, apparently so. They describe it as being the stage where one's life has value. You know, where people make a difference to the world, and especially to other people." She drew the book away, flicked through a couple of pages and began reading. "But the key to all of this, to unlocking the three parts, so they say, is authenticity. That being authentic is where you can truly come to understand the meaning of life. That only through being yourself can you find sense, purpose and significance, and that when you perceive increasing authenticity in your own life, it can be a marker that you're moving in the right direction."

Dirk snorted, causing Nia's lips to thin. He immediately waved his hand in a lacklustre apology. "Sorry, but my bullshit radar is going off. I can't believe our man Mason here has such a book lying around. Or any book, for that matter."

"You don't think I'm intelligent enough to read?" Mason asked impassively.

"I don't think you *need* to read – not this, anyway. Look around you, my man. This place is heaven. You grew up privileged and wealthy beyond most people's dreams. The meaning of life? It's already here. You're living it. Why would you need to read about it?"

"For what it's worth, I've never seen that book before."

Nia closed the book and put it down next to the board game in the centre of the gathered circle. "It wasn't his. The tower left it here for us. The other books are all empty, set dressing. This was the only real book among them."

"But why would the tower do that?" Monique asked, picking the book up and turning it over in her hand reverently, as though it was made of magic.

"It's a clue to why we're here," Alden said, holding Nia's gaze. She nodded as he spoke. "The tower is challenging us in ways we don't really understand. We know it's testing us. Perhaps *this* is what it's testing. Seeing how well we measure up – whether we're good, authentic humans or not. Whether we're wasting our lives or not."

Earl's eyebrows rose. "You're saying this is all a challenge to see how *human* we are?"

Alden gave a little shrug. "I guess it's possible. Like an intergalactic pub quiz. We've been picked to represent humanity, and maybe we're playing against someone else or maybe we're playing against each other. But we're here and we're being posed questions about ourselves and our ability to survive. With each level we get past, some of us get to move on to the next. Until there's a winner."

"While the rest... fall by the wayside?" Earl said.

Rakie sighed theatrically. "Just say they die, Dad. We all saw what happened."

Dirk stood up, knocking the board game. His little car fell on its side and all the pegs fell out, spilling his family across the painted hills on the background.

"Jesus, you guys, you're actually buying into this insanity? You're seriously saying this entire experience is a fucking *game*? That we're all risking death with every step we take in order to... what? Prove a point that we're good people? That's ridiculous."

"Kim was a good person," Dev said quietly, staring out through the window. "And she still died."

"Exactly!" Dirk exclaimed.

Nia looked between them both. "Maybe there's more to it than that. But whoever did this has gone to an awful lot of trouble. What would be ridiculous is if that tower beamed into our world, kidnapped us, made us climb it, used whatever kind of magic or technology it had to conjure up levels pulled from our memories... and it all be for nothing. There has to be a bigger reason."

As she spoke, Alden felt the truth of her suggestions solidify and take form. She'd found it. He was sure of that. Even if it wasn't *the* reason, even if they'd never understand what that was, it was *a* reason. Something tangible to cling on to as they tried to survive this place. A known within this unknown.

Except, the more he thought about it, the more the implications took on a darker turn. This tower hadn't been a place of risk and reward. What if it wasn't about winning, but not losing?

He shuffled to the edge of his seat as he looked around the group. "We know there's a countdown and we're in a race to get to the top, right. So, what if this *is* all to save the world, like we said before? What if we're representing everyone, the entirety of humanity, and if we fail to convince the tower we're worthy, maybe we all pay the price?"

There was silence as they all considered that. Until Casey blinked and grinned.

"*Or* maybe there's a reward for whoever gets to the top!"

"Like… a prize?" Dirk said, eyes brightening.

She shrugged. "Why not? You thought it was a reality game show when we first arrived. Maybe it is. Maybe this isn't a good versus evil struggle for our souls, or whatever. Maybe it's just a race, with winners and losers and a prize for those that make it."

Alden wanted to say something against the idea. This was a dangerous moment, potentially creating competition between them where they really needed to hold together as a team. The tower's challenges had been terrifying and deadly. It would be sadistic to put them through this for a bloody prize. No, this was something else. Bigger. More important. The end of all things, a last throw of the dice – a challenge put to humanity for them to prove they were capable of banding together to succeed, or risk being blasted from existence.

The mood had already lifted, though, and he felt the moment to argue against this idea slip through his fingers.

"It wouldn't be a cash prize," Dirk pondered, taking this more seriously than he had mostly anything else so far. "No, man. That would be too *human*. These guys aren't humans. This tower is better than that. It's fucking *magic*. So. Huh. Maybe the prize is, too." He started tapping the table, beaming at whatever his mind was conjuring up. "OK, I'm on board! That's more of a reason behind bringing us here and trying to kill us than the fucking meaning of life." He picked up his car again and placed it on the board game path, sweeping the pegs aside. They rolled onto the floor, and he gestured to Earl and Rakie to throw the dice. "Come on, then. Let's play."

Alden didn't like the shadow that flitted across Dirk's eyes as the game continued. It felt like a storm brewing on the horizon.

CHAPTER SEVENTEEN
There's Something in the Storm

It was Rakie who saw it first.

At dusk, she and her father had wanted to take a walk along the beach to soak in the last of the sun's warmth. Nia decided it was probably safe enough to join them, as the day had been uneventful so far. Alden and Casey tagged along, too.

Mason, Monique, Dev and Dirk stayed back at the house to nap, eat and drink.

The wind had picked up, but the sky was still clear and there was only the barest cold touch of the coming night drifting in off the water. It was a soothing, delicious evening. The kind that stuck in the memory and kept you warm in later years.

That they were afforded such luxury had made Nia a little uncomfortable. It felt too good, too perfect. If they were still in the tower, it had been strangely quiet and calm this entire level. Perhaps it was mining their brains for new nightmares to have them traverse. Or... maybe they were being given space. Maybe the tower was allowing them a chance to recuperate and regather their strength. A save point. Every game needed them.

It had also been an opportunity to learn more about why they were here.

The book had stood out. It was the only actual book in the towering stack kept on the kitchen breakfast bench – the perfect place for a group of visitors to notice them – and the title *The Meaning of Life* had leapt out, with its bright colour and striking font. It had begged to be slid from the pile and investigated. Nia knew it was by design, as so much had been already.

"The tower doesn't want us to get lost," she told Alden quietly as they walked along the beach, following Rakie, Earl and Casey. The laces of their pairs of shoes were tied together and slung over each of their shoulders. Nia felt the warm sand giving way beneath her toes, trying to soak in the sensation, reminding herself this might all disappear at any moment. "It's not trying to test our navigation skills. It wants us to be able to figure out which paths to follow."

"While also trying to kill us," Alden reminded her.

"Perhaps that's the point, though. It wants to push us to the limit, see how we overcome the obstacles in our path. Determine whether we fall apart, work together, save each other, let each other fall. The ultimate test of humanity in the face of death. It's like some twisted reality TV show combined with your pub quiz idea."

They walked in silence for a moment, enjoying the lapping of the waves at the shoreline. Until Alden sighed. "None of us volunteered for this. We didn't put ourselves forward as representing anything. We were chosen, blindly. Why us? That's what I can't figure out."

"Maybe we did something in our lives that made us worthy of the challenge."

"I can't think the aliens, or whatever they were that built this place, were like 'Choose your fighter' and they chose Mel or Bryan – or Dirk," he said with a wry smile. "I absolutely cannot imagine any higher power would make the mistake of thinking *they* were worthy of this, Nia."

"Well... true. Bollocks. That's a good point."

She lifted her face up to the sun, enjoying the light on her skin. A perfectly normal feeling juxtaposed against the horror of the last few hours. She found herself wishing the tower *had* let them escape back home again, even though she knew it couldn't be the case.

"So," she continued, determined to lay this out so at least the pair of them were on the same page. "The most likely scenario is the tower chose thirteen of us at random and put us on this ascent to test us individually and collectively. And *then*, after putting us through absolute hell, it pulled the most idyllic setting from our minds to allow us a place to rest and talk and discover the book." She nodded to herself, happy that this all seemed to fit. "I think it makes sense, Alden, don't you? The beings who sent this tower and brought us here would have wanted to give us a fighting chance. To eventually figure out what we're trying to survive, and why. Otherwise, it's just sadistic!"

At this, Alden laughed. It was a light, beautiful, boyish sound and she suddenly wondered what it must be like to hear him sing. If they ever made it out of this, she was determined to drag herself out of her house and into society to see him perform. He was sweet and caring, brave and compassionate. And he seemed empty, too, a figure alone in the world, in need of a friend. It wasn't a feeling alien to her; she'd always been alone by choice. With him, though, she felt a kinship she hadn't felt in years. She wanted to be there for him. To be that friend.

They continued talking for a few more minutes, of everything, and nothing. Nia linked her arm in his and they walked together with a casual ease. She didn't have many friends, hadn't in a long time. But Alden was different. Younger, with a maturity that allowed him to be open to the possibilities of life and the views of others. He wasn't a steamroller in conversations. He was a garden, welcoming whatever words you showered him with and blooming through it.

He would be a good friend back in the real world.

He was the friend she needed in this one.

After a while, they found themselves catching up with the others. Nia thought nothing of it at first, until she saw Rakie paused at the edge of the water, stopped dead still, pointing out to sea.

"Dad?"

He'd been chatting with Casey. "Yeah, Rakie?"

"What's that?"

She was pointing to a streak of darkness across the horizon. The antithesis of the glorious orange hues of the sunset and far more than a smudge of cloud. A storm, maybe. It was almost palpable in its threat. And as Nia watched, the wind blew stronger around them, the sunlight grew dim, and that dark streak continued to billow outwards unnaturally.

The waves against the beach changed in a split second. The water that had been gently lapping at the shore grew choppy, and began hurling itself at them as they stumbled back.

"Storm?" Nia asked, tasting the salt on her lips.

Earl shook his head slowly, a look of foreboding in his eyes. "Lived on the Welsh coast all my life and I've never seen a storm come in like this. That thing out there looks solid. I don't think it can possibly all be cloud."

"Then what is it?" Rakie asked.

"I don't think we want to know, kiddo."

It was Casey who voiced what they were all thinking.

"We're still in the tower," she said despondently.

Nia took the shoes off her shoulder, untied the laces, and began to slip them on. The others followed suit. Maybe they'd all been harbouring hope this was real, that they were back home, but that hope was most definitely being dashed. Their respite was over. The break in play done. The game was to resume.

The skies ahead – orange and red a few seconds ago – were grey, heavy with murderous intent. She felt her heart thump out a distress signal as she watched the change rolling towards them. And then… *There*… A shadow moved within it.

"Shit, did you see that?" Alden said.

Nia had. Whatever it was, the thing was *gigantic*. It writhed across the horizon.

Getting steadily closer.

They all turned and ran. On the way, Nia tried scoping the beach out in the hope that there was some kind of clue as to where exactly they needed to go. But there wasn't anything that she could see. So far, they had always escaped up, but where was there to go up on a small desert island? None of the trees surrounding the house stood out. They were small and currently bowing to the strength of the wind.

The spray from the crashing waves chased them up the beach, even as they skidded across the porch and into the house. As a rumble of thunder shook the island, another strong blast of wind sent sand whipping sideways into the house. The five of them dived through the door with it stinging their necks and the backs of their legs.

"Weather came in, then?" Dev said with a grin, sitting at the kitchen bench with another glass of whisky in his hand. His eyebrows lifted as he watched the outside blow in with them. "Bloody typical, I was going to go swimming in a bit!"

He gestured to his Bermuda shorts, which he'd obviously borrowed from Mason's wardrobe. The notion they might not be real clothes didn't seem to bother him. He looked like a young man on his holidays. Deliriously happy and not about to let a bit of a storm get in the way of a good time.

Nia envied him his ability to let go of all sense.

Alden rifled through the cupboards, pulling out glasses, mugs, containers. He grabbed a flask with a lid and quickly filled it with water.

"Dev, man, look outside. This isn't the place you think it is, or even want it to be. We got a bit of time to chill, but it's over now. We need to grab some supplies, take water with us, and get the hell out of here. The tower is telling us we need to go on. The quest isn't over."

"Fuck the quest, *bitches*!"

Dev said it with drunken joy and raised his drink as he did so, sloshing it over the counter.

"Yeah, I don't think we have a choice to do that," Alden replied.

"Alden, come on, buddy. This has been a nice level! Just trus' me... The storm will blow over soon, and then we'll have ourselves a *fucking barbecue* and more drink and, shit, maybe go for a midnight swim, even."

"Dev, no. We have to go."

Dirk stepped up behind Dev and placed a hand on his shoulder. His lips curled upwards with his usual charm, but Nia saw there was nothing but daggers in his eyes for Alden.

"If this awesome dude wants to enjoy himself here, none of us should stand in the way, y'hear? Who are *we* to get in the way of Dev having a good fucking time after all we've been through? Let him stay. Like he said, the storm will probably be over quickly. Then he can cook some good shit and go for his swim."

Dev took a sip and patted Dirk's fingers with an air of comradeship.

"Yeah, come on, Alden. Don't be a party-pooper. I'm done with all the running and climbing. This place is *paradise*, baby! I'm never going to get a chance to hang out here back home. Might as well enjoy it now, right?"

"But the storm?" Casey said.

"It's not a storm," Earl warned. "This isn't an island and what's coming isn't weather. We need to go."

"Ah, fuck that," Dev said. "It's just a bit of rain."

"Exactly," Dirk said, patting the boy on his shoulders and giving them a squeeze.

Alden leaned over the breakfast bar, ignoring the shit-eating grin Dirk was wearing, fixed on Dev. "I know this has all been awful so far. But we've been through too much together to give up now. I know you don't want to face what's ahead. I don't either. I *know* how you're feeling, Dev. But the tower brought us together, and I want us all to leave together. We have to at least try to keep going."

"Dev, please," Nia echoed. "He's right. We need you."

She saw a crack appear in the boy's façade, the fear behind his forced good humour leaking through. But there was too much of it. All built up and clogging his thinking, and he was trapped by it. She could understand that. He'd been broken by the tower. By what he'd seen. By losing Kim. This place offered him more than togetherness could. It was a place to see things out on his terms.

"I'm sorry, Nia," he said, shaking his drink and his head at the same time. "But you really *don't* need me. And I don't really want any more of this. So... yeah, I'm done. I'm going to stay here, and when the storm is over, I'm going to have some damn fun." The grin returned. "What d'you say, Mason? Shall we get a nice grill going outside later? This is your home, brother, you should want to stay as much as I do. Your folks aren't here, you can finally enjoy the place as it was meant to be enjoyed, yeah?"

Mason's chiselled jaw was fixed as he stared around the house, seemingly torn over the opportunity to do what Dev had just suggested. He hadn't seen what they had. Maybe he figured this could be just a storm after all, and there was yet some peace left to mine from his childhood home.

His deep blue eyes flicked to the woman at his side, then to the windows vibrating with the force of the rain hammering against the panes.

"If we leave, where would we even go?" he asked.

It was a good question, and Nia didn't know if she had a convincing answer. "I haven't seen anything like a way out yet. Maybe it's inland, far from whatever's heading our way across the sea? There might be a big tree waiting for us. Or something else we can climb. All I know is that the tower wouldn't have put us in this level without providing a way out."

Dev smiled at him sadly, as one might a child who'd said something stupid.

"Who of us can say what the tower would do, though? You've already said it probably wasn't made by humans. What if this is the end of the journey and there's no next level, only an exit back to our crummy lives? Why would I leave paradise if death or going back home to a dull job and crap family are the only alternatives? What if *paradise* is the reward?"

Alden pressed his fingers into the edge of the counter, clearly trying to maintain his composure. His face kept turning to the windows and the lashing rain. Then he flinched as a crack of thunder shook the house and there was a tremendous roar.

"What the hell was that?" Rakie cried.

"It's nearly here," Nia said, looking to Alden and Earl. "Things are not going to improve when it arrives, I think we all know that. If we're going, we should go now."

It was Dirk who led the way, though. He gave Dev another squeeze of the shoulders, before striding to the front door. "Good luck, buddy. Hopefully we'll see you in the sun soon enough."

Dev raised his drink, forcing a smile to his face. "Cheers to that. Mason, you staying, then?"

But Mason was already following Casey after Dirk. "No, Dev. This place has always had a hold on me. I think I'll take my chances with the tower."

"We don't even know what the tower is!"

"You're right, we don't. But it feels like something important, and I need to go with my gut on this one." Mason walked back and gave Dev a hug. "Help yourself to whatever you want. The place is yours now."

Dev nodded. Nia could see his eyes grow watery, pleading at each of them to stay as he looked them over, yet he maintained his confident demeanour as they gathered in the spray coming through the door, readying to rush out into the storm.

"You sure?" Alden said over his shoulder. Nia felt the desperation in his voice as he gave it one final try.

The whisky was raised in salute. "No, man. I've got everything I need right here. Try not to get too wet out there, OK?"

Alden's shoulders sagged as he turned without another word.

Nia followed him out of the door and into hell.

CHAPTER EIGHTEEN
Beyond the Sea

Nia held as close to Alden as she could, pushing through the rain and sand whipping along the beach. She shielded her face and mouth as best she could, while wrapping her arm in his. She hoped he was doing the same with whoever was in front of him. Such was the power of the wind, it was threatening to rip them apart and toss them across the island.

The ocean churned and sprayed over the shoreline with the ferocity of a shaken can of fizzy drink. Nia could barely see anything other than Alden and the indistinct figures in front of her, with Mason hopefully leading the way to the path inland. But she could hear just fine, and in the midst of the howling gale came that roar again that she could feel in her bones.

A deep, reverberating noise, ancient and primal.

"What *is* that?" she yelled in Alden's ear. He shook his head and pulled her onwards.

As they rounded the house and gardens, and pulled a little way inland from the beach, they found enough shelter for Nia to lower her hand.

And then she looked back and saw it.

A bank of cloud held just off the coast, perhaps half a mile out. As the wind tossed and swirled the billows of darkness around, they revealed a presence in their midst.

A gigantic face rising from the ocean.

It was as big as the island itself. A nightmare of slick slime and seaweed, with valley-wide crevices of coral, eye craters of the purest night, and thick, writhing tentacles surrounding a cavernous mouth.

These limbs were slipping from the churning waves, too, black like eels, sliding up the beach. She saw that each was covered in suckers, filled with what looked like clacking teeth.

Another horrendous blast of noise erupted from the vast being.

Alden barrelled into the others ahead. "Keep moving!"

Nia followed in his wake, trying not to think about leaving Dev behind. There was no time for regret. She had to keep her focus, especially as they moved around the peninsula and she realised there was not a batshit's chance in hell they were going to be able to move through the woodland behind the house. The damage being wrought across the ocean had spread. The trees were being ripped from the island, torn to shreds, and flung around at speed.

"We'll be torn apart in there," Dirk called through the chaos. "Where the fuck do we go?"

"We can't go back to the house!" Earl yelled back through the rushing wind. He held Rakie close, trying to protect her from the elements as much as he could. "That Cthulhu Kraken thing will see us."

"Mason?" Casey shouted. "Where do we go?"

But Nia could see Mason had checked out, staring blankly at the ocean monster. She swore under her breath, then looked around, hoping to see something, *anything*, that could help them.

Then Alden squeezed her arm and pointed across the sand.

"There!" he yelled.

She followed Alden's rain-lashed squint towards the sea, expecting to see yet another thing that might be trying to kill them, only to see a tiny figure materialise at the edge of the waves.

A beautiful black-and-white border collie.

It was standing alert, its tail wagging as it saw they'd seen it.

"Leia!" Alden cried, the word a heartbreaking wail underpinning the swirling snarls of imminent death around them. He seemed on the edge of breaking down, losing his mind, staring in disbelief at his dead dog.

Nia's focus, however, was drawn beyond the pet, where she could see a grey mass growing simultaneously from the waters below and the clouds above, forming about half a mile out.

It met in the middle and began to whirl viciously.

A waterspout.

When she looked back, the dog had vanished. Alden moaned, having lost her again, until he saw what Nia had. He straightened and pointed.

"The way out!"

She shook her head. "Have you lost your mind? That can't be it. There's no tree, no leaves."

"And it's a fucking water tornado!" Dirk added, screaming through the wind as it rose again.

The creature was getting closer.

But Alden was fixed on the sight, utterly convinced. "That's what Leia was showing us, though. She showed me the door in the ship. Now she's showing us that. *And* it's going up!" He gestured around them. "It's the only thing going up. So if anybody has a better suggestion, let's hear it."

To Nia's regret, none of them did.

The group turned inwards, huddled against the elements, faces meeting in the middle.

Dirk was raging. "Who the *fuck* thought this was a good idea? We shouldn't have left the house! Fuck your waterspout, you musical asshole. And your dog, quite frankly. What the fuck was *that* even doing here, and where'd it go?" He shook his head as Alden began to speak. "No, I don't care, dude. There's no way we're swimming out that way. Even if it is the way out of this hellhole, we'll drown before we reach it. It's all a trap and we fucked up. The tower tricked us into leaving so it could kill us easier."

Nia wanted to agree with the bastard. Every fibre of her being wanted to stay on land, even with the giant squid face trying to devour it. But with a sinking feeling she realised Alden had to be right. Again, the tower had given them a sign. Got them to see the spout, which, yes, was going up. They needed to ascend. That was the rule.

Shit.

"I think Alden's got a point," she said.

"Fucking *fucknuggets* he has," Dirk yelled back. "We'll never make it!"

Then Mason's eyes lit up and he held out his hands to get them to stop.

"My parents' boat should still be here. It's kept in a hidden cove around the corner from here. Not far."

Nia glanced back to see a tentacle snaking through the trees, pulling them out by their roots and tossing them away.

"Then we go!" she shouted. "Quickly!"

She pushed Mason to lead the way again. As the group moved off, the decision made, Nia could have sworn the winds eased just a touch.

We're moving in the right direction, she thought. *The tower wants us to know it.*

It was incredible to think this was all by design. Such an incredible, sadistic, evil feat. Was it all predestined? Did the tower already know which of them were going to die and which would survive? Would she ever find out the truth?

She hoped so. If only to meet who did this and learn why and how... and then beat the living shit out of them. Even if they were gods, and this was some kind of rapturous challenge to gain entrance to heaven, she was not above visiting violence upon the mind or minds that had turned them into lab rats and put them in this maze.

The eight survivors crested a rise in the beach and then they saw it. Below them, to the left and hidden from the view from the house, was a little hut, seemingly sheltered enough to still be standing. Just.

The door to the boat shed had already been torn from its hinges. The wind whipped through, causing the roof to shudder, its nails barely clinging to the frame. The roar came again, closer, angrier, the creature sensing they were about to get away.

But the boat was there and it was intact. A sturdy white speedboat with three rows of seats and a windscreen that would offer little protection where they were going.

Mason jumped in and helped Casey after him. If he started it, Nia couldn't tell, as she and the others climbed aboard and huddled in the back seats. There was a steady vibration through the seat, but she only knew it was the engine purring when Mason pulled out of the deteriorating shed at speed.

The roof was finally torn free with a fearsome screech behind them, sent swirling into the sky, before it was plucked from the air and crushed within a black, oily tentacle.

Nia felt instantly sick as the boat lifted and fell, slamming against the waves repeatedly, at the mercy of the ferocity of the sea and sky as they fought to batter the crap out of the tiny, insignificant people in between them. Mason's knuckles were white as he gripped the wheel, his face slick with sweat and spray, as he ducked behind the glass windscreen, driving them towards the waterspout.

That this was their way out was inconceivable to Nia. But so much of what they'd experienced was, and she trusted Alden enough to know he must be right about this. Hell, she trusted *herself* to know this was right. The tower had guided them. It was a vicious prick, but at least it was playing by its own rules.

The water tornado ahead was the only thing going up. It had to be the way out.

Another roar, and Nia looked back to see the creature *eating* the island. Jesus, how was that even possible? The face had risen so high in the sky, it was blocking out most of the light, its mouth widening along the shoreline, and its long writhing limbs winding across the beach and through the trees, tugging and pulling what it could and throwing it back into its gaping maw. Then *CRUNCH*, it bit down on the sand and rock, and everything around them shook.

Nia thought of Dev in the house. She hoped he was passed out, drunk, dreaming of his barbecue.

"What do I do?" Mason shouted from the front seat. His face was gaunt, with little colour in his cheeks and eyes wide with fear. He wiped the water from his face, trying to see where he was going. "Are we just driving into the spout?"

"What other option do we have?" Alden shouted.

Please let this work, Nia thought, huddled in the footwell. *Please don't let us die here.*

She gripped Alden's hand tightly and felt his fingers crush around hers, too. The boat neared the spout. The water spray was ferocious, coming sideways, pummelling them. The waves rose and fell. It became almost impossible for her to keep her eyes open, and she covered them with her forearm, wondering if Mason was doing the same and just hoping the boat would maintain the heading.

Suddenly they crested a wave and rode hard through a wall of water. The boat was flung sideways, knocking the breath out of Nia and slamming her head against the handrail on the side. She expected to feel the floor break away, the boat splinter and fall apart, to tumble through it and lose herself in the ocean. In any other reality, it should have done. But this was only a semblance of reality. A copy of it, created by a life form that wasn't familiar with how things worked on Earth.

The boat held together as it was lifted and spun around and around in circles, the force of it pressing everyone into their seats as it rose into the sky. A watery *Wizard of Oz*, Nia decided, but without the terrifying witch, and only a moderate chance of flying monkeys appearing to tear their limbs off.

Up and up they spun, Nia's head a mess, her sense of direction shot. She wanted to vomit, hurling it outwards, not caring where it went. With nothing to lose, she opened her eyes and witnessed the terrifying sight of the boat leaving the wall of water and being flung into the air at the centre of the spout.

Where they fell... before Nia's deathly scream was cut short as the boat came to a juddering halt and she was slapped in the face with a wet green leaf frond. Gagging and spitting the salty slime out of her mouth, she realised they were all still in the boat, which was wedged in the branches of a gigantic sea plant stretching high into the sky.

It had been hiding in the centre of the swirling waterspout.

"What the fuck is *this* now?" Dirk moaned in the front of the boat.

Nia echoed the sentiment as she looked to the others. Mason gasping for breath, Casey weeping. Earl, Rakie and Monique behind them, close to tears and hugging one another tightly.

"Jesus," Alden breathed, pulling the frond away from Nia's forehead. "I can't believe that worked. It might not be a tree, but it's nature and it has leaves, and this has to be the way out, right?"

"I guess it must be? Your Leia showed us the way."

"She did, but now we should–"

They both lost the air from their lungs as the boat suddenly shifted and dropped a few feet, coming to a jarring halt again. Another rumbling roar crossed the ocean.

They both looked over the side of the boat to see one of the creature's tentacles, far below, sliding out of the ocean and wrapping itself around the plant.

It shook them again.

"Climb!" Nia shouted.

They all scrambled out onto the oceanic beanstalk. Nia didn't care whether this was a real thing or artistic licence by the tower. She figured a marine biologist would probably have a field day with it, but she wasn't one, and at that moment she didn't care. There were slick wet branches to stand on and colourful leaves showing the route up, and that was all she needed. Even if it led up to giants and golden geese, it was preferable to being eaten alive by the squirming cosmic horror below them.

.

Another shake and the boat creaked and fell from its ridiculous mooring, whistling all the way down to the water. Nia looked between her feet, hoping it would crush the tentacle.

Nope. It missed. Then there were two of them down there. They swiped the boat's remains aside and started slithering up the stalk. Nia gasped with exhaustion, wondering if they were going to be able to escape in time, and then she saw the waterspout around them was closing in, too.

Give us a chance, she pleaded to the tower.

They moved as fast as they could. Nia could only hope it would be enough. Her lungs were bursting, cold with exertion, but she kept her hands and feet active, lifting her up, not seeing an end to this sea tree above them but knowing she couldn't give up.

In the distance, through the maelstrom of water and wind trying to squeeze them out of this level, Nia heard a crash and she looked out, over the sea, towards the island. The house had been wrecked, torn apart, splintered and collapsed. The slithering limbs were slamming against it, crushing and consuming the remains.

Nia slowed just for a moment, stalling, a sob wanting to work its way out of her throat. She wondered if Dev was lying there, whisky still clutched in his hand, Mason's shorts riding up his skinny legs. He'd found no paradise in this fucking mousetrap of a game, but at least his torment was over.

Hers was still ongoing. She faltered against her wet branch, exhausted, unable to muster the energy to go on. The hope in her dwindled.

Why couldn't the tower have picked anybody else? That

stupid director. Or Matt, for pity's sake. Both deserved to suffer like this. She was a good person, wasn't she? What had she done to warrant being put through this absolute *shit*?

Alden pulled up beside her. "Nia, we're almost there. You have to keep moving."

"I can't," she cried, feeling herself fade. The drop below her beckoned. *Just let go and it'll all be over.* Alden reached over and she pushed him away. "Go on, Alden. I can't move. I'm done."

There was a cry from above and they both looked up to see Rakie, who was still young enough to have the spirit and energy to climb, begin to disappear. First her top half, then, as she lifted her right foot and stepped up again, she vanished completely.

The exit.

Nia was spent. Physically, she just couldn't move. But the spike of hope, knowing they were so close to getting out, allowed her to let Alden grab her arm and guide her upwards.

Around them, the waterspout continued closing. She felt the spray intensify, doing its best to impede their climb. Some of the outlying branches of the stalk shook with the impact of the water and were torn off.

Below, the tentacles continued climbing.

The tower had taken Dev and it wanted to see if it could take more lives.

Nia couldn't let it.

Half climbing, half being dragged, she did her best to follow the others as they, too, disappeared into the clear blue sky above the waterspout one by one. Until it was just Nia and Alden left.

They went up together, neither willing to let the other slip, escaping the roar of the water and the creature and the howling of the winds across what had once been paradise.

Into the nothingness, once more.

CHAPTER NINETEEN
Space Wars

Nia skidded across a polished floor and smacked into a sheer white wall. It felt like a metallic plastic, with a little give in it, and some warmth. She bounced off it and twisted to the side, tripping over the heap of bodies that made up the other survivors.

The air was muffled and still. It was a touch artificial – recycled, perhaps – but Nia would have taken this over the Cthulhu hurricane they'd driven a boat into any day of the week.

It was quiet. She could hear herself think.

At least until the sounds of blaster fire fizzed close by.

She flinched and pressed herself back against the wall, checking their surroundings. They were in a small room, the floor grey and the walls white. To her right, there was an open doorway and what looked like a corridor outside. She couldn't see much from this angle, but she could at least tell that was where the sounds were coming from. Metallic chimes, almost musical, shooting back and forth not too far away.

The others cowered alongside her.

"That sounds like guns... Is it guns?" Rakie asked in a whisper. Nia could hear the tightness in her voice, as though trying to control a sob. The poor girl had been through so much, Nia was surprised she was even able to speak. By rights, she should be catatonic. Her father had his arm around her, and she looked up at him. "Why would there be guns here, Dad? And if we're all here, who's shooting them?"

It was a question that Nia also wanted answers to, and yet she was beginning to wonder if she already knew them. Because this place... There was something to it. A hint of familiarity about the clean lines and the smooth, almost reflective, surfaces.

"I don't know, kiddo," Earl said, offering a helpless shrug to his daughter's question. It was clear the weight of parenting through this gruelling experience was getting to him. The rest of them had only themselves to look after. Nia couldn't imagine having to worry about trying to protect your child through this nightmare.

"We're close to some kind of battle," Nia said, trying to offer some calm, despite the shooting continuing nearby. There was a gruff cry. Then silence. She dropped her voice. "The tower has conjured up some scary stuff for us before. It's a good bet it's filled this level with soldiers or warriors or something. Don't worry, Rakie. Just think of it as more set decoration for us to try and avoid."

"*Set decoration?*" Dirk hissed. "You're badly underselling the fact that this phallic fuck of a tower has sent all those creatures to kill us, not create a fucking *vibe*."

Nia stared at him. "I was talking to Rakie. But maybe it's worth reminding ourselves that, as *adults*, we need to keep our heads and stay cool if we're going to get through this together, yeah?"

A strange look passed over his face as he drew himself up, straightened his T-shirt, and tugged his running shorts out of his arse. "Sorry, but let's not kid ourselves here, sweetheart. We're just randos thrown together into the worst reality TV show imaginable. Don't try and bullshit yourself that this is a bonding experience. We're not friends. We're in this to get out of it. End of story."

"Somebody wants the prize for himself," Alden muttered.

"Fuck you, Baby Spice."

Alden's cheeks reddened, but Nia was glad he'd acknowledged what she'd been feeling. Dirk was clearly in this for himself, like he probably was most things in life. She refused to play that game. Just because the narcissistic author wasn't intent on making friends, it didn't mean the rest of them weren't capable of looking out for one another.

Look at you, she thought to herself. *Championing the idea of other people.*

There was an irony to her being the one to go up against his individualist attitude. She'd been plenty happy during the pandemic to lock herself away at home, conduct life through video screens, avoid getting close to others. But this was different. This was a game of death, and she had been forced together with other people who, like it or not, she had bonded with through the trauma of their experiences so far. She wasn't going to give up on them, like she hoped they wouldn't give up on her. *Hope.* That was the all-important word. They had to work together to keep their morale up – to ensure they held on to hope. Without it, they wouldn't get through this. Hope was everything.

The blaster fire grew closer. The tower was testing her to hold on to her own hope.

"I hate to keep repeating myself," she said. "But we need to keep moving."

"Do we even know where we are?" Dirk said, getting up and looking around with disdain. "Shouldn't we maybe figure that out first, before we run into this geeky cliché of a science fiction movie? Seriously, what the hell is this place? It's more retro than a Saturday morning serial…" His voice trailed off as he peered out through the doorway. "Well, I'll be fucked."

Nia suddenly knew what he was seeing. She closed her eyes with a sigh.

A geeky cliché of a science fiction movie might as well have been the tagline to the original straight-to-video film whose sequel she'd been working on this weekend. It had been a job she'd begged her way into directly from secondary school, where she'd been one of the junior designers who worked for free for "the experience" and "a credit at the end, isn't that cool?", according to the creepy producer with roving eyes and – so she'd heard – roving fingers who'd hired her.

She knew that the view through the doorway went straight out into space, towards a dying planet resplendent with glowing lava-filled cracks forming across its surface and two rings of stardust circling each other.

She knew because she'd designed it. Painted it. Her idea, inspired heavily by countless other artists' works.

"I know where we are," she said, as they all stared out of the doorway and through the window in the corridor beyond. "It was a movie I worked on long ago, doing concept art. It was a terrible film, but it's how I got my break as a designer."

"You did *that*?" Alden asked, pointing at the slowly deteriorating planet, clearly impressed.

She felt a rush of pride beneath the general anxiety. "Yeah, I did. And I think I know where in the story we've been dropped into, as well. It came at the end of Act Two, where the heroes are trapped aboard the space cruiser orbiting the planet, trying to rescue survivors, only to be boarded by the enemy. There followed a huge, confusing firefight through the cheap set of corridors and chambers, and it all came to a head in the botanical gardens."

She stopped there, remembering that some malevolent life form was eventually roused and ended up destroying the ship from the inside out. Everyone in the scene died.

So. This level was hers. What did that mean? Was she responsible for getting the others through it? Or did this mean she was destined to die here?

No. They'd just been on Mason's island and he'd walked away. Found the strength to leave his idyllic home and survive. Dev had been the one to lose the will to go on.

Just breathe, she told herself. *And try to remember the bloody plot so you can get us all out of here alive.*

Flashes of light – reds and blues – could be seen lighting up the corridor floor outside the room. There was yelling again. Distant and muffled, but enough to cause Nia's heart to race. The battle from the movie was heading their way.

"So what do we do?" Alden asked calmly, patiently. He must have seen she was going to take the pressure of helping them survive on herself. He was trying to give her a moment to think before the others panicked and jumped in. She could have hugged him for it. "You said the heroes in the movie head to some gardens, right? Probably makes sense we head there ourselves, then."

Nia poked her head around to check the coast was clear. "That's what I remember. Some botanical gardens at the centre of the ship."

"Which way, then?" Dirk asked.

"Well, we're on the crew deck, I think," she said as the others turned her way. It felt good to be their focus, knowing that even Dirk had to pay attention without interrupting, because his life might depend on it. She felt a grim sense of justice in that. "The battle is mostly contained here, in these corridors, so if we can avoid all that and reach the lifts, we should be safer when we get to the upper floors. At least for a while."

"OK, then, let's find the elevators," Dirk said.

"What about the fighting, though?" Monique asked, frowning. "Who's out there and what's going on? Do we need to worry?"

Nia shrugged. "I'm sorry, but I can't really remember. I think there were two factions... the bad guys who were destroying the planet and the good guys trying to save it. Both were these weird, mostly human people with big shoulders and horned scalps. Like devil gammon. To be honest, I think the reviews might have pointed out not even the director seemed to understand what the plot was about." She took in a deep breath, readying herself to lead them out there. "Oh, and it was one of those gory, edgy science fiction films, so there was a lot of blood and dead bodies lying about. Be prepared."

She looked to Rakie, only for the girl to shrug.

"I play horror games. I'm good."

"Then you can look after *me*," Nia joked.

Rakie seemed to appreciate the levity. Then her face pulled serious again. "You guys were all talking before about that book on the island. The different meanings of life. So, what's this one? Maybe that will help us."

"There were nine sections in that diagram you showed us," Earl said. "And three different aspects of meaning, I believe?"

Nia nodded. "Coherence, purpose and significance. And if there were nine sections, I guess there must be three levels for each–"

"We've done four already–" Mason said.

"...which means we're into purpose here," Nia finished.

"Jesus *fuck*, I've dropped into a real-life *Rain Man* convention," Dirk muttered, staring around at them all. "The meaning of life? Finding your purpose? I might seriously walk out there and tell whoever is shooting to just finish me before I have to listen to any more of this verbal ejaculate." He sighed and gestured to the doorway. "But seeing as I actually *have* a life to get back to, I guess I have to trust you on this. Go on then, nerds. Lead the way."

CHAPTER TWENTY
The Death

Dirk couldn't help but gag like a bitch every time they found another fucked-up alien body.

He'd seen twenty or so corpses along the way to wherever they were going. So much death, he almost thought Nia was leading them *into* the battle.

It was a lot of gagging.

The aliens were all ugly as sin, not helped by the ragged, charred flesh, popped eyeballs and coils of intestines spilling through torn holes in their armour. They were all roughly humanoid. Heads made up of rolls of pale flesh, noses like bricks, and horns curling from their scalps. And they were all identical, except for the colour of the armour that was clearly useless in the face of whatever weapons they were using.

Some wore a deep ruby red, some a cerulean blue. That seemed the only difference between the warring factions.

Stupidity everywhere, he thought, stepping around a slumped figure and almost losing his footing in a pool of blood and innards.

As they hurried onwards, he realised the sounds of this pointless war were coming from both behind and in front of them. The screams of the wounded and dying. The roars of the victors. All of it echoed through these clichéd corridors.

All of it driving him insane with fear – a fear of dying in this cheese-fest.

"This way," Nia said again, ahead.

"You sure?" Dirk asked.

She shot him a glare, but didn't respond. Because she couldn't. He was pretty sure she was lost.

Fuck this, man. Should he take over? He didn't want to take his last breath in this cheap *Star Wars* knock-off. He hated the idea of any science fiction, with its dumb lasers and weird aliens and barely contained political wokeness. It was all so trivially *meh*. Certainly not the kind of "bold, imaginative, character-driven children's stories with lots of oomph" the *Sunday Times* had said of his latest instant bestseller – thanks to what he imagined was a not-inconsiderable sum of money slipped their way by his publishers.

He continued onwards, following their hapless leader. Trying to set aside the voice reminding him he hadn't actually written any of his books… or even read them. But his people had said they weren't faff, and he was fine with that. People shouldn't want to enjoy faff. It was junk food for the soul, making it weak and stupid.

Just like this place Nia had unwittingly imprisoned them all in.

The group skidded to a halt at the corner of this corridor, which was much like all the others. White walls, grey floor. Just enough reflection to almost see yourself and realise you were indeed living through a fucking nightmare.

At least you're living, dude, he thought, thinking about Dev. Dirk had done them all a favour back there, making sure they could escape the level. It hadn't taken much convincing, either. The poor sap hadn't even understood the sacrifice he was making.

Dirk hoped the others would go as easily. No way was he going to let anybody get in his way of reaching the top of this fuck-fest. The more he thought about the idea of a magical prize awaiting them, the more he knew it had to be something incredible. Maybe the winner would be bestowed with some insane powers. Maybe he could become an actual fucking *superhero*!

The thought made him hard.

"Are we close?" Casey asked Nia, interrupting Dirk's daydreams of grandeur. She was a wet blanket of a woman, with a squeaky voice and a haircut that was way too good for her. She was still cuddled up to the tall handsome drink of a dude, Mason, despite discovering his sexual preferences lay in a different direction. Dirk supposed she might be hoping to sway him straight before the end.

They held at the junction, Nia looking between this indistinct corridor and the one that cut across it. "There are blue lines marked at the corridor edges near the lifts. I added those in as a little decoration, tried to give it some kind of sense. We find them, we'll find the way up."

"Which way, then?" Monique asked.

"Follow me," Nia said, leading them left.

Dirk was sure she didn't know where she was going, but he might as well sit back and let this unfold. Enough of this and they might get another dropout, someone who would willingly give up and let the rest move up the tower. If not, at least it allowed some space for him to find opportunities to thin the herd.

The weird thing was, he didn't even feel guilty about thinking such things, like he'd thought he might. The sting of it had hit him with Kim, sure, but it had faded quickly. This was an unprecedented situation. It called for unprecedented measures. They had been beamed to this tower and challenged to survive, and yeah, it was primal, but sometimes life was like that. You had to adapt to the rules quicker than everyone else to win. Which meant doing what needed to be done to reach the top before anyone else.

It wasn't his fault. He was just playing the game.

The game turned upside down a few minutes later.

They were hurrying away from another gun battle when the entire world shook. Debris and smoke blasted outwards from a wall fifty yards ahead, the shock wave throwing Dirk into Monique, whose firm, uniformed figure clattered into a wall while he fell on his ass. As bursts of blaster rays started shooting through the ragged hole, lighting up the smoky haze, his instincts kicked in and he scrambled behind her prone, crumpled body.

The teenage girl, lying against the opposite wall, saw him using the woman as a shield. The look in her eyes as she saw the real him should have cut deep, but he didn't care. He peered over Monique's shoulder to where Nia, Alden, Mason and Casey were scooting backwards as the blaster fire grew fiercer ahead.

Five strange shadows leapt through the hole in the wall. One stumbled and fell across the jagged white plastic, struggled for a moment, then fell still at the feet of its comrades.

At least, Dirk thought they were feet.

He watched with a slow, creeping nausea as one of the figures stepped backwards through the smoke towards them, growing more distinct. The creature was nearly as tall as the ceiling, rising up on six legs like a centaur, with four thick, muscled arms, claws for hands – two carrying blasters – and its head...

Nope. That's not a head. That's a mass of bulging eyeballs.

They were like dandelion seeds on a stalk.

Dirk convulsed, the dregs of his last meal attempting to empty themselves all over his lap. He ducked back behind Monique, feeling all bodily senses malfunction. If he made a mess in front of everyone, he wouldn't even care.

I want to go home, his brain whined.

The other alien bodies they'd come across made sense in this generic spaceship. They were clichéd, dumb, dull. Whatever the *fuck* these things were, they weren't part of Nia's design. They were too imaginative, too recklessly insane. Too expensive for CGI in this kind of movie.

They were the kind of coked-up doodles of a life form only an actual god could have jacked off into being.

A glance at Nia confirmed it. She had seen them and was panicking, digging her fingers against the hard floor and scurrying away from it as fast as she could. There was no familiarity. She was just as shocked and repulsed as he was.

It's aliens, he thought as the creature moved through the smoke, and time seemed to slow. *Actual aliens. We're not alone in this challenge.*

Dirk didn't know why the feeling struck him so hard. The tower had clearly shown them its power in creating the worst asshole monsters for them to deal with. But these *things* were so wildly random, and clearly not of Nia's making, that he couldn't imagine the tower had dreamed them up just for this level. The torture chamber hadn't been in Earl and Rakie's game, but contextually it made sense in the dungeon. The giant squid with tentacles for teeth almost certainly hadn't been part of Mason's childhood at his beach house, but there was a recognisable Lovecraftian sensibility to it.

These insanely terrifying creatures made no sense.

Unfortunately, as the smoke cleared, Monique took that moment to regain consciousness and let out a groan. The response was instantaneous. A cacophony of click-clacking from far too many limbs echoed around them as the four alien creatures spun to determine the source of the noise.

With all those eyes, it didn't take long.

A noise issued forth from one of them as it spotted the humans, a sonic growl that Dirk felt trying to burrow its way inside his ear, bending his brain over to fuck it good. He threw his hands up to try to block the sound out, but there was nothing to stop. The sound wasn't in the air. It was inside *him*.

The closest Eyeball Head reared back on its legs and raised the glowing silver blaster in its grip. Its thousand eyeballs blinked simultaneously at them. Then it fired, shooting out a fizz of intertwining blue lightning streams that scattered across the group, rippling fire across their heads. Dirk felt the heat cook his hair, as the wall just above him cracked and melted. Monique screamed and turned to bury her face in his chest, and he let her, ensuring she did it well enough to keep shielding him.

On the other side of the corridor, he saw Earl take a hit to his shoulder, bowling into Nia and Alden. They fell onto Dirk's legs, pinning him to the floor.

It left Rakie all alone.

Seeing her father get shot, her face contorted with terror and rage. She barely registered the Eyeball Head stomping towards them, lifting its gun for another shot. Her focus had switched to her father, clutching his sizzling shoulder.

She leapt up and made for Earl. Right into the path of another stream of blue fire.

The girl's eyes grew wide as she must have felt it hit her back. The heat burned through her clothes, her skin, her bones. There was a brief moment of realisation, of agony, tugging at her lips, pulling them over her teeth in a grimace, as she glowed from within.

Dirk wished he'd been looking anywhere else in that moment, but as she looked to him in desperation, their gazes met and he was forced to watch as her face bulged outwards and fire erupted through her skull, chest, stomach, bursting her open and exploding charred pieces of teenage flesh across the adults.

For a second, all that was left was a silhouette of light where she had been standing. The sight burned into Dirk's retinas.

A couple of blinks later, she was gone.

Another guttural sound shook him from the inside out. The Eyeball Head that had killed her stomped towards the rest of them, blaster still raised. Its eyes blinked simultaneously as they pivoted between each human – sizing them up, perhaps. Maybe gloating.

The blaster swung towards Dirk and Monique.

He kicked his legs, but someone was still lying on them. Monique was still clutching him.

He couldn't move.

He couldn't get away.

He watched as the silver tube lit up again.

Then two strange things happened, which no amount of mental gymnastics could help explain.

The alien blaster glowed a bright blue. The streams of fire left the barrel. *Fuck*, Dirk thought… His last thought, he was sure of it.

Only for the blue fire to vanish in mid-air. One moment it was there, the next it was gone. Then there was a horrendous *CRUNCH* as the blaster instantly crinkled and imploded, folding in on itself – and crushing the alien claws still wrapped around it.

It didn't end there, though. A sonic scream sounded inside Dirk's head again as the alien's limbs began to fold in on themselves. The skin tightening, then tearing, while the muscles beneath popped like firecrackers. The limb with the blaster finally grew so small it was ripped out of existence. Then its other arms followed. Before its shoulder and torso snapped and caved inwards, too.

That there was no blood seemed almost more horrifying to Dirk. Something inside the creature was pulling it inwards, as though a black hole had opened in its stomach and was sucking it in while it was still alive.

He wanted to look away, but he couldn't. Even when the legs folded and all that remained of it collapsed to the floor – a mass of eyeballs… which began to pop, one by one, into nothingness, until the last vanished with a sickly, squelchy, sucking noise.

Dirk could feel Monique's sobs soaking his T-shirt. He could sense one of the others trying to scramble off his legs. He could hear Earl's screams for his daughter.

But all he could focus on was the heat on his face as the silhouette of light returned in the midst of them.

Weak, pale, but real.

Nobody else had seen it yet. Earl was wailing inconsolably, pieces of his daughter still sticking fast to his clothes. The others were looking between him and the other three aliens approaching.

Then Dirk blinked again and the light before him grew

stronger, more distinct. He wondered if it was some form of delayed reaction. Shock at what he'd seen. But as he watched, it grew more powerful, and suddenly the chunks of kid he could feel sticking to his legs grew fainter and disappeared altogether.

The silhouette burned in the dark behind his eyes. It was so strong the others had finally noticed. The aliens fell back once more as it lit up the corridor.

A figure of light burning with a scalding heat.

A miniature thermonuclear explosion in the shape of a teenage girl.

Dirk shielded his eyes, feeling for a moment like he might have escaped death just to be melted right where he lay. Until the heat dissipated in an instant, so quickly it might have been a memory all along. The blood thumping in his ears grew dim.

And then a cry cut through the air.

"Dad, *Dad*, are you hurt? Talk to me!"

Rakie was back, as though she'd never left. She ran to her father's side, leaning over him, staring with horror at the smoking wound in his shoulder.

"What the *shit*?" Dirk mumbled, kicking his feet against the smooth floor, sliding helplessly as he tried to get away from the vision.

"Rakie?" Earl gasped from the floor, the age in his face showing as it wrinkled in confusion.

"You're going to be OK, Dad, I promise," Rakie continued, as though she hadn't just come back from the dead. "I'll get you out of here."

Dirk looked back to the Eyeball Heads. He felt their language reverberate within him again, though much less intense this time. They weren't talking to the humans anymore; they were talking among themselves. Trying to figure out what had happened.

One of them lifted the silver blaster it carried. Pointed it towards Rakie.

Another reached over with a claw and pushed it down again.

There was another rumbling of alien dialogue, then they turned around with little more fanfare and scurried up the corridor, beyond the smoke.

Dirk let go of Monique and pushed her away, sitting up and continuing to stare at the girl in case she might explode again at any moment. She didn't, though. And the aliens didn't come back. They were alone again, and they were somehow all still alive.

"How the *fuck* did you do that?" he blurted out.

Rakie stared at him in surprise.

"How'd I do what?"

"You know what I mean." Dirk gestured to the air around them. "*That.* You fucking exploded. How did you just come back to life like that?"

"Dude, don't be an NPC. I've been right here the whole time."

NPC. He knew that reference. Non-playable character. The kind in a video game that was there to spout nonsense for the sake of it. He looked around at the others as though he might be crazy, but saw them staring in shock, too.

Earl's hand reached up to his daughter's cheek. His fingers caressed her gently, as though any more pressure might make her drift off again, a wistful dream in this hell. But her cheeks, her hair, her skin... Dirk could see they were all real.

"Rakie," Earl said. "You died, just now."

She shook her head firmly. "No, I didn't, Dad. I think the pain of getting shot is causing you to lose your mind a bit. We need to get out of here to a hospital." She looked to Nia for help. "I think he's got a concussion or something."

For once, Dirk realised Nia was speechless. She simply stared at the girl, who had died, then come back to life again, all within the space of a few seconds.

They all did.

And as Rakie retreated under the spotlight, Dirk's thoughts turned to what it meant for this level. Because if the rule was that someone had to die to escape, and Rakie *had* died, but her killer was the one to be erased from existence, what in the absolute *fuck* did that mean for Dirk's plan to off the others and be the one to get to the top of the tower?

CHAPTER TWENTY-ONE
Purpose

It took Dirk and the other adults a few minutes to get their shit together after Rakie's resurrection.

There was no time to sit around trying to talk it out, though. What they'd just witnessed meant there was a new, bizarre dimension to the rules, and the sooner they made it out of this level, the better. So they got up and got moving again, following Nia through the interior of the ship, until finally, *mercifully*, she spotted what she was looking for.

"We're here," the woman said, the relief that she hadn't entirely fucked all this up clear in her voice. She picked up the pace as she pulled up to a corner of the wall that held two navy-blue stripes in stark contrast to the rest of the white. The group held firm as she peered around it into a hall to see if the coast was clear, before gesturing for them to follow her quickly.

Dirk held to the centre of the group, making sure he was covered on all sides. He didn't make a fuss about it, just ensured he held to a pace that would keep Nia and Alden ahead of him, Earl and his daughter behind him, and Casey and Mason slightly to the side.

Nobody noticed it. They were all too concerned with getting to the lifts in one piece to realise he was playing the game.

Purpose. That's what they'd said, right? That's what the book had told them the tower was trying to get them to realise. Fair enough. Well, his purpose was to avoid any of the shit being flung around this tower and *get out*. He wanted his normal life again. To get a phone call from his agent telling him about more plaudits, more requests to take the stage and let people adore him. This was all so utterly *NOPE*, he didn't care how he escaped anymore. There was no guilt over what he'd done, what he was doing at that time, or what he was going to do. Guilt was a triviality for the weak. He would be a survivor, whatever it took.

They reached the elevators, whose doors were set back into the wall with a thin diagonal slice across them. Nia pressed her palm onto a shallow triangular button on the frame and the doors slid open sideways, just in time for them to dive into the cabin as more blaster fire crackled behind them. Dirk pressed himself to the wall, hiding in the shadow of Mason, until the door slid closed again and he felt the floor rising.

"How far up do we need to go?" he asked, frowning at the panel of lights on the wall and not making sense of any of the icons on it.

"We're going right to the top, will probably take a minute or two. It's a big ship." Nia didn't look at him as she spoke, her focus on Rakie. The teenage girl was still very much alive, with Earl's big hands clutching her shoulder and holding her close. "How are you feeling, Rakie?"

The girl shrugged. "Fine, I guess." There was a moment of silence as they all looked down at her and she pulled an awkward face, moving closer to her dad. "What's up with you lot? Look, I didn't die, all right!"

Earl's fingers gave her a squeeze. "We don't know what happened, kiddo. But all that matters is you're here again. You're fine, thank God."

"Of course I'm fine. I wasn't hurt or anything. *You* were the one who was shot. Are *you* OK?"

He looked puzzled for a moment, then glanced at his shoulder. Dirk noticed there wasn't a mark anymore. Earl rolled his shoulder to test it.

"Huh… Yeah, I'm fine. Can't feel a thing."

A series of glances passed between him, Alden and Nia. Dirk bristled at being left out of their little band of leaders, but said nothing. He didn't want to be part of their inept clique anyway. He was just annoyed he had to follow these douchebags at all.

"Well, whatever just happened…" Alden said in what must have passed for his teaching voice. "The main thing is, we're all still here."

"Yes, *sir*," Dirk added. Monique grinned beside him. Nia stared at them both for a moment, then went back to focusing on her beloved Alden.

Let them have their little love-in, Dirk thought. There would be time to deal with those two later.

"Are we going to talk about the other group now?" Mason asked. He looked more confused than usual. "I mean, that's what they were, right? Those things were aliens, but they didn't feel like they were part of that set."

"They weren't," Nia confirmed. "There were only those red and blue grunts in the film. I've never seen those other creatures before."

"And why did that one *implode* like that?" Casey added, her lips twisting like she'd eaten something sour. "At the end, after it killed… uh, after it shot Earl, it just folded in on itself. It was pretty gross."

"There was nothing in the film about that either. Nothing imploded. And nobody was resurrected. This is all on the tower."

"Please make all this make sense," Monique said, half joking, looking to Dirk. Only now did he realise she'd not seen much of what had happened; even after she'd regained consciousness, her face had been buried in his chest. He could still feel her warm nose pressed against his collarbone, her gasps on his skin.

He'd protected her. Kept her safe during that little attack. That would surely count for something later, when he needed it.

He offered her a smile. She smiled back.

Alden took that moment to answer her, killing the moment, and Dirk had a sudden compulsion to punch him in his throat. He flexed his fingers, wondering how the young man's blood might feel across his knuckles.

"I'm with Mason," Alden said, oblivious to the beating he was taking in Dirk's mind. "They felt different to everything else here. All the monsters we've seen. One of them even died as they came through the wall at the other end of a firefight. They were battling against someone else, and they seemed surprised to see us. And then *more* surprised when the one that shot us was crushed out of nowhere. They have to be another group, struggling through the tower, just like us."

"Other contestants," Earl mumbled. "That makes sense if this is a competition."

Dirk felt the elevator begin to slow. Nia was right – this had been a heck of a long trip. How big was the damn ship?

Casey shook her head, eyes pinched shut. "But the tower's on Earth and they were definitely *not* from Earth. If they're not part of this simulation, or vision, or whatever it is the tower is putting us through, then why would they be in the same tower with us? How, even?"

"I don't think the tower *is* on Earth," Alden said.

They all looked at him.

"What the fuck are you on about now, Vanilla Slice?" Dirk spat.

"We all saw the tower on the news, yes? And we saw it when we got here. Did you notice the red and purple swirling clouds around it, hiding the top half? I don't think they were real clouds. They were something different, something *other*, and on the TV I remember thinking sometimes it looked like the tower wasn't even here. Not properly. What if it just appeared to be floating above England, but in fact the clouds were like a portal to somewhere else, an interdimensional rip, and there is only one tower, but it appeared in a few different places simultaneously. Like a tower at the centre of a variety of paths coming in from different directions."

Monique sighed. "Portals now? Please, I can barely keep up. I just want to get back to my plane, my crew, my life. I really detest all this."

"It's a lot to take in," Nia said, agreeing, though a little less sympathetically than Dirk thought she normally would. He wondered if she was jealous of him and Monique growing closer. "But there's merit in the idea. And we need a foundation of an idea to hold on to as we go up this bloody tower. Some semblance of what we might be dealing with. Perhaps Alden's right. Perhaps this place was a beacon, calling to more places than just Earth, and we were just one group invited to ascend."

"'Invited' makes it sound like we had a choice," Monique said briskly. "Kidnapped, I think is the better word."

"Fine, but if there's an additional team of challengers, you can bet we were right before. There is either a massive reward at the top for the winner–"

"...or some huge consequence for the losers," Alden finished. He and Nia shared a glance. "So not only do we have to survive the levels now, but we're in competition with whatever those aliens were."

"Fucking great," Dirk said.

Rakie looked up at her dad. "I think the lift's about to stop."

It was.

They'd arrived.

CHAPTER TWENTY-TWO
Nature Calls

Dirk had to admit the botanical gardens were pretty insane.

On multiple levels, foliage of blended colours that defied reason spilled forth, overhanging balconies, falling from the glass ceiling several storeys above them, and rising from the segments of mossy foam coating the floor.

As a child, Dirk had travelled a lot with his parents and been to many botanical gardens around the United States. He'd experienced the thrill of wandering into the glass-contained heat and instantly feeling like he was in a faraway land, seeing exotic plants he would otherwise have to cross the world to find. But this was beyond all that.

Nia had outdone herself. Although, obviously, he wasn't going to say anything.

The woman herself was staring around with as much dumb awe as the others.

"They asked me for this," she said quietly, reverently. "For an elaborate garden, sort of like a universal catch-all of all these incredible species the people on the cruiser found. It was supposed to be like Noah's Ark. In the end, I went too big, and the budget wasn't accommodating to turn it into a set, so most of it ended up being cut from the movie. But this? This is all as I drew it in my mock-ups. They were a thing of beauty, and this is beyond anything I could have imagined!" She spun in a circle, soaking it all in. Until she stopped and sighed. "However, it was designed to be intense and dangerous, too. So, please, watch yourselves."

As they spread out over the wide path, moving between the drooping red leaves and rows of blue spiral stems, Dirk stared at the bizarre flora filling the cavernous hall. Which is when he noticed the flowers – some his height – moving in real time. He'd seen flowers move on Earth before, in time-lapse videos. He'd seen the way they grew and stretched and reacted to their environment over hours and days.

These flowers were moving very deliberately. Turning their heads as if they were following the scent of the humans through their midst.

Anxiety seeped into his fascination.

"Uh, what exactly did you mean by 'watch yourselves'?" he asked, hurrying to catch up with her. "Those flowers look hungry. What kind of danger are we in here, sweetheart? You going to be the death of us in here?"

"Hopefully not," she replied, in a way that wasn't entirely reassuring. "You know, I didn't design this place to be realistic, and I didn't figure I'd have to navigate it one day. It's meant to be fictional. The tower pulled this out of my brain and I'm going to do my best to make sure we get out, OK? The best I can tell you is that we shouldn't dawdle. It's all very pretty, but there's a risk of spending too much time being entranced by what's here. That's what *it* wants."

"Jesus. *It?* D'you mean the tower?"

A pause. "Sure." Nia then pointed up, to where they could see a platform hanging from the beams above them, accessed by a single gantry to the right. "Come on, that's where we need to go."

As the group picked up the pace, Dirk allowed the others to move around him, until he was back in the centre of the human food parcel. Because if he was going to be eaten, he'd at least ensure he wasn't the motherfucking appetizer.

Alden kept pace behind Nia along the winding path through this beautiful, enchanting world. The garden was truly ethereal in its scope and vision, and he could see the pride in her face as she took in her creation, staring all around her as though caught between the familiar and the fantastical of her designs.

He wanted to feel the same. But he could also sense the underlying note of darkness lurking beneath the vibrancy she'd been asked to include. It was like a shadow on a sunny day, in which anything could be hiding.

It didn't help that the foliage kept moving. Or that he was aware there may be another team racing them up the tower. Or that his dead dog kept showing up.

Leia. She was there, on the beach.

What the hell did that mean?

Earl drew up alongside him, perhaps sensing his quiet. "How you doing, son?"

"Oh, you know, fine," Alden said, trying to collect his senses. He hadn't been called "son" in years. It felt like a hug. "We're trapped in a tower, in a spaceship within that tower, fighting our way up it against spider-centaurs with eyeballs for heads. I've had better days."

He wasn't going to mention Leia.

"Yeah, I've been thinking about that."

"Which awful part in particular?"

Earl smiled and scratched a finger against the hair at his temple, as if trying to figure out how to say what was on his mind. They both ducked under a stray frond with sticky, wiggly "teeth" on it that looked like thousands of bluebottle fly legs.

"I like to read a lot, you know that? I don't always get the time. But when I do, I like to read. Everything. Fiction. Non-fiction. Educational stuff." He gave Alden a sideways glance. "Mythology, too."

"I don't suppose you came across anything in mythology about a tower that kidnaps people and pits them against creatures from other worlds, all the while trying to kill them?"

Just ahead of them, Nia laughed, clearly listening in. But Earl's smile had faded. He held Alden's gaze. "Maybe."

"Wait, you're serious?"

"Yeah, kind of. You see, there's an old Norse myth about a tree sitting at the centre of nine realms. It involves a lot of Thor and Asgard and the underworld. But, at its heart, it's about a conduit between worlds."

"Oh." Alden thought about the tree engraved on the outside of the tower. The one they'd found in the dungeon. The forms of nature that had led them up between levels each time. He frowned. "A conduit in the form of a tree. For real?"

"Yup."

Nia looked over her shoulder. "You think they might have been talking about this tower? That maybe it's appeared on Earth before?"

"It's a hell of a coincidence otherwise, wouldn't you say? What if this challenge has been set for humanity before? We might not be the first to have ascended. There could have been others who've been through this and survived to tell the tale. A tale that was then passed down through the generations and became myth."

Alden blinked. "If that's true, you know what it means? There *is* a way out."

Earl smiled. "Exactly."

As Alden felt something akin to hope rekindling inside him, there was another rustle in the bushes and his face whipped around, scoping for the source. Again, it was nothing, and his momentary good cheer faded. He badly wanted to see Leia. To hear a bark, a growl, anything that would let him know she was close.

"You searching for anything in particular?" Earl asked.

Alden didn't know how to answer that question honestly. What was he supposed to say? *I keep seeing my dead dog and I think she's trying to help us.* How would that go down in the midst of all this?

Luckily, Earl seemed to understand. A supportive hand found Alden's shoulder and the man's voice dropped low so nobody else would hear.

"We all saw the dog on the beach. Yours, right? I overheard you talking to Nia about your dog dying recently."

Alden nearly stumbled from the path into a bush. Only Earl's fingers tugging at his shirt kept him upright.

"I–I…" he stammered. Then, "Yeah. Leia. Her name was Leia. I'd heard her barking before, too. On the ship. I think she's been following me through the tower. Maybe even helping us. I don't know why, though. Why would she be appearing to me? To *us*? I thought the tower might be pulling random things from people's heads and decorating the levels with them, but each level has been particular to a person and Leia has now appeared in two of them!" He sighed, feeling the grief welling up again. "Am I going nuts, Earl? Am I losing my mind? It feels a bit like I might be."

"Son, given what we've been through today, I'm surprised none of us have completely flipped our shit!" Earl laughed and Alden felt the warmth of his words, the compassion in them. "You seeing your dead dog is the least of our concerns and, possibly, like you say, she's here for a reason. The tower is drawing on our experiences. I guess that means it's able to access our thoughts, memories, feelings even. When you stepped into this place, perhaps it drew from you in other ways, too. Maybe it felt the grief you carried. Maybe it gave it form."

"She's an expression of my grief?" Alden said, eyes widening.

"Yeah, maybe. Proof of your enduring love."

Was that it? Was that the truth of what was happening?

Alden suddenly felt it surely must be. He knew Leia's appearance couldn't be part of the levels. She'd been helping to guide him, to get through these challenges; her appearances transcended the settings they were being thrown into. His beautiful, smart dog *must* be proof of the love he still carried with him every day since she'd died.

Whether it was by fate or a mysterious quirk of the tower's magic, she had been brought back to him. And that love, that grief, they were both guiding him, helping him to survive. Both equally important. Reminders not only of what had been lost, but also what was possible.

It made him want more than anything to escape this torment. To help everyone get home, to go home himself, where he could teach his class of kids, could get out to sing and play guitar in dingy pubs and clubs... Where he could *live* again.

Before the tower, he had nearly succumbed. Loneliness was normal, part of life, but the empty void it hid within its dark heart had almost consumed him. He had seen it for real: in the waters of a sinking ship; in the agony of a dungeon; in the shadows beyond open doors; in the mouth of a tentacled storm. It was the emptiness of loss, beckoning you closer, wanting to feast on what life you had left.

Before the tower, he had let it eat. Not now.

There's always another sunset, Nia's voice in his head reminded him.

"You going to be all right?" Earl asked, looking concerned.

But Alden smiled. "Actually, I think I might be. Thanks, Earl."

"Good. Just remember, grief can play a useful role in the world, too. It can show you what's important. What matters. So keep looking out for her, OK?"

"I will."

Nothing more was said for a moment, as they continued along the path. Until Casey – always Casey – asked, "Any idea how far we still have to go in here? Only we haven't stopped for a rest for a while and it would be really good if we could do that soon. I go to the gym twice a week, but this has all been a lot. I can't be the only one flagging."

Nia pointed ahead to where the path was coming to an end. Before them, through the wafting fronds and twisted stalks, Alden could see the other side of the gardens – a series of galleries built into the wall, rising several storeys high, each overflowing with exotic plants and with a set of stairs zigzagging up them. "We need to go a little further still, up through those galleries, to the bridge above us. We can slow down, if that helps, but it's probably too dangerous to rest anywhere here."

"And we're still in a race to the top, sweetheart, remember?" Dirk said to Casey. "Gotta keep climbing ahead of those Eyeball Heads. We gotta hustle here. No way am I going to let them reach that prize before us. So, keep your shit together and let's all crack on, OK?"

There was a snarky edge to his tone that made Alden's skin crawl. He didn't understand how the man was so popular with anyone. Not the children who read his trashfire books, nor the women he was constantly seen with in the media.

From the look on Casey's face, she didn't get it either.

They climbed the first set of stairs and reached the first-floor gallery, following Nia along a path between what seemed like upside-down trees, with flowers at their bases and long, wriggling roots just above the humans' heads. Then they hit the next set of stairs and headed up again. The group continued like this for another few storeys, hiking up from gallery to gallery, Alden noting the canopy of the gardens fall further below him, while taking care not to brush too closely against the most imaginative plants, flowers and trees adorning these galleries.

"You really are a genius, do you know that?" he said, catching up with Nia halfway to the bridge.

"Oh. What made you say that?"

"Just to have the creativity to dream up these gardens in the first place. I know this isn't the kind of place you want to hang about in, but it's truly spectacular here. I almost wish we could spend more time wandering, having you show me what everything is. You're an incredibly talented artist."

She blushed as she tucked her hair behind her ear to see him properly.

"Well, I don't know what to say. Thank you. I just love creating, I guess. Taking the visions in my head and getting them down somehow. I've always been compelled to draw and create, knowing the end result was *mine*, you know? I enjoyed the control of creation. At least, until I began doing it for work and other people had to have their input." She gestured around them to the gardens. "Still, this was my favourite part of that particular job. I've always loved the outdoors, the wilds of nature, and here I got to make my own version, more or less. I think I'm more at home in nature than with people, if I'm honest. I love being out there, alone."

"You like being alone?" he asked, staring at the glow in her face, the passion for her craft pouring out of her as she talked. Feeling the warmth of her energy. Sensing it spark some recognition in him of what he'd been missing from his own life lately.

"Oh yeah, being alone is the best. Don't you like it?"

"Not really," he said honestly.

"Huh. I've just always found something freeing about it. Just you out there in the wild, following your own path, nobody else around getting in your way. I tried to bring that kind of feeling in here. A natural space, as freeing as you can get within the confines of an unnatural spacecraft." Nia chewed her lip. "Of course, the director wanted me to weave some deadly plant life in among the alien beauty I drew. For dramatic tension. Otherwise, I would have loved to hang out here some."

"Got to entertain the masses," Alden said with a smile.

"I guess," she replied, before being bowled over by a flash of movement.

* * *

The impact knocked the wind out of Nia, but it was the sensation and texture of what had hit her that freaked her out.

A thick mass of scales. Hard, like a suit of armour, but rough and slick with some kind of sticky goo oozing between the overlaps. And dozens of flailing tentacles surrounding it, flinging out in all directions. So black they seemed to suck light from the immediate vicinity.

Her first thought was that somehow the Cthulhu monster had found them, but as it scrambled away, she saw this was a much smaller creature. Its flexible, rope-sized limbs stretching up to the ceiling above and the path below, holding the reptilian ball in the middle.

It had been swinging through the foliage around them, like a fever-dream Tarzan. If it had eyes, she couldn't tell. Clearly it hadn't seen her closely enough to avoid the impact, and as it backed off, she got the impression it was just as surprised and wary as she was.

Three of the limbs flew up in front of its body and formed a variety of shapes.

Someone shouted and Nia flinched. But there was no attack. The tentacles kept making their signs, then stopped and held fast. The creature left, bobbing up and down.

Did it just... talk to me? It made the signs again, then stopped and waited, and she knew – she just fucking *knew* – it was waiting on a response.

Silence reigned, broken only by the breeze of the air recycling units blowing through the gardens. Nia twisted to see the others, eyes wide, mouths agape, watching to see what would happen. Earl had pulled Rakie behind him. Mason had done with the same with Casey. Dirk stood a little behind Monique.

Nia was relieved to find Alden by her side.

"What *is* it?" she whispered. "It's not like the others."

"There's a third team," he replied, and Nia felt his fingers find hers, feeling the warmth, the comfort, the humanity in his touch. It grounded her. Allowed her to accept that this was happening.

But even as he gently encouraged her backwards, away from the alien, she resisted.

"Nia?"

She didn't respond, tilting her head to look in the direction the creature had come from. There was no more movement.

"I don't think it's going to hurt us, Alden. And I think it's alone. Maybe its team were killed already?"

There was a note of pity in her voice she wasn't expecting. A stirring of compassion inside for this... Well, she had no idea what to call it. An octolouse?

The thing signed again. Same three limbs, same shapes, but slower this time, as if desperately trying to get her to understand.

It finished by raising the end of one of the tentacles and it flattened, much like a hand.

"We come in peace," Earl said.

"Fucking *Christ*," Dirk muttered. "What B-list piece-of-shit movie is this?"

Nia ignored his insult, drawing in a deep breath and hoping it wouldn't be her last, before she stepped closer to the alien. She raised her own hand, holding it in a mirror of the gesture, a foot away from the creature's, and held it there, not willing to press against the being in case she had some kind of alien allergic reaction. But she hoped the gesture was enough. The creature needed to know she was trying to communicate back. That she wasn't about to pull out a blaster and shoot it.

They held there for what felt like centuries, the others watching, perhaps waiting for this to end in disaster.

But it didn't. And as the creature slowly retracted its limb, Nia raised her hand and extended her finger to point to the ceiling. Specifically, the bridge.

Alden leaned in.

"What are you doing?"

"I'm telling it where we need to go as simply as possible. I can't imagine it sees this level as we do. If this is a single tower, with multiple ways in for these other teams to gain access, and we see this level in the form that was extracted from my mind, it doesn't make sense that the aliens see it the same way, does it?" She glanced back at him. "What if they are here as we are, existing in the same physical place, but the tower presents their levels in a way that speaks to them – in a way that only they can see? What if we are all in the same tower, but experiencing it differently? Like life itself."

Alden nodded slowly, but behind him Dirk's face contorted into a sneer. "Even if that is all true, honey, what – and I cannot stress this enough – *the fuck* will pointing accomplish?"

Nia's lips thinned, wishing at that moment one of her director's man-eating plants would grow out of the foliage and gulp the bastard down. She was getting tired of the way he was talking to everyone.

"Because, *Dirk*, pointing is the simplest way I know of

showing which way we need to go to get out of this level. And chances are the other teams need to head in that direction, too. The levels might not look the same, but I bet the exits to the next level are aligned somehow." She paused in wonder, her heart racing, as the alien slowly raised its limb, copying her. "Yes, yes! You got it, we need to go up there!"

"Fuck me," Casey gasped. "She's having a conversation with an alien."

Nia thought for a moment, then looked to Alden. If anybody here would properly listen to what she had to say, it would be him. No matter how wild an idea it might seem.

"What if we have to work with the other teams on this level?" she said. "What if that's the purpose of bringing us together here – to show we can work alongside one another, despite our differences or being in competition? Think about it. When that giant eyeball monster shot Rakie, *it* died instead. It was like the tower was undoing what had been done, rewinding the act of violence between one team and another. And this one is all alone…"

"So we should kill it while we can. Good idea." Dirk reached into the undergrowth and pulled out a hefty blue branch.

Nia stepped protectively in front of the alien, glaring at him. "No. That's not going to happen. Did you even listen to what I just said? I think if we hurt it, *we'll* be the ones who get hurt. And while I don't mind you being sucked back up your own arse, I wouldn't want this creature to think we mean it harm. Look at it – the thing is scared and alone. We should let it join us."

Dirk snorted, a noise that made all the alien's limbs tense as it turned his way.

"Are you fucking kidding? That's a huge leap to make, assuming it's safe just because it's alone and playing its cards close to its scaly chest. What if it *wants* us to do that? What if its plan is to lure us into being friends, and then while we least expect it, one of those tentacles slips into our dicks and fucks us from the inside out?"

"Then we'll have time to get away while it tries to find yours," she said.

Dirk's knuckles whitened as he tightened his grip on the branch, madness in his eyes as he stared her down.

Then blaster fire seared through the air and exploded against the ceiling, raining debris all over them. Nia fell forwards, only to be caught in a hammock of alien limbs.

The creature held her for a moment. She stared at its shelled interior.

"Thank you," she said.

Alden reached over and pulled her to her feet again, as a commotion grew from the gardens below. The sound of multiple feet clicking against the path.

"No time for love, Dr Jones," he said. "We're leaving."

More streams of fire singed the plants around them as the group of humans and their alien counterpart moved quickly to the next set of stairs. Nia didn't know why they were being shot at. Was it the same team that had "killed" Rakie earlier? If it was, hadn't they learned anything from what had happened? Or were they just the alien equivalent of lads out on the town – aggression-fuelled, setting aside logic to focus on their debased desires and inherent need for shooting their load?

The humans moved as fast as they could, flowing through the paths across the balcony up to the stairwell. Their alien ally swung through the foliage, zipping with speed, and as Nia watched it disappear *through* a wall and appear on the other side, unscathed, she knew her theory was right. This level was perceived differently by the alien. It wasn't navigating the garden as they could see it, which made her wonder exactly what it saw or felt. What scene had the tower pulled from its mind and forced it to race through?

Up they went to the next gallery, then up again. More streams of blaster fire followed them, keeping pace. Not yet on target, but Nia knew it was only a matter of time.

She could only hope the rules still applied as they had before. That the tower would bring back anybody who got hit – although she really didn't want to go through what she'd seen of Rakie's disintegration.

Panting and gasping, she pulled herself up the railing of the last staircase, to the top level of the botanical gardens. Above them, an expanse of stars twinkled through the glass roof, their lights ebbing and flowing, blinking and flashing. While ahead, hanging below the roof, was a platform with a built-in array of seats and panels, accessed by a single gantry only footsteps away.

"Are we here?" Monique asked desperately. "Where do we go?"

"In the movie they go onto the bridge..." Nia's voice trailed off as she looked around. She'd been hoping for something more, some sign of where to go once they got up here. There was nothing on the bridge – it was the one place clear of plant life in these space gardens. Had she missed something along the way? A tree or vines, or something weird they had to climb.

"You've led us into a dead end!" Dirk snarled, staring around in disbelief. "There's no way off that bridge platform. No way up from it. Why'd you bring us this way again?"

Nia's hope flagged as the others looked to her for some answers – an explanation. She had nothing. All she had been going on was the movie this was all pulled from. What if that had been the wrong call? What if there had been something she'd forgotten?

"But this is where the movie's climax happened," she tried to explain. "The heroes got onto the bridge and then something came to life below and they had to fight it to get out. It all happened here."

"Wasn't there an escape pod?"

It was Alden who reminded her of what she'd brought up earlier.

"That's it! Yes, they escape in the pod."

"Which is?"

Nia spun around desperately, trying to remember where it was. But if it was obvious in the movie, it wasn't here. There was nothing around them. No doorway or emergency markings indicating an escape route.

"It needs to be above us," Alden said, beginning to wander onto the bridge, looking up. "We need to ascend, and all our ways out have been upwards. So, look up. Look for leaves, trees, anything like that. A symbol. It will show us the way out."

"There's nothing above us, though!" Casey said, jabbing her finger upwards towards the glass. "That's fucking *space*! It's a vacuum and we'll die!"

"Just keep looking," he urged.

Nia knew Alden was using the tower's logic. Their perceived reality was that there couldn't possibly be a way out above them because there was nowhere to go. But the tower wouldn't let that get in the way of its rules. It hadn't yet.

Unnoticed by the rest, the alien was swinging around the bridge as the humans fanned out across it. Nia kept an eye on it, getting the feeling it understood what they were doing and it was trying to help. Or, perhaps, it thought they were helping it. Either way, the thing was covering more ground than they were, and thanks to its vinelike limbs it was able to swing from the curving beams above them, out from the safety of the bridge, over the long drop to the gardens below.

Which is where it found the escape hatch.

It was a few seconds before Nia realised. When she saw the alien vigorously signing to her, flinging its limbs into very deliberate patterns before pointing directly above where it hung.

There, it seemed to say.

"Fucking hell," Nia said, racing to the edge of the bridge platform to find a gap of just under two metres between this and the handle of the hatch that had been hidden in the beam above the gaping chasm. A hatch bearing the symbol of a tree. "How do we get to *that*?"

CHAPTER TWENTY-THREE
Roots

Nia tightened her fingers around the railing. The cold metal bit into her skin, keeping her present, focused. She could hear the galloping below them getting nearer, the blasts louder as they fired upwards. Were they in danger from the shooting? She didn't think so. Not after witnessing Rakie being brought back to life. But she couldn't take the risk they *weren't* in danger, either. They had to get out *now*.

"That's a hell of a leap," Alden said, joining her at the railing.

"Big leap, bigger drop," she said, trying to wrestle control of her emotions. To stay positive. "But we can do this, Alden. The tower wouldn't have put it out there without giving us a shot, right? We must be able to make it."

He looked like he wanted to muster up reassuring words, but quickly surrendered in the attempt. "No. With that hatch closed it's too high, too far. If we could maybe get it open somehow, with it hanging down, we could do it." He glanced at her. "Can you get your alien friend to help?"

The thought was ridiculous. She wasn't an alien linguist! What was the universal tentacle sign for *open the hatch or we're all going to die*?

And yet it made perfect sense.

"It has to help us," she said, nodding to herself. "What we said before about working together, helping the other teams. We found the hatch for the alien. Maybe it wouldn't have known where to look without our help?"

"And in return, it needs to open it for all of us?"

"Bingo."

Nia looked out to the creature, prepared to wave her hands in whatever way she could to get the alien to do what must be done. But the thing was smart. It was alone, the only one left of its team to keep ascending the tower, and it knew this was the way out. And it was already slipping its limbs through the thick handle and yanking on it hard.

Her heart leapt, then dropped, as there was a little give and a shower of paint crumbled from it, but the hatch didn't move. *Fuck.* Was it welded shut?

It pulled again. Then again.

A crack appeared.

"Come on, mate." Nia waved at it encouragingly, lifting her hand above her head and yanking down. Mirroring its actions. "You're close. You can do it!"

Wrapping more of its limbs through the handle, the octolouse readied itself and then pulled again with all its strength. With a wailing screech that swallowed the closing sounds of blaster fire, the square hatch door was yanked open hard.

Nia was so overwhelmed with relief, she barely cared for the piece of frame that came away with it. She only half watched it drop harmlessly past the creature, tumbling end over end to the garden far below. Only half heard the distant crash as it must have hit the ground.

In the back of her mind, as she prepared to rally the others and get them to jump, she heard the silence that followed.

Before the loud, thick scratching of something stirring filled the entire chamber.

"The *fuck* was that?" Dirk shouted over.

Nia didn't want to think about it. They were so close to getting out of here. She kept her eyes fixed on the alien hanging from the hatch door and the opening above it. In the midst of a glass ceiling, through which was the endless vacuum of space, it looked like they would be climbing to their deaths. To be boiled alive, or frozen, or whatever happened to humans in space. But she knew the darkness in the hatch was a different kind of nothingness. One that would transport them up through the tower. To the next level.

She waited for their alien friend to slip up and through by itself. It had done its job; there was no need to wait for them. But it didn't. Instead, it held fast, limbs still wrapped around the handle, several free tentacles gesturing first to her, then up.

Pointing, in the way Nia had unwittingly taught it.

"It wants to help us go through," she said in grateful disbelief. "It's going to wait there to catch us!"

"Can it do that?" Alden asked incredulously.

She'd felt it before, though. When it had caught her. Those slim tentacles were stronger than they looked.

"Yeah, I believe it can." She turned to the watching group, as another shot of blue blaster fire burst overhead. "Hey, everyone, we're leaving and we've got some help. Let's fucking *move*."

She made her way along the bridge, one eye on the hatch, trying to find the closest position to it where she could kick away the railing. She didn't need to, though. The tower had already kept a gap in the right place, just wide enough for one person to leap through.

Very thoughtful of you, Nia thought sourly. *Probably would have been easier not to beam us here and try to kill us in the first place, though?*

The tower must have heard her. At this point, she knew it had been inside their heads. It was probably still in there, a silent passenger, watching them, studying their reactions to its design. Probably changing things on the fly to provoke new and interesting emotions in them. She could have laughed at the irony. *The designer caught in the design.*

In response to her snark, the tower increased the rustling from the gardens below. Made it louder. Gave it vastness and strength as it filled the air, until Nia's skin was itching with the sound and she wanted to claw it off.

Something was moving down there. Something big.

She peered over, seeing a rip in the thick canopy below. What lay beyond it mirrored the nothingness above them – darkness and shadow, except she saw movement in it. Lots of movement. In all directions.

As her eyes adjusted, she saw it was a writhing mass of purple roots growing before her eyes, hundreds of them, twisting around one another, pulsating with what felt like eagerness. Rising as one, legion. Tearing through the strange plants and ripping aside the upside-down trees. A tangle of death climbing up towards the hatch.

"Let's go, let's go, let's go!" Nia shouted. She looked to Mason, who was closest. "You, jump!"

To his credit, Mason didn't hesitate. He'd been a man of few words for most of this journey, but there was nothing wrong with his ability to take action. His run and leap was straight and true, his fingers catching the hatch, while the alien's tentacles caught his body in the way they'd caught

Nia earlier. There was a moment where he looked like he was slipping free, but the creature wrapped around him tighter and hoisted him just enough to reach the handholds she could see on the inside of the hatch.

Dirk drifted into the space between Alden and Nia, watching Mason as though his life depended on it. He was suddenly muttering to himself.

"Wait, but we're all still here? Can he even go through? Nobody has been killed."

"What?" Nia asked.

He ignored her, continuing to talk to himself, almost waiting for something to happen as Mason heaved himself up rung by rung.

"Rakie died, but that doesn't count, surely. No, no, the tower brought her back. She came back! That's not the rule." He sighed. "*Fuck*. We're missing something…"

Nia and Alden looked at each other.

"What rule?" Nia asked more firmly. "What the hell are you talking about, Dirk?"

But just then, Mason reached the last rung and reached up and dragged himself into the hatch. His dangling legs quickly followed, as though he'd been pulled up by some invisible force. Then he vanished.

Dirk leapt and punched the air. "Fucking hell, yes!" He turned to the pair as though only just seeing them. "Nothing, don't worry about it," he called back, moving away to join the others.

"What rule?" Nia asked Alden, keeping her voice low. By the look on his face, he was just as concerned by what they'd heard. "What does he know that we don't?"

"He was talking about Rakie and being killed?"

"And Mason not being able to get out."

"Do you think...?" Alden paused, his hair dropping over his face, eyes seeking answers in some unseen memory. Until suddenly he looked back up at her. "Back in the haunted house, the stairs wouldn't let us out. Then they came to life for no reason. And I thought we all made it out of there..." He brushed his hair behind his ears. "But Kim didn't."

Nia stared at him. Then looked over to Dirk.

"Bloody hell, Alden. What are you suggesting?"

But she already understood. She could see it in Alden's eyes, in the horrified curve of his lips, and she could feel the truth of it inside her. As though the tower was in there, nodding along.

You figured it out, it might have been saying.

Alden followed her gaze to the children's author as the man pushed Monique aside and readied to jump. "I think there's a rule about these levels we've overlooked. One he's been using to his advantage."

"Someone has to die?"

Alden nodded. "Yeah."

Nia felt the idea seep inside, tainting her with its cruelty. It felt so wrong, so pointlessly horrible, and yet completely in keeping with what they'd been through. There was a logic to it that made her want to vomit.

And yet... Dirk was right. If that was the rule, why had Mason been allowed through?

More blaster fire ricocheted off the glass above them as Dirk leapt for the hatch. He was older than the rest of them, but in better shape. Being a celebrity, with all that money and time on your hands to work out, clearly paid off. He grabbed the handholds straight off, without help from the alien, and gave the faintest glance back at the others, as though not expecting to see them again. Then he was gone, too.

"He seemed confused, Alden," Nia said. "He thought he'd missed something critical."

They all ducked as the glass cracked above them and shards of it rained down. Nia knew it was only a matter of moments before it all gave way. She could also hear the scratching of the roots growing closer from the gardens below.

Glancing over, she saw the wall of them spread up and out, weaving around the balconies and wrenching them from their moorings. The eyeball aliens must have seen it, too, because their blaster fire was raining down into the gardens, trying to halt its advance.

One of them stumbled as the balcony below was knocked. The roots seized their opportunity and snaked across it, pushing aside the plants and flowers, until they wrapped around the body of the prone alien. It was pulled into a mass of vegetation, and although Nia couldn't see it, she could hear what must be happening. There was a sonic boom of agony reverberating through their bodies as the roots went to work on it.

"Nia?" Alden shouted, as the noise faded with the creature's death. More shards of glass clattered to the bridge around them. "What do you think he'd missed?"

"No time." She gestured to the waiting Casey. "Go!"

Casey leapt more nimbly than Nia would have given her credit for. The octolouse caught her and she wasted no time in scurrying up the rungs on the hatch door to vanish into the darkness.

The remnants of the other alien team were on the balcony immediately below. Their fire was indiscriminate, in all directions, and Nia should have realised it was only a matter of time before one of the shots got lucky.

A fizz of the blue fire came straight up and clipped their alien friend holding the hatch open. One of its limbs spun away while the rest of it flailed, pulsing outwards with what Nia figured must be pain.

Still it didn't leave. It hung on, waved them to continue. Another blast came close and the alien slipped as it tried to dodge.

It almost fell.

Nia waved wildly to get its attention. "Go!" she said, pointing towards it and then upwards, towards the hatch. "It's your turn."

"What?" Monique shouted.

"It's helped us enough."

"But how are the rest of us supposed to get through?"

"Monique, just listen…"

But the flight attendant wasn't going to hang around any longer. She ran for the opening, leapt over the drop, and grabbed the alien before it could move. She levered herself up onto the inside of the hatch, grabbed the handholds, and began to climb.

"No, Monique, you have to wait," Nia shouted. "We need to work together! Let it climb up and then you need to…"

But Monique was already gone, up to the next level.

Only Alden, Earl, Rakie and Nia were left.

The alien held where it was. A weary sign indicated more should jump, but then another blue bolt rocketed past and slammed into the beam. The explosion rocked the alien, and as more blaster fire came its way, it knew it couldn't wait.

"Go!" Nia urged.

It slipped under and around the hatch, moving from the handle on the outside to the handholds on the inside. Then, with a brief gesture in her direction, it escaped the blaster fire and squirmed up into the hatch.

At which point the door was free of the weight holding it open.

It began to swing closed again.

Nia cried out, a wordless sound, as if the horror in her voice alone might hold the thing open. And in that agonising, terrible moment, she realised what it was Dirk had been trying to figure out. What had surprised him.

This level had let them escape even though Rakie hadn't stayed dead. He must have been wondering if that had done it – if it had ticked the box to allow them to get the hell out of here. And it might have seemed like it when Mason had gone through.

But no. The tower wanted what it wanted. A sacrifice. Someone to remain behind, holding the door open for the others to escape.

She didn't know what to do. What to say. One of them had to jump and grab the outer handle of the hatch door, swinging it back open, or they were all going to die.

Could she do it? Could she rouse herself to do the right thing?

Yes, I can.

She stepped back, ready to make the leap. To do what must be done.

Only for Earl to beat her to it.

The father with greying hair, who'd often been out of breath when they'd had to run, rushed past her and leapt with both arms outstretched. He grabbed the handle of the hatch door before it closed, pulling it back down again, before he jerked to a stop in the air, legs dangling over the chasm.

"Dad!" Rakie screamed.

"Hurry," he called back through gritted teeth, as he carefully adjusted his grip and turned around to face them, his face creased with exertion. "Rakie first."

Nia blinked, unable to comprehend what he'd just done.

"Hurry!"

She shook herself back into focus and turned to the girl. "Quickly, sweetheart. You think you can make that leap?"

"I'm on the athletics team at school. I do long jump."

"You got this," Earl said, ever the encouraging dad, even as Nia could see the death-by-roots sweeping up towards them. "Just a regular meet. Jump for the other side of the door, for the handholds. I'll catch you if you miss."

Another bolt of fire shot past them.

"Come on, Rakie, you can do this."

But as the girl stepped back, readying herself, a strand of purple thread wove up from the gardens. Nia watched in slow motion as the end of it, waving back and forth like a sightless worm, found Earl's shoe.

Curling up around his foot, it swelled with intent. Earl yelled, trying to shake it off, but the root had him. Its tip snaked around his ankle, then tentatively pressed against the man's skin… before burying its way inside.

Earl screamed, a pained, panicked noise that threatened to finally shatter the glass above and rain death upon them all. Rakie joined in, Alden barely holding her back, as her father fought and kicked, trying to free himself.

It was no use. He was caught.

As the root snaked through his body, he forced himself to stillness and looked over at his daughter.

"Jump, girl."

Rakie knew she couldn't wait. She couldn't rally against this twist of fate. She was a smart, capable child with nerves that would put most adults to shame. And she did as her dad had asked.

She ran and planted her right foot cleanly on the edge of the bridge, easing through the gap in the railings and arcing through the air. Her feet kicked in slow motion. Her arms windmilled.

She caught the hatch as deftly as any of them had.

Hanging from the handholds, she held face to face with her father.

"Dad?"

His face was etched with fear and pain in equal measure.

"Climb, Rakie. I'll follow."

"Promise?"

His body convulsed as the root continued burrowing up through his legs. Nia saw blood spill down its length, slick and dark.

"Go," he groaned. More a noise than a word. His eyes were squeezed shut. "Please?"

Rakie kissed him on the cheek, crying. Before she could think twice, she heaved herself up the handholds and disappeared into the next level.

Alden was closest to the gap. He started to back away, but Nia put her hand on his waist to stop him.

"You go first, while he still has the strength for you."

"But–"

"Just go!" she shouted.

Alden's landing wasn't nearly as clean as Rakie's. His fingers slipped down a couple of the handholds. Only his boot, digging into Earl's leg, halted his fall. Alden used it to push himself up.

Earl didn't seem to even notice. Nia saw his hell was internal, as the second root caught and burrowed into his other foot.

Still he held on.

Alden gasped an apology as he climbed and disappeared after the girl.

Now it was just Nia and Earl, and no matter the danger she was in, her brain was racing to take stock of what was happening and figure out a way to save him. To at least *try*. All these years she'd been shutting herself away from people, retreating from connections, not wanting to get hurt. Now she had to do just that, but she couldn't. She couldn't leave this man to such a fate. He was decent and good, and he didn't deserve this. She wanted to scream with the injustice of it.

But the survival instinct was a powerful thing. She might feel powerless, but *it* wasn't. She was the product of an infinitely long line of humans who had let their instincts do the same – to fulfil their one purpose and survive, come what may.

So Nia didn't think. She let her instincts take over and leapt.

As she arced through the air, she saw Earl's body convulse again. His eyes bulged. More roots had found his legs, pulling him, stretching him. The roots going in through his legs burst out of his stomach and wrapped around his torso. She could see his bloodied skin beneath his clothes change, harden, thicken with the same purple shell as that which was killing him. The roots were making him part of them.

Nia landed clumsily, half on the hatch, half on Earl. She smacked away a root that tried to pin her wrist, then kicked out at another as she scrambled up, using Earl, the roots, whatever she could to give her leverage.

As she came face to face with him, she saw Earl's eyes roll back in his head, as his eyelids closed and his skin thickened and grew into bark. He shuddered one last time, gave a last gasp of earthy air, then the roots pushed from what had been his lips, sprouting leaves, one of which caught on Nia's shirt as she scrambled up.

"I'm so sorry," she gasped.

As Earl finally became one with the gardens, he let go of the hatch, and she clung to the inside as it lifted, ignoring the guilt that accompanied her. But as she felt the coldness of the void above brush against her wrist, and the eternal nothing pulled her inwards, she felt something knock past her shoes and hoist itself up through its own version of the hatch.

There are still three teams in this, she thought, before the tower took her.

CHAPTER TWENTY-FOUR
Role Players

Alden landed on a circular patch of grass, digging his fingers into the soil, gasping for breath. Despite being flung through the emptiness between levels, ceasing to exist for the briefest of moments in time, he couldn't shake the sight of Earl being consumed by the roots, nor rid himself of the feeling of them convulsing beneath the man's skin as Alden had climbed up him.

He retched hard, only to discover there was nothing but bile in him. Again and again he spasmed, the liquid burning his throat, until he thought he must be done. Then he rolled over and collapsed on his backside.

Rakie was staring at Nia, who had appeared last, and saw by the look on the woman's face that her father wasn't going to follow. She began sobbing violently. Nia dragged herself over to the girl and enveloped her in a tight, fierce hug.

"I'm so sorry," she whispered, brushing the teenager's hair from her face. She glanced over to Alden, tears welling in her own eyes. "I'm so very sorry, Rakie. He's gone."

The other survivors were sprawled around on the grass, looking on guiltily, Alden sensed. Monique quickly shifted her gaze away. Casey's cheeks were flushed, and she gratefully allowed Mason to wrap his arm around her shoulder and pull her to him.

Only Dirk stared with those beady eyes, impassive to her grief. Alden couldn't tell if he was looking at the girl or staring into space, lost in thought.

He wiped his lips with the sleeve of his shirt and hugged his knees, watching Nia offer comfort where there couldn't possibly be any to be found. She did it anyway. The trauma of the tower had altered her chemistry, taken this older woman who was a little frosty, maybe even reclusive, and opened her up enough to actively comfort this grieving child with so much kindness and warmth. That was often the measure of a person, he decided. How they carried the burden of responsibility for others when it was needed most.

Rakie, meanwhile, as brave as her father, simply let herself be held. She cried into Nia's chest and eventually the wails began to fade.

Feeling a little like a voyeur of her trauma, Alden got to his feet and decided to inspect their surroundings.

The grass patch they'd been transported to was not very large, contained entirely within a small circular hillock, like a henge. Above them grey clouds hung low, while to one side the grassy rise opened up and a path ran from it to a wide, foreboding forest.

Set against the twisted trees in the background, there stood a stone spire, built with blocks of sheer white, rising to meet in a point. A little like those Egyptian needles he'd studied at school. Except this one wore a tree engraved in emerald and gold on its surface.

The tower wants us to go in there, he thought. *There's something inside it needs us to see.*

They'd been there long enough for him to have an idea of the kind of signposts Nia had been talking about. She found hers in game design, in storytelling, and now he thought about it, he supposed he had always felt it in music – knowing when to follow the feel of the tune, the chord progressions, the rise and fall of the piece. He had grown up listening to music constantly, before playing it on his parents' piano as soon as he was able to sit on the stool unsupported. That's how it had all started. How he'd immersed himself in the patterns of the art.

Someone had once said he had a good ear for such things when composing, but he knew it went deeper than that. He'd sometimes heard fiction authors say "I'm just the instrument, the universe is playing the tune" when it came to describing how they wrote books. Maybe there would be people who didn't get it. But he did. It was same with his music. There was a magic to it, directing him.

"There's a spire ahead," he said to the others. "I think that should be our first stop here. Unless anybody recognises this place and has any objections?"

There was no answer forthcoming, because as soon as the words had left his lips he felt the ground shake beneath them. A strong rumble, like thunder in the earth.

It stopped, then it came again.

"What the fuck now?" Dirk sighed. "I swear to Christ Almighty, if one of you has let the tower conjure a *T. Rex* out of your brain, I will hand-feed you to the toothy motherfucker myself."

Alden looked to Nia. He didn't want to say anything, but there was definitely something coming their way. He indicated they needed to go and she nodded, while rubbing the back of Rakie's head.

"Listen, Rakie," Nia said in a soothing, composed voice. Alden didn't know how she was keeping her shit together, but he was so grateful she was. "Your dad saved us. He's a hero. If he hadn't done it, we all would have died back there. Instead, he made sure we were safe. That *you* were safe. I think you know that he wanted you to be able to carry on and get the hell out of this tower." Rakie mumbled something against her and started crying again. "Yeah, I know, kid. And the last thing you're going to want to do right now is get up and walk. I get it. If there was a way we could just stay here for a bit, we would. But we're still in a race and still in danger, and we need to move. Can you do that, do you think?"

Alden knew the shroud of grief was thick and little anybody said in these moments ever helped. It was often just noise, and you were so saturated with grief there was no room for anything else to sink into you. Words, feelings, music, emotions, real-life responsibilities. None of it seemed to matter anymore. It all became droplets in a flood.

He could still feel the enormity of Leia's loss. Others just saw a dog, a pet, something replaceable. But to him, she'd been the entire world. A tie to a past where he'd been happy. The last link to memories where he'd been loved and safe. The well-meaning platitudes of colleagues and friends hadn't been able to fix the emptiness or stop him spiralling out of his own life, unable to grasp on to the person he needed to be.

But this wasn't a normal situation. The thing Rakie needed more than anything was time. And they didn't have that.

Her grief was going to have to wait.

The ground shook harder and Alden went over to her, leaned down.

"Rakie," he said quietly. She looked up at him and he gave her the barest flicker of a smile. A note of understanding, as best as he was able. "I don't want this tower to win. Do you?" She shook her head, sniffed, and wiped her eyes. "Good. Because I think something bad is coming to kill us and I know you don't want to just sit here. Your dad wanted you to live. So let's get up and beat this tower together, OK?"

Alden saw the mental walls going up as he spoke, as Rakie shut away her grief. He was sad that kids these days were better at it than most – with so much horror available to them 24/7, they had to compartmentalise their shit just to get through the day – but at that moment it was a good thing.

"OK," she said, easing out of Nia's grasp and getting to her feet. Nia quickly joined her.

Leading the way, Alden got to the entrance to the henge and then looked around in case he'd missed something. Aside from the spire and the forest, though, there was only mist in every direction. A soupy, grey cloud that–

No. He stopped himself. There *was* something out there.

A shadow in the haze. A towering humanoid figure.

"Seriously, what the *fuck* is wrong with you all?" Dirk said, adjusting himself with one hand, while the other gestured towards whatever was coming for them. "Why can't we just have a normal level instead of... of... whatever the spooky forest, fairytale fuckery this is? I take it that's a giant, then?"

"Troll," Monique said quietly, but firmly.

Dirk's eyebrows tried to climb up his face as he turned to the woman in the uniform and looked her up and down.

"*You're* the secret dork? Jesus, sweetheart, I never would have pegged you for that."

Monique raised her chin, her French accent more pronounced as she defended her honour. "I may look good as a flight attendant, but that's not to say I do not enjoy a little *Dungeons & Dragons*. You writers do not have reign over imagination or the realms of fantasy. They are open to all."

The ground shook again, then again.

Alden stepped in between them. "Look, we don't have time for this. Unless the troll is friendly and is going to help us, we have to get moving. Monique, which way do we go? Because I'm thinking we need to visit the spire."

Nia was nodding along as he spoke. "I think so, too."

"Yes, the little tower," Monique agreed.

Dirk rolled his eyes, took her arm, and guided her ahead of him. "Right, come on, then. Let's cosplay the shit out of this and get the fuck outta here."

As the rest followed, Nia and Alden held either side of Rakie. Nia tried to put her arm around the girl, but she gently pushed it away.

"I'm OK," she said, then she tilted her head curiously at Nia as something caught her eye. Reaching over to pull something from the woman's shirt, Rakie lifted it up and inspected it sadly. It was a leaf. She very carefully slipped it into her pocket, then gestured at them to hurry. "I won't let Dad down. Come on, let's get this done." She pulled her face straight and put on an American accent, copying Dirk. "We need to cosplay the shit out of this, mother*fuckerrrrs*."

Alden and Nia both laughed, and the smile it elicited from Rakie was everything.

A brief glimmer of hope.

* * *

The ground continued to shake, as the troll's shadow pursued them across the countryside.

As they ran down the path, Alden watched the spire rise ahead, bleak and ghostly. The darkness of the trees beyond added to the effect. It was both uncomfortable and comforting, the way he'd always thought forests tended to be.

Nature could be terrifying, but also a place of life and magic... and protection.

He wondered which this would turn out to be.

They arrived at the base of the spire and found a small wooden door with iron hinges. It was open, and they pushed their way inside, slamming it shut behind them.

They were in a small hall, as wide as the base of the building, with a low-beamed ceiling over their heads. To one side there was a spiral staircase leading up to the next floor. At the back of the room, a polished table held a miniature tree on its surface, as small as a bonsai and seemingly entirely made of gold, from the root poking through the hessian bag to the branches that stretched out into an arc over its trunk.

It could have been a priceless artefact. A majestic work of art.

But as Alden stared, he realised it was alive.

More of the sparkling roots were pushing their way out of the bag, tiny tendrils teasing apart the weave and slipping through.

Just like they did to Earl, he thought, swallowing back the bile rising in his throat.

"This is your D&D campaign, Monique," Mason said. "What do we do now?"

Dirk was staring up the stairs. "Please don't let us have to fight orcs or something."

Monique scratched her cheeks with long fingers, each with chipped red nail polish. "I am sorry, but I don't remember very well. My friends and I... we are in the middle of our quest. Our games are long and tend to be played over several months, as we are all travelling for our jobs. When we come back, we are reminded of where we got up to by our Dungeon Master." Monique stared around the interior of the spire and her eyes rested on the tree for a moment. "I think *that* is familiar, but I do not know why."

Alden didn't need her to confirm this was why they were here. It was the only thing in the room. It was gold. It was a tree.

Judging from the look on Nia's face, she understood that, too.

Frustratingly, the others had already turned their attention to the stairs.

"Should we not go up?" Casey asked, venturing away from Mason for the first time in a while and peering upwards to where the stairs led. "Everything in the tower has made us climb things. We were told to ascend, weren't we? Surely we go up?"

Mason nodded, and Dirk grunted in the affirmative. Even Monique shrugged, going along with the idea.

"So we go up," she said.

Rakie shook her head vehemently.

"No."

Dirk raised a finger. "Shush, kid, let the adults talk."

"I said no. We don't go up."

The author's lips pulled wide with amusement. "Sorry, little girl. I know you've just been through some trauma, but you don't get to say what we do or don't do here. You had your level. And also, Casey is right. Everything leads up. It has done this entire time. You just be quiet. We'll do our best to get you out of here."

Our best.

There was something about the tone of those words – a disquiet – that made Alden's insides crawl. How this author had managed to become beloved across the nation, he didn't know. The guy couldn't be trusted – not out there in the real world, and definitely not in the tower, where so much was at stake.

Nia seemed to feel the same.

"How about *you* be quiet, you arrogant tit?" she said, standing beside the girl and fixing Dirk with a look that could have melted the gold right off the little tree. "Rakie has done more to help us in the tower than you have. She has more right to offer guidance than you. You've done nothing to help us with any of this, so how about you be the one to shut the fuck up and hear her out?"

It was the first time Alden had ever seen Dirk speechless. The man stood there, mouth a little agape in a smile of disbelief that anyone dare talk back.

Rakie had no more fucks left for Dirk either. With a very deliberate huff of irritation, she strode over to the tree and pointed to where several long golden leaves had sprouted and were unfurling.

"See these? Leaves. On a tree. It's been the motif for what's important this entire time." She counted them one by one. "There are seven leaves here. *Seven* leaves on this tree that's been left for us." She looked around the room. "And seven of us left."

Alden smiled to himself, glancing at Nia to see her doing the same. But apparently Dirk had been too busy being an arse the entire time to pay attention. He frowned at the girl, not grasping what was happening.

Not until Rakie pulled up her sleeve to reveal the leaf marking the tower had given them all.

"Dad said the leaves on the outside of the tower represented us – thirteen of them, for thirteen of us who were brought here. But they've been us inside the tower, too. The tree that led out of the dungeons had real ones. The Christmas tree that lifted us up out of the ship had decorative ones. The stairway in the haunted house had them carved into the railings. Even the seaweed had them." She reached into her jacket and, to Alden's surprise, pulled out a handful of all the leaves they'd come across. All different types. She laid them on the table carefully. "These are the ones who didn't make it. They fell when those people did. I've been collecting them."

Alden's heart ached to watch her as she gently touched the one she'd taken off Nia after arriving in this level.

Rakie met his gaze, eyes watery. She stayed silent. He didn't say anything.

The ground rumbled again outside. Dust fell from the ceiling.

"You've been collecting them all this time?" Mason asked, frowning. "But why?"

"Because it felt right. I wanted to bring their memories back with us. With whoever gets to leave this tower. I didn't want to leave them behind." She slipped them all back into her pocket gently. "This tree is important because it contains our leaves. That staircase is a distraction. Maybe a trap."

Dirk threw back his head and let rip a loud howl of frustration. "For *fuck's* sake!" he exclaimed, walking to the stairs and jabbing his finger up them. "That's a lovely fucking fairy tale and a neat coincidence, but rules are rules. The tower wanted us to go up all this time. So, we should go up the stairs. Why would it change the rules now?"

"Maybe it hasn't," Nia said, backing Rakie up. "But she's right. Those stairs are too easy. We wouldn't have been given the way out this quickly. We should save the tree."

The floor shook again. More dust rained down and the tree shifted on the table.

"Listen, *sweetheart*–" Dirk began, speaking through gritted teeth.

But Nia's blood was up and Alden could see the real her climbing out of the shell she'd constructed for herself. She held her calm, kept her emotions in check, but there was an energy to her, a confidence, and she faced the man without looking away. "I'll rip out your throat if you call me 'sweetheart' again. Yes, at every stage, we've gone up. But I'll lay good money on the tower wanting us to get used to that physical dynamic, to challenge us to focus. The actual clues to our ascension were written in nature all this time. The trees. The vines. The sea plants. The space gardens. And here we're being given a choice. Between physically climbing this building, as we've been taught, or focusing on the sign from nature. The tower is testing us, seeing if we're paying attention. And if we're not, we're going to die."

Alden felt himself nodding along as the spire shook again. He could see the puzzle pieces come together in his head.

"Purpose," he said. "The book Nia found on the island suggests that's where we are in the tower – we're supposed to be looking for our purpose here. The tower is making us choose what we think it is."

Casey let rip a loud, hysterical laugh. "*This* is all nuts, *you're* all nuts, and *none* of this makes sense! You're all just guessing at this insanity. It's all conspiracy theory and bullshit. None of you actually know what the tower wants, do you?"

Alden felt his face grow warm. "We only have so much to go on, Casey. We've done the best with the information we have."

"But maybe that's the point," Nia said, growing in confidence as she walked towards the tree. "Life is about trying to understand the rules of the world and society and survive it all. But nothing is definitive, it's not all rigid in the ways we'd like. People do the right thing by others, live kind lives, and they get sick or injured or killed. Others do the wrong thing by everyone and live long, rich lives. There's no conceivable justice and often nothing makes sense. But there are still rules underlying it all. One of them is that nature is everything. We might have forgotten that back in the real world, but it's an immovable, irrefutable fact. Nature is life. And if we're being made to pick between the only two rules in the tower we've identified, I pick life. I pick the tree."

"What the absolute fuck are you saying?" Dirk shouted, throwing up his arms and shaking them at the heavens. The spire creaked as the thunder was closing in on them outside. One of the wooden boards beneath their feet cracked. But the author was too fixated on trying to be right. No – more than that, he wanted to mock them for being wrong. His cheeks were burning a furious crimson as he finally lost his shit. "Are you two some woke, lefty hippies who got bent over and pegged with Mercury's retrograde last time it was in season and it's still stuck up your asses?"

"What I'm saying, you prick, is that maybe the tower has seen the chaos of humanity and is testing us on what's important here. Hoping we see that in order for humanity to ascend, we don't need to be going up. We don't need to climb over each other to get as high as we can go. Maybe we ascend as a species by choosing to live a more balanced life. Perhaps we need to choose nature over perceived success."

"Bullshit," Dirk said.

But Alden could feel the logic of Nia's words. A rock to cling to in the storm of everything else being thrown at them. She may have just revealed what the tower wanted them to understand about all this.

Casey stomped over to the stairs, rolled up the sleeves of her jumper, and grabbed the railing. A roar split the air outside and Rakie covered her ears. Casey had to shout across it. "We're wasting time and I want to get out of here. I'm going up. You coming, Mason?"

Mason's tousled mousy-brown hair flopped around his eyes as he gazed around the room, to the tree and then to Casey. He nodded and strode across the wooden boards with those long legs of his, the knees poking out of his ripped jeans. He gently pushed past Casey to lead the way up.

Dirk and Monique were quick to follow, though Alden couldn't help but note Dirk picking up his pace to edge just in front of her and behind Casey – wedging himself in the middle to ensure some kind of protection.

He watched with disgust as the three of them clanged up the iron steps after Mason, just as the model reached the top and looked back to the remaining three holding fast on the ground floor. He gave an almost apologetic smile. Then he took the next step.

The white wall broke apart.

The stones fell inwards as a colossal grey hand burst through and curled thick, scaled fingers around him. There was a tremendous howl from outside, and the hand squeezed.

Mason's head exploded as his insides were forced up through his neck.

Casey's scream of horror was so high-pitched it barely registered. It disappeared quickly, though, as she, Monique and Dirk fell backwards when the stairs collapsed under the weight of the falling wall.

Alden was momentarily frozen. Unable to stop looking at the dust and debris billowing into the spire. Until Nia shook him into movement. He turned to see Rakie already had the tree, carrying it in her arms like a baby.

"We need to protect it, Alden," she said. "Where do we go?"

"Nature," Alden replied, grabbing her and Nia and shoving them towards the door.

CHAPTER TWENTY-FIVE
Into the Forest

The three of them ran for the trees.

Shadows rose ahead, twisted limbs rising above as if ready to reach down and grab them. But compared to what was behind, Alden knew running into the forest was an easy choice. It held the unknown. The big, ugly troll, which was half the size of the spire and twice as wide, held the known. Which, as it pulled its hand free of the spire, visibly consisted of the crushed, bloody goop that had been Mason.

Alden tried to sort the thoughts swirling in his brain as his legs pumped and his lungs burned.

The stairs *had* been a trap.

The tree *was* what the tower needed them to focus on.

But the important part of all this still eluded him:

What were they supposed to do with the tree now they'd saved it?

"Keep going, into the forest. Troll's too big to follow us in there," Nia said in between gasps, running alongside him.

Alden didn't think that was the case. He was sure trees wouldn't hold back a troll who could put his hand through stone. But there was nowhere else to go, and the thick mass of branches and trunks might at least slow it down a little.

He heard shouts behind them. Dirk, Monique and Casey were scrambling free of the spire just as a crack shot across its midriff and the top half began to fall. It crashed down behind them, as the lumbering grey troll stomped through the cloud of dust in pursuit.

Casey screamed again, as she tripped and fell. Neither Dirk nor Monique stopped.

"Wait for me!"

Nia slowed. "We can't leave her."

Shit.

Alden pushed her onwards, after Rakie. "I'll go back."

He skidded to a halt and backtracked, every fibre of his being rejecting the idea of running towards the giant troll with the bloody hand storming straight for him. Yet still he went.

Dirk and Monique shot past in the other direction, neither looking his way. Guilt or callousness, he couldn't tell.

As the horizon was swallowed up by the giant, Alden reached Casey, slipped his arm around her, and spun them both round towards the forest again.

"Mason's dead. Alden, *Mason's dead.*"

"I know."

"We're all going to die!" she wailed, and suddenly he was taking the strain of her grief, carrying her along.

"No, we're going to keep going," he said firmly, trying to get her to pull her shit together. "That's our purpose right now. Get the fuck away from that thing."

His lungs ached and his breath was coming in foggy gasps. Was it growing colder? Looking ahead, he could see the inexplicable growth of frost patches across the grass. Ahead, the leaves on the trees were also beginning to turn and fall, whereas before they'd been green and lush. Winter was suddenly claiming this level. Another part of the tower's tricks? Alden wondered. Another aspect of Monique's abandoned D&D game?

Just noise, he thought. *Ignore it. It's all just noise and set decoration.*

The only thing that mattered was reaching Nia and Rakie and getting that tree wherever it needed to go. Then they could escape.

He and Casey were crunching through the frosted landscape, their progress slowed. Alden felt the chill seep up his legs and into his skin, icing his bones. Casey's teeth began to chatter. But they were close to the trees and within seconds burst into the relative warmth of the shadows.

Another deafening roar shook the world behind them. The trees wavered, their branches shaking loose what leaves were left. They fell around and were quickly absorbed back into the earth.

Alden tried not to think about the metaphorical implications of *that*.

He could see the others ahead, gathered in a small clearing. Rakie was in their centre, still clutching the tree as if her life depended on it. She looked distraught, though.

"It's losing its glow," she said, waving it at Alden as he reached them.

He let Casey go and she fell to her knees. His head swayed and grew faint; he put a hand on a nearby trunk to steady himself.

"What do you mean, Rakie?" he breathed.

"The gold on the tree was bright before and now it's not. And it's not just being in the forest. Yeah, it's dark here, but it's not that. Something else is happening, Alden. I think the tree is dying or something. We must be running out of time?"

It began to snow.

"Then we need to get moving again."

"Where the fuck to, if you don't mind me asking?" Dirk snapped, hugging himself to stay warm in his T-shirt.

"Further into the forest," Alden said, without a better idea. He could still feel the footsteps shaking the world behind them. There was a *crack* as a tree fell. Then another. The troll was intent on getting them. "And, Monique, if you have any ideas about what we do with the tree, anything from the game you were playing, now's the time to share them. We think we need to do something to save it. Protect it from that… *thing*. But what?"

Casey was crying. Whimpering for Mason. She got to her feet and began to stumble away, into the forest. Alden had no energy to go after her. He decided to let her grieve for a minute.

"Monique?" Nia persisted. "Do you remember anything that can help us?"

"Look… I don't, OK?" the woman said. "I don't remember much at all. It's been weeks since I played! Yes, maybe there was a tree and maybe our quest was to rescue it, to protect it. It's young. A baby tree. And you always protect the young."

Alden caught Nia glancing quickly at Rakie. He didn't want to allow the thoughts in his mind to take root; there was no room to consider anything but the present. But after their realisation back in the botanical gardens about what each level demanded from them, he could tell Nia was thinking about what might lie ahead.

If there was one aspect of humanity that rang true across the entirety of its existence, it was that you were born, you grew, some of you procreated, and society collectively protected the next generation to allow them to repeat the cycle. That was the only possible future. Without ensuring the children's protection, there was no future to be had.

You always protect the young.

A crunching of snow from beyond the clearing drew his attention back to the moment. It was in the direction of Casey, but too far to be her. He swivelled his head, hoping desperately it was only the friendly tentacled alien stumbling across them again.

Instead, he saw a figure stepping from the shadows towards the weeping woman.

A tall, chiselled, naked figure they all recognised.

"Mason!"

Casey's cry of disbelief echoed around the forest.

Impossibly, it actually seemed to be him. His hair impeccable, his body sculpted as if by Michelangelo himself. Alden caught himself staring and blushed, shifting his gaze away. Nia had wrapped her hands across Rakie's eyes, but couldn't help looking herself. Dirk was staring with his jaw open, his mouth twisted with very obvious jealousy at the body of beauty he saw walking through the forest.

That they'd witnessed Mason mashed to a pulp a minute ago meant nothing. They had all seen Rakie die and be reborn. Why not the model?

But Alden quickly felt something was off. He shivered as he looked back and caught the winter's light filtering through the trees across Mason's face.

The eyes.

They were open, but there was no life there.

"Casey, be careful," he called out.

Mason reached for her, his lithe, muscled arms stretching out, long fingers flexing.

"Casey," the man said in a monotone voice that brushed through the forest like the wind.

"Mason?" She stumbled towards him as though lost in a dream. "I thought you were gone. Oh, God, thank you for coming back. Thank you, thank you…"

She reached him and his hands slipped over her shoulders, around her back, and pulled her into him. Her face pressed against his chest. His chin rested on top of her short blonde crop and those soulless eyes wandered lazily to the others as she wept against his skin.

Mason-that-was-not-Mason smiled.

Before any of them could even move, his chest tore open and Casey was pulled inside with a muffled scream, his ribs wrapping around her like elongated teeth. Her hands slipped against his bloodied flesh, trying to find purchase. Her legs kicked out. But his strong hands held her in place as the ribs began chewing, tearing through her clothes and shredding her back.

There was only silence from the onlookers. Too exhausted, horrified, shocked to do anything but watch as Casey was consumed alive. Until, finally, she thrashed with one last violent spasm, suffocating on Mason's innards, and went limp.

Mason kept smiling at the group, his face shimmering into something altogether more reptilian. In the darkness behind it, more movement. A rush of it.

"Goblins," Monique whimpered.

Dirk swore, and the pair turned tail and ran. Nia followed suit with Rakie.

Alden picked up a branch about the size of a baseball bat and joined them, hightailing it through the trees, through the snow, knowing he wouldn't last long against whatever was coming. But resolving to give the others enough time to find the way out.

It was Monique who stumbled across it, quite by accident.

As Alden caught up with the others, he saw the woman ahead rush straight though another clearing. This one was free of snow, a ring of grass circled by trees that seemed like they were keeping a respectful distance from the centre, offering reverence and protection to what lay inside – a half-dug hole, barely a foot deep.

Monique was too terrified beyond reason to be paying attention. This was her level, but she'd either forgotten or didn't realise the significance of what this place might hold for them. She simply ran straight through and out the tree line on the other side.

Rakie knew, though. The kid was intuitive and smart, and she skidded to a stop just before the hole in the ground. She put the tree down beside it, then began digging with her hands.

"Help me make this bigger," she shouted, digging with her hands in the pit.

Nia immediately bent down to join her, even as Dirk followed Monique back out into the snow, towards a small bridge, half-hidden in the trees, that arched over a gushing river.

"Where the fuck are you going?" Nia yelled at them. Neither stopped.

She looked back to Alden.

"I've got you," he said.

Breathless and terrified, but still clutching the branch in his hands, he turned to face the hordes at their back. He caught glimpses of the goblins, an army of almost translucent, pale beings, half his height, with no eyes or noses, only gawping mouths filled with pointed needles.

They'd come from the shadows and Alden knew that's where they belonged. An evil dreamed up by one of Monique's friends. Maybe even Monique herself. Whoever it was, they had issues.

"Dirk, I need help!" he yelled out, knowing it was pointless but trying anyway. "Rakie and Nia need time to plant the tree!"

"No fucking *way*, man!" the voice came back. "Suck a bag of dicks."

Alden adjusted his grip on the branch, grabbing it with both hands and lifting it over his shoulder, preparing to swing. A cold inevitability gnawed at his gut. The fingers of death marking him as theirs, no doubt. If there was anything left of him after these goblins had their fill.

"Shit," he muttered. This was not how he'd envisaged going out.

Someone shrieked.

The noise carried through the forest, but to his surprise it came from behind him.

It was Monique.

Full of shock and fright, the noise peaked and then immediately became gurgling. Alden knew he should keep his eyes front, but he'd already glanced back over his shoulder. Towards the bridge.

A long, grimy arm was reaching out from under the arch and a spiked finger had impaled Monique through the chest. Her body went limp as she was lifted up like a human canapé and pulled over the wall, down towards the river, and back into the dark underneath the bridge.

A crunch of bones filled the air.

Dirk was crying, scrambling back, returning to the clearing.

Coward, Alden thought, wanting to wait a little longer to see if the author would be taken next. But he could hear the gasps and snarls of the goblins, and he turned back to see the army of white, mindless evil closing in on them.

"Rakie? How you going?"

"I'm planting it now!" the girl shouted.

"Hurry!"

"It's in the soil. Cover it up, Nia!"

Please let this work, Alden begged.

He steadied the branch, ready for the first swing, feeling the rough bark graze his fingers. The cold was bitter, but the blood was rushing through him, the adrenaline feeding him just enough warmth to get through what was coming.

"Alden!" Nia shouted in warning.

He'd already seen it.

The first of the goblins to reach them had slowed a little, almost hesitant to breach the circle of trees. Then it gave a high-pitched screech of defiance and stepped through.

Alden went to meet it. He wasn't a fighter; he was a teacher, a musician. His fingers were meant for art – for creating, not destroying.

But there was only so much death you could witness before it changed you. He had lost people. He had nearly lost himself. And this tower had chosen him to witness the violent deaths of people it had flung together to fight for their lives in a galactic game.

He'd had enough.

Not waiting for the goblin to reach him, he rushed at it, swinging the branch with a ferocity he didn't realise he possessed. The creature's head burst open like a grape and it fell to the floor. Another appeared behind it and Alden spun back, twisting around to knock the little shit back out of the clearing again. It almost dodged, getting its claws up to swipe at him. A white-hot burst of pain shot across his shoulder as his skin tore, and he immediately felt the warmth of his blood soaking his shirt.

The goblin fell away, but as Alden blinked back the tears, he saw others reach the edge of the trees. He stumbled over, half-blind, to meet them, knowing this was going to be over quickly. Behind him Rakie and Nia yelled something. They were shouting wildly, but the blood was rushing in his ears and he was too consumed with what was about to happen to hear them.

Rakie. You have to protect Rakie.

It was enough to keep him fighting for a second or two more.

Then there was a howl and from out of nowhere a big, furry mass leapt into the fight.

A dog. But not just any dog. She was unnaturally large – bigger than a wolf, perhaps even the size of a car – but as her jaw snapped and her claws flew, he saw she was still the black-and-white border collie he had raised from a pup, with a red collar and a shiny tag in the shape of a bone.

Leia.

She had returned, manifested in the kind of physical form that made sense only in dreams, in a way that couldn't have been more needed.

The dog's teeth found her first victim, tearing the face from one goblin. Then she turned over her shoulder and bit through the neck of another. Snarling and lashing out with her gigantic paws, she defended Alden, Nia and Rakie as best she could.

All this time in the tower she'd been an ephemeral presence. A sound. A glimpse. But Alden could feel the breeze from her movement. The heat of her growl. The sudden, glorious *WHOOMPH* of her fur on his face, as she swished her tail, knocking him back as another goblin leapt his way.

He staggered back, stunned.

Was this real? Was she really here?

Had the tower brought her back to life?

Earl had said she might be the manifestation of his grief. What if that was true? What if he had brought her with him into the tower somehow and his persevering love had made her real again?

He stretched out to touch her fur again, to grab it, to *know*. But something wrapped around his waist, and he was yanked backwards and lifted up before he could reach her. His breath was squeezed from his chest as her name fell uselessly from his lips. All he could do was kick out his legs at the goblins jumping for him, before he was turned to see Nia, Rakie and Dirk had all been grabbed, too.

By the golden tree.

It was the same tree that Rakie had planted, and yet it had grown a hundredfold in the space of seconds. And was still growing. Its branches had wrapped around the survivors, pulling them from the fray, as it continued to expand up and up and up, glowing with light as it did so.

This was the way out. They were about to escape.

But Alden didn't want to go. His dog had saved him, but who would save her?

"Leia," he gasped, the word nothing more than a wisp of need.

The tree pulled him closer, towards its sparkling trunk. He could hear the fight continue behind him, the snapping of Leia's jaws and the howls of her victims.

The anger of his grief made real.

Then he was lifted beyond the canopy and vanished.

CHAPTER TWENTY-SIX
The Starry Night

They were in a painting.

That was Dirk's first thought as he opened his eyes. The transition between levels was still jarring, but such was the beauty of where he found himself, the *horrendous* fucked-up trauma he'd just experienced faded far quicker than it should have done.

Lying on his back, he stared up, soaking in the most insanely glorious whirls of stars splattering the night sky.

One of his favourite paintings was hanging over him, stretching around and beneath him. He was in it. Almost able to feel the stickiness of Van Gogh's paint on his skin and breathe in the fragrant scent of the oils. He shoved himself up onto his elbows, rising from the grass, trying to wrap his brain around the details. He was fucking *inside* one of the most famous paintings in history! There were the trees, the houses of the village, the spinning stars and the glorious moon. It was unmistakable.

"This is mine," he said proudly. "My level."

He'd been wondering all this time if that suburban horror show of a haunted house had really been drawn from him. It hadn't felt quite right. The others all had direct ties to their levels, and while there had been moments in that house, familiar in part because of those stupid books he'd read as a child, the appearance of Kim's husband meant it was most likely hers. Maybe an old home she'd forgotten in her senility, one she'd shared with the old asshole who would eventually pull her into his portrait and crush her tiny body.

This place, though? This was his. Pulled from his beautiful brain.

He knew this setting as well as he knew the sight of his own face in a mirror, which was to say: incredibly well. That this level – *his level* – was the most tasteful and grown-up they'd visited felt right.

"You're welcome," he said to the other three survivors, unable to help the grin creeping across his face as he saw they were similarly awed.

As he got to his feet, he saw the painting wasn't the only thing here. Other creative works of art began to shimmer into existence as he swiped his gaze across the landscape and slowly wandered across the hill.

He recognised most of these, too – objects and artefacts of exquisite detail and stunning design. Chief among them a statue of a veiled lady – an exquisite marble carving of a woman who appeared to be wrapped in light material; he remembered being awed by it at some English estate.

He ran his fingers lightly over her form, only to be immediately distracted as a poem drifted on the wind towards him.

"...and half the seed of Europe, one by one."

He felt a knot in his chest as the words of Wilfred Owen wrapped around him, barely whispers, but potent enough to sink into his soul, filling him with their sadness and beauty. Closing his eyes, he shivered with the tickle of each sentence.

Is this heaven?

Dirk had never been very religious. His parents had been, though, and they'd drilled into him an appropriate respect for all the clichés that came with believing in the unbelievable. Now he wondered if they had been right. Because, *holy fucking balls*, this place was everything he'd expected heaven to be like. He was consumed with creative joy, and wanted to devour more of what he saw, greedy for the confidence it gave him to be in the presence of these masters of art, feeling worthy as one of their peers.

He wanted to explore. To live. To experience everything this world had to offer.

Jesus, it was so good to be among his people. He gazed at everything like a famished man at an all-you-can-eat buffet, trying desperately to consume every visual morsel, unable to wipe the joy from his face as he did so. He was filled with so many emotions, he didn't know what to focus on next.

The wind continued to brush against his face, carrying with it even more words. Not only poems, but stories, too. The passion of a thousand writers spilled over the hills towards him, wrapping them up with their experiences, while more works of art – from photographs to paintings, sculptures, architecture, and even visions of some of his favourite films – were splashed across the sky in glorious technicolour.

"What is this place?" Nia breathed, holding Rakie in front of her. Both were staring up at the flash of colour in the sky, as a heart floated away from the reach of a child-shaped cloud. "It's beautiful."

"This is art, baby!" Dirk crowed. "Writing, poetry, paintings… Finally, we get to a level with some class."

Beyond the two females, he saw Alden staring at a long stick balanced on a few tattered sheets of paper. Alden leaned over it, unable to contain his fascination.

"Oh, wow. I know what this is."

Dirk walked up to him, frowning a little as he realised he didn't recognise whatever it was. Oh well. Not every level was perfect. Maybe some of their stuff had crept in here, too.

"I knew you'd be some kind of wizarding freak, Lady Gag-Gag. Whose wand is it, then? Fucking Gandalf's?"

"It's a composer's baton, you dipshit." Alden gestured to the paper beneath, careful not to touch it. "And this looks like original sheet music to one of the world's greatest compositions. Khachaturian's 'Adagio of Spartacus and Phrygia'. Look, it even has little notations in pencil." He stared at it lovingly. Then the wind picked up and they were assailed with a gust of the most beautiful, sweeping music. Alden's face lifted and he closed his eyes to it, letting it wash over him. "Bloody hell, I've been listening to this all my life. Never thought I'd hear it so pure, though."

The power of the music was incredible. It was like being courted and taken to bed by the universe. Every emotion they could imagine was dancing through them, lifting them up, spinning their insides around. As if in tandem with the sweeping feeling, Dirk saw the eddies of clouds above suddenly grow fierce with colour, burning brightly in reds and oranges. The sky became a blazing sunset and mountains appeared in the distance. Nia gasped as they were built up in strokes, as if they were at the end of an invisible paintbrush.

"And I recognise that happy little artist," she said wistfully.

Dirk thought he did, too. But there was so much colour and sound around him, he felt like he was spinning out of control. His knees buckled with the force of flashbacks through his life as he was dragged backwards to catch glimpses of who he'd been, the moments that had made a difference to who he was now.

Not all of them good.

One memory stuck fast, like a pebble in a drain. Him in his apartment in New York, playing with AI prompts, trying to piece together passages for his first children's book. The publisher had given him explicit instructions not to use it, but they'd already used it for the cover, and so why the fuck shouldn't he do the same for the words? Besides, the blank page had been too big a wall for him to scale, and the pressure of a deadline and the huge advance he'd been given on the strength of his celebrity had been a real stick in his pee-hole.

The publisher had offered him a ghostwriter, sure, but he had some semblance of pride, wanting to do this himself. Ha. Fat fucking chance. Turned out he wasn't quite the creative genius he'd thought.

Not until he discovered AI, the delicious entity jerked into existence by some tech bro, just at the right time for Dirk to type some shit into a prompt and have it trawl whatever it could find to present him with a story. And it was fine. Yeah, simplistic, stupid and pointless, but what children's story wasn't?

His editor had flipped out. In a good way. The thing about being a celebrity, he'd come to know, was that it gave you passes for everything. He wasn't even sure the editor had read it, they just cared he'd given them words. They also understood, regardless of how good the words actually were, that the books would sell, because he was famous. Win-win.

"AI steals other creative work," his girlfriend at the time had told him. "You feel OK with that?"

Turns out he did.

"The real genius is the guy who gets the book out without doing any of the work," he'd replied, burying his feelings of inferiority beneath the new contract for a series of ten more books. He was Dirk *fucking* Gentson, influencer and famous AF. It really didn't matter how he'd come up with the book – only that he had. And in the end, people loved him for getting their kids reading, and his publishers loved him for making them all shitloads of money.

"Dirk? Dirk!" Nia's nagging voice roused him from his reverie. "Come on, the other teams are probably still in this race, so we need to figure this out quickly. If you think this is your level, what do we need to do? Where do we go?"

With a contented smile, Dirk stuck out his chest.

"Of course it's my level! This shit is all famously beautiful. It's all art. Art for the artist."

Not for the crappy singer or budget designer, he thought defensively, as he saw Nia and Alden glance at each other.

"Art," Rakie repeated, nodding as though she understood what was happening, as she walked around inspecting it all.

Dirk bristled, knowing she couldn't possibly understand the true beauty in any of this. The others thought the kid was clever, had some kind of intuition about this shit. She'd got lucky a couple of times. But he wasn't going to let her take the lead.

She's going to get us killed, he thought. Then, more hopefully: *unless she dies first.*

He suddenly smiled at them all. "Come on, my dudes, let's get walking."

"Do you remember the movie *Return to Oz*?" Nia asked the group as they wandered the ever-changing hillside.

Dirk shrugged, not giving much of a shit about whatever she was saying. He was too engrossed in the thoughts in his head. How to get out of this level. What was the key that would unlock their escape?

Who would be left behind this time?

Artefacts, jewellery, majestic painted canvases… all were appearing and disappearing around him, seemingly at will. It was fascinating to watch. Especially as he saw so much of what he'd admired throughout his life. Craft he had tried so hard to emulate.

"Never saw it," he muttered, not really remembering if he had or not.

The other two – No Direction and the kid – both shook their heads.

"Why?" Alden asked her.

Nia paused at one artefact. Dirk glanced back to see her stroke a finger across the crescent curves of a particularly stunning metal piece, with strange writing covering its face. "There was a scene in that movie where all these treasures were laid out around a chamber and Dorothy, our hero, had to touch the right ones to escape with her life." Nia indicated all the temporarily present objects around them. "This place feels a bit like that. She had only a few chances to pick the right objects, the ones that best represented her friends, or she would become part of the collection."

Dirk chewed his lip, feeling that somehow the description rang a few bells. Maybe he had seen that movie before. Still, who cared? Her rambling was an annoyance, getting in the way of his planning.

"Look," he said impatiently. "If I don't really remember the movie, I don't think this can be what you think? This level is a physical representation of all the goddamn beautiful shit inside me."

"Honestly, Dirk, if this level is yours, I'm surprised it's been able to contain your ego."

"Honey, this *is* my ego. It's everything I am. An international superstar comedian and author of everyone's favourite children's books. A bestseller in too many countries to mention and adored the world over. *I am art itself!*" He lifted his arms out, gesturing to everything around them. "Maybe there are one or two things from your tiny little brains that made it in here, too. I guess the tower needed you to not feel left out. But be in no fucking doubt, this is a world of my creation. I'm the only one here worthy of it. Let's be honest, you shit out clichéd designs for low-budget movies, and our very own Elton Bomb here is such a talent he's had to resort to teaching."

He watched the words strike Alden, hoping they might pierce him enough to let the last vestiges of the boy's pride seep out of him, into the hillside. That would have been the cherry on the icing on this delicious visual feast of a level so far.

Alden narrowed his eyes a little, half hidden beneath his emo haircut. But otherwise he stood there and took the hits. *Getting a little backbone finally?* Dirk wondered. *Or just too chickenshit to say anything back?*

Nia wasn't, though.

"You're a real cunt, Dirk. You know that?"

It was a one-star review delivered with such emotionless force, for a second Dirk didn't know what to do with himself. He just stood there blankly, as eons passed. Nia staring at him, Rakie smirking. Until finally he cranked a grin back onto his face.

"Whatever, *sweetheart.*"

She balled her fist. "I fucking warned you..."

The threat was real enough that he put his hands up in a gesture of surrender before he'd even thought how it might look. Still. He'd riled them up enough, got under their skin. He could potentially use that soon enough. But best to calm things down a bit for the moment. He had no idea how to get out of this place, after all, and the others might still prove useful.

"Woah, fine, settle down!" he said. "Carry on, then. What were you saying?"

She took a breath, let her fingers unclench. "There are things I recognise here that you could never. Not just famous pieces of art, but real, personal things to me. We know the tower is challenging us every step of the way. If that book was right, we've entered the levels of significance. Now, that's a pretty subjective thing, don't you think? Each of us will find significance in different things. What matters to you doesn't necessarily matter to me." She looked him up and down derisively. "In fact, I'm fucking sure it doesn't."

"Easy now, tiger."

"*Whatever,*" she repeated in a terrible approximation of an American accent. All nasal whine. She stepped closer to him, and for a moment he readied himself for the swing of her fist, but she stepped past him with a wry smile and moved to a pedestal holding a small teddy bear atop it. "See this? To you it's just a cuddly toy of no value. But *this* was the toy my grandmother gave to me before she died. I was only four and I've kept it all these years. The real version is at home, sitting on my rocking chair." She looked around the group. "So why is it here, if this is truly Dirk's level?"

Dirk stared at the bear. The teddy was scruffy, brown and worn. There was only one good eye and the other was simply stitches. He'd definitely never seen it before and there was certainly no value to it compared to all the other works.

Fuck.

As if adding salt to the wound, the tower began bringing into existence more objects that meant nothing to him. A small Casio watch in a glass cabinet, its back open to reveal a tiny array of spinning parts. A toy car from an old TV show on a shelf. A faded photograph with a torn edge, hanging in mid-air.

Nia was right, these weren't his.

The glow of victory in her eyes as she saw his acceptance of the truth was almost too much to take. Dirk felt the humiliation rising in him, barely restrained, encouraging him to lash out. It would feel so good to slap the smug from her bitch face once and for all. To beat them all to a pulp and leave them to whatever evil death the tower had planned for them.

But he held himself back, for the moment. Straightened.

"So… what? This level is meant for all of us – is that what you're saying? You think it's part of your subconscious putting us in that movie you remembered?"

"Yeah, that's what I'm saying. That maybe we need to be careful here, because if it is what I'm thinking, we're being confronted with items of significance. Things from our very best memories."

"And we need to find what is most significant to us and that'll allow us to escape?" Alden asked.

Her voice softened. "That would make the most sense."

"And if we touch the wrong thing, we become part of this place forever? We die?"

"Perhaps."

Dirk laughed. "That's all you can offer us? Fucking risking our lives for *perhaps*? Jesus Christ on a stick, I actually thought you knew what you were doing for a minute."

"I've been more use than some jumped-up influencer who doesn't even write his own books."

Dirk felt like he'd been struck. How the *fuck* did she know?

His cheeks began to burn fiercely. He willed the heat to go away, but it just seemed to make it worse. It was one thing reliving the flashback in his own mind, quite another to be confronted with it here, with these assholes.

"Whoever said that will be hearing from my lawyers. That's a heavy accusation and I've got a ton of money to throw at making them pay."

She saw right through him, though, a glimmer of power flashing in her brown eyes as she stepped closer. "People say a lot of shit in the creative world, Dirk, it's true. But I work with a lot of writers, and one of them said he recognised some of the cues in your books. Some of the patterns of word use. They were pinched from another author. He figured you'd used AI to draft it. He was right, wasn't he?" Dirk's features tightened, giving him away. She nodded. "All your success boils down to you being famous and failing upwards. You've got nothing else up your sleeve, have you? No talent, no skills. Just a pretty face, some tattoos and bags of fame. I already knew your covers were AI-created. And given what I've heard about your writing, it doesn't surprise me to learn you got some software to spit that out, too."

Dirk's hands formed fists at his sides. A torrent of comebacks raged in his head, ready to spill out.

"Figures," Rakie said, though there was a look of genuine disappointment there. That was perhaps the worst of it. The moment that killed whatever shred of integrity he'd got left.

Never meet your heroes, kid.

"Times change," he said through gritted teeth. "Shit works differently now. I use AI. So what? Everyone does in some way. I just use it to get words down, and it doesn't make me a fraud or a sell-out or a cheat. It makes me *smart*, you dumb fucks. I used the tools to get ahead. To create a career for myself. Sue me!"

"I'm sure somebody will," Alden said, and Dirk almost leapt for him there and then.

Nia's jabbed finger in his chest was enough to keep him where he was, though. Her voice rising in pitch, with strength and fervour.

"You're the worst kind of self-proclaimed artist, Dirk. What you create isn't your own. It doesn't come from within you, it's siphoned off from everyone else – those who actually lived their lives and expressed their experiences in ways only they could. In ways only *people* could. Art is meant to be authentic. All this," she said, gesturing around them, "is who we are. And you play no part in that. You've twisted what art means. You're its antithesis."

Dirk flinched as he felt something hit him. A large splat of cold, icky damp on his cheeks. Putting a finger up to wipe it off, he stared in confusion as it came away in a stringy streak of silver goo.

He looked up. The stars were melting.

The picturesque work of art they'd been placed in was changing, twisting before his eyes. The night sky was darkening, the silver of the stars beginning to run as though paint down a canvas. The moon unravelling.

It wasn't just affecting the sky, either. The craziness was happening all around them. A *crack* like a gunshot went off next to him and he threw his arms across his face, only to realise it was the pedestal with the teddy bear on it that had broken in two. The teddy had fallen into the grass, but what had been waves of green around their feet was decaying into brown mulch, and slowly the toy was sucked into the mud.

The others stared at him as though this was all his fault.

"Fuck you," he snarled.

Nia ignored him, turned to Alden and Rakie. "Go and find what matters to you. Something of great significance, probably related to nature in some way. A lot of this stuff is materialistic, sentimental. Ignore it. I don't think that's what we're looking for. Stuff like the teddy bear is here to trick us, tempt us into screwing this up."

The pair nodded, not even bothering to question the order.

As Nia moved off, Dirk called after her.

"So how will we know what we're looking for? I don't have a fucking favourite tree or anything!"

She didn't answer him.

"Nia, come on, help me!"

"Significance isn't always obvious," she bit back. "Maybe it's a flower or an animal or a nice fucking view. Why don't you use your imagination for once, instead of letting everyone else do the work?"

The four of them spread out. Dirk's eyes wandered over the slowly dying world, the cold fear of panic now a raging typhoon inside him. Was this his fault? Was the revelation of him as a fraud responsible for the destruction of this beautiful world?

Focus, you dick!

Who cared about what was happening. What the fuck was significant to him? He hadn't cared about much in so long. Everything in his life was a temporary hit of dopamine and that was it. One-nighters, social media likes, his fraud of a book hitting lists and being lauded as the latest celebrity success story. There was nothing he could think of that actually *meant* something real.

What was going to get him out of here? He had to think, and think quickly, or the others would all leap ahead of him and he was going to be the one left behind to die.

Unless...

Wait.

He caught sight of Rakie moving from piece to piece as the objects appeared and disappeared from this decaying realm. She was moving away from the other two. Any discomfort over the sudden thought that popped back into his head was short-lived. His survival instinct drowned all else out.

Pretending to be looking at a picture hanging in the air, he took a step in the girl's direction. There was no guilt, no nervousness. Yes, he would rather have left Rakie until the last level. He was a children's author, for fuck's sake. But there were few opportunities presenting themselves to him, and he wasn't going to give up the chance to give the tower what he knew it would demand to let him move upwards. Towards that grand prize. Superpowers and shit.

When he was a god, if he felt benevolent, maybe he'd bring her back.

But if she and the other two found their significance before he did, they'd disappear and leave him to die. He might not even have to die first for them to be able to escape. Perhaps they were at a point in their journey up the tower where, once it knew it had bested him, it would let the others leave.

Perhaps it already knew Dirk had nothing of significance in his life. It was going to let the other survivors go and melt him away with everything else.

No. Fuck *that*. He hadn't come this far to die here.

"Hey, kid, found anything yet?" he said casually.

His footsteps through the wilting landscape had been deliberately soft until he appeared right behind her. There was a painting not far ahead, stuck at an angle in the mud. One that he knew very well. He didn't believe it held any kind of special place in his heart, and it certainly wasn't significant to him, but he knew it was pulled from *his* memory and not the girl's.

Which made it dangerous to her.

"Go fuck yourself," she replied, still looking.

"Look, Rakie, I'm sorry. This is all stressful and I shouldn't have taken it out on you." He moved closer. "But we need to help each other get out of here. What do you think you're looking for? Let me keep an eye out for you."

She grumbled something under her breath. Then said, "There was a flower my mum loved. She had a fresh pot of them in the kitchen window when I was growing up. It was her favourite."

Rakie barely gave him a glance as she explained what they looked like, and he felt a kind of envy of where she was in her life. Where he was no longer. A time of youth, when everything was simple. Where you more easily saw the significance in the things of your existence, before it all got cluttered and confusing with age.

"OK, got it," he said encouragingly. Then, pretending to wander for a moment, he stopped near the painting ahead and gasped. "Wait, do you think *those* are the flowers you're talking about?"

She looked up with a start. "What? Where?"

As she joined him, he put a careful hand on her shoulders, just enough to nudge her forward towards it.

"There, in that big old painting. There's a bunch of flowers gathered in the middle of the scene!"

Such was his enthusiasm, she went like a lamb to the slaughterhouse yard, squelching across the mud with a confused look on her face, before stopping just a couple of steps short. Her hand reached out to the frame of the painting, but she pulled it back. *Smart*, he thought.

Rakie looked back at him.

"I can't see anything in there. Just a horse and cart and lots of mud."

He reached his arm over her shoulder to point at a smudge of what could have been flowers, but were certainly not the ones Rakie was looking for.

"Look closer. That's them, I'm sure of it. That's your ticket out of here!"

The thing about lies was that they were often designed to contain the hope people were looking for. It made them more malleable. More susceptible to believe what they should not.

Rakie should have known better than to trust him. But, then again, he was a beloved celebrity. Who wouldn't fucking trust him?

Sorry, kid, he thought, placing a hand on her back and shoving her forward into the painting.

CHAPTER TWENTY-SEVEN
An Eye on the Future

Alden knew what was going to happen as soon as Dirk moved towards Rakie.

All thought of finding his own significant item left him. He knew he wasn't going to make it out of the tower alive. There were four of them, and three levels left. The maths was so simple even he could figure it out.

It was up to him and Nia to make sure Rakie made it. To protect her from the tower and anything that might harm her.

Including Dirk.

Alden started across the hillside to intercept the author, weaving around the objects that blinked into existence and then popped back out again. The tower was trying to distract him, keep him focused on getting out, but there was no point to any of this if the girl didn't make it. He knew what the man had planned. There was a tension to Dirk's gait, the kind of predatory deliberation that didn't bode well for anybody in his way. He could see the painting he was ushering Rakie towards – a painting she looked confused by. No way was that the item she needed to find.

Alden could have shouted at him, tried to distract him, but he was too far away if his calls went ignored. Which he knew they would be.

Shit.

He picked up the pace.

The grass had become mud and was slick and sticky. Once or twice, Alden felt his boots slipping, but somehow kept his balance. A distant part of him realised it was raining, fat droplets of blue water. Paint? The beauty of the world was disappearing, being washed away. Perhaps Dirk was the catalyst. Perhaps this was his level, after all, and the revelation that he had risen on the crest of a wave that wasn't his to ride had been made real by the tower. Art destroyed in real time by the corruption and taint in its presence.

Alden wondered if his own exit was going to be around for much longer. Maybe his significant item had already disintegrated. Vanished. Leaving him stranded.

Doesn't matter. Save her.

Dirk was standing behind Rakie. Reaching over her shoulder, pointing to something in the painting they both stood in front of.

Alden tried to run faster.

The author put his hand on the girl's back.

No, you can't, Alden thought desperately. *You can't!*

Dirk pushed her.

Alden bundled into him from the side, knocking him flying down the hillside. But he made sure to grab Rakie by the shoulders and bring her with him as they flew past the edge of the frame. He let go almost immediately once he knew she was safe, and he scrambled to his feet.

"What the f–" Rakie groaned from the ground, then, glancing up at him, "Look out!"

Dirk came at Alden from behind. A coward's attack and Alden should have known it was coming. He'd been in a lot of the rougher pubs across Manchester with his band and witnessed his fair share of fights. But he'd never actually been in one.

After the impact of the author's shoulder in his upper left back, feeling like it cracked a couple of his ribs, he knew that was about to change.

Dirk's face was twisted with rage, the real him bubbling to the surface.

"You little fucking turd. You rancid, poisonous, soy boy cuck. I was only doing what needed to be done. What you don't have the balls to do."

Dirk threw his fists, one after the other, and Alden only just managed to swing clear of both, gasping as pain erupted down the left side of his chest, beneath the skin. Movement, even breathing, was agony.

He retreated as Dirk stalked towards him like a jungle cat. The children's author might not have been able to sacrifice Rakie to the tower, but it looked like that didn't matter. He was going to kill Alden instead.

"You shouldn't have stopped me," Dirk snarled, his lips curling and flecks of spit flying everywhere. "I'm going to throw you face first into whatever I can here. Let the tower do what it wants with you. This entire time you've been a know-it-all prick and it'll be a pleasure burying you where you belong – with all the other pieces of shit created by people who died poor, not smart enough to get what they deserved. You don't represent humanity, you silly little fuck. You don't represent *me*." Dirk raised his fists again. Sweat glistening against the tattoo on his chest as his T-shirt pulled lower. "I am so much more than you'll ever be. I took what life had to offer and I made it mine. Can you say that? No, of course you can't! Whoever built this tower wanted to find the best of us, and that ain't you. It's not the poor, starving teacher who isn't good enough to make it big in his band. It's people like me. The winners in this life, who do whatever it takes to get ahead. *That's* what being human is all about. And I'm going to win this, not you."

He flung out another attack. Alden slipped in the mud, unable to get out of the way. The knuckles snapped his jaw sideways, along with the rest of his face. He fell backwards, narrowly avoiding a plinth with a wood carving of a fox on it.

"Life isn't about winning," Alden moaned from the ground, spitting blood into the sodden, paint-stained soil. His fingers sank into the mulch as he struggled to get upright. "You've got it all wrong."

"That's what *losers* always say. Face it, you're done here. And as soon as I've finished with you, I'm going to finish the other tw–"

Alden pushed himself up as fast as he could. It was messy, slippery, but he got enough purchase to leap with as much power he could into Dirk's midriff. They went flying for yards, then collapsed in a heap, before Alden pushed himself up just enough to knee the author in the balls.

"You're not going to get near them," he shouted into Dirk's face, letting the anger surge through him, before cracking him again with a punch. There was a satisfying snap of cartilage and a spray of blood across his once-white shirt as Dirk's nose broke. The man moaned and swore, before Alden hit him again. "*You* don't get to decide this. They do. They will go on. You won't. I swear to whatever gods brought us here, I won't let you leave, you talentless hack."

"Fuck you." Dirk spat into Alden's face, trying to kick him off. Alden held firm, though, one hand on the man's shoulder, the other raining down punches. Leia had shown him the way. His grief and loneliness had become his strength.

Even as Dirk cracked Alden's damaged ribs and he fell off, even as the man got up and kicked Alden hard in the thigh, then in the stomach, Alden kept channelling his pain into rage. He sprang up and went in again, grabbing Dirk's T-shirt and pulling him forwards, yelling into his face.

"No, fuck *you*! This life isn't about winners versus losers." He smacked him hard in the stomach. "This isn't about you versus us. It was only ever supposed to be about us, together." He pulled Dirk up to face him again. "And you fucked everything up!"

Alden pushed him just far enough away to get a final shot in, then swung in from the right.

Dirk's face shuddered and he fell sideways, eyes rolling back up in his head as he landed hard in the paint.

Only then did Alden let himself go. He fell back on his behind, chest on fire, lungs burning, knuckles bleeding and bruised. His throat sore from screaming.

Two shadows appeared over him, and he hoped it was the tower come to claim him. He was done. Over this. He'd stopped Dirk from doing the unthinkable and that was enough. Fuck. He was so tired. His body hurt.

It was time to rest.

He looked up through eyes stained with tears and paint.

Rakie and Nia leaned down to lift him to his feet. Pulled him into a hug.

The girl was weeping into his shoulder, whatever grief she'd been storing up bursting forth into him. Nia was silent, but her squeeze was fierce and she pressed into him, lightly kissing his cheek.

In that moment, Alden felt the colour inside him once more, gentle tangles of connection growing and pulling him back to the bigger picture, the world that grief had stolen him away from.

He'd let Leia's loss be the flood that swept away the foundations of everything he'd built. The void within him, probably the same that lay within everyone, a place of fear and disconnect and emptiness, had expanded unchecked – and created an inward pull so powerful, he had collapsed upon himself like a dying star.

The tower had shown him that grief and love were two sides of the same coin. It showed him his grief and allowed it to guide him back to love.

He'd forged a new family here.

Nia touched her forehead to his. Her breath soft on his skin, her words full of warmth and comfort. It felt so damn good.

"We have to get out of here, Alden. You good?"

He nodded, unable to speak. His jaw was swollen, his lips burst and full of blood. Everything hurt.

The three of them pulled away from each other. Alden looked down at Dirk to ensure the bastard wasn't going to surprise them, but the beloved celebrity children's author was still lying unconscious in the mud, where he deserved to be.

"Dickhead," Rakie said, as they walked away.

The tower could be a place of great cruelty, Alden had discovered. Yet as the three of them wandered the remnants of this painted world, he also saw it deliberately giving those in its midst what they needed to survive. All this time, it had tried to kill them, while simultaneously offering clues and direction, and even hope.

That's life, he thought.

He felt a shift in the energy of the place – a sense that good had won against greed.

A vase of flowers appeared directly in front of Rakie. She yelped in surprise, before her eyes went wide as she seemed to recognise them. A quick look back to Nia and Alden confirmed she'd found what she needed. Nia gave her a smile and a nudge to be quick.

Whispering something about her mother under her breath, Rakie grabbed them and vanished.

Nia and Alden had barely taken another couple of steps before they came across the wooden carving of a fox Alden had nearly clattered into earlier. A sad smile of recollection claimed Nia's lips, lighting her up with a pure glow Alden couldn't help but stare at with love. The purest, sweetest love of friendship.

Nia reached for it, then stopped herself.

"We should find yours first," she said, putting her hand on his arm.

But he slipped out of her grip and stood back.

"I'll be fine. You go."

"Alden, you can barely stand! Let's not do this."

"The only thing that matters now is Rakie," he said. "You need to go and make sure she doesn't go on alone. I'll find my way out of here. There's still time to find what I need."

"Alden–"

"Please?"

He held firm and Nia could tell he wasn't going to be swayed. So her hand reached for his and she stared at him for the longest moment, her eyes drifting over his face. It felt like a caress and his agony subsided just enough for him to enjoy it. A final moment of being seen by another. Its own particular kind of magic.

With one final squeeze of his fingers, Nia let go. Touched the fox. And disappeared.

Alden was alone.

He moved slowly, agonisingly. The painted skies continued to rain themselves to darkness. The ground continued to turn to mush. The light grew dimmer with each step and the visions of art around him became more sporadic and spread out.

Finally he couldn't walk any further and he collapsed to his knees, head bowed, fingers pressing into the earth, almost willing himself to sink into the ground and be done with it.

Which is when he saw it.

Just a small thing. A green shoot of hope in the mire.

A tiny four-leaf clover.

He was beset by a strong memory: that class of kids he'd had to leave when he'd moved schools. That little girl who'd looked at her friends, who all nodded, and who silently agreed to get off her stool and come to the front of the class, to hand him the four-leaf clover she'd found on the school field that day.

"For good luck, sir," she'd said.

He'd been left standing there like a dork, unable to believe the gesture she'd made on behalf of them all. A drop of time in their day, a moment he'd never forget in his life.

He'd taken that delicate clover back home, twirling the stem between his fingers as he stared at it at his kitchen table, before slipping it into a fold of tracing paper, which he then pressed into the middle of one of his favourite childhood books.

A memory, preserved for all time.

One of his favourites.

Alden reached out to touch the clover. Not to pluck it, but just to feel, even for a moment, that connection again.

His finger carefully brushed a petal.

And he felt himself carried away.

Dirk woke, feeling like he'd drunk an entire fucking writers' conference worth of alcohol.

Then he remembered why he ached from face to feet and he groaned loudly, feeling blood bubble from his lips as he did so.

Fuck. He couldn't move. He didn't *want* to move. So he lay there in the muddy paint and opened his eyes to see the last vestiges of *The Starry Night* rain down upon him.

There was no sound anymore. No wind carrying music, no swishing of the grass or chirp of bird song, or anything like that.

There were no voices, either. No footsteps. Whispers. Breathing.

He was alone.

He began to cry. The tears finally given permission to escape. His bravado broken and his insecurities laid bare, allowing him one final act of humanity. He was alone and he was going to die, and fucking hell, he was scared, he didn't want to go, but the stars had fallen away and the darkness creeping over him was as empty as it had ever been.

The void had claimed the art and beauty of this world.

Now it would claim the taint at its centre.

Dirk shifted against the mud, feeling it sucking him in. A

last sob fought its way up his throat before the paint of this world flowed down it, and he began to choke and struggle as he was swallowed whole.

The sound of his own fear was the last thing he ever heard.

CHAPTER TWENTY-EIGHT
Different Paths

Alden woke in another meadow.

This one wasn't painted. There was no music on the breeze and no swirling stars above him. No artefacts of any kind of significance popping into existence and fading away around him.

It might as well have been a hillside back in the Peak District, where the grass was sporadic across the peaty moors and broken up with clutches of pinky-purple heather and clumps of moss. Where the wind was chilly and strong, buffeting you with reminders that it was just you and nature, and nature was stronger.

He sat up slowly, cursing the pain he'd carried with him from the last level. His ribs were definitely broken, maybe his jaw, too. Dirk might have been older, but he was fitter and taller, and he had left Alden a mess.

Groaning, Alden blinked away tears and looked around for Nia and Rakie. He couldn't hear anything, so assumed they'd maybe walked away to get a feel for their surroundings.

Not so.

The diagonal horizon was grey and empty. A fine mist clung to the lush countryside hill he found himself on and there was nothing of note breaking the immediate view. No figures standing around.

Nia and Rakie weren't here.

Shit.

He got up and spun in awkward circles, clutching his chest like some wheezy old man.

"Nia? Rakie?" He cleared his throat. "*Nia! Rakie!*"

Nothing.

"Anyone out there? Hello?"

The echoes fell short of the mist holding fast on all sides, Alden's words daring to go no further, as if something bad lurked beyond the grey curtain.

Or perhaps there was no further to go.

He didn't care so much that he was alone, but his worry grew for his friends. If they had all touched the right items in the painting, they should have all been brought here together. Why weren't they here too? Had he done something wrong? Was the clover not the right choice?

Don't panic, he told himself. *Hold it together. You found the item meant for you.*

Which left… what, exactly?

They must have been taken somewhere else. Perhaps their own separate levels.

Maybe they've been let out?

Alden wished it might be so, but he couldn't imagine it being that easy. As for this place, that he was still in the tower he had no doubt. He could feel it. There was a familiarity to this hillside, but everything about it just felt slightly off, inauthentic. You could *feel* nature when you were out in it. The sense of immersion in the wild, the insects in the ground, the birds in the sky, the chittering and chattering of creatures, the rustle of the grass and bushes and trees, and the howl of the wind through it all.

The gusts pushing across the mist, blustering past him and

whipping at his clothes with teasing hands, were powerful, but carried little life about them.

Alden set to walking. He chose to climb up the hill, rather than down. He supposed there was some unconscious part of the design that made him decide that, but he didn't care to think about it. Who really knew? He felt like walking up and the tower had probably known that he would. Which meant he was going the right way.

Step after step, over fallen stones and across small brooks of fast-flowing but silent water, Alden climbed the hillside, wondering just how far he might be rising above this fake, artificially generated landscape should that mist ever clear.

It didn't, though. In fact, it seemed to be following in his wake. Whenever he looked back, there was the exact same distance between him and the line of grey. It was eating up the greenery as he moved, never catching up, but not falling behind either. Had he not been paying attention, he might have thought he hadn't moved at all.

"I see you," he called to it.

The mist didn't respond.

But unless his eyes were playing tricks, there was a glimpse of a shadow within it.

Nia woke on cobbles, to the sound of Christmas music.

It was cold and there was frost on the surface of each stone around her. She blinked and pushed herself upright, taking care not to slip.

"Nia?"

Rakie was already up and standing next to her. The girl reached down to help Nia to her feet and the pair then stared at where they'd arrived.

It was a market, resplendent with hundreds of stalls, each decked out with all kinds of festive decorations. Holly and ivy hung from store façades, with bunches of mistletoe draped over awnings. All set on cobbles that led up to a distant outline of a mansion. A house she knew well, nestled as it was in the hills of the Peak District.

"Chatsworth," she said, half confirming it to herself, half explaining it to Rakie. "These are the Chatsworth Christmas markets. I came here once. With a friend."

"I remember when we first got to the tower, I heard you tell my dad you didn't have friends," Rakie said.

"Jesus, you've got a good memory," Nia said with a smile. She shrugged a little. "But this… This friendship was a long time ago. A different time."

They began to walk around, and Nia realised she couldn't see the estate beyond the stalls. The house took up one side of the area, its sandstone façade tall and imposing. But the stalls were low, short, and she knew from memory that in the distance in the other direction, there should be rolling green fields, a bridge, a river at the centre of the valley, and clumps of wooded areas rising on the other side.

There was nothing. They were completely encircled by cloud.

There was also nobody else here. Not on the stalls and not meandering between them.

"Alden?" Nia called out in panic, annoyed she hadn't noticed his absence sooner. They usually landed all together in each level. Had he not made it to his object? Had he not been able to escape the level? "Alden!"

No response.

"Do you think he died?" Rakie asked.

Nia shook her head, defiantly ignoring the seeds of doubt in her mind. "No, I saw him and he was OK. A little battered after the fight, but he told me to escape. He wouldn't have done that unless he was confident he could find his own way out. Alden wouldn't have given up. He would have made it. I promise you."

"OK, so where is he?"

"I wish I knew. Maybe we should look around. He could have appeared anywhere around here. Maybe in a stall, behind one, in the cloud somewhere."

She knew she was clutching at straws, but they had come too far for her to give up on him. They were friends.

Friends. It seemed a strange word for her to use about anyone these days. A little distant and almost unrecognisable, like a half-faded memory. But that's what they had become.

What's more, the bright, festive market was reminding her this had been the place she and another friend had come, once upon a time. Saanvi. Perhaps her greatest friend. Certainly the last she remembered having.

They had spent a beautiful day here, wandering the market, buying way too much arts and crafts and artisan foods. Laughing and joking and having the very best time, as the winter sky darkened and the Christmas lights grew with fervour.

It had been the last time Nia had enjoyed another's company, before that person had subsequently disappeared from her life. Not taken away in an accident or by illness, but simply carried away by other friends and priorities and distractions. That was probably the worst of it. The friendship had died through neglect. Saanvi's and her own.

"Oh," she said, as she happened across one stall filled

with wooden frames and carved animals within them. "You again?"

It was the fox from the last level.

The shadows in the mist remained as Alden continued walking.

He could see them flitting around him. Sometimes distinct, sometimes barely a flicker of life. But they *were* life. They weren't quite of the mist, but seemed images reflected through it. The grey shroud had a feeling of being impassable, a place he could not venture, so it was likely the beings weren't *in* there. Rather, the tower was letting him glimpse the others in their own versions of this level.

For a second he could see the shapes of Nia and Rakie, and was overcome with a flood of relief. They were side by side, although where they were he couldn't tell. Didn't matter. He didn't need to call out. At least they were together. The girl wasn't alone and for that he was grateful. Perhaps the tower had deemed her in need of a guardian of sorts. A protector.

Then the next shadow appeared, this time one of multiple limbs flinging out in all directions, swinging across the mist, carrying the scaled body in its centre. The alien that had helped them out of the space gardens! Alden was strangely relieved to see it was still alive, though the tension in him grew, knowing they were still up against the others. What if that wasn't the only contestant left?

He wanted to shout out to Nia and Rakie to hurry, find whatever they needed, and get to that last level. But they were already gone. Soon, so was the friendly alien.

The cold grew in his gut as it was replaced by another fleeting shadow.

A single Eyeball Head. The shape of it all too distinct within the mist, enough that Alden was unable to help the nauseous shiver when he saw the eyeball silhouettes bounce around on their stalks.

He slipped backwards involuntarily, trying to get away from it.

The noise of his movement carried.

The eyeballs turned his way.

It was the same fox as the previous level, but that's not why Nia was staring at it so intently.

It was because this was the gift Saanvi had bought her, from this very same stall. A symbol of friendship and love and companionship. Bloody hell, it was so lifelike, it was almost as though Nia had been thrown back in time, to that exact moment and place in her life.

She had been so taken aback by the gesture, perhaps more than the gift itself; it had punctured her emotional shell and truly hit home. It had been one of the few times in her life she'd felt cared about. Which was perhaps why, when the friendship drifted, it had left a gaping wound behind that festered and spoiled. Enough to cause Nia never to open up again. To keep her head down, avoiding social situations and the hell of other people.

Until the tower had forced her together with a whole bunch of them.

"Nia, are you OK? Is that fox what we're here for?"

Nia honestly didn't know. There was a chance, perhaps, but this fox wasn't as vibrant as the one in the previous level and she knew what that meant. It wasn't a focus of the design. It must just be a reminder, a token marker, nothing more.

"I'm sorry," she said. "No, I don't think that's what we need. Yes, it means a lot and it *is* significant. But I get the feeling it's not our goal right now. Plus, it's my thing. And we're here together." She gestured to the entirety of the markets. "This is *all* me. It's my memory, I think? Unless your dad ever brought you here?" The girl shook her head and Nia gave her a smile. "Right, then. We need to find something that speaks to both of us. Something that carries weight for you as well as me. Deal?"

"What might that be, though?"

"Honestly, kid, I've no idea. I guess we should keep looking?"

Rakie looked up at her. "For Alden, too?"

"Yeah, for Alden, too."

Yet as they walked some more, slipping over the cobbles from stall to stall, Nia suddenly understood they weren't going to find him. Because as she turned, she caught a glimpse of his lean, slightly dishevelled figure between two of the stalls, shimmering through the surrounding cloud.

A vision in the mist.

"Alden!" she called, before realising what she was doing. Could he even hear her in there?

Rakie pulled up at her side and gasped with relief at the sight.

"Alden, it's us," she yelled, jumping up and down and waving. "Over here! We're at these markets."

But if he heard them, he showed no sign. And although Nia wondered if he might see them, his face was fixed in one direction, staring at something beyond the stalls that they couldn't see.

He turned and flitted away into the grey.

Fucking hell, she thought. She missed having him around, the togetherness she felt when he was near. Somehow he had slipped under her skin. He was a good friend and she didn't like being here without him. Nor did she like the idea that he was somewhere else in this hell palace, alone, without them to back him up.

Rakie's shoulders sagged. "Shit," she said. "Where'd he go, Nia?"

"I think the tower let us see that he's alive. Maybe he's in another part of this level."

"Can we get to him?"

"Maybe," Nia said, unwilling to admit she didn't think they could. "But for now we need to focus on our own goal here. We have to keep moving." She looked around the stall with the fox, but the other cabins were all beginning to grow more indistinct, as though someone was turning down the brightness on their display. The only life was the lit path away from the market, through the wall of the stately home and into the garden.

Nia remembered: that's where she and Saanvi had gone after the market, for a wander around the festive lights that illuminated the path through the estate. A path that had taken them into the maze. It was at its centre that she had been given the fox as a gift.

She and Saanvi had only ever been just friends, nothing more. But the gesture was as sweet as a marriage proposal, and certainly Nia had been as happy as if it had been. It was a moment of pure friendship that in that moment meant everything to her.

The memory lingered, taking root in her mind.

"We need to get to the maze," Nia said, gesturing for Rakie to follow her towards the lights. "Come on, the sooner we get out of here, the sooner we can see Alden again."

CHAPTER TWENTY-NINE
The Last Leaf to Fall

Alden watched the eyeball alien push against the wall of mist.

Then it lifted the weapon it was carrying and fired, and a wisp of cloud drifted away from the impact zone.

It's coming through, he thought. *Should that even be possible?*

But it was all possible here. That was the point. And to his surprise, he wasn't panicking. What really was there to panic about now? He'd found what he needed through the tower. Friendship, family and purpose, allowing him the chance to feel himself again.

All that was beyond this creature's reach, even if it could break through. And despite what he'd been through along this ridiculous, horrifying journey, he wasn't afraid anymore. He was alone, facing death, yet he felt nothing but peace.

"About fucking time," he said to himself, and laughed.

He stayed where he was, balanced on a rock on that hillside, making sure the alien knew he wasn't scared and wasn't going to run. He watched the creature shoot again and again, causing more of the mist to dissipate. Then he turned his back on the nightmare and began up the hill again. If there was more blaster fire, he didn't hear it. He didn't really care now. This place was his. A calm in the storm of life. The eye of the tower.

As he climbed, pushing through the scratchy heather, wading through brooks, and stepping around rugged boulders of all shapes and sizes, the sense of familiarity about where he was grew. This place was home, like any of the hills in the Peak District. But it was more than that. There was a sense of direction to his route, a path ahead, though he couldn't see it. It was felt. Instinct.

Somehow he knew where he was going.

A tree soon came into view ahead, lifting its arch of twisted, wintry branches above the horizon until the thick, curved trunk revealed itself. He realised it was the oak on the hill he'd frequented with Leia. The walk he had often taken up the slope and through the fields behind his house.

This tree was different, but the same. Taller, stronger, yet it had the same knots in its trunk and the hole in the upper branches where he knew an owl often resided. He knew that because Leia had sat on her haunches and barked at it incessantly one evening, and the thing had got scared and flew off to hoot accusations at them from an old gatepost nearby.

Alden might not have been panicked or afraid, but he felt the pinch of sadness.

This is where we came for our last walk, he thought.

Blinking away tears, he kept focus on the tree and moved towards it until he was able to place a hand on its bark, as if greeting an old friend.

That's when he realised the branches weren't completely bare. Not any longer.

There were three leaves left. Each a curious swirl of amber and ruby, like the deepest autumn colours. Three curled sunsets waiting for their time to fall.

One for each of the humans left.

"They're still alive," he said.

The sadness was tempered once more and he began to smile, knowing Nia and Rakie were on the other side of that mist somewhere.

He knew they would make it to the top. They'd been the smartest ones on this journey. And if the tower wanted proof that humanity still had worth and value, Alden knew they were the ones who deserved to pass the test. To save themselves, to save everyone.

Maybe even every*thing*.

He was still smiling when he heard the rustle of the grass behind him.

Alden turned calmly, expecting death. For that's all he seemed to find.

Yet it was Leia.

His beautiful dog was padding up the hill towards him. No longer the beast from the last level, who had saved them from the goblins, a manifestation of the strength of his grief and anger. No, this was the Leia he knew and loved. Who he'd raised from a troublesome puppy and had been around for every day of her life. She was smiling, as she always was after a run – she *loved* running, it was her favourite thing – and then she paused to tilt her head at him.

Alden broke down as he fell towards her, happiness and sadness clashing in a starburst of emotions. Leia sped into a trot and ducked her snout under his outstretched arms, to get at him. She whined with joy, excitement and love, licking and nuzzling him wherever she could, while he grabbed handfuls of her black-and-white fur and buried his face into the softness of her neck.

She pushed her head against him hard and he fell back on his behind with laughter, even as the tears streamed down his cheeks. Then she pawed at him and climbed immediately onto his lap, though she was far too big for it. Curling around in circles, she eventually collapsed in a ball, her head resting on his chest, gazing up at him.

"I missed you, too," he whispered, trying to catch his breath. The weight of loss lifted from him for a glorious moment. "Thank you for not leaving me."

The horizon to his right suddenly burned a bright gold. A sliver of sunset light that burst across the grassy hillside, burning away the mist and beckoning him onwards.

The tower wanted him to complete the climb.

To reach the final level.

Leia nuzzled his chest one final time, then slipped from his lap and out of his grasp. She didn't disappear, though, merely pulled away a few steps and waited for him to leave.

Alden got to his feet. Glanced towards the light, then back to Leia. Then to the mist which was still surrounding them on all the other sides.

He could see the figure of the alien growing more distinct by the second. In fact, he could even hear the screech of the blaster as it continued to burn a hole towards him. Whatever barrier the mist had formed was being broken by the rage and hatred and need to kill of the creature beyond it.

Alden knew he needed to leave at that moment, if he was going. He could get out of there and reach the final level, and humanity might yet be saved. All he needed to do was step over the hill and enter the light beyond the tree.

He looked back to the three leaves.

* * *

Nia and Rakie hurried along the gravel path, through the gardens of Chatsworth House, passing majestic statues and waterfall steps and pristine lawns.

That bloody cloud followed their every move.

Nia wished it would leave them alone and disappear, if only so she could see Rakie's face take in the stunning countryside. It had never failed to delight her when she visited, and she figured the girl could use a distraction from the torment of what Nia knew she must be feeling.

The girl, though, was hardy. Had proven it this entire time and carried the same courageous spirit her father had shown. She was still upright, when many would be slumped. She hadn't complained or whined, where the others had constantly. She was a joy of a person, and Nia was honoured she'd been chosen by the tower to watch over her in this level.

The tower needed her to have a guardian, she thought. *Even the tower knows that's how the circle of life should work.*

"It's growing darker," Rakie noted, as they entered the rock garden. Stones as big as cars dominated this little enclave of the estate, with a slick waterfall down a rockface that was the centrepiece. Yet the flow had reduced to a trickle and the girl was right – it was much darker around them.

"We don't have much time," Nia said. "The maze is close. Let's hurry."

They picked up the pace, Rakie making far less work of it than Nia. But then again, Nia was in her forties, didn't get out much, and spent her time in front of screens, poring over pads, drawing and designing. Maybe she could have made more of her time. Spent it better than she had. Got out and kept fit instead of retreating from the world.

I gave up control of my life, as well as those in it.

It was a difficult thing to tell herself, she thought, as they made for an arched stone gateway, but it was no less true. After Saanvi, Nia had shut herself off, stopped herself from getting out where people were. Disconnecting from a world where she felt helpless, adrift on the currents of other people's decisions and actions. She'd lost so much of her life, so much potential goodness and joy, because she had allowed herself to feel so damn afraid and out of control. The tower had shown her what was possible. That she had the power to decide for herself where her fate lay, if only she faced the fear and took the risks. Because this was all part of the journey. It was all part of life itself.

They emerged from the arch into another part of the gardens and the maze rose ahead. The walls were taller than in reality. Exaggerated and more imposing, especially in the deteriorating light. Menacing and full of danger, a world of the unknown awaiting them, so much so that she felt her spirit weaken. She wanted to retreat again, to withdraw from this place, into herself, away from the risks of being at the whim of the tower.

No, she told herself. *Not this time.*

"Rakie?" The girl looked up at her as they paused at the entrance. "It's going to get dark in there, kid, but stick with me and I'll get us to the centre while we can still see. Then let's get the hell out of here into that last level. Deal?"

Rakie nodded. Nia offered her hand and the girl took it, her fingers warm within Nia's grasp. She was responsible for this human being. And as much as it might have worried her in the real world, right now it buoyed her confidence to take charge.

She led them in.

It was darker in the maze than she'd expected. For a moment she wondered if this had been a mistake and this was where they were both going to die. But soon her eyes adjusted just enough to allow her to discern the path in the gloom. Enough for them to keep moving.

"Hurry," she whispered, not wanting to speak too loudly for fear of calling monsters their way. For there must surely be monsters in the dark. There always were. "Left up ahead, then right, I think."

"Do you actually know where you're going?"

Nia knew there was no way she could remember the directions through the real-life maze, but she'd always been good at picking them apart. Been able to put herself into the mind of their designers, working out the path she might have created to lead to the centre.

Of course, nobody was perfect, and after turning left, then right, they immediately hit a hedge wall.

"I guess not as well as I thought," she said to the girl as they backtracked. But she wasn't dissuaded from carrying on. "Keep moving. The light's getting worse, if that's possible, but I promise you we'll get there. There will be wrong turns, but we'll keep going. Come on, Rakie. We can do this."

The minutes felt like hours, time dragging out in the overwhelming nothingness that had Nia wondering if they'd been swallowed whole by the void between levels. Maybe they'd end up doing this forever? Only the feel of the ground beneath her trainers – hard and uncompromising and full of the twists and turns of roots trying to trip them up – kept her from spiralling into panic. They were still in the level. Still in the maze. They *could* do this.

Until, finally, after eons more walking, arms stretched out to follow the path, and several more wrong turns, Nia realised they were moving in smaller circles. Closing in on their goal.

That's when she saw a glow nearby. A real light, not some trick of her mind.

The brave adventurers had taken the risk, and the maze was guiding them to their goal.

When they eventually took the last turn and saw the light spilling through the gap ahead, Nia almost cried with relief. Shoring herself up, she ushered Rakie along beside her, until the pair stepped through to where they needed to be.

It was not quite as she remembered at Chatsworth. In reality, there was some kind of statue here. Something to climb on, to shout to everyone else that you'd made it. A reflection of how life seemed to be in the social media age, she'd always thought.

But this space was devoid of statues or ego.

They were enclosed by the towering hedge, but the smothering darkness was being held back by a glorious beacon in the form of an old-fashioned lamppost. The kind that might stand at the entrance to Narnia, leaning crooked but proud, its fire a symbol of hope and warmth to any who might venture across it.

And directly beneath the light was a tree.

But not any tree. It was *her* tree. A bookshelf in the shape of a towering tree she had designed many years ago for Saanvi, in return for the fox. A gift created with her own hands – the first time she had ever brought her designs to life.

Even here, in this unreality of the tower, she recognised so much of herself in it. The memories contained in its creation. The shelf in the trunk that had almost cost her a finger to cut out. The sweep of the three branches that would hold the books, but only after it had taken several attempts and more than a month to get right. It was the purest labour of love. A Tree of Life, which might well store the books her friend loved to read, but also represented more than that. It signified friendship, the roots of which could and should be enduring, even when you couldn't see them.

It gave Nia heart to think Saanvi might still have this in her home. Maybe she looked at it still and thought of their friendship. Nia hoped so. It didn't mean a thing that they were no longer in contact. Their roots had been strong enough to endure the drought, she was sure of it. All they needed was a little watering from time to time.

She resolved not to let that opportunity slip by again if they made it out of here.

Rakie stepped closer to the piece and Nia let her go, knowing they were safe.

The girl pointed to the bottom of it. "Another fox?"

Nia smiled and nodded.

It was. Similar to the one her friend had bought her at the markets. It was their little sign to each other.

The girl then squealed and jumped up and down in shock and delight, pointing to the few books the carved tree held in its curling limbs.

"Look at them, Nia! It's *my* name on them. It's *my* name! These are my books!"

Nia's eyes widened as she bent down to study the spine of one of them, realising Rakie was right. It was her name.

"Holy crap, Rakie. You wrote these?"

"No. I mean, I always wanted to be a writer, Nia. But I've never written an actual book. I've only written little things. Short stories. A few poems. Scribbles in notebooks. Never anything like this."

"This is why you were gaga over Dirk when you first met him?"

Rakie stuck two fingers in her mouth and pretended to gag. "I thought he was a role model. His books were only OK, but he was famous, so I figured he must be a great writer. Stupid, huh?"

Nia placed a hand on her shoulder. "No, not stupid. He fooled a lot of people who should have known better. People who will happily be fooled by fame. But don't worry about him now, Rakie. He's gone and doesn't matter. *This* is what's important. Look at all your books! I think the tower is telling us your future is bright!"

The pair grinned at each other, until Nia noticed something on the tree. A part of it that wasn't of her making.

The original had been formed of a trunk and branches curling outwards like waves. And those branches all had carved leaves in the wood, maybe twenty of them in total. All small and not entirely significant.

This version of the tree carried only three leaves. All distinct, with the most exquisite detail. And they were so delicately carved, they looked as though they were a splinter or two from falling away.

"Those are us, aren't they?" Rakie said. "Three leaves. Three of us left?"

Nia didn't answer. Because, as she watched, one of them broke free.

It drifted slowly, falling as though in a dream.

And her heart broke.

She knew what that meant. They both did. Neither said a word, too saddened to speak, only able to stare helplessly and imagine what must have happened.

Nia wanted to cry, but she couldn't. She mustn't. This

was on her – and her alone. She had to get Rakie out of this bloody tower. That was all that mattered. Rakie's future.

"Touch your leaf," she told the girl softly.

Rakie moved, but only to pick up the fallen leaf and slip it into her jacket as she had been doing the entire time. Nia's eyes welled up at the act, knowing the girl was collecting their memories. Making sure they weren't forgotten.

Then they held hands and both reached out.

"Ready?" Rakie said, fingers hovering over her escape.

"Ready," Nia replied, doing the same.

They touched the two hanging leaves and moved to the last level.

Alden stared at the leaves, dazzling brightly in the light over the hill.

You can get out of here, he told himself, that old survival instinct kicking in. *Grab your leaf and live!*

But he did not. He let his gaze linger for only a moment, picturing all the things his future might hold if he just reached out, before he spun around slowly and sat down again, resting his aching back against the mossy trunk.

He beckoned Leia over. She came willingly.

The mist seemed to be drawing in around the tree, no longer maintaining its respectful distance. Still the alien attacked it, and was quickly breaking through.

Alden knew if he reached up to touch any of the leaves, he would have been able to get away and escape the creature's wrath. But then Nia or Rakie wouldn't have been able to leave. The tower still needed its sacrifice. Three had entered this level. In separate places, but still…

Only two would be able to leave.

He wasn't about to take Nia or Rakie's place. And he wasn't about to leave before them, and let the alien turn its wrath to finding and killing them instead.

Alden pulled Leia into his lap again, gave her a tickle behind her ear and a kiss on her snout.

"You OK, girl?"

She responded with a lick up his cheek and curled up into a ball again. She had always been far too big to sit on him comfortably. But this felt so good, he didn't care. He rested his hands on her back, holding her tightly, and she gave that long, deep sigh of contentment he'd always loved. He felt the relief of it flow through his entire being.

"Yeah, I'm OK, too," he said happily.

Together, they remained under the tree. Watching as the alien's colourful blaster finally ran out of juice, but seeing the rip in the mist now big enough for the beast to claw its way through. Alden figured this must be just another part of the tower's design. Perhaps it had known his fate before he had. He wouldn't have been surprised. There was so much about the universe he didn't know, and the thought that he had been chosen to be a player in this interstellar game awed and humbled him, no matter what awaited him.

Maybe that was the point of everything, he thought, stroking Leia's fur, feeling the soft warmth between his fingers. The rise and fall of her breath. The sense of colour returning to him.

Maybe it was just about being born into this blip of a life and simply allowing yourself to experience the wonder of it all, while doing your best with what you had.

If that was the meaning of life, he felt it a good one.

The mist continued to close in rapidly. Even as the alien finally dragged itself through and galloped the short distance towards Alden, its sonic roar reverberating in his bones, he knew the tower's trap was about to be sprung.

The alien had lost its focus. Like Dirk, it wanted to beat the others, rather than seek its goal, which went against everything they had all been brought here to understand. The thing was filled with hate or evil, or simply a desire to kill.

Either way, Alden had allowed himself to be a nice little distraction.

He bent down and hugged Leia tightly, breathing her in one last time.

Then she faded away to nothing, as he'd known she would, and he sat and waited, a smile on his face.

Alone at the end, he thought brightly, accepting his fate as the alien leapt towards him and the mist decided in that moment to swallow them both. *But the others got away.*

That thought was enough to keep him company as the tower finally claimed him for itself.

CHAPTER THIRTY
The Top of the Tower

Nia felt warmth.

Dappled sunlight fell across her face, and with her eyes closed she could see flickering shapes in the rays. The movement of clouds across a sun beating down on her skin.

The only thing was... she felt the heat from three different directions. There was no wind, no sounds of nature, nothing but Rakie's gentle breathing nearby and three sources of light.

She opened her eyes and sat up.

They were in a wide chamber, circular in shape, with a polished floor of crimson stone, a pedestal in the centre, and a domed glass ceiling. A single window wrapped around the entire circumference of the room, and what she saw through it was spectacular.

We're here, she thought, unable to quite believe it. *We made it to the top.*

As she looked straight ahead, she saw home. The real world. The lush green hills of the Peak District, with long stretches of water within valleys, and the towers of Manchester shimmering in the distance. The sun rose above it all in the clearest blue sky, bathing the grass and trees in light and allowing them to shine with the most vibrant colours she'd ever seen. It was a sea of emerald, split by navy waters, on a glorious spring day.

She felt the tears well again and her chest grow tight with need. *Fuck.* After all this time in the tower, not knowing if she'd ever see Earth again, she could hardly believe it was still there. The real world, beyond the glass, continuing to exist even if they hadn't been entirely present in it.

Now it was calling her. Beckoning her back.

"We won," she said, then louder, "Rakie, we *won*! We beat the tower. We–"

"Nia," Rakie whispered, sitting up beside her and staring to the other side.

There was a note of wariness in the girl's tone that made Nia's eyes dart around the window to take in the scope of the view. But as she did, she saw what Rakie had seen.

Everything was not as it seemed.

It was a single window, but the view of the English countryside did not continue all the way around. It suddenly merged into an entirely different view. Of what? That was the question. She could only guess what it must be, but the logical part of her brain was having trouble processing the idea.

It was another place. Another sun. Two of them, in fact. Both drifting through what seemed like a purple sky – but the more Nia stared, the more she realised that "sky" had a tangible quality to it. It was some form of gas. Maybe even liquid.

Creatures of shapes she couldn't begin to describe floated or flew past, while in the distant murk there appeared to be thousands of blinking lights within an undulating pocket of air filled with dark mass. A kind of… bubble city. An impossible place, alive with life.

Nia looked back to the Peak District view and noted a marker of transition between Earth and this other strange underwater world: the same wisp of crimson cloud she had seen wrapping around the tower when it first appeared on Earth.

"Is that another universe?" Rakie asked quietly. "Do you think that's one of the homelands of the other aliens?"

"Yeah, I think it must be."

The pair of them were witnesses to another world. The first humans to look upon a completely alien place, perhaps in another universe, perhaps in another dimension entirely.

One that must have been chosen for this galactic test, just like theirs.

But there were three teams, Nia thought.

She instantly twisted on the floor, following the purple seas around the window, until they crossed another strand of cloud and fell into a whole other land. A chaotic mass of blue and orange mountains filled with movement.

Peering closer, she saw the rippling colours were hundreds of thousands of beings fighting one another across the terrain. Explosions rippled through their ranks. Fire rained down from fearsome machines blanketing the skies.

Nia's mouth gaped as she looked from the hellscape to the bright red star blazing across this world. A star that was beginning to darken.

The light faded over the battlefield below, but the fighting continued. Suddenly the war machines began to spiral out of the air, crashing down into the mountains. The armies raced in all directions, making their escape, but Nia could tell there was no escape to be found. The more the light of the star faded, the more she could see the fissures shooting across it. Flares seeped from them, draining it of its power, until barely anything could be seen other than the fires below.

Nia and Rakie were witnesses to the end of the world. The destruction, in real time, of an entire planet, happening so quickly it was as if someone had flicked the off switch to it.

Then she understood.

This was the answer to the question they had been asking all along.

What happens if we don't reach the top?

In the corner of the chamber, something moved. Nia's heart momentarily stopped and she panic-grabbed Rakie, pulling her back behind her before she leapt to her feet, ready to fight.

There was nowhere to go, but she was determined not to give up the girl.

Then she blinked and saw what was moving.

She took a breath and watched as the octolouse rolled into sight.

Held within a ball of its tentacles, their alien friend seemed not to have seen the humans. Instead, it rolled towards the purple world, caught up in the same wistfulness Nia had felt upon seeing Earth.

As Nia allowed herself a moment to recover, letting go of Rakie a little, the creature finally turned their way. Two limbs lifted and flattened. Nia and Rakie raised their hands. Then the alien went back to staring through the window.

"These are our worlds," the girl said, looking up at Nia. "It's just like Dad said, about that Viking myth, the one with the tree at the centre of the realms. I think... I think this tower is the tree."

"And these are three realms chosen for the challenge?" Nia said.

"Right! Where teams were picked to come here and climb. Or ascend, or whatever. And now we've made it. We're at the top and I guess we get to see what we win."

"Or what we didn't."

Nia gestured to the horrendous catastrophe unfolding in the world to the right of them, unable to help the revulsion at what they were witnessing. The six-legged eyeball aliens had been aggressive and nasty, trying to kill those they were against rather than reach the top. Clearly the team in the tower had all died. But did their entire world deserve this fate? Did any of their fellow beings truly deserve to be blinked out of existence like this, on the failure of those chosen at random?

The tower had chosen thirteen strangers from Earth, among them the likes of Bryan and Mel and Dirk. There had been no logic to those choices that she could see. They were not the best or the brightest, nor the kindest, nor the most compassionate. Those three men had been part of the challenge by accident, and any one of them could have ensured failure and doomed the Earth to destruction.

It didn't seem fair. And yet... it was entirely in keeping with this whole fucking place. With life itself.

History was resplendent with so many instances of failures of leadership – of failures to elect the right leaders in the first place – and the suffering wrought by those who relied on them. Nia often stared at her social media feeds, realising how badly the inhabitants of Earth had screwed up in recent years, and occasionally she had wondered if maybe theirs was simply a flawed world. A place where they hadn't quite got the hang of looking after one another.

Maybe we were the outliers in the universe, because *surely*, there must be others doing it better.

No. It turns out they weren't alone in their struggle.

Yet you're still here, she reminded herself. *You and Rakie made it, with the help of Alden and Earl and the others. You did it together. You survived and showed the tower what humanity was capable of. You ascended!*

Nia took a long, deep breath as the world before her was extinguished with minimal fanfare. As it all went dark, the visions of the two remaining worlds grew around the window to fill the void. Three realms began the challenge. Three species.

Two remained.

Nia felt no sense of threat. No vibe from the tower that they were still in a race. The eyeball alien world was gone and they remained.

"I think we just saved our worlds," she said to Rakie.

But the girl wasn't looking at her. Her face was crinkled in a frown as she peered upwards.

"I don't think it's over yet," she said.

Nia followed her gaze to the dome above, to see those peculiar purple and pink clouds swirling in a circle beyond the glass, an eerie vortex framing a background of stars and spiral galaxies.

Is that where the tower has come from? Is that where it will return when all this is over?

Then Rakie dropped her gaze and Nia did the same. And they both looked more closely at the pedestal in the centre of the room.

It stood about chest height and on it was a shadowy tree, as dark as the vacuum of space above it, from which three leaves of the purest white were hanging.

Nia and Rakie walked over to the tree and stared at the two leaves on their side.

Sensing the time was near, their alien friend slipped across the marble floor, facing them on the opposite side.

Its long, sweeping limbs signed something, pointing to its own leaf – or at least, that's the form it took for Nia; she was sure it must look different to the alien – then it pointed to the plinth, where a small imprint could be seen.

Nia realised she and Rakie had one as well. An imprint on each side.

But just the one on theirs.

Fuck! FUCK!

She began to panic, looking between the girl and the alien. "What do we do?" she asked urgently, knowing full well as soon as the words were out of her mouth that neither of them would have the answers she needed. "There's only one place for our leaf. I don't know what to do?"

The alien repeated its movement, pointing from the leaf to the imprint. Nia nodded. "Yes, I get *that*. We have to put the leaf in there to complete this bloody task. But we have two leaves and only one place to put it!" She gestured to herself and Rakie, and held up two fingers. Then she pointed to the imprint and held up one.

The alien swayed, as if understanding.

But Rakie didn't. "What do you mean?"

"Oh, sweetheart. I'm sorry, I don't really understand what's going on." She sighed. "But it looks like only one of us can do this. Only one of us can press our leaf to end this."

"So what happens to the other one?"

Nia couldn't answer, feeling the panic seize control of her thoughts, the anxiety rush through her body. She began to pace, trying to figure this out. Yet as she did so, the colours of the clouds above her began to grow in ferocity and light, bathing the chamber in an urgent glow. They began to spin faster. Through them, the stars grew brighter.

The tower was telling them time was running out.

They had to make a decision.

For some reason, again the alien didn't leave them. It held fast, regarding them intently, as though waiting around to give them the support they needed.

Rakie understood what it was doing and reached out across the tree. One of the limbs crept across and wrapped around her wrist. Nia held her breath, but nothing happened. Only the gentle touch of a cosmic connection, a fleeting bond between two beings who couldn't have been more different, yet who had survived the tower together.

The pair imprinting on each other was a moment she would never forget, as long as she lived.

One that gave her hope.

"Rakie, take your leaf," Nia said, trying not to let her nerves show.

"What?"

The girl and the alien let each other go. The creature knew what was happening somehow and plucked its own leaf, as if to show Rakie what to do.

Rakie didn't move.

"What about you, Nia? What about your leaf?"

The colours grew more intense around them. It was growing oppressive. Nia could feel the blood thumping in her ears.

She gave the girl a sudden hug. "You need to be the one to put the leaf in, Rakie."

"Wait, what? How do you know?"

"Because I think that's how you show the tower you made it. You need to give it your leaf to prove that you reached the top. That you climbed its terrors and you beat its challenge. You need to connect with it and show it what humanity is made of, to prove you're worthy. That we're all worthy." She pulled back, holding the girl's shoulders. "You're going to save the world."

The atmosphere became thick, the air vibrating.

"What's going to happen to you, though?"

Rakie's voice was quivering.

Nia ignored the question and pointed to the leaf. "Quickly, Rakie. You can do this, I believe in you."

"I don't want to leave you."

Nia's smile widened, and she plucked her own leaf and gave it to the girl. "Then take me with you, OK? Get me out of here."

"I don't think that's how this works—"

"No time to argue," Nia said firmly. "You have to be the one. Grab your leaf now and press it into the stone. Imprint yourself on the tower, Rakie. Show it humanity's strength. Show it how significant you are."

She stepped back. There must only be moments left. The swirls of clouds seemed to be coming *through* the glass above, into the chamber. It was getting difficult to breathe. Whatever was happening, it was happening fast. But Rakie needed to be left to get this done.

"Come on, Rakie!"

The girl stared at her for a moment, tears escaping and running down her cheeks. But she didn't cry. She straightened and turned to the tree.

Plucked her leaf. Held it up to the alien.

Attagirl, Nia thought.

The pair pressed their leaves without hesitation into the stone plinth, and a blinding light erupted from it. Not just light, though. There was life within it. Knowledge. The universal truths of everything, everywhere and everyone. A force of such immense power that Nia was struck blind with the joy and the terror and the love it held.

And in the midst of it, she had a sudden, terrible realisation.

The rules still apply, even here, even at the top.

This is the last level.

"No!" she screamed, a soundless cry into the void that was about to retake the tower. "Noooo!"

It was the anger that carried her through. Anger that allowed her to fight against the intensity of the light and push forward through it, towards the girl. Anger at the tower. Anger at herself.

Ascend, they had been told. The tower had given them the challenge and it had seemed so simple.

But along the way, they had come to know that the tower demanded more of them. It wanted sacrifice. It wanted blood. On each level someone had to die. Which meant that even here, at the pinnacle of the climb, death still lay in wait.

Nia threw herself at Rakie.

She had thought it so obvious that, by stepping back, it would be her death that would sate the tower. Rakie would have her moment, showing the tower she had conquered it.

But what if Nia hadn't been here? What if, like the alien, only one of their group had reached the top. Alone, they would have had to complete the task and press their leaf into the plinth to save their world.

Someone always has to die.

Nia slammed into Rakie, pushing the girl aside. The light was so all-encompassing, time seemed to slow within it. The girl slipped and fell as though through the vastness of space. Her cries of shock echoed distantly. And she let go of the leaf in the pedestal.

Nia's fingers stretched over it instead and pressed down hard, connecting with the tower. With the tree. With the realms beyond and everything that had ever been.

The light intensified until she couldn't see. White fire poured up her fingers. But it didn't matter. She knew what was about to happen, what had been inevitable from the very start.

That whoever made it up here had to sacrifice themselves to save their world.

Death was a part of life, and hadn't that been what the challenge had been designed to test? The meaning of life was not about escaping death. It was about accepting it and living anyway, working hard for the benefit of those who came after, while you fell away. One leaf among a thousand leaves, all falling from a tree in order that it might blossom again.

The tower had demanded they ascend. And the winners would ascend with it. Giving their one little blip of a life for countless millions. The ultimate act of significance.

Nia screamed as the light reached a crescendo and blasted outwards, swallowing the chamber and everything in it. She had given everything she had for this moment.

But in the end, it was worth it.

EPILOGUE

Rakie fell through the light into a blanket of long grass. It shouldn't have been there. What it should have been was the hard floor of the room at the top of the tower. A floor she had been falling towards only a second ago, after Nia had bundled into her.

She sat bolt upright, rubbing her side where she'd been hit.

The grass was spread out across another hillside. But immediately she knew this one was real. This wasn't just another landscape stolen from their brains. She was back home again.

For in the skies above her was the tower, where she had just been. It hung above the Earth like a dagger, lit from behind by the setting sun.

I escaped, she thought almost absently. Then, frowning: *I escaped?*

How? How was she here and not up there? Where was Nia? Was this another trick?

The confusion made her feel sick. Had she done something wrong? She'd been pressing the leaf like she'd been told, so why had she been knocked aside by her friend like that?

Then it struck her.

She was here, in this meadow.

Nia wasn't.

Rakie's mouth gaped in despair as the tower far above began to blink in and out of existence, like a fading transmission. The spooky clouds spinning around it became faster and thinner, before disappearing entirely. Then with a *shwoomp* sound the tower vanished and the rays of the sun blasted through where it had been, lighting up Rakie's meadow.

She threw her hands up to shield her eyes, peering through her fingers to see where the tower had gone. But there was no sign of it. No sign of the tower or her father or Nia or Alden, or any of the people she'd been trapped with inside. It had taken them all.

It was over. They were gone.

This high up on the hill, she could see the city of Manchester sitting quietly, almost lifeless in the distance. She'd heard the others talking about whether they were the last ones left in the world. Right now, it felt possible. Perhaps she was alone now. All alone in this country. Maybe on the entire planet.

Rakie thought she might still be crying, but the heat from the light in the chamber had dried her tears. And despite everything, she felt a strange, sudden quiet inside her.

The meadow was full of life. Bugs sweeping through the air. Bees bouncing from flower to flower. Somewhere a bird cried and was answered by two others. In the woods behind her, she heard an owl.

Am I… dead?

It was a silly thought. She knew that. A silly, ridiculous thought, and one she wouldn't normally pay attention to. But this place was warm and cosy and felt like a dream. It was too nice to be real life. It felt like heaven. Except, she could also feel the realness of it, the sounds and the touch of the wind and the scents of the flowers. Maybe she'd just been in the tower too long? And only now she was out did she see how life had always been.

She stood, letting the breeze from the tower's departure blow across her face and ruffle her jacket and skirt. The branches of the trees behind her creaked and groaned pleasantly, and Rakie turned to see their leaves fall like confetti across the meadow.

It reminded her of something.

Reaching into her pocket, she gathered the leaves she'd collected in her hand.

There were twelve of them. Nia's, the latest, sat on top.

She stood there for the longest time, staring at them, remembering who they'd belonged to. Picturing their faces and smiles and grimaces, and the way they had acted towards her and one another, and the way they had made her feel.

That she was still in the world was down to the sacrifice of them all. Those she had loved and those who had loved her. Those who had been awful and mean and a disappointment. And those with whom a connection had been fleeting.

They had all played their part in protecting the future – her future – and she felt an immense gratitude for that.

She held Nia's leaf up, twirling it by the stem.

Should she keep them?

Dirk would have. To talk about at one of his book events or on Instagram Reels or whatever. Alden might have taught his class about them, or maybe written a song. Nia would probably have drawn them and made them look even prettier than they looked right now.

But Rakie's father?

She knew he would have felt the same way she did. That she had saved them from the tower and brought them back home, and that it would be wrong to hold onto them.

So she pulled each one from her hand in turn and placed it on the ground among the roots of the nearest tree. As she did so, she pressed it into the soft earth and mulch, until it disappeared. She only hesitated once, with her father's leaf, holding it a little longer against her chest before letting go.

The ritual made her feel a little better. It had been the right thing to do. As people had always done with those they cared about, and even those they didn't. She had remembered them. Now they were at rest.

With a sigh, she leaned back against the trunk, looking out across the landscape, this dreamy land where nothing but the breeze and the bugs and the leaves stirred. It was warm in the light, comfortingly so. As she rolled her sleeves up, she noticed the sycamore leaf tattoo had gone from her wrist. Vanished, along with the tower.

She ran her fingers over the tender skin where it had been.

Maybe she'd get another for real one day.

Her eyes grew tired, so she closed them, breathing in the smell of the meadow and listening to the music of the world around her. She reached her hand lazily across to the graveyard of memories, thinking this would be a good place to die.

But as she drifted off, hearing the strange and distant sounds of what seemed like sirens, she knew she was not dead. Not yet.

Life was still stretching out before her, and she intended to live.

ACKNOWLEDGEMENTS

These acknowledgements, to the disappointment of at least one of my friends, will not be that long.

A huge thank you to my editor Eleanor Teasdale, assistant editor Desola Coker, and the wonderful team at Angry Robot for continuing to take a chance on my words and being the very best to work with – and to artist Sarah O'Flaherty for a wonderful cover. Thanks to my agent, Sara Megibow, for being in my corner and constantly pushing me onwards. Thank you to the booksellers and bloggers and readers who are so supportive of all authors. And, as always, thanks to my boys Elliott and Noah, and their mum, Fiona, for their continued backing in all the ways.

To my writerly friends, thank you for your jokes, help, and making light of the ridiculous situations I sometimes find myself in. With extra thanks to Chris Panatier, Sarah J. Daley, Ginger Smith, and Khan Wong, for your input to this book. Indeed, Khan is responsible for a short, brilliant note right at the death of the process, ensuring this story got the ending it deserves. Seriously, if you're a writer, find a group of likeminded folk to share your journey with - they will make you better.

Finally, thank you to Noelle Salazar, who championed this book from the moment I was struck with inspiration for a tower in the sky that needed climbing and hastily wrote a ridiculous prologue (which made it in here almost intact), to the end when I needed someone to read the whole book to make sure it didn't suck balls. Your encouragement, adventurous spirit, fake British accent, and love is everything.

We are Angry Robot, your favourite independent, genre-fluid publisher, bringing you the very best in sci-fi, fantasy, horror and everything in between!

Check out our website at
www.angryrobotbooks.com
to see our entire catalogue.

Follow us on social media:
Twitter: @angryrobotbooks
Instagram: @angryrobotbooks
TikTok: angryrobotbooks

Sign up to our mailing list now: